THE BOSS KILLERS

THE BOSS KILLERS

Keith Gillison

Copyright © 2015 Keith Gillison
The Boss Killers

Published 2015.

All rights reserved. No part of this book may be reproduced or transmitted in any form or by any means, electronic or mechanical, including photocopying, recording, or by any information storage and retrieval system without the written permission of the author, except where permitted by law.

This book is a work of fiction. Names, characters, places, and incidents either are products of the author's imagination or are used fictitiously. Any resemblance to actual persons, living or dead, events, or locales is entirely coincidental.

First printing: 2015.
ISBN-13: 978-1511776035
ISBN-10: 151177603X

British Cataloguing Publication Data
A catalogue record of this book is available from
The British Library.

Also available on Kindle from Amazon

For Tammy

Chapter 1
Meet Charles Belvedere

Ross Ackerman watched the large wall clock outside Charles Belvedere's office tick to 9:20am. He had now been sitting on one of the six chairs outside his boss' office for exactly 26 minutes. Nobody knew why there were six chairs outside Belvedere's office as this was one of only two occasions that any of the chairs had been used.

As he waited for his 9am annual appraisal, Ross displayed a calm, laid-back appearance, his whole body oozing a bored indifference to this understandable and unavoidable delay. This was at odds with the seething rage flowing through his veins. His mind was wandering again, thinking about things it shouldn't. They weren't good things; he didn't think of good things anymore. Not since ...

He allowed himself a smile as he continued to enjoy the vivid fantasy in which he was torturing his boss with a variety of household appliances and industrial building tools. He grinned at the mental image of Belvedere begging for his life as he approached him with a wallpaper steamer in one hand and a nail gun in the other.

Ross had been fantasising about harming Belvedere for some time now. His fantasies never stopped short of torture and degradation, with a good deal of creative flair displayed in the methods used. The disturbing progression from torture to murder was a more recent development.

Charles Belvedere was 46 years old and head of the Fraud Detection division at the Browns of London bank. It was an important job. There was much responsibility. A waiting area with six leather chairs was the minimum requirement for such a role.

Not for the first time that morning, he glanced out of his office window to check that lots of people were watching him hard at work. He'd insisted on his office being surrounded by glass on all four sides for this very reason. To his annoyance, only Ross was currently enjoying the privilege of observing his productivity. This may have been something to do with Belvedere's executive office being located at the end of a disused corridor that led to nothing other than his executive office. The nearest working human was at least a hundred yards away, around several corners and through numerous sets of fire doors. Everyone who worked for Browns was happy with this arrangement – everyone except Belvedere.

The strange location of his office was the result of a long night of drinking between Ross and the building architect, who also despised Belvedere on account of having met him once. Ross was pleased with his role in the farce that was Belvedere's office. It was a small victory in the ongoing war against his boss. As he shifted in the chair, the new and unused leather irritating him, Ross wondered how much longer he would be satisfied with small victories. He glared at Belvedere in his goldfish bowl office.

Look at him there, acting like he's Donald Trump. Bloody middle-aged anorexic dwarf. I know what you did.

Ross was growing increasingly irritated at the charade playing out before him. Belvedere was on the phone and making hand gestures to say that he would be with him in a minute. Ross couldn't hear what was being said and, perhaps sensing this, Belvedere obliged by speaking louder so he could.

'Yes, sir, I agree, and I can assure you that we in the Fraud Detection team treat the safety of our customers' money with the utmost gravity. I have some new fraud prevention strategies I'd like to discuss with you as soon as is convenient. Three o'clock is fine for me, sir. I must go now, sir, I have to appraise one of my team. See you at three, sir. Goodbye.'

He put the phone down and beckoned Ross to enter. 'Come in, sorry to keep you waiting.'

'No problem, Charles. Anyone important?' Ross sounded calm but the few seconds of the phone call he'd just heard had pushed his anger over the edge. Too weary to resist his instincts anymore, he had decided to have some fun with Belvedere.

'That was the Chairman,' beamed Belvedere. 'He wants to see me at three today.'

He was as excited as a foreign office diplomat whose opposite number had, after three weeks of intense negotiations, turned around and said 'I tell you what, you seem like decent chaps, why don't I just sign this page here at the bottom and you write the rest of the treaty.'

Ross took a deep breath. Then another one. Then he grinned maniacally.

'No it wasn't,' he said.

'What?'

'That wasn't the Chairman you were speaking to.'

'I can assure you it was. I think I know who I was talking to, thank you very much,' Belvedere replied, with maximum pomposity.

'But it can't have been,' said Ross, relaxing now, relieved the decision had been made.

'And why not, pray tell? Were you listening in to my phone call? Do you have x-ray hearing?'

Belvedere laughed at his own joke. By his own low standards it was the funniest thing he had ever said.

'No, I don't have x-ray hearing. X-ray hearing, like x-ray vision, is an imaginary power that fictional cartoon heroes have; it doesn't apply to real people. The reason I know that wasn't the Chairman you were talking to is because you weren't talking to anyone. The Chairman's phone is dial out only; he doesn't take incoming calls. Your phone didn't ring, so you were not talking to the Chairman. For the last 30 minutes you've been having an imaginary conversation with yourself and pretending you were talking to the Chairman. You did this in order to keep me waiting for half an hour and make me think the Chairman sees you as a valued colleague. He doesn't.'

'Yes he bloody well does, he's just been talking to me. I've just been talking to the Chairman, you cheeky bastard.'

'No you haven't, Charles. The Chairman left the building an hour ago.'

As Belvedere protested, Ross removed a small rectangular object from his jacket pocket. It was a photograph. 'This,' he said, 'is a Polaroid picture of me and the Chairman outside the building at 8:32 this morning. If you use this,' he said, handing Belvedere a magnifying glass, 'you can see the time the picture was taken by looking at my watch, and just for completeness I'm holding up a copy of today's paper.'

'You've doctored that photo, that's what you've done. Very clever, trying to make me look stupid like that.'

Belvedere gurned in embarrassment. There should be strict rules forbidding subordinates from making him look like an ignoramus in his executive office.

'OK Charles, if you say so. Here is a memo from the Chairman's PA, confirming his schedule for today. You'll notice his 9am appointment with the Bank of England. Also interesting is this signed statement from our Head of Security that the Chairman left the building at 8:30, and he's confirmed I can have a copy of the CCTV video tape for this morning.'

Belvedere was flustered. The argument he had been so looking forward to was lost. Recovering his poise, he took out his bespoke handkerchief, embroidered with his initials, wiped his receding brow and polished his steel-rimmed spectacles. Glancing at his reflection in the glass window, he straightened the Windsor knot in his silk tie and steeled himself in readiness for round two. He may have lost the battle but there was still the war. He glared at Ross.

'Congratulations, you've had your little joke at my expense. Now let's get on with your appraisal, shall we?'

'Of course,' Ross smirked, his mind chalking up the victory.

Belvedere began the tedious process of the appraisal. He liked meetings. It was what being a boss was all about. If you attended lots of meetings you must be important. For this reason, he insisted on calling lots of meetings for the Fraud Detection team. They responded by competing to say as little as they possibly could, whilst distorting as many hackneyed business clichés as possible. Belvedere liked it when they did this. To him, a meeting was truly valuable if his colleagues were using phrases such as 'low-hanging vegetables', 'thinking inside the box' and 'mauve-sky thinking'. He would make notes of these excellent phrases and use them at future meetings, passing them off as his own. This impressed a grand total of nobody.

'Ross Ackerman's annual appraisal commencing at 9:34am on the 23rd July 1989,' Belvedere began, as though conducting a police interrogation of a mass murder suspect. No recording device was present.

'Now, I want to start by reviewing your targets for the year.'

Yes, let's discuss targets; the round red ones I'm going to paint on your forehead and groin to help me practise my archery skills.

'I see that you have not only hit all your annual targets but have exceeded them. I think perhaps we need to make your targets more specific.'

OK, but only if I can make your targets more specific. How about I make a small dot on the end of your nose with a marker pen and throw darts at it?

'We need to stretch you more, Ross.'

Coincidentally, Charles, I'd quite like to stretch you too; across a medieval rack until your limbs are ripped from your torso. That way I can kick you up the arse with your own feet.

'I'm thinking of moving you off credit card and cheque fraud and putting you on money laundering. Much more of a challenge for you.'

Nothing to do with money laundering cases being much harder to prove and therefore impossible for me to hit my targets. I'll give you a challenge, you bureaucratic bastard. You've got 60 seconds to exit this building before I hunt you down, disembowel you and feed your innards to stray dogs.

The appraisal continued for another two hours of monumental dullness, during which Ross kept a thin grip on sanity by enjoying his inner monologue's frank replies to Belvedere's dreary interrogation.

Nobody knew the appraisal process better than Belvedere, with the possible exception of Ross, who had been preparing for this meeting for the last month. He'd come armed with a large file full of colourful graphs and charts illustrating his performance against his actual targets, as well as a whole host of additional performance measurements that he knew would be thrown at him. He had detailed feedback from all of his clients and updates on every case he was currently working on.

All this was just to counteract Belvedere's obsession with policies and procedures. If there were two things Belvedere loved, they were policies and procedures. The only thing he liked more than policies and procedures were processes, particularly if they were unnecessary, bureaucratic and cumbersome. What gave Belvedere the most pleasure in the world was to work a sixteen-hour day producing extensive reports outlining lots of unnecessary policies, procedures and processes, supported by dozens of flow charts, Gantt charts and other indecipherable statistical analyses that would make all potential readers want to hang themselves.

By the end of the appraisal Belvedere was unable to hide his frustration at failing to find any aspect of his job that Ross was poor at. He knew he had to get rid of him, that his position would never be safe while Ross was around.

Everyone knew Ross could do Belvedere's job standing on his head. He outperformed every other member of the Fraud Detection team, they all respected him, all his clients were personal friends and he was on first name terms with every member of staff at Browns, including the Chairman. By contrast, Belvedere was hated by every member of staff he had ever met and those he hadn't met hated him by reputation. Ross and the rest of the Fraud Detection team saw to that. In Belvedere's mind, it was just a matter of time before his younger adversary was forgiven for past misdemeanours.

'Well, I think that's everything,' Belvedere said, concluding the appraisal. 'Once again I congratulate you on an excellent year's work.'

Ross grinned as he collated his many supporting documents, which were strewn across the desk. He had won.

'On a personal note, I must say,' Belvedere began as Ross prepared to leave, 'how impressed we all are with how well you are doing after that,' he said, pausing for dramatic effect, 'well, you know, after that unfortunate episode. Terrible business, truly terrible. Well that's about it, unless there is anything else. Thank you for your time.'

Ross pretended to drop his file and knelt down to pick it up. Behind the desk he clasped his hands over his head, put his head between his legs, began counting slowly down from ten and practised his breathing exercises. Everyone knew which subject to avoid with Ross. Belvedere was baiting him. He would pay for this.

When Ross reached number one he was now only angry enough to kill a man with his bare hands. At ten he could have charged a pride of hungry lions. Belvedere smirked, pleased with himself for finally breaching Ross' defences.

Rising from behind the desk, Ross produced a stare that was not so much aiming daggers at Belvedere as aiming a full squadron of testosterone-fuelled, psychotic, tooled-up Special Forces personnel who'd just found out their wives had left them for tax inspectors, their daughters were on the game and their only sons hung around Hampstead Heath of a night.

'Now that I think of it there was something else,' Ross ventured.

'Yes?'

'I'm afraid I'm going to have to kill you. Don't look surprised. You know you're a jumped-up worthless bureaucrat. It's an offence against nature that you're using up perfectly good human organs that could be donated to more worthy cases. Goodbye, Charles.'

With that, Ross pulled a small hammer out of his jacket pocket and lunged at Belvedere, who jumped out of his chair to dodge the attack. Ross' arm swished through the air before Belvedere had time to retreat and the hammer smashed into his temple. The blow cracked his skull clean open and Belvedere slumped to the ground, blood spurting from a small hole in his head. He was dead but Ross didn't care. He stood over Belvedere and smashed his face with the hammer until there was nothing left to smash.

Breathless and drenched in blood, Ross emerged from his trance, his mouth smirking, his eyes glinting with madness. He stood over the mutilated body of the late Charles Belvedere and felt no remorse.

Ross left Belvedere's office and headed back to work. As he strolled down the corridor, his heart pounding, he thought about the murder that had just taken place and how he wished it had been real and not just in his head. Fantasy and reality: he could no longer distinguish between the two. He worried that he might have to kill Belvedere, and soon.

Chapter 2
The Badger's Eyebrows

Friday night was drinking night at The Badger's. The Badger's Eyebrows was located on the corner of Hurst Street, about 100 yards from Watkin Station.

When asked to describe The Badger's the word most often used was 'rough' but this was unfair. Lots of pubs are rough. The Badger's Eyebrows was a complete toilet. It was the kind of pub that decent people crossed the road before walking past to avoid being struck by missiles, both bottle- and people-shaped. The clientele of The Badger's were what you might expect, a weird and wonderful assortment of degenerate drunks, benefit cheats, con men, bikers, skinheads, prostitutes, truck drivers, travelling salesmen and students.

Ross arrived at eight, late for the agreed seven thirty meeting time. Alice and Stuart had already ordered drinks and secured one of the larger tables in the corner.

The design of The Badger's Eyebrows had been conceived with the needs of its target market very much in mind. It had more nooks and crannies than a mature rabbit warren. It also had more corners than seemed architecturally possible by a simple mathematical calculation of the building's total number of walls. Places like The Badger's needed lots of corners on account of the colossal amount of clandestine meetings and black market trading that took place. It was a place where petty criminals went to drink and meet with other less petty criminals. Packages would be brought in by one person and leave with a person bearing little resemblance to the one they arrived with.

There was very little you couldn't get your hands on in The Badger's for the right price. Sex and drugs were always in plentiful supply, as were competitive rates for money laundering, commodity trading and trafficking of people and endangered species. The landlord's general approach to all this blatant crime taking place on his premises was one which combined indifference and leniency with a certain hardness of hearing and shortness of sight that he really must get looked at one of these days if only he could find the time.

Ross joined Alice and Stuart and thanked them for having a pint ready for him. Adam had yet to join them; he was holding an impromptu open legal surgery in another corner. Adam was a solicitor who specialised in contract law. He had been friends with Ross since his time working for Browns' legal team but was now employed in the contracts department of Wilson, Wilson, Wilson, Wilson and Wilson solicitors' group. None of the Wilsons were related.

Adam prided himself on his 'contacts' with the criminal underworld. To cultivate these contacts he offered free legal advice to the regulars in The Badger's Eyebrows. The serious criminals in The Badger's already had their own bent lawyers on the payroll willing to swear at a moment's notice that their client had spent the evening with them enjoying a steak dinner followed by an enjoyable game of billiards and therefore couldn't have been seen standing over a bloody corpse brandishing a butcher's knife at the aforementioned time, your honour. That left Adam with the desperate scrapings of the criminal barrel as his ad hoc clients. On a typical night he would be asked about sentence lengths dished out for various crimes, help in fiddling benefit claims, and some legal technicalities of evidence produced in court cases. Adam's specialist knowledge of contract law in no way qualified him to answer any of these questions.

His surgery ended on an angry query about divorce law and he joined the others, regaling them with tales of the numerous fictitious Mr Bigs who had been hanging on his every word. Stuart was unimpressed with Adam's tales. He suspected, with good reason, that almost every word spoken by Adam's mouth was a massive lie.

As Ross guzzled his first pint in a futile attempt to keep pace with Alice, Adam moved the conversation onto daytime television, in order to wind up Stuart. Ross and Stuart had been best friends since nursery. Stuart was a senior IT manager for a large insurance brokers.

What Stuart didn't know about computers had yet to be invented. As well as computing, the other topic Ross and Alice knew to avoid at all times with Stuart was the TV detective show Columbo. Stuart was the head of the official UK Columbo fan club and had an encyclopaedic knowledge of the show. His life's goal was to meet Peter Falk.

'All I'm saying is that for me Quincy is the king of daytime TV detective shows,' Adam said.

'You talk a lot of crap, Adam. Quincy is inferior to Columbo in every way and you know it. Anyway, Quincy isn't even a proper detective, he's a doctor,' Stuart replied, rising to Adam's bait.

'No he's not, he's a pathologist. Anyway, he solves crimes, doesn't he? And he's clever. Columbo is a buffoon. He bumbles his way through each episode and just gets lucky every time.'

'What! That's it. This conversation is over. You're a moron, Adam,' Stuart snapped.

'OK children, that's enough fighting. My round. What you all having?' Ross asked, keen to bring the hostilities to a swift conclusion. He smiled at Stuart and frowned at Adam, like he was scolding a naughty boy. Adam just grinned and shrugged his shoulders.

It was Friday night and The Badger's was at its demented best. Not that a large proportion of the customers were relaxing after a hard week's graft. Apart from the bar staff, Ross and his party were the only people present in legal employment. Ross ordered his round of drinks at the bar and studied the room full of crazies around him. At the end of the bar the singing vicar was entertaining a small audience. The singing vicar was no more a vicar than Ross was a circus lion tamer. What he was though was a charismatic con man. He sung, he told jokes, he regaled the regulars with funny stories. When he was really drunk he delivered mass and took confession. When he was steaming drunk he would stagger into nearby churches to perform these ceremonies. On such occasions, the confused parishioners wondered why their usual priest had been replaced with one who was much more sober.

Opposite the pub's entrance and near to what could loosely be described as the toilets was the pub's resident gang of skinheads. They were drinking pints of high-strength cider and being given a wide berth by all who enjoyed the experience of not having blood pouring out of their heads. In the absence of anyone within arm's length to pick a fight with, the skinheads were engaging in one of their ancient cultural activities, traditional to their ethnic roots. They were running as fast as they could and smashing their bald, scarred skulls against each other. The winner would be the one who remained conscious or was bleeding the least. The reigning champion of this game was the gang's unofficial leader, Igneous. Near the end of a mammoth session one evening, a kamikaze Ross had approached Igneous and asked him how he got his name. The skinhead pressed his large index finger into the centre of his temple and, with genuine madness, screamed: 'Because I'm fucking rock!'

These mad characters were what Ross loved about The Badger's and why he kept coming back. It was the opposite of corporate. Here you had real life, real people. It might not be pretty and it didn't smell nice but it was real. It also had the added benefit that never in a million years would he ever bump into Belvedere in The Badger's Eyebrows.

Ross returned with the drinks and took his usual place next to Alice. 'Busy today, Ally?' he asked.

She smiled at him. 'So-so. It was quiet this morning but picked up later.'

Ross and Stuart had known Alice since school. She was a few years below them but had made her presence known. Alice was 28 years old, petite at five foot one, had long black hair and, by anyone's standards, was good looking. She was a sales assistant on the hosiery department of an old-fashioned department store that would give Grace Brothers a run for its money.

Despite spending all day ordering them, answering questions about them and selling them, Alice never got bored of discussing tights and stockings. Ross had tried hard to show an interest in hosiery but found it difficult. Talking to Alice about stockings and suspenders stirred thoughts and feelings in him that he was trying to avoid and he had to force himself to think about re-grouting the bathroom or the terms and conditions of his home insurance to avoid visualising Alice trying on the items she was describing.

'I had another tranny in earlier,' said Alice.

'Are you sure it wasn't just an ugly woman?' asked Ross.

'Oh no, it was a man alright. He was dressed in men's clothes, had a beard, an Adam's apple and a deep voice. His name was Trevor.'

An escaped marmoset was paid little attention by Alice as it scurried across her lap in a bid for freedom.

'So if he wasn't dressed as a woman, how do you know he was a tranny, and how do you know his name?' asked Adam.

'We just got chatting; people tell you anything when they're buying tights. He was definitely a tranny. He was six foot five and 'buying for his girlfriend' who just happened to be …'

'Let me guess, also six foot five?' ventured Stuart.

'Correct. So he's saying to me, "What have you got in my size? It's not for me, it's for my girlfriend and she's the same size as me," and as I'm showing him some tights he asks "Haven't you got any Woolford in my size?" Note *my* size, not *this* size.'

'What's Woolford?' asked Adam.

'It's a luxury brand of hosiery. See, you just proved my point. How many men can name even one brand of tights?' asked Alice.

'I see what you mean, Ally,' said Ross. He was the only one allowed to call Alice Ally.

'He could just be well informed, you know, done his research before he got to the store?' Stuart offered.

Without the slightest amount of surprise the four of them lifted their drinks off the table to avoid the skinhead flying across it on his way to an important appointment with the wall.

'No Stu, he was a tranny,' Alice continued. 'How many six foot five women do you know? Anyway, the clincher was when I went out the back and found the Woolford in his size and brought it back to him. He started to drool, then broke the world speed record for paying and getting the hell out of the store. No doubt dashed off back home, put the tights on, dressed himself up like a six foot five bearded man wearing women's clothes and spent the rest of the morning having a ham shank over his copy of Cocks in Frocks Monthly.'

Ross grinned. Whilst Alice had the looks of a sweet girl next door, she had a slight tendency to talk filth at every opportunity. If he didn't know any better Ross would have made an educated guess that Alice was the offspring of a docker and a sailor.

'Alice dear, could you please not talk about masturbating transvestites. Thanks, darling,' Stuart said in his best upper crust Brian Sewell impersonation.

Stuart abhorred Alice's potty mouth; he had often lectured her on how she should try to be more of a lady and less like a football yob. He was thanked by Alice for these efforts by being told to 'Fuck off, Stuart.'

****

Isolated from the hubbub, two men sat in a secluded alcove, away from prying ears. Everywhere in The Badger's Eyebrows was away from prying ears, even the parts that were in the middle of a throng of noisy drinkers. People learned to train their ears to avoid hearing things that were not meant for them or suffer the very real prospect of being unable to wear spectacles on account of lacking the minimum number of ears required for such a task.

The older man was a regular at The Badger's. He had the look of a man who had seen far too much life than is good for one person. His face was craggier than the Himalayas and more leathery than a tanning factory. He was also in possession of a voice that, if it could be solidified, would be put to very good use by the highways construction industry, such was its gravely quality. He had dispersed with a name many years ago and was known only as the intermediary.

The intermediary provided logistical and administration support, as well as the customer face, for an organisation of underground contract killers known as the Boss Killers. Their success was in no small part down to the work of the intermediary. He ensured it was very hard for the average criminal – and almost impossible for Joe Public – to find out any information about them. If you wanted to employ their services you had to be serious and put the effort in to find them. The intermediary saw to it that clients paid in full and were left in no doubt about the speed and severity of the repercussions if they were to ever open their mouth to the law.

That the intermediary was still alive to perform this role with such efficiency after so many years was in no small part due to the complex network of additional intermediaries he had established to ensure he also never came into contact with his employers. These were people you wouldn't want to bump into in broad daylight at a busy street carnival with a heavy police presence, never mind in a dark, deserted alleyway. You had to respect people who carried out cold-blooded murder for a living but even the intermediary thought they were a bunch of bloodthirsty bastards who would shoot you in the face as soon as look at you. He was getting too old for this; he needed to get out.

The man sitting opposite him was one of his network of middlemen. He enjoyed breathing and being alive very much and was therefore patiently awaiting his instructions. The intermediary handed him a briefcase under the table.

'This is a new job. William Phillips is the target. Rest of the details are in the case. The first instalment's also in there, minus my fee of course.'

The man nodded his understanding.

'Tell them this here's a foreign job so it's more than the regular fee. Everything they need should be in there but you know the drill – if they need more or there's any problems I'll be in here every Tuesday and Thursday from two till three.'

The man nodded again and began to stand.

'Before you go, quick question.'

This was unexpected. The man froze to the spot, gripped by fear.

'You got a garden where you live?'

'Er yeah,' replied the man, praying the intermediary didn't know the location of his home.

'Then take this,' said the intermediary, placing a handful of greasy white matter into his shaking outstretched palms.

'It's... it's not Semtex, is it?' he whispered, looking over his shoulder to check no one could hear.

'No, you daft sod,' chuckled the intermediary, 'they're fat balls. Stick them in your garden. The birds love 'em. Hang them up though so they don't get pounced on by some bloody moggy.'

The confused man thanked him, stuffed the fat balls into his coat pocket and left in haste with the briefcase. *So serious, these kids*, the intermediary thought to himself. *Roll on retirement.*

The evening wore on and many more drinks were consumed. Stuart left early and went home to collapse in a drunken fog on his sofa after showing a Chinese banquet for two no mercy. Adam tried and failed to ingratiate himself with some dodgy-looking characters. He then tried to score with a few ladies, only to discover after buying them several drinks that they were on the game. Ross just chatted to Alice and enjoyed the effect the alcohol had on blotting Belvedere out of his brain. Alice hurled abuse at students, much to the delight of the rest of the pub.

****

At the end of the evening Alice supported Ross as he staggered his way out of The Badger's Eyebrows, stepping over the detritus of skinheads on the floor.

Ross winked at Igneous. 'Still the guv'nor, Iggy,' he slurred.

Igneous pointed at his solid cranium and yelled: 'Rock, son. I'm made of rock,' and for no apparent reason smashed a glass bottle over his own head.

Alice hailed a taxi for her and Ross and helped him out when it reached his flat. As the taxi drove away, she blew a kiss towards the inebriated man attempting to open his front door with a key. *One day*, she thought to herself.

Chapter 3
Murder, Torture and Toast

Detective Inspector Harry Christmas sat in his office on the third floor of New Scotland Yard and sipped his first cup of coffee of the morning. It had come from the staff canteen, and was therefore deeply unpleasant. Everything that was produced by the canteen was an abomination as far as Christmas was concerned.

He took another sip from the cup and winced. How could you go so wrong with a simple cup of coffee? His drink had a full one-inch head on it and Christmas knew for a fact the canteen didn't possess a cappuccino machine. It also tasted of pork chops. His coffee tasted of pork chops. Christmas wondered what possible culinary process could result in a cup of coffee tasting of pig. He would complain if he thought it would make any difference but suspected this would only lead to his next coffee tasting of something much less pleasant than pork chops.

He pushed the cup aside and turned his attention to his ever-growing mountain of case files. Another file had landed on his desk yesterday afternoon while he was absent from the building. Christmas wasn't the least bit surprised. He knew his DCI monitored his movements so he could identify the most appropriate window of opportunity to dump more crap on his desk.

He picked up the new file and read it once more. He'd read it three times last night and twice this morning. He liked to be thorough with his cases. It was this relentless attention to detail that had seen him rise to the position of Detective Inspector. He knew it must be this and his knack for solving unsolvable crimes, because it sure as hell wasn't his charismatic personality or popularity with colleagues. If it was, he would still be hiding behind a bush at the side of a dual carriageway somewhere pointing a speed gun at sales reps returning home at two in the morning.

The case file Christmas was now reading had been well-thumbed and defaced by numerous incoherent scribbles in the margins from previous readers. A British man had died in an apparent accident whilst on holiday. The fact that the location was the Seychelles was the reason for the considerable interest from his colleagues. The file had been passed around every detective in CID in a flurry of excitement yesterday morning and then, one by one, when they had learned from the DCI that this case did not involve a trip to the Seychelles to 'liaise' with the local law enforcement they lost interest and the file found its way to Christmas' desk. Most of his case files had followed a similar journey. All the dead end cases, the odds and sods that no one else wanted ended up on his desk. They were his children. Christmas never gave up on a case until the perpetrator of the crime had been apprehended. He was that sort of detective.

On the face of it, no crime had been committed in this new case. William Phillips had died as the result of a freak accident. The jet ski he was riding on his private beach had malfunctioned and exploded, scattering parts of Mr Phillips across a wide area of the idyllic sea.

The Seychelles police seemed to have done a thorough job. They concluded the jet ski didn't appear to have been tampered with and they had interviewed staff at the luxury resort at which Mr Phillips was staying. The staff had all co-operated in full and such was their desire to help the police, they had even offered to have their homes searched for any evidence of foul play. This had been carried out and unearthed nothing untoward. The hotel staff records showed no member of staff had a criminal record and all could account for their movements in the hours before the accident occurred. The company who supplied the jet ski had been investigated and found to be long-standing suppliers of leisure equipment to the island with no prior complaints about the safety of any of their goods going back over a twenty year period. The manufacturers of the jet skis met all the required international standards and had an impeccable safety record.

The Seychelles authorities concluded that this was a tragic accident whose cause was most likely to have been a spark from one of the oversized Cuban cigars that were found in Mr Phillips' personal effects in his hotel suite. Phillips' wife was devastated by his death. He appeared to be a loving husband and father, respected in his place of work and popular with friends.

So Harry Christmas had on his hands a case that had no motive, no suspects to investigate, no insightful forensic evidence and no proof that a crime had even been committed. His job was to tie things up this end so the Seychelles authorities could close the case. This was the exact opposite of what he was going to do. A man had died and the case had dropped into his lap. It would receive the same thorough investigation that all his cases received. Besides, Christmas' nose was telling him this was no accident, and his nose was never wrong. He rummaged through the Everest of files on his desk and pulled out three more. Jerry Stapleton, fell off his fifth storey balcony whilst drunk; Evan Johnston, run over by a truck; and Stephen Baxter, whose private plane had crashed into the side of a mountain. All accidents. All held senior positions in the corporate world. All the files had ended up on the desk of Christmas, the only man who would pay them more than lip service.

****

Adam perused the menu yet again, his irritation plain for all to see. He couldn't decide between the roast guinea fowl on toast or the beef stroganoff on toast.

'Come on, Adam. Hurry up, will you? It's called a lunch hour, not a lunch fortnight,' said Ross.

'There's plenty to choose from,' added Stuart.

'Yes, that's all very well Stu, if you happen to like toast, which I don't,' snapped Adam.

As they had done every day so far this month, Ross, Adam, Stuart and Alice were dining in World of Toast, one of the batch of new restaurants leading the grilled bread culinary revolution sweeping the capital.

About four months ago they had decided to spice up their lunch hour. Lunchery of the Day entailed eating at a different restaurant each day, to be chosen at random by a member of the lunch group. The venue would then be scored against varying criteria including diversity of menu, value for money, service, quality of toilets and, for no apparent reason, the reaction of the establishment to a request for a dish that was not only absent from their menu, but went against the entire ethos of the restaurant. This included dining at the exclusive Chez Mange restaurant and requesting a chip butty, asking for quail's eggs in Pizza Hut and ordering four large bloody steaks in the Mange Tout, the double Michelin star vegetarian restaurant.

Reactions to these requests varied from bad to appalling, and as a result they had now been banned from six restaurants. It soon became clear that Lunchery of the Day was unsustainable so Lunchery of the Month was born and the scoring chart very sensibly dropped the 'ask for something they would never in a million years serve' column. At the first opportunity, Stuart had chosen World of Toast, just to annoy Adam.

'I hear their grill is over a hundred feet wide,' Stuart said, bursting with excitement. The angrier Adam grew, the greater Stuart's enthusiasm for World of Toast became.

'Right, that's it. I've decided. It's the sausage and egg on toast,' barked Adam.

'That's a bit basic, isn't it,' frowned Stuart. 'Isn't that from the children's menu?'

While Stuart and Adam continued arguing, Ross had something on his mind. 'Ally,' he asked, 'have you ever wanted to kill someone?'

'Oh yeah, loads of people. Why?' asked Alice.

'What about at work – ever thought of killing your boss?'

'All the time, she's a right slag. She's always *accidentally* getting my time card wrong so I don't get all the lieu time I'm owed and I'm sure she's on the fiddle. Sometimes I have to cash up and the till is always out by the same amount. If I cared I'd report her but I know she'd only blame me and she's been there longer so who are they going to believe? Bitch.'

A waiter arrived with their main course orders and obligatory sides of complimentary toast.

'Would you ever do it though? You know, go through with it?' Ross continued.

'No, I'd just think about it, get angry for a bit then go out, get pissed and forget about it. Why? You thinking of bumping off Belvedere?'

Adam and Stuart had ceased hostilities and they were all now looking at Ross.

'No, don't be silly. I'm just talking hypothetically, of course,' Ross lied.

Alice wasn't convinced as to the innocence of Ross' questioning. 'Look, he may be an odious creep who deserves to be done in but is it worth doing time for? You're a pretty boy and I don't want you going inside and being some big lifer's bitch in the showers. You'll have an arsehole like a wizard's sleeve by the time you get out.'

Adam roared with laughter while Stuart buried his head in his hands.

'Thanks Alice, you foul mouthed harlot. I feel sick now,' garbled Stuart in between enormous mouthfuls of duck a l'orange on toast, Alice's comment not affecting his appetite in any way.

'Don't worry guys, I'm not going to do anyone in,' Ross said, he hoped with conviction. 'It's just that I thought it might help if I talked about it a bit. Something I learnt in anger management – talk about it rather than keep it in. Helps to soothe the anger.'

They were all surprised by this admission as Ross never talked about his treatment. This was the nearest he'd ever got to asking for help and they quickly responded.

'Sure Ross, no problem,' said Adam.

'Now then, young man,' said Stuart. He sometimes called Ross this even though he was only a few months older than him. 'When planning a murder there are three things we need to consider. Means, motive and opportunity. That's what Columbo always says. So OK, let's say you want to kill Belvedere. First of all you need to decide your method.'

'Poison him,' said Alice.

'Too difficult,' said Stuart. He was on happy ground here. He spoke with the knowledge and authority of an experienced forensic scientist, but he was just repeating things he had seen in episodes of Columbo, without the faintest idea if any of it was true. 'You have to know what you're doing with poison – they don't all kill, you know. And where are you going to get it from – Poisons R Us?'

'You could shoot him,' added Adam.

'That's better,' said Stuart 'but it still raises lots of difficulties. First, where are you going to get a gun? Second, you've got to get rid of the gun. If they find it, they can match the ballistics to the body. You've also got the noise of the gun, so a silencer is a must and where're you getting one of them?'

'I know a guy,' said Adam.

Ross stifled a smile. Whatever the topic, whatever was needed, Adam always knew a guy. If they were discussing assembling a nuclear bomb Adam would 'know a guy' who could lay his hands on some plutonium.

A waiter arrived to collect their empty plates and take their dessert orders. He sneered at the pathetic half-eaten children's portion left by Adam.

Stuart continued. 'OK so you got the gun, the silencer and of course you're wearing gloves so you don't leave any fingerprints. You've still got to shoot a man dead at point-blank range. Not many people can do that. It also places you at the scene of the crime at the time of the crime, which brings me onto the second thing you need to take care of.'

'What's that?' sighed Alice, already bored with Stuart's detective speak.

'Opportunity,' said Stuart. 'You need an alibi. The best chance you have of getting away with it is to make sure you are somewhere else when it happens and with plenty of witnesses. If you get the first two right you don't have to worry about the third.'

'Which is?' asked Ross. It never occurred to him that Stuart's knowledge of Columbo might prove useful.

'Motive, of course,' said Stuart. 'You could have the best motive in the world and be the number one suspect but it won't matter a damn if you've got a watertight alibi and they've got no murder weapon.'

Stuart beamed; for a brief moment he was a smart detective with an audience and not a computer nerd. He decided tonight he would watch the 'Any Old Port in a Storm' episode of Columbo, starring Donald Pleasance as the murderous vineyard owner. It was one of his favourites.

'Hmm. Interesting,' said Ross.

As the waiter served Stuart's dessert order of apple pie and custard on toast, Alice nipped to the ladies' and Adam made a hasty exit from the restaurant, mentally chalking off the number of days remaining in the month.

'Listen Ross, all that talk is just talk, you know. Just for fun,' said Stuart.

'Of course. Hypothetical, like you said.'

'If you're that wound up why don't you take up a hobby or something to let off some steam? Or if Belvedere is doing your head in that much can't you just leave? I'm sure you'd be snapped up by one of your competitors.'

'Maybe, but I like Browns, I like the people. The Fraud Detection team is *my* team, not his. Anyway, even if I didn't work with him I'd still want him dead,' Ross snapped through gritted teeth.

It was a rare moment of Ross letting his guard down and Stuart missed it because his attention had been diverted by the tantalising aroma of chicken chasseur on hot buttered toast being served to an adjacent diner.

The meal finished and Ross returned to work, his brain alive with new possibilities for murdering his boss.

****

Belvedere was in a deluded state. He didn't know where he was and wasn't even sure if this was real or some sort of disturbed nightmare. His head was spinning, his vision blurred. He was trying to stay conscious but couldn't manage it. When he came round again he felt like a patient waking up from an operation, unsure of what was happening and helpless. This time he achieved consciousness, or as near as possible given the circumstances. His eyes regained some clarity and before long he was able to focus. What he saw made him wish he hadn't.

Ross was sitting on a chair in front of him, grinning, mania in his eyes. The sight of Ross triggered several horrific flashbacks that brought Belvedere to his senses. His fight or flight response kicked in and he summoned all his strength to run away as fast as he could from his predicament. His effort was unsuccessful. His whole body felt like he had just run 58 consecutive marathons with no food, water or sleep. He was in quicksand, not even possessing the strength to move his little finger a millimetre.

'A brave effort, Charles, but you'd be wise to conserve what little strength you have left. Your chances of escape are less than or equal to zero. First, there are the solid iron shackles around your legs, which are chained to both your chair and the concrete floor. They could keep King Kong restrained. Then there are the steel handcuffs, to stop your hands getting up to any mischief. These are very special; I went to a great deal of trouble to acquire them. I have it on good authority that only two escapologists in the world could wriggle their way free. You're not one of them. Last, there's the colossal quantity of drugs I've pumped you full of. It's a unique cocktail. There will be another ice age before their effects on your muscles wear off, but – and here's the good part - they have no effect at all on your ability to feel pain. That's going to be an important detail over the coming hours and days.'

Pain. The mention of the word induced another flashback for Belvedere, waking his shocked pain sensors from their temporary coma. He screamed in agony and began to slip from consciousness again.

'Now, now, wakey wakey,' said Ross, pouring a bucket of ice cold water over his head.

It had the desired outcome. Belvedere screamed again. Ross just smiled. He liked hearing Belvedere scream.

'Scream all you like. Nobody will hear you here.'

'Where …am .. I?' whispered Belvedere, exhausted from the effort.

'Geographically, there is no living soul within at least five miles in any direction so you'll have to scream louder than that for anyone to hear you. If you want me to be more specific then I believe the factual term would be dungeon.' Ross picked up a large dictionary, flicked through to the desired page and read out loud. 'A dark, often underground chamber or cell used to confine prisoners. Yep,' he said, looking around the dark, underground chamber he was holding Belvedere prisoner in, 'I'd say we're in a dungeon alright.'

Belvedere grimaced in pain and was overcome by nausea. Unable to move or stop himself, he vomited down his chest.

'Now let's recap,' began Ross. 'It's been a long day and I wouldn't want you to miss anything. As you can see I'm going for a whole new look for you, Charles. Kind of bringing you into the twentieth century. I'm calling it torture chic. You'll be quite fashionable by the end of the programme. You won't be alive of course, but we all have to make sacrifices.'

Belvedere grimaced, his body shivering with cold. 'Please Ross, let me go,' he pleaded.

Ross ignored him. 'Now, as you recall we started with your hair. I'm no hairdresser so I had a bit of a hack job at it; nicked you a few times, I'm afraid. It's always the same when you don't quite have the right tools for the job.' Ross held up a blunt machete and miniature axe. Both had dried blood on them. 'Then I thought, it's not just the style that needs changing but also the colour. I didn't have any hair dye so I used bleach instead, quite a bit to be honest. Makes you look quite distinguished.'

Belvedere could feel his skull burning.

'Then I gave you a bit of a facial. It took some time but I managed to pluck every one of your eyelashes out with some tweezers. I think that may have stung a bit because you were hollering quite loud at that point. Then we moved onto your eyebrows, which I removed with the help of some boiling hot hair removal wax. I used a bit too much so you've got some nasty burns to the face.'

Ross stroked his chin in thought.

'Let's see, where did we go next? Oh yes, I remember. I know how busy you are with work, Charles, so I thought I'd save you a trip to the dentist. Of course I don't have anaesthetics or proper dentist tools so I had to use a bit of elbow grease with my hammer and chisel. You've got some stubborn buggers in there so I took the power drill to those ones.'

Belvedere had flashbacks of the drill and lost consciousness again. A foul-smelling aroma brought him back to his nightmare as Ross held smelling salts under his nose.

'This is no time for a nap, Charles. We've still got a lot of work to do. OK I'll speed the rest up for you. I broke a few of your ribs with my steel toe-capped boots, bashed up your fingers with a mallet and then removed your fingernails with the pliers. That's about it so far.'

Belvedere became aware of fluid on his hands. He knew it must be blood.

'So, ready for phase two of your makeover?' Ross enquired, as if he was asking Belvedere if he took sugar in his tea. He held up a metal cage in front of Belvedere's face. It contained rats. 'These beauties haven't eaten in days. They get quite ferocious when they're hungry, you know. In a few minutes I'll be cutting your trousers and boxers off and opening the cage door just in front of little Charles. I'll not lie to you; that's going to hurt. First though, I'm going to liven you up a bit.' Ross started attaching electrodes to various parts of Belvedere's anatomy.

'Please Ross, I'm begging you. Please don't,' Belvedere sobbed, partly because of the pain but more in fear of what was to come. There wasn't going to be any further time. If he was going to plead for his life, it had to be now. 'I'll do anything you want. Please don't,' he begged.

'Anything, eh?'

'Yes, anything, anything,' Belvedere pleaded.

'Well, there is one thing I've been meaning to ask you for some time. I think you know what it is. This might be a good time now that I have your strict attention.' Ross glared at the broken Belvedere with malice, relishing the moment. Finally, the truth.

Just as the interrogation was about to commence Ross became aware of a loud beeping noise. As it got louder and louder he looked around but couldn't locate the source. He couldn't think straight. He put his fingers in his ears and closed his eyes, waiting for the noise to disappear. Moments passed and he opened his eyes. This wasn't right. He closed his eyes and opened them again. Belvedere had gone, and so had the dungeon. The beeping continued.

****

The dream had been so real in every sense it took Ross several minutes to comprehend what was happening. When he did, he sat up in bed, reached over to his bedside table and switched the alarm off. He got out of bed, walked to the bathroom and took a shower.

Whilst the hot water sprayed his face and returned him to full consciousness, Ross experienced mixed emotions. He was relieved that a quite sickening nightmare had ended. This was followed by some guilt at the depth of depravity to which his fantasies had sunk. Then he experienced emotions he was not altogether comfortable with. Regret. That he was now awake and still desiring to torture Belvedere in a dungeon was not good and he knew it. He finished his shower, got dressed and made himself some breakfast.

As Ross sat at his kitchen table sipping his tea and eating cornflakes, he stopped and said out loud: 'I need professional help.' The assembled furniture in his one bedroom flat chose not to reply.

Chapter 4
Extra Curricular Activities

Dr Stephens shifted in his chair, looked at his watch to see how much more of this bile he had to be subjected to, and repeated a difficult tongue twister in his head to prevent his brain from having to process the words his ears were hearing. The hour was nearly up and he'd already had to excuse himself twice to dash to the toilet and relieve his stomach of its contents. *This man is seriously disturbed*, he thought to himself.

He'd only taken the appointment as a favour to a fellow psychiatrist who'd had to leave the country at short notice because of a family tragedy. Stephens was now suspicious of the legitimacy of his colleague's emergency and was comparing the demographics of his relatives to see which one would be most appropriate for him to pay a visit in the immediate future. *They need to live very far away and have one foot in the grave.*

'So, after I've removed two of his ribs without pain relief and with the bare minimum of stitching, I stick some of my favourite rock songs on and play along to the drumbeat by bashing his cranium with the ribs. I make sure he hasn't eaten in several days, then I knock him out with some strong drugs, peel a large piece of skin off his face and bake it in the oven so it gets nice and crisp. Then, while he's still out, I remove one of his eyeballs with a tablespoon, mash it up with a pestle and mortar and add to it some finely diced red onion, fresh lime juice and a pinch of garam masala. When he comes round I stick a gun to his head and tell him if he doesn't eat this poppadom and chutney then I'll blow his brains out. After he's eaten it I blow his brains out anyway, piss on his fresh corpse and sell what's left of his carcass to a travelling necrophiliac ring.'

Stephens excused himself again and dashed to the gents, only just making it in time. When he returned his face was the colour of unripened bananas.

'So what do you think?' asked Ross. He'd spent the best part of an hour describing his dreams and daytime fantasies of torturing, mutilating and murdering Belvedere. Sharing his thoughts was therapeutic but it didn't make him want to carry out the acts any less. Only one thing was stopping him, and his will was being tested to breaking point.

'That's very interesting, Ross,' said Stephens. 'And how long have you been having these thoughts?' Ross told him. 'I see, and why do you think you have this enmity towards your work colleague?'

Ross told him why. Stephens gasped in shock and helped himself to a stiff brandy. Were there no depths of depravity to which man will not sink? He wished he'd listened to his parents and become a dentist. He looked at Ross, so full of hate, so tortured, and he genuinely felt sorry for him. This feeling in no way diminished his desire to never set eyes on him ever again.

'If I were you I'd try and make your peace with Mr Belvedere. Hate can consume a man until there's nothing left.'

Ross sneered at Stephens. *That's alright for you to say. What if it was you it had happened to? Would you be so willing to forgive then, you pompous arse?*

The clock struck the hour. Stephens let out a relieved sigh. He'd made it.

'Well, thank you for coming, Ross. I hope you found this session useful. My secretary will take care of the fee. I'm afraid I won't be able to see you again for quite some time now as I will be moving to Inner Mongolia to care for my sick mother. I'll refer you to a colleague, of course.'

Stephens flicked through his contacts and prayed his blatant lie wouldn't result in any dire consequences for his mother. This would prove difficult, as she was already dead.

Ross remained in his seat, rubbing his forehead with his hands in exasperation. He was getting the distinct impression the psychiatric fraternity didn't want to treat him. This was the fourth therapist he'd seen in the last two months and none of them had seen him twice. Pretty soon London would be bereft of psychiatrists at the current rate at which they were leaving the country to tend to sick relatives.

None of the therapists he'd seen were a patch on his old anger management counsellor, John Oldham. There was a proper man, thought Ross. Kind, thoughtful, and with a caring nature. He questioned your beliefs and helped you work through your issues until everything seemed so much more straightforward. You had to listen to John as well; everything you were going through he'd been through before. He'd killed a man with his bare hands. When he passed away last year Ross lost more than just his mentor. He'd been lost ever since. Maybe this was all trying to tell him something. Maybe this time therapy wasn't the answer to his problems.

Stephens handed Ross a business card of another psychiatrist. This one had a double-barrelled surname and his first name was Giles. After writing the secretary a cheque, Ross strolled out of the building and tossed the card away. He'd had it with therapists.

****

After ditching his attempts at therapy, Ross decided to take up Stuart's suggestion of finding a hobby to alleviate his anger. This was a novel concept to Ross, whose typical leisure pursuits involved drinking alcohol in The Badger's and visiting the cinema with Adam to watch shoot 'em up movies.

Being a large corporate organisation, Browns of London had a range of social and sporting clubs that employees were encouraged to join. Ross joined the company football team. It was a brief affair.

At the first team training session it became apparent that Ross was in possession of approximately no footballing ability whatsoever. He couldn't head or trap the ball and he couldn't dribble. He could kick the ball but not in the direction he wanted the ball to go in. The one area he seemed to excel at was tackling. He tackled anyone who didn't move quick enough to get out of the way, including his own team mates. No one was safe. Yet somehow Ross had failed to grasp the concept of tackling and he proceeded to hack down and kick as many players as he could. Little or no attempt was made to win the ball. After tearing the captain's cruciate ligament, he was given his marching orders from the football team.

Ross took this setback on the chin and instead joined the company rugby team. Again he was let down by his total inability to catch or throw the ball in a specified direction. This proved to be less of a problem than his failed attempt at football though as the rugby team were much more encouraging of his psychopathic tackling. *This is more like it,* he thought, as he walloped another player. *You can kick, punch, bite and gouge your opponent and as long as the ref doesn't see it you get a hearty slap on the back from your team mates.* The team's love affair with Ross didn't last long though.

After three training sessions Ross had hospitalised half the rugby squad. Although serious, this was less of a sacking offence than his refusal to take part in the team's compulsory drinking games with their adolescent forfeits. He refused to strip naked, stick a firecracker between his bum cheeks and sing God Save the Queen. He refused to participate in the 'last man not to be sick has to drink from a bucket of the other men's sick' game. When he refused to put his knob in a pint Ross was asked to leave the team.

Having failed to master rugby and football, Ross concluded that team sports might not be quite his cup of tea. He investigated the wider range of leisure pursuits offered by Browns and opted to join the company rambling society. When Stuart found out he also joined and the pair of them accompanied fellow ramblers on several weekend walking trips. Ross enjoyed the walking but found the pastime a bit sedate as an activity to help relieve his frustrations. He also found the group a little too obsessed with brewing obnoxious homemade nettle wine, trespassing on farmers' land and growing obscure organic vegetables and bushy beards for his liking. Stuart kept on insisting that they go off the beaten track to experience nature so he could use his compass and ordnance survey maps to navigate their way around the countryside at their own pace. This always ended up in them getting very lost and very wet.

At the end of one trip to Wales where they walked in the pouring rain for eight hours, Ross decided he'd had enough of the walking club. Nature's fine, he thought, but you can't beat being warm and dry, knowing exactly where you are, and not being chased by rural types brandishing shotguns.

****

One evening on his way to The Badgers' Ross was thinking that perhaps the right hobby wasn't out there for him when he spotted a gym and decided to pop in.

He saw lots of men punching. Men punching punch bags, men punching thin air and men punching other men. Ross could see they were letting off a lot of steam. A grizzled old trainer named Patch approached him and asked if he'd ever boxed before. Ross told him he hadn't but he thought he might like to try sometime.

'How about now?' asked Patch.

'I was on my way to the pub,' said Ross, pointing in the general direction of The Badger's Eyebrows. 'I'll pop back some other time.'

'I don't have time for some other time son, I might be dead tomorrow,' Patch said, coughing his guts up. Ross thought he might not be exaggerating if he kept coughing like that.

'Joey, fetch him some training gear. Medium. What size shoe are you, lad?'

'Eight,' replied Ross.

Joey headed off to grab a change of clothes for Ross, who refused to argue on account of Joey looking like the kind of man the police called when they needed to arrest at least 20 unruly bouncers but couldn't spare the officers.

A few minutes later Ross had changed into a pair of shorts, a vest and boxing shoes. Patch fitted a head guard over Ross' head and fastened a pair of boxing gloves onto his hands.

'Now son, you watch what Joey here does and see if you can do the same into this bag.'

Patch was standing the other side of the bag, braced to take the impact of the punch. Joey threw a few right hand jabs, followed by a left-right combination. Ross looked slightly confused but tried to copy what Joey did. The punch bag barely moved. Patch and Joey looked at each other and smiled.

'OK,' said Patch, 'let's not run before we can walk. Step into the ring, lad.'

Ross climbed into the empty boxing ring. Joey stepped into the other side of the ring.

'Er, I don't think so,' said Ross in a panic, moving swiftly to exit the ring.

'It's alright, son,' Patch said, blocking Ross' path out of the ring. 'He's not going to hurt you, are you Joey?' Joey shook his head and grinned. It was one of the biggest heads Ross had ever seen. He wondered if Joey suffered from gigantism. 'You've got no technique, lad and you don't know the first thing about the noble art of boxing. Your physique needs a lot of work as well. We're going right back to basics. I want you to walk over to Joey there and hit him as hard as you can.'

'What?' shrieked Ross.

'He won't hit you back, will you Joey?'

'No,' boomed Joey.

'See Joey there, son? He's been in with all the greats, haven't you Joey? He fought Sonny 'Iron Ore' Lewis for the British title, he took Sugar Ray Planet the distance in Vegas and he even went in with Razor 'Nuclear' Bunker at Madison Square Garden when no one else would go near him, didn't you Joey?'

'Yes,' yelled Joey. The years of taking thousands of heavy blows to the head had taken their toll on Joey's vocabulary.

'Joey here's what we call a human punch bag,' said Patch. 'His strength was always to let his opponent get knackered punching his head and then when he could barely stand Joey throws a few punches and knocks him over. You can't hurt him; he's never been KO'd in his life.'

Ross edged towards Joey; he really didn't want to do this.

'Let's see some aggression,' shouted Patch.

The rest of the boxers had stopped their punching and were staring at the ring. They'd all been in with Joey on their first visit to the gym and it was always a good laugh to watch the new guy's fist rebound off Joey's head and his body shoot backwards.

'Hit him,' yelled Patch. Ross froze. 'Come on, hit him, lad. Think of the thing that makes you mad as hell. Who do you wish he was right now?' he bellowed, pointing at Joey.

Ross looked at Joey and concentrated. Belvedere stood before him, all arrogance and pomposity. Joey saw the change in Ross' eyes and stopped smiling.

'Er, Patch,' he started; he'd seen that look before when he fought Kid Nitro-Glycerine in Honduras.

'I'm going to kill you,' Ross whispered as he stepped forward.

A nanosecond later the building shook with the force of Joey's massive frame slamming into the canvas. Had synchronised gasping been a recognised Olympic sport, those present in the gym at that moment would all have been awarded gold medals. All the boxers stood there open-mouthed. None of them had seen Ross throw the punch but they'd been around long enough to know that when a man hits the deck like a sack of spuds and doesn't get up then he's been hit very hard. Ross was the only other one in the ring.

Patch was slapping himself hard across the face and pinching his skin. 'Shit boy, where have you been all my life?' he screamed incredulously.

****

Over the next few weeks Ross was at the gym every night. Patch was running around like a kid in a sweet shop. He'd ditched all his other boxers and was now working exclusively with Ross. Joey had been released from hospital with his jaw wired up and was on light duties in the gym. He made sure to give Ross a wide berth.

Patch was trying to teach Ross some basic boxing skills and working on his fitness. He'd had to hire some sparring partners from out of town as nobody who'd seen what happened to Joey would set foot in the ring with Ross. Patch called in some favours to get Ross fast-tracked for his first fight.

'We'll just let you knock over a few nobodies and then you can go in with the big boys,' said Patch. 'They won't know what hit 'em.'

Ross was enjoying the training and it was making a big difference in calming his anger. What he really wanted though was for more people to line up against him in the ring and pretend to be Belvedere. After the first guy had been floored, the other sparring partners had made a hasty exit. Patch was frantic in his search for another sparring partner before Ross' upcoming debut fight the following week. When he entered the gym one night Patch ran up to him, beaming.

'I've got someone, lad. He'll go in with you and I've been told he's a tough sod so you've got some punching practice tonight.' Ross stepped into the ring and waited for his latest victim. 'Now just remember what we've practised, lad. Use some of those combinations we've been working on and then hit him with the big one.'

The gym was packed out with boxers who just happened to want to train that evening and make sure they didn't miss the latest sparring partner to get walloped by *The Almighty*, the nickname they'd given Ross. The horde of boxers parted as the new man made his way towards and then stepped into the ring. Ross had his eyes closed and was trying to focus on Belvedere's face to prepare himself. When he opened his eyes he found himself staring at the last man he wanted to be in a boxing ring with. He turned to leave the ring. Patch and a hundred boxers blocked his way.

'Come on lad, don't be nervous. You've knocked over bigger fellas than him,' Patch reassured Ross.

'I'm not going near him.'

'Look son, you're showing me up now. All these lads want to see you do your stuff. Now get over there and hit him like you hit Joey.'

'You don't understand. He's insane. He demolishes houses with his head,' Ross pleaded.

Igneous grinned. That had been a happy day. He'd been passing a house due to be demolished and overheard the builders saying the wrecking ball was broken. Igneous had offered his services. The builders laughed in his face. They stopped laughing when he started head-butting holes in load-bearing walls. After about 10 minutes the house had been nutted into submission and collapsed. Igneous now had a retainer contract with several building firms for human demolition services. At first the firms had a job preparing a contract that didn't break every existing health and safety law as well as making their entire company insurance null and void but eventually, many waiver clauses later, Igneous signed all his rights away and they provided him with a hard hat which he could choose not to wear. It wasn't seen as cool for skinheads to be in employment but the other skinheads agreed that if you're going to have a job then head-butting houses to death was the job to have.

Patch was getting emotional. 'Look lad, if you don't go over there right now and clobber him, you're finished in this gym, and any other gym round these parts,' he said, tears in his eyes. Ross was breaking his heart.

Ross turned to face a beaming Igneous. He squinted his eyes to look closer at the mouth of shining teeth. If he didn't know any better he would have sworn Igneous had super-glued bits of broken bottle to his gums where he had missing teeth. He concentrated again and tried to picture Belvedere. He couldn't do it. He stepped onto the ropes, leapt into the sea of boxers and fled the gym, running all the way home, still in his boxing gear. Patch was inconsolable. Igneous refused to leave the gym until he'd been punched in the head at least 200 times.

Sometime later, when auditing the A & E incident log, an NHS manager reported a suspected case of deliberate misreporting. It just wasn't possible for 63 incidents of broken hands to occur in the same evening.

****

Ross was depressed. He'd enjoyed the boxing but the one-on-one aspect of it was too problematic. He also felt guilty for maiming people just because he was pretending they were Belvedere. He was running out of ideas for ways not to kill his boss. His will was gone; he couldn't fight it any more.

'I'm so sorry,' he said, as he sat alone in his flat, tears running down his cheeks. He picked up the phone and called Adam.

'Hiya mate, I need you to do me a big favour please.'

Chapter 5
Brown Free

A few months ago, the marketing department at Browns had the brainwave of producing a staff newsletter. The Chairman had been told by one of his fellow Masons about their staff newsletter and thought this was just what Browns needed. A newsletter for staff, informative articles about banking and some nice personal interest stories about the troops. Just the job to help boost morale, thought the Chairman. It was a rare display of thoughtfulness for the hundreds of employees he was responsible for by a man whose every waking thought was dedicated towards devising more and more elaborate ways of fiddling his personal expense account.

So the marketing team set to work on bringing the Chairman's vision to life and six weeks later every member of staff was issued with the pristine first issue of *Brown Free*. The Chairman had been persuaded by the Head of Marketing that *Brown Free* would make an ideal title for the newsletter as they could tie it in with their corporate sponsorship of protected Kenyan safari reserves. It was Browns token nod towards international development and the environment and they milked it disproportionately in relation to the pittance they paid to the reserves.

As the brains behind the newsletter, the Chairman agreed with his marketing team that the perfect way to launch *Brown Free* was to include a special personal feature about the Chairman. He would show his nice side and prove to all at Browns that underneath his expensive suit and Bentley, behind the entire floor he had to himself, here was an everyday chap who was just one of the guys.

The Chairman agreed to being interviewed by the marketing people, his plan being to tell them just enough about himself to write their article. Focus on the family, that sort of thing, was the Chairman's thinking. He had almost got through the ordeal of the interview when he was asked a question that threw him.

'Interests?'

'Yes, sir, if you could just tell us what things you like to do outside of work, we think that would finish things off nicely, show the staff you're not all business.'

'Er, yes of course, of course,' the Chairman said, panicking, desperate to think of some interests that would be palatable to his staff.

This was one he couldn't tell the truth on. The troops wouldn't be too keen on a Chairman who awarded himself an annual pay rise of twenty per cent if they discovered his outside interests were foxhunting, the Freemasons and sailing around on a million pound yacht bought out of his Browns expense account for the express purpose of entertaining the company's super-rich clients. That not one of the company's super-rich clients had ever set foot on the yacht in five years of the Chairman owning it was what would finish him off if anyone ever found out. He consequently decided against mentioning the yacht, and owning up to foxhunting and the Masons wouldn't endear him to the workers either. So the Chairman did what he did best. He lied through his teeth.

****

When he received *Brown Free* with his payslip, Belvedere did a very rare thing. He left work at five o'clock prompt. On watching him leave the building, Stephen Cleary, Browns' Head of Security, retrieved a first aid kit and took his temperature and blood pressure, just to check he wasn't hallucinating.

Belvedere had been excited about *Brown Free* for days. He'd seen the posters about this new staff newsletter and heard how the Chairman was right behind it. He knew it; such a fantastic idea could only have been the Chairman's. Belvedere was in awe of the Chairman. He wanted to have business meetings with the Chairman, attend gala luncheons with him and throw dinner parties for him and his family. This was Charles Belvedere's dream and all his hard work and not even thinly concealed toadying was driving him towards this goal.

Charles Belvedere had a busy evening. The Chairman's article had him buzzing with excitement; he had so much to do and couldn't wait to get started. He now knew more than he ever thought possible about the Chairman, about what made him tick. The joy he experienced reading about the Chairman's interests... he hadn't felt this happy since his glorious 72 hour shift at work when he hid in the stationery cupboard to avoid Cleary and his cronies. Being five feet six inches tall and weighing less than a wet towel was a distinct advantage when it came to squeezing into cupboards, Belvedere had discovered. He closed his eyes and experienced comforting warmth and happiness as he reminisced about those exquisite 72 hours. It had been when he first joined the company. Aided by the odd catnap and a box of Pro Plus, he'd spent every hour of those perfect days doing what he loved doing most in the world: working. If it hadn't been for his blasted appendix bursting he'd have stayed in work a lot longer than 72 hours. Browns had never before been confronted with an employee who refused to go home. HR had to draft a new policy and all security staff were now instructed to be on the lookout for stationery cupboards that might be concealing Charles Belvedere.

Now he could be that happy again. The Chairman had given him a blueprint to his dream. The Chairman's passions would become his passions and this way they would have so much in common that it would only be a matter of time before he would be hobnobbing with the Chairman on the fifth floor.

What a guy the Chairman was. Belvedere was so impressed with him. Not only was he responsible for over 500 employees and billions of pounds of investors money, not only was he a family man with a beautiful wife and three lovely daughters, but on top of that he also found time to go fly fishing with friends and was an experienced beekeeper. If that wasn't enough, there was the coup de grace: the

Chairman was a senior member of the Magic Circle.

****

The Chairman had cracked under the pressure. He simply blurted out the first three obscure hobbies he could think of. He thought he was on pretty safe ground with fly fishing: how hard could that be? If anyone questioned him further he would say he fished in private rivers that cost obscene amounts of money to access. The beekeeping had been a bit silly but how many beekeepers were there? If he was pushed he would say he had private hives on his estate and that would end the matter. Nobody was getting onto the Chairman's estate; his armed security guards and attack hounds saw to that. The big mistake had been mentioning the Magic Circle; that was just foolish. You could do magic anywhere. One of his fellow Masons was in the Magic Circle so he would ask them to confirm him as a member if needed. The Chairman hoped nobody else at Browns was interested in magic; it was probably a bit too exotic and strange for a bunch of bankers. He started to relax a bit as he thought more about the predicament he had placed himself in. Who reads these staff newsletters anyway? Tomorrow's fish and chip papers.

****

As Belvedere lay on the single bed of his bachelor flat, his thoughts raced ahead to the bright future opening up for him. He knew nothing about beekeeping, fly fishing or performing magic but as God was his witness, he was going to learn.

Chapter 6
Festive Frivolity

Without the courtesy of a polite notice in the editorial column of the Times, winter descended on England. It was a time of mixed emotions for many. For the intermediary it was boom time. Snowstorms, heavy fog and black ice were tailor-made for accidental fatalities. For Ross, the approach of Christmas was not a happy event. It was a reminder of times gone by.

****

For Detective Inspector Harry Christmas, the arrival of December was the start of the period of the year he could best summarise in one word. Hell. His request for the maximum amount of annual leave permissible during December had been rewarded by his boss with the absolute minimum of holidays granted. None whatsoever. This was the fourteenth year in succession his requests for holidays in December had been declined. After the sixth year Christmas complained to Personnel. It turned out that he'd just been unlucky during those first years but after the complaint his boss made sure every member of staff was granted holiday during December except DI Christmas. It was the start of the relationship between the two men becoming frostier than a penguin's freezer.

As December progressed, Christmas' visits to the staff counsellor verged on stalking. In addition to the prescribed anti-depressants and valium, Christmas took up smoking and carried about his person a hip flask full of whisky. While he was high as a kite, all his drug consumption achieved was to balance out the dangerous stress levels he was experiencing. Still the ridicule continued. During one nightmare winter he kept a record of the abuse to support a discrimination claim he intended to bring in the New Year. In a single day he counted over 300 occurrences of his colleagues shouting 'Harry

Christmas' at him in a jolly voice. Then there were the cards.

At first it was just a few but in recent years an organised campaign had developed. Each year, every single member of staff would send him a card which had been edited to replace the words 'Happy Christmas' with 'Harry Christmas'. He received thousands of them from all over the country. His detective skills led him to discover that his boss had struck a deal with a local printers to purchase the cards at a reduced cost per unit for an annual bulk order. When he complained that he was being victimised, Christmas was told it was good for staff morale. The morale of other staff, that is – not his. The claim was supported by statistical analysis showing that staff absenteeism dropped to its lowest level during December. Nobody wanted to miss the annual piss-take of DI Christmas. It was the one time of the year he truly loved his assistant. Sergeant John Major was loyal to his boss and had refused to join in the elaborate festive mockery of Christmas. Perhaps it was because his earnest and ambitious assistant knew what it meant to have a silly name.

Sergeant Major had not been immune to name calling of course, but unlike his boss, the pattern of his abuse was the exact reverse. At first he'd been bullied remorselessly but this had soon slowed to a trickle and now it was rare if Major received a token comment throughout the whole year. It wasn't as if he was any more popular than DI Christmas, or even any more respected. It was because everyone was scared of him. He never smiled. In the seven years he'd been at the Yard nobody had seen him smile. Then there was his encyclopaedic knowledge of the law and his ruthless enforcement of it.

For Sergeant Major there was never another cheek to turn. He would arrest anyone and everyone. Motorists driving a mile over the speed limit were arrested. He made the other officers nervous. If there was one thing that united the officers of the Yard, it was the common knowledge that far more crime was being committed by police than any so-called criminals. Everyone gave Major a wide berth for this reason.

Despite being doped up to the eyeballs and half-cut, Harry Christmas did some of his best work during December. At any normal time he had an ability to focus that few could match, but during the festive period he could achieve Zen-like states of concentration, such was his desire to block out the world.

Christmas had been doing some research, painstaking and meticulous of course, the only type he was capable of. He had discovered a strange pattern over the past 30 years. The number of senior bankers and corporate business leaders dying from fatal accidents was massive. The number had been similar each year, with no real fluctuations of note. Except that before 1975 there had been only one every four or five years. His investigations also found that the number of accidents of UK bankers and corporate types was much higher, with little or no fluctuations compared to their European counterparts. The USA had an equivalent number of accidents, but a population five times that of the UK. Many of the deaths in the US and Europe had been declared suspicious and prosecutions had occurred. This had happened in almost none of the UK cases. Why had nobody else discovered this?

As far Christmas was concerned there was only one logical explanation for this anomaly that didn't involve a crime. UK residents would have to be unusually accident prone compared to residents of other countries. It had taken some serious digging to test this hypothesis but Christmas had tracked down all manner of statistical analysis from the same countries from which he'd been comparing the accidental deaths. It showed that as a percentage there was no variance of statistical significance to support the theory that people in the UK were more accident prone than their foreign equivalents.

This left DI Christmas with one avenue of inspection open to him. Somebody somewhere was committing a great deal of murders over many years and passing them off as accidents. Christmas liked statistics. They didn't lie and they didn't shout 'Harry Christmas' at you every five minutes. He rubbed his head and sipped the cup of coffee Sergeant Major had brought him from the staff canteen. It tasted of walnuts.

****

The month of December was an important one for the employees of Browns of London. It included the annual Browns Christmas bash. Depending on your point of view, this single evening of merriment-come-debauchery was either the high or low point of the year's social calendar.

For Charles Belvedere it was very much the social high point of his year. Not that it had much competition. Every member of staff from the cleaners to the Chairman was invited to the Christmas bash, which made it the only social event of any description that Belvedere was invited to in the entire year.

Browns had toyed with numerous ideas to stop Belvedere attending. One year they made it fancy dress thinking he would never go for it. He turned up in a smart suit and tie, claiming he'd come as a TV newsreader. Another year they changed the venue at the last minute and accidentally on purpose told everyone except Belvedere. He still turned up. In the end they resigned themselves to the thought that it was the only night of the year they had to put up with him.

The irony was that the presence of Belvedere had spiced up the Christmas bash to the point that nobody wanted to miss it. The senior managers were guaranteed to get plastered before they even arrived – it was the only way any of them could face an evening of frivolity with Belvedere. The widespread drunkenness of senior staff had led to many a wedding proposal, sacking, disciplinary case, criminal prosecution and bitter paternity suit.

****

Less excited about the prospect of the Christmas bash was the Chairman. The thought of having to mingle with the drunken proles for a whole evening made him shudder with revulsion. He'd already tried several strategies to get out of it.

In his first year as Chairman he didn't turn up. Of all the Browns Christmas parties, that was his favourite. The following year his plans were scuppered when the Board invited themselves. The Chairman was answerable to the Board. If they went, he had to go. Since then he had tried, and failed, to ensure his presence at the bash was kept to an absolute minimum through various cunning schemes. He had fallen down a flight of stairs, faked a heart attack, and even had his wife fake a heart attack but every time he got found out. He did manage to get away early one year when he paid a criminal gang to steal his car.

These days he resigned himself to his fate, and with the help of his good friends Jack Daniels and Ron Bacardi he would try his best to make it through the ordeal. This year was different though. The Board wanted to raise the Chairman's profile internally at Browns. The Chairman thought he'd fulfilled that request with his less than truthful interview in Brown Free. The Board wanted more. The PR team hatched a plan for the Christmas bash.

The Chairman poured himself a substantial brandy and drained the glass. He looked in the mirror, and started to cry.

****

For one evening of the year, Browns' head office was turned into party central. At 7pm the doors were unlocked and the waiting guests ushered in. They were queuing round the block.

In years gone by, attendance at the Christmas bash had been poor. Only the senior managers had turned up – because they had to – along with a few lonely souls with nothing better to do. Then, four years ago, the Board had one of those rare flashes of genuine inspiration and consideration in which, for one brief moment, they made a decision that didn't involve increasing their own salaries, awarding themselves non-performance related bonuses or turning a blind eye to their own gross misconduct. *We're a bank,* they thought. *We have more money than sense. Let's pay for the bar at the Christmas bash.* Since then you had to fight your way in. Employees were getting up off their sick beds to attend.

The scrum at the entrance was managed by Browns' security team. Early entrants bundled through the revolving doors in a mad dash to the bar to order a quadruple whisky and six pints of lager each to keep them going for the first hour. Most of them paid little attention to the figure dressed as Santa Claus who was standing outside the entrance to the main bar and dance floor on the first floor, giving out presents whilst unconvincingly trying to sound jolly when saying 'Ho ho ho'.

The last of the partygoers entered the building at 7:10pm. Over 500 people had crammed through the entrance in less than 10 minutes. They weren't hanging about; there was free booze at stake.

As the last of the employees received their free gift and passed into the now heaving bar area, the Chairman took a deep breath and sighed with relief. He reached into his sack and rummaged among the remaining presents. His hand emerged victorious, clutching an expensive silver hip flask that he gladly relieved of its alcoholic contents. He looked ridiculous. Here he was, Chairman of the company, dressed as Santa Claus and giving out cheap crap to morons. Still, at least nobody had recognised him. His spirits were further raised when it dawned on him that he hadn't seen that cretin Belvedere. Things were looking up if he wasn't putting in an appearance.

****

Belvedere was busy working on the task currently occupying number one on his to-do list. He was concentrating on keeping his hand still. There was a faint clicking noise and the office door opened. It had only taken half an hour. His technique was improving.

In preparation for the Christmas bash, Browns' staff were required to finish by no later than three, to give the party organisers and caterers time to prepare. Belvedere didn't finish work early under any circumstances. It hadn't been easy, but he succeeded in locating a disused office on the fourth floor and avoided the detection of security staff by hiding in a cupboard for four hours. To ensure he wasn't short-changing the company he took a boxful of reports he was working on and a torch.

****

Things were hotting up at the bar. The huge queue of customers were getting tetchy. In time the men would be sorted out from the boys, with only the hardcore degenerate drinkers still ordering half pints of spirits for themselves after hours of heavy drinking.

Ross fought his way back from the bar and through the crowd with a tray of drinks and set them down on the table. He'd been fortunate to be near enough to the front of the queue to secure a table. As with every party that has ever taken place in human history, there were more guests than there were tables and chairs, even though the organisers knew well in advance the maximum number of people attending.

The invites for the Christmas bash were given to every employee of the company, who in turn were each permitted a guest to accompany them. As Stuart provided freelance IT support to Browns, he'd received his own invite to the bash. Against his better judgement and, after weeks of being pestered, Stuart had invited Adam as his guest. As his best friends were Stuart, Alice and Adam, Ross hadn't thought anything of inviting Alice as his guest. Alice had.

Ross felt awkward, nervous. Alice looked stunning, knockout, sensational. Gone were the scruffy jeans, t-shirt, Dr Martens boots and lack of attention to hair and make-up. In their place were a beautiful red party gown, professionally styled hair and make-up, exquisite jewellery, brand new heels, perfume, perfectly manicured nails and a dainty handbag. She was feminine in a way that made all the men in the room want to go out, club the nearest animal to death and present it to her for approval. A cleavage that Ross never knew she had was on display, as were luscious legs he couldn't take his eyes off. When she turned her head the ringlets in her hair bounced off each other. Adam wasn't even being discreet. His mouth was wide open, drool forming in its corners as he stared at Alice.

Ross sipped his drink and tapped his foot. He was trying to think of something to say. He saw Alice all the time and they chatted for hours about everything and nothing. Now he was sitting next to the most beautiful and sexy woman in the entire world. Alice had dressed to impress. It was the first time Ross had asked her to anywhere classier than The Badger's and she wanted to make an impression. She wasn't sure if this was a first date and had decided to make sure that if it was, there would be a second.

Her presence hadn't gone unnoticed. Nobody was looking at her, but everyone was glancing around the room on a regular basis, their gaze stopping for just long enough on Alice to get a good eyeful. There were some unhappy women in the room. They'd spent all day getting ready and still looked like they were wearing an old sack and had slept in a dumpster compared to Alice. Many were there to bag themselves a rich banker. All the rich bankers were too busy sneaking cheeky peeks at Alice every couple of seconds to even notice them.

Ross decided on a course of action. He would drink at an increased pace until he stopped feeling petrified to talk to the beauty sitting beside him.

Stuart broke the ice. 'That's a beautiful dress, Alice. Is that one of your lines?'

'Oh what, this old thing?' said Alice, pouting. 'Just something I threw on before I came out.'

Now Ross knew something was up. The normal four-letter-word vocabulary and venomous delivery had been replaced by the voice of a softly spoken 1940s-style submissive movie siren. Squirming and feeling hot, he tried to look at anything except Alice. Adam hadn't closed his mouth yet.

'I love your hair,' continued Stuart. 'Did you get it done at Marsha's on the high street?' he asked matter-of-factly.

'Oh, it's just a new look I'm trying,' said Alice, finishing with a well-rehearsed pout.

'Well I think you look beautiful,' said Stuart.

'Thank you, Stu,' said Alice, glad that at least one person had noticed. She'd gone to a great deal of effort to look her best and was getting a bit annoyed that nobody seemed to have noticed apart from Stuart. 'I need to powder my nose,' she purred.

Stuart pointed her in the direction of the ladies' and she floated across the room, her hips moving hypnotically from side to side as her hair bounced up and down. Hundreds of pairs of eyes followed her. Ross allowed himself a quick glance. Her legs, her hair, her sexy walk, her dress, her voice. He needed an ice cold shower very soon – or at least a bigger size of underpants and trousers than he was currently wearing.

While Alice was in the toilet and Stuart was busy at the bar, Adam took the opportunity to have a quiet word with Ross.

'It wasn't easy,' he whispered, 'but I got that number you were after. Real pros they are,' he said, tapping the side of his nose. 'Only call them if you're dead serious though,' Adam warned him, as he slipped the intermediary's business card along the table to Ross, who quickly put it in his pocket. Tonight was about merriment; Belvedere could wait for another day.

****

As the evening wore on, the atmosphere became more raucous. Ross consumed many drinks and managed to persuade himself that the woman he was talking to was in fact Alice and not the number one in a poll of the hundred sexiest women alive. It helped that Alice had dropped the siren act and reverted to form by drinking pints of lager and whisky chasers and abusing lecherous bankers.

In the few hours between Browns' staff leaving work and them fighting each other to get back in, the company hired to organise the party had made a pretty decent fist of it. An enormous Christmas tree sparkled in the corner of the hall. A substantial buffet was brought in that everyone was waiting to be unveiled. A makeshift stage had been erected at the back of what was normally a huge open plan sea of identical workstations, but was now a dance floor surrounded by tables and chairs with a bar of insufficient size in the corner.

'Testing, testing, one, two,' a voice screeched into a microphone as a group of musicians stood at the back of the stage tuning their instruments.

'Who's the band, Stu?' asked Ross, knowing that Stuart would have somehow acquired this information during the course of the evening.

'Diarrhoea,' said Stuart.

'Diarrhoea? What sort of a name is that? They'll never sell many records with a name like Diarrhoea, will they?' Adam said.

'He's right,' Ross agreed.

'Er no, I think you've got the wrong end of the stick,' Stuart replied. 'It's Dire Rhea, not Diarrhoea.'

'You've lost me there,' said Ross. Adam nodded in agreement.

'Dire Rhea,' said Stuart. 'They're a Dire Straits and Chris Rhea tribute act.'

The lights went down and the band burst into the opening bars of Money for Nothing.

'Come on, you,' said Alice, grabbing Ross by the hand and pulling him towards the dance floor. Ross wasn't much of a dancer but at least he knew it was a sure-fire way of avoiding any possible contact with Belvedere.

****

As luck would have it, Belvedere wasn't too keen on bumping into Ross anyway. His cunning plan of moving him onto money laundering to lower his profile had backfired in spectacular fashion. In his first few months in the new role, Ross had discovered a Browns business account was actually a giant ponzi scheme filtering millions into offshore tax havens. Those responsible were arrested and charged.

The Serious Fraud Office was delighted. Belvedere wasn't.

The party wasn't going well for him. His attempts to stalk the Chairman had been thwarted by a small army of discreet bodyguards, hired to ensure Belvedere couldn't get within 50 yards of the Chairman. His plans scuppered, he'd spent the evening circling the dance floor, trying to push his way into other people's conversations, desperate to find someone, anyone who would talk to him. Instead, they all shuffled off to a Belvedere-free part of the room. His quest continued.

****

After growing bored of winding up Stuart, Adam had tried, with varying degrees of failure, to ingratiate himself with several of the attractive young ladies who worked the counters in Browns' high street banks. He was getting fed up of being given the cold shoulder. He was a lawyer; they should be queuing up to snog him.

****

The Chairman checked his watch. It was almost time to take to the stage to swallow an extra large slice of humble pie and deliver his annual message of thanks to the staff of Browns. He took the hip flask from his pocket and drained its contents. He hated having to mix with ordinary staff, the people who made the place run, the people who kept him in Rolexes and Bentleys. He hated even more having to thank them whilst dressed as Father Christmas. The members of the Board had insisted. It was no good just handing out presents dressed as Santa if nobody knew it was him. He had to show them publicly that he was their servant and they his master. He sipped the dregs of his hip flask and staggered towards the stage.

Already it hadn't been the greatest of evenings for the Chairman. After the doors had opened and everyone had entered the main hall, he'd ditched the fancy dress and proceeded to phase one of his plan. His plan had three phases. Phase one was to spend as much of the evening as possible chatting up the sexy girls from the high street banks. Phase two was to get tipsy whilst carrying out phase one. Phase three would come into play after his speech. He thought it was a good plan. Nice and simple. Not much could go wrong. He hadn't counted on Deborah.

The Chairman had spent the evening trying to avoid Deborah by making sure he was always in a crowd – a crowd of attractive young ladies wearing revealing outfits, of course. As he hid from view behind the stage, changing back into his Santa outfit in preparation for his speech, Deborah sneaked up on him.

'I think it's time for my present now,' she said. 'I've been a naughty girl, Santa – but you like that, don't you?' She started to undo his robe.

The Chairman glanced at his watch. He had never been so relieved to find it was time to give a speech in his life. 'It's time for my speech, Deborah. This will have to wait until later,' he said, giving her his most charming smile. Later was later and he would think of something else by then. Deborah swore in frustration, furious her prey had succeeded in escaping her clutches.

****

The Chairman was a prolific fraudster. He'd taken Browns for millions down the years. To achieve this he either had to fool many people some of the time or one person all of the time. He'd chosen the latter.

Deborah Phillips, the Chairman's PA, knew what he was up to but chose to turn a blind eye because of his undeniable charm, his regular showering of her with expensive gifts, but mainly because she was in love with him. She couldn't help it. He was rich, powerful, handsome in a distinguished way, and had more charm than an amulet factory. The fact he didn't have an ethical bone in his body didn't bother her in the slightest. She'd fallen for him and she meant to have him.

The Chairman was aware of Deborah's interest and had a tendency to encourage it when he required her help with concealing outrageous scams. His mistake was to think he could control the situation. He was a loveable rogue who thought he could keep her dangling on the end of his string for as long as required. A year earlier he crossed the line. At a luxury expenses jolly in Tahiti, or key fact-finding mission to give it its official title, the Chairman had brought Deborah along as a reward for standing by him over the years. On the last night he overdid it on vodka and slept with her. He'd regretted it ever since.

Now, as far as Deborah was concerned, they were having an affair. The Chairman had been giving her the slip for some time since. He was trying to keep matters to playful flirtation that didn't go anywhere. Deborah wanted anywhere.

****

It wasn't a great speech. It wasn't up there with Martin Luther King's 'I have a dream'. The Chairman bumbled his way to the end with a less than heartfelt 'three cheers for the workers' battle cry. As the final 'hooray' died down the assembled throng turned and began a stampede towards the buffet. If there was a world record time for removing kitchen foil from industrial quantities of food, the caterers smashed it before diving for cover. Stuart was at the front of the stampede.

Meanwhile, Adam was taking advantage of a quiet bar. His evening was improving – he'd found a girl who would let him buy her a drink. After an evening of countless knock backs, he was in no mood for another one. While everyone focussed on the Greco-Roman wrestling taking place at the buffet, Adam removed a small glass vial from his pocket and, checking he was unobserved, emptied the contents into a vodka and orange.

The relieved Chairman made his way off the stage as the band launched into On the Beach. It was time to put phase three of his plan into action. Phase three was simply 'get twatted'. There was no phase four. He wandered over to Ross and Alice.

'Ross my boy, how goes it? What did you think of the speech? Better than last year's, wouldn't you say?'

Ross was considering whether he should lie to the Chairman to protect his feelings as Adam returned from the bar. 'Right guys, I'll see you all later. I've pulled.' Adam nodded his head towards a pretty blonde over the other side of the room who smiled back at him.

'Good show, man,' said the Chairman. 'She's a fine young filly. Here,' he said, grabbing the vodka and orange out of Adam's hand, 'I'll have that.' He knocked the contents back in one. 'I'll get you and your lady friend some champagne. Nothing impresses the ladies like champagne my boy, you mark my words.'

The Chairman wandered over to the bar and returned moments later with a bottle of champagne and two flutes. He handed them to Adam, slapped him on the back and slunk back to the bar. Adam stood there open-mouthed, replaying the last few minutes in his head and hoping for a different outcome. Sheepishly, he made his way over to the pretty blonde, armed with the champagne, and received a delighted hug and peck on the cheek. Perhaps he would get his end away after all.

****

The Chairman was busy caressing and whispering sweet nothings to a pair of quadruple whiskies at the bar as Deborah sidled up beside him.

'Come in for the kill, have you dearest?' he asked, no longer possessing the energy or mental ingenuity to evade her any longer. 'Lead on, my girl, lead on,' ordered the Chairman as he followed her towards the exit, still nursing his whiskies.

As they entered the hall and turned left towards some uninhabited offices, the lift opened and out stepped Detective Inspector Harry Christmas.

'Can I help you?' asked the Chairman.

'I'm Detective Inspector Christmas and this is Detective Sergeant Major,' said Christmas, presenting his credentials.

'Christmas eh,' remarked the Chairman. 'Be funny if your first name was Harry,' he said, sniggering.

Sergeant Major winced and turned his back. He couldn't watch.

'Funny how?' asked Christmas.

'Oh you know, Harrrryyy Christmas,' yelled the Chairman, roaring with laughter at his own joke.

DI Christmas was unamused. 'Oh I see,' he exclaimed, striking his forehead with his palm. 'You made a hilarious reference to my surname and how it would be even more amusing if my first name made my entire name both a joke name and a festive yuletide greeting. How very clever of you. With your permission, I'll laugh at a later time when it's safe to do so, for instance when I'm in the immediate vicinity of a hospital that specialises in emergency abdominal surgery. I wouldn't want my internal organs spilling onto the floor as a result of my sides splitting, unless I could guarantee an experienced surgeon was close to hand.'

If he wanted to, DI Christmas could be sarcastic professionally. Such was the arid nature of his humour that the world's cactus population and the policy of certain Middle Eastern states towards alcohol consumption were all jealous of its lack of moisture.

A confused Chairman failed to comprehend Christmas' meaning but had a sense that he should somehow feel embarrassed, and duly obliged.

'Er, yes well, I'm the Chairman of Browns, gentlemen. How may I be of assistance?'

DI Christmas looked at the man standing before him, dressed as Santa whilst bouncing off the walls, and doubted the validity of this statement. 'Just the man we're looking for,' he said. 'Is there somewhere private we can talk?'

The Chairman led the way to an office at the end of the corridor. *This is it,* he thought, *they've rumbled me. My last act as Chairman is going to see me marched out in handcuffs dressed as Father Christmas.*

They reached the office and the Chairman opened the door and switched the light on. A startled young man sitting behind a desk looked back at him. There was an uncomfortable pause while the Chairman waited for the man to explain himself.

'Er, I don't know what you're doing but do you mind leaving? I have some official business to attend to,' said the Chairman.

Another pause followed during which the man said nothing. He then made an audible groan, fumbled with something behind the desk, stood up and darted out of the room. The Chairman invited the detectives into the room. He was just about to address DI Christmas when the part of his brain associated with problem solving managed to come up for air from beneath a sea of alcohol. He turned to the desk.

'If you wouldn't mind, this is official business.'

There was a momentary shuffle that sounded not unlike a middle-aged woman trying to get up off the floor with the aid of a leather chair. The lady in question emerged from under the desk, grinned at the Chairman and shuffled out of the room sheepishly. All that was missing was a comedy innocent whistle as she left. Sergeant Major took out his notebook and began writing. Perhaps he would get an arrest out of the evening after all.

The Chairman had forgotten the incident already. 'Are you chaps from the,' he paused, 'Fraud Squad?'

'No, sir, we're from the Murder Investigation Team at Scotland Yard.'

The Chairman was so relieved he broke out into an enormous and inappropriately broad smile. DI Christmas dispensed with the pleasantries and got to the point. He explained to the Chairman that they were there to ask him some questions about a friend of his, a Mr William Phillips who had died in an apparent accident on holiday in the Seychelles.

The Chairman listened intently but at some point after the first few words his attention was drawn to more pressing matters. These included a sudden racing of his heart, the violent spinning of his head, the inability of all his senses to work and the loss of all voluntary control of his muscles, bones, joints and ligaments. Less than a second later he collapsed face down onto the floor, foaming at the mouth. The detectives looked at each other. Christmas reacted first, instructing Major to administer first aid while he called for an ambulance. Browns was near Westpoint General and the ambulance arrived within ten minutes.

The Chairman would have been most relieved that he wasn't conscious to witness the crowd of people gawping at him as he was carried out on a stretcher, loaded into the ambulance, and driven at high speed to Accident and Emergency. His bad turn had caused a great deal of excitement and concern amongst the staff of Browns. One person who wasn't the least bit concerned was Deborah. She'd been standing outside the office, eavesdropping. When the Chairman collapsed and paramedics rushed into the office to whisk him away, she strolled over to the bar and ordered an extra large gin.

She had to hand it to the Chairman; he had some nerve. To think that he could get away with a fourth bogus medical emergency at the Christmas bash took the biscuit. She wondered how he'd done it. On the previous three occasions she'd arranged for the fake ambulance to turn up and getting hold of phoney ambulances wasn't easy. She had to admit it – he'd gone to town with the deception. Recruiting fake detectives was the work of a real pro.

****

Ross watched Alice saunter away from the dance floor and head in the direction of the ladies', briefly turning back to smile at him. He returned the smile and strutted off towards the bar. He couldn't remember the last time he'd smiled so much. Maybe a bit of fun was just what he needed; perhaps he might not need to kill Belvedere after all.

As he ordered a couple of drinks at the bar, he felt like a load had been lifted off his shoulders. Then he saw Belvedere attempting to talk to Alice. A rage rose in him so fierce he struggled to maintain control. Alice ignored Belvedere's ramblings and looked around for Ross. Her eyes glanced past and then back to a Ross look-alike who stood rooted to the spot, shaking. His face was crimson with a hint of purple.

Stuart's sixth sense alerted him to the danger. He spotted Alice and Belvedere together and then saw an about-to-explode Ross at the bar staring at the two of them. He darted over to him, grabbed him by the arm and bundled him out of the room and into an empty office next door. Ross was still shaking with rage. Stuart sat him down on a chair, crossed himself several times, took a deep breath and then slapped Ross hard across the face. A few moments passed during which Ross ceased his Incredible Hulk impersonation and returned to his senses. He clutched his cheek in pain.

'Why do you let him get you so worked up like that?' Stuart asked.

Ross frowned. Stuart was his best friend but he'd never told him the real reason why he had to kill Belvedere.

'It's no good, Stu. I thought I had it under control but there's no getting away from it. I'm going to have to kill the bastard.'

'Just ignore him; he's so pathetic he's not worth the effort.'

'Believe me, he's worth it,' snarled Ross.

'Why?'

Ross felt the uncontrollable urge to unburden himself. He had to tell someone. He told Stuart.

Chapter 7
Pedagogic

Stuart sat on his family-sized sofa, helping himself to the family-sized picnic he'd assembled on the seat next to him. Stuart's family of one was switching between a tempting array of his favourite delicacies. He was also watching Columbo. Eating food and watching Columbo were the two things that gave him a warm, comforting feeling, something he needed right now. He had thinking to do.

Stuart had promised to help Ross. He'd made a promise. Stuart didn't enter into promises lightly. If he made a promise then that was what he would do. The problem was he'd promised to help his best friend and the help his best friend wanted was to commit murder. Stuart wasn't the violent type. He kept goldfish. He grew orchids. He'd never been in a fight in his life. This was in part because he went out of his way to avoid confrontation but also because anyone who picked on him at school had received a hiding from Ross.

Stuart spent his working days solving technical problems, using a combination of logical and creative thinking. If a problem couldn't be solved with the tools available then a different look at the problem was needed. How could he help Ross in a way that would spare Belvedere's life? He had to come up with something because now that Stuart knew the truth, he knew Ross wouldn't just forgive and forget. He crammed another mini pork pie into his mouth and watched Columbo at work. What would *he* do? Then it came to him. *It's a bit of a long shot*, he thought, *but it's worth a try.*

****

Stuart's research led him to the Institute for Creative Computing, a research centre at the University of Shepherds Bush. He arrived early for his appointment with the Institute's Head, Professor Shambles, and waited outside his office.

Before embarking on his career in the commercial IT sector, Stuart spent a brief and unhappy stint as a junior university researcher. The experience taught him two things about university academics. First, they were monumentally arrogant and self-absorbed and the higher up the food chain they got, the more colossal were their egos. The second thing he knew was that every one of them had a price. No matter how many hundreds of letters they had after their name, if you offered to fund their research they'd bend over backwards to accommodate you. Satan could walk in with a horrible 'Englishman who's spent far too long on the beach in Spain' crab-coloured tan, sporting prominent horns and an inconspicuous tail, and providing he was carrying a suitcase full of cash he would be welcomed into the boardroom of any university.

It was this knowledge that secured Stuart his appointment with the man heralded as being at the forefront of revolutionary new strands of computing. Stuart had suggested his company was interested in funding some new research and was given an appointment for the following day.

When he arrived, Stuart was surprised to be greeted by a man who was not only clean-shaven but wearing a smart suit and smiling. This was alien behaviour for any of the professors Stuart had encountered before.

Shambles began the meeting with an extensive lecture on the many excellent qualities of the Institute. Stuart couldn't help thinking that he could have saved them both a lot of time by summarising all of this in two words: 'We're great'. When the professor eventually had to stop for air and to re-moisten his salivary glands, Stuart took this as his cue to get a word in edgeways. He outlined the area of research he was interested in.

'It's a very interesting area,' began Shambles, without the slightest hint of sincerity. 'It's very much science fiction of course at this stage and a great deal of research needs to be done before it can be brought anywhere near to fruition.'

Stuart nodded, waiting for it. Shambles began scribbling some figures in a notebook and muttering to himself.

'Let's see now, you'd need ... mumble ... professors ... mumble ... researchers ... mumble ... ... pedagogic research ... mumble ... use of facilities ... mumble mumble.' Stuart couldn't help comparing the experience to that of a cowboy builder plucking random figures out of the air when preparing a farcical quote for services.

Here it comes.

'Yes, that's it,' mumbled Shambles. 'It's just a provisional estimate of course but for a thorough research project on this topic to deliver your outputs I'd say we are looking at a starting budget of at least five to six million pounds.'

Stuart nodded and pretended to consider the figure. Shambles had seen enough. He'd been in enough of these meetings to know that Stuart didn't have a pot to piss in. Stuart was in luck though – Shambles had just been on a people skills training course. Before the course he would have told him to bugger off. Instead, he did the world's worst impersonation of an absent-minded professor remembering he has another far more important meeting he has to be at. This gave him an excuse to bring the meeting to a swift close without offending his guest. Shambles made his apologies to Stuart, thanked him for his time and asked him to consider the project and get back to him. With a bit of luck he would still have enough time to make the faculty's executive committee; there was someone there from marketing he wanted to persecute.

He was at the door when something stopped him in his tracks. *This man has come here proclaiming to have money to spend on research. It may not be very much money but your job is to take that money from him and award yourself a pay rise.* He stepped back into his office, picked up a file and flicked through it. He found the page he wanted.

God, not those two.

'We have a few junior researchers who have some interest in your area. They may be in a position to do some exploratory work for you.' Shambles scribbled down the names on a post-it and instructed Stuart to speak to his secretary for their location. Then he disappeared.

****

It took Stuart some time to locate the offices of the researchers he was looking for. It would appear the building had been designed by an architect who specialised in labyrinths. There were lots of corridors. The corridors just led to more corridors, which then led back to the start of the first corridor. There were no clear signs indicating where you would arrive at if you ventured down a particular corridor. Stuart thought this would be a good place for juvenile rabbits to prepare for their advanced warren-making exams. A few of the office doors had names on them but they were either empty or populated by people who hadn't recently been on a people skills training course.

As he progressed in what he guessed as the correct direction, Stuart noticed the offices becoming pokier. The general state of décor and housekeeping resembled that of the slum accommodation estate agents were never able to shift. He hadn't seen any natural light for some time.

Stuart reached the end of the corridor and thought he must have made a wrong turn as there were only what appeared to be a couple of dingy broom cupboards. He opened one. It contained an assortment of low-quality cleaning equipment and a broom that had seen better days. He opened the second door. The room, if you could call it that, was even smaller than the first broom cupboard. It contained two junior computing researchers.

The room barely passed as office accommodation for a small squirrel, yet somehow two men were squeezed into it. The room had no window, no ventilation and there was just the tiniest space between the two desks. *They must have to breathe in before one of them can enter or exit the room*, thought Stuart.

'Er hi, I'm Stuart Davies. Professor Shambles sent me. I'm looking for...' He squinted at the indecipherable scrawl on the post-it; *that can't be right,* he thought, *the Prof is having me on.*

'Rum and Black?' One of the researchers performed some complicated contortionism in order to adjust himself enough to extend his hand to Stuart.

'I'm Black,' he said, shaking Stuart by the hand. 'Matthew Black. This is my colleague Dr Lo Rum.'

Matt Black and Lo Rum, occupying an office smaller and darker than my airing cupboard, thought Stuart. It was possible for this scene to become more ridiculous but Stuart failed to see how.

'You can tell Shambles,' said Black, 'that we've got until the end of the week to organise our affairs and I've got confirmation of that in writing.' He brandished a dog-eared piece of official-looking paper in his hand.

'I think there might be some confusion. I've just come from a meeting with Professor Shambles about a research project I'm interested in funding and he recommended I speak to you.'

Rum and Black looked at each other in confused silence for a few seconds and then attempted to simultaneously scramble out of the room. This resulted in what looked a lot like a pair of grown men playing Twister in a miniature cupboard under the stairs.

Breathless, the two men reached the freedom of the corridor and introduced themselves to Stuart. Now that they were in more normal, albeit artificial, lighting Stuart could see at least one possible reason for them being hidden away. Black was the hairiest man Stuart had ever seen. It was impossible to distinguish between the competing areas of hair on his body. The hair on his head had no clear boundary with the hair on his face, which in turn seemed to be fighting some sort of turf war with the hair on his neck and chest. Stuart couldn't bring himself to look at Black's hands. Instead, he looked at Rum's hand as he shook it – and wished he hadn't. He was missing a finger on each hand.

'Triads,' said Black by way of explanation. Rum was of Asian descent and wasn't coming across as much of a talker. His petite stature seemed to be of benefit to him in his present office accommodation. Whereas Rum was standing up, Black was hunched over and in dire need of a lengthy session with a chiropractor. Stuart stopped staring at Rum's hands and appraised his face instead. He looked behind him to see what Rum was looking at but there was nobody there. *Oh God,* thought Stuart; *he's got a lazy eye. Stop staring, Stuart. Stop staring at his lazy eye.*

Black ushered them all back down the corridor until they found an empty meeting room. As they sat down around the table Rum and Black entered into a whispered conversation. Whispering appeared to be the standard means of communication for Rum. Stuart couldn't hear a word Rum was saying to Black but when it was Black's turn he could hear every word, although he couldn't understand it as it wasn't in spoken in English.

These guys have no social skills at all and they look like rejects from a circus freak show. Let's just hope they're brilliant at computing.

'Erm, perhaps you could er you know, erm tell us about this research project you are interested in,' said Black, trying not to come across as too eager.

Stuart gave them the spiel he'd given Shambles. More whispering followed from Rum to Black. Stuart watched the dynamics of their relationship unfold. Rum was the brains and the one who made the decisions while Black did the talking for them both.

'Erm, yes we are interested in that area of research but ... well, the thing is it's a broad area. Could you tell us exactly what you want to do?'

Direct, thought Stuart. *More direct than Shambles was.* He noticed that Rum was wearing a discreet pin in his shirt collar that he recognised as a CND logo. He'd also spotted a 'save the whale' poster on the wall of their 'office'. *At least one of these guys is pro-life. Honesty might be the best policy here.* Stuart told them what he wanted them to do and, more importantly, why.

'So as you can see, gentlemen, the lives of two men are literally in your hands. If you are successful then one man's life will be spared and another will avoid going to prison for a long time. That man is a very dear friend of mine and knowing him as I do, he won't make it in prison. He'll take his own life.'

Stuart had stretched the truth a little bit with the last point but with Ross' fragile mental state who knew what he would do. More frenzied whispering took place between Rum and Black. They scribbled notes on a pad of paper and animatedly pointed at each other. They turned back to Stuart.

'What's the deadline?' asked Black.

'Two months,' said Stuart.

The two men stared at each other. Black frowned and Rum looked like he was about to have a nervous breakdown.

'How much?'

Stuart told them his budget. Rum shook his head while Black muttered obscenities to himself.

'I'm afraid we can't do it that soon or for that amount,' said Black, disappointed.

'What's the issue? Is it time or money?'

'Both,' said Black. 'All research projects have to be approved by the Institute's committee and because of the size of this one, they won't look at it for at least a month. A more pressing matter though is that our contracts of employment are terminated at the end of this week so unless it could be approved by Friday then it's a non-starter.'

'Why are they terminating your contracts?' Stuart asked.

'The official reason is they're downsizing the department but we overheard they want to knock through to make a bigger broom cupboard. Also, erm, there have been some complaints.' Black didn't elaborate but Stuart could take a fair guess as to the nature of them.

'What about the money?'

'That's more of an issue for the Institute,' said Black. 'All research projects have to be costed out and approved by the committee. There's equipment, travel, admin costs, insurance, marketing and it has to make at least a three hundred per cent profit after all that.'

'I see. And how much of the project budget goes to you two?'

'I don't understand,' said Black.

'You know, for doing all the work. How much do you two get?'

Black translated this to Rum. There was a pause followed by a roar of laughter from both men. Rum wiped the tears from his eyes.

'What's the joke?'

'We don't get a penny,' explained Black, still giggling. 'All the money goes to the Institute and they just extend our contracts for the duration of the work. Then when it's finished we go and they keep the profits.'

'I see. And what will you do after Friday?'

Rum whispered into Black's ear.

'He said he'll be spending the last of his money on a one-way ticket back to Korea if nobody offers him a job. He's Korean, you see,' said Black.

'That would certainly be a good reason to travel to Korea,' said Stuart. 'And what about you?'

'Well I'm mulling over a few offers. Got to make the right decision you know.'

'Got a few irons in the fire, have you?'

'That's right.'

'So you wouldn't both be interested in an offer of employment then?'

The two dispensed with the whispering. The excited head nodding between them somewhat gave the game away.

'Yes,' shouted Lo.

'I thought he didn't speak English?'

'He knows that word,' said Black.

'Congratulations,' said Stuart. 'Just to be clear though, this is nothing to do with the Institute so not a word to Shambles. You'll be working for me. And to make the budget go as far as possible, we don't need to make this official and bother the taxman; it's a strictly cash-in-hand job. I'll pay your expenses and purchase any equipment you need.'

'You got it,' beamed Black.

He clasped Stuart by the hand and shook it vigorously. Stuart wished he hadn't. The three men, now partners, continued their meeting and agreed the finer details of what would be needed to get started. Rum and Black didn't have the luxury of being concerned about the questionable morality of what they would be doing. They needed to eat. The meeting concluded with the men exchanging phone numbers and arranging to meet on Saturday at Stuart's flat to start work. Rum and Black then went to the nearest pub to get pissed.

'No more broom cupboards for us anymore, Lo,' said Black as they chinked their pints of beer in a darkened corner of the pub.

Chapter 8
The Council Meets

The intermediary made his final preparations. The room that would host the meeting had everything required of it. It had a table. It had four chairs. It had a trolley in the corner with an assortment of beverages. He'd pushed the boat out a bit by laying on a plate of custard creams. Alcohol was absent from the menu. People have a tendency to talk a little too freely when they've had a tipple or several. They might say something they wouldn't get the chance to regret.

The intermediary paced up and down the room. Something was bothering him. Had he gone too far with the biscuits? The presence of food could result in the meeting being prolonged further than the absolute minimum amount of time it could be concluded within. None of the four attending this meeting wanted to be there one second longer than was necessary.

It must be the biscuits producing the anxiety; he'd been fifty-fifty about whether to have them. There was two minutes before his first guest was due to arrive. He grabbed the plate of biscuits, dashed into the hall, unlocked the tiny utility room, threw the biscuits in, locked the door and dashed back into the room. They would have been too much of a temptation.

He sat down at the far end of the table with his back to the wall and a clear view of the door. In the opposite corner, just to the right of the door, a small television attached to the wall showed the street outside the building. It was a private lock-up garage on an industrial back street, chosen for its excellent location of being far away from, well, everything really.

The intermediary watched the first of his guests arrive on the screen. A car pulled up outside the lock-up and its passenger wasted no time in exiting the car and opening the lock-up with their key. Each of the four had one. As he watched the guest enter the lock-up the intermediary realised what was causing his stress. He'd forgotten something. He searched his coat pocket and found it. As guest number one made their way down the flight of stairs to the concealed basement where the meeting was taking place, the intermediary pulled the balaclava over his head and adjusted it, just in time before the door opened.

A short, stocky man entered the room, all dressed in black, with a black balaclava covering his head. You didn't need to hear him speak to know this character was male. He was as wide as he was tall. Whilst by no means fat, he had a 25-inch neck and arms so large that his diet almost certainly included the appetising dish of raw meat, raw eggs and steroids blended into 'power' shakes.

Following the strict protocol agreed between the parties prior to the meeting, the figure in black made his way around the table and sat down on the chair opposite the door, with the intermediary sitting to his right.

'Intermediary,' said the man, acknowledging his host.

'Middleman,' replied the intermediary, returning the acknowledgement.

'Drink?'

'I'm alright thanks.'

This discourse concluded the informal pleasantries. The two men never took their eyes off each other.

The middleman was, unsurprisingly, a middleman. He performed the same role as the intermediary did for a criminal organisation known in the underworld as The Pugilists. His true identity was a well-guarded secret.

If you wanted someone killed and it made to look like an accident you went to The Boss Killers. If you wanted someone to be given an almighty kicking then you hired The Pugilists. Their particular field of speciality was violence, stopping just short of actual death. How short was determined by the client. The Pugilists offered a comprehensive portfolio of services ranging from a black eye right through to permanent paralysis. They were well trained and for the right price could break any specified bone in their victim's body.

The Pugilists liked to think of themselves as more than just mere thugs but there was no getting away from the fact that they did employ an awful lot of burly men who were covered in tattoos, preferred a military-style haircut and were not unsympathetic to the views of certain far-right political groups. In short, they were a bunch of thugs, albeit a bunch of highly skilled thugs with an encyclopaedic knowledge of human anatomy.

Of the other three groups due to be represented at the meeting, the intermediary had the most time for The Pugilists. There was always a market for a gang of violent thugs and, as a paid up member of the old school of criminals, he appreciated their no-nonsense administering of justice. You knew where you were with The Pugilists; usually face down in the mud being kicked in the bollocks by big leather boots and beaten about the body by baseball bats.

Compared to the two representatives yet to make an appearance, the middleman was the intermediary's best mate. It went without saying that neither man trusted the other as far as they could throw them but, despite this, they had an unwritten alliance between them to watch each other's backs against the other two.

He wasn't supposed to know the identity of any of The Pugilists but through his spies the intermediary had it on good authority that several were former members of The Boss Killers who had grown weary of faking accidents and yearned for some knuckle-on-nose action. The Pugilists didn't earn as much as The Boss Killers, on account of them leaving their victims still alive, but they did provide a more comprehensive dental package.

Right on cue, five minutes after the arrival of the middleman, footsteps were heard coming down the stairs of the lock-up. The door opened and in stepped a tall, wiry individual. Like the other two, he was dressed all in black and his facial features were identical to that of a balaclava.

'Intermediary.'
'Go-between.'
'Middleman.'
'Go-between.'

Acknowledgements over, the man took his seat to the right of the door, opposite the intermediary and with the middleman to his right. The atmosphere in the room had changed since he entered. Before it was tense; now it was electric. The three men stared at each other. The middleman and the intermediary hated the go-between. They also feared him. There wasn't much the intermediary feared; he'd been tortured on many occasions. The men the go-between represented though – there was no other word for it: they were evil.

The go-between was, believe it or not, a go-between. His role was that of liaison between the aptly named Gang and their clients. Like The Pugilists, The Gang dished out violence for clients with a severe grudge against their victims. It was the method used by The Gang that was so abhorrent, so sickening to the other men present in the room; men who arranged murder and torture for a living. The Pugilists tackled their victims head on, welcoming the inevitable confrontation that would occur as a result of their target seeing a group of angry-looking hard men approaching them. The Gang preferred to approach their victims from the rear.

By all accounts, the members of The Gang were well paid for their work. These generous financial incentives in no way made it easy for them to recruit new members. There were many gangs in London and across the UK. As in all industries, there was a good deal of movement in personnel between them. Star performers were headhunted and won or lost in high-stakes poker games. Some were spies for other gangs who wanted to see what the competition was up to. None of this horse-trading ever applied to The Gang. Nobody wanted to work for them

Like The Pugilists, The Gang stopped short of murder. It wasn't necessary for them to kill their victims. Most didn't make it past a couple of years before they could no longer live with the shame and took their own life. The others were so dead inside they might as well have been killed.

The intermediary wished he could get rid of The Gang from The Council but it was too late now, they knew too much to be allowed to operate unchecked. When they first joined the alliance of criminals known as The Council they were merely rivals to The Pugilists, giving people a good hiding. Somewhere along the line they saw a depraved gap in the market and decided to fill it. The intermediary couldn't understand how they could do what they did. He had it on good authority that the members of The Gang weren't even homosexual. He wasn't taking any chances though; both he and the middleman had agreed that they would enter the room first, that the backs of their chairs would be so tight against the wall there would be insufficient room for an amoebic stick insect to squeeze past, and that the go-between would be in front of them at all times.

The intermediary looked forward to a time in the not too distant future when, if all his plans were executed, he would never again have to sit in a room with a deviant freak like the go-between. As far as he was concerned the only redeeming feature the go-between had going for him was that he wasn't the secretary.

The secretary waltzed into the meeting room and took her seat next to the door. It was a stipulation of the meeting that she was not allowed to be within arm's length of any of the others present at any point. At five foot two inches tall, her arm's length was not very long, but when calculating the room dimensions in preparation for the meeting, the intermediary had taken his best guess at the secretary's arm's length and quadrupled it to be on the safe side.

In yet another in a long line of incidents engineered to infuriate the other members of The Council, the secretary had turned up ten minutes late. In recognition of this affront, none of the others even bothered to acknowledge her. She helped herself to a tall glass of mango juice, confidently assuming it wasn't poisoned, and muttered to herself, loud enough for the others to hear, about the lack of biscuits. The intermediary was fuming. She wasn't even wearing a balaclava.

As they waited for her to finish adjusting her black bobbed hair, check her make-up and take out a notepad, breaking yet another of The Council's rules, the three men fantasised about taking out a contract on her. The intermediary attempted to achieve calm by considering which type of accident he would arrange for the secretary and settled on the combination of man overboard/boat propeller/hungry sharks luxury yachting accident, one of his favourites. The middleman considered the order in which he would like to break her bones. Alphabetically perhaps, or maybe in order of size, starting with the smallest. The go-between's thoughts about the secretary were best left unsaid.

The intermediary had the best reason of all to despise the secretary. She was a former employee of The Boss Killers.

The secretary was, that's right, a secretary. She was employed in an exclusive private medical practice as an administrator. When arranging large numbers of fatal accidents, as the intermediary did, it was necessary to have access to a wide range of individuals in certain professions who, for not inconsiderable sums of money, could aid you in your endeavours. The secretary was one such person. Through her contacts she could handpick those colleagues who had no interest in the welfare of patients but were in it purely for the money and had no moral qualms at all about what they would have to do to earn as much of it as possible .

The secretary had helped the intermediary. If a man fell down a flight of stairs for no apparent reason, the police investigating the case might find about the victim's person a hospital letter for an upcoming appointment with an ear, nose and throat consultant for vestibular tests to address the source of their dizziness. Case solved. Fatal car accidents could be written off when victims were taking prescribed drugs with dangerous side effects. She even put him in touch with bent coroners who, for the right price, would sign anything off as an accident or natural causes. Then one day, like so many others before her, she got greedy. The intermediary knew very well the danger of greed. The reason he was still a free man after all these years was because he *wasn't* greedy. Yes, he could make a fortune by arranging more accidents but sooner or later he'd be caught. Being rich beyond your wildest dreams was jail bait. Much better to be wealthy and free.

So the secretary stopped returning the intermediary's calls and when he did get hold of her, she announced she was now the official representative of an organisation known as The Medics. A written request was submitted for The Medics to join The Council. The secretary made it clear to the intermediary that if this request was turned down she had enough dirt to put him away for a long time. The Boss Killers' executive committee accepted the request on agreement that the secretary continued to assist them in covering the tracks of their accidents. It was a decision the intermediary accepted but disagreed with. He'd pushed hard for them to do her in. The Pugilists and The Gang went along with the deal to keep the peace. By the time they all learned of the true nature of the services The Medics would be providing it was too late, they were on The Council. Once you were on The Council the only way off was to start a war. Nobody wanted a war with The Medics.

The true nature of what The Medics did sickened The Council, even the members of The Gang. The intermediary thought this somewhat hypocritical of The Gang given what *they* did for a living. It was a low individual who wished cancer upon someone. It was an even lower individual who paid someone to make good on that wish. The intermediary despised The Medics' hypocrisy. While he and his colleagues skulked in the shadows, The Medics were being publicly thanked for their excellent charity work while hob-knobbing with other high-level sycophants at Masonic lodges and rotary clubs.

Nobody knew *how* they did it but The Medics offered their clients the opportunity to select the paralysing or fatal disease of their choice for their unlucky victim. Cheaper offerings included a dose of swine flu, measles or some uncomfortable sexually transmitted diseases. As the price increased, so did the seriousness of the ailments. Exotic diseases such as dengue fever and Japanese encephalitis were all available for the right price, as were diabetes and pneumonia.

In the top price bracket came the biggies: meningitis, AIDS and cancer. They were working on Ebola but it wasn't quite ready yet.

At some point everyone has to visit the doctor or hospital and it was for this reason the arrogance of the secretary was tolerated by The Council. They were all shit scared that a routine visit to the doctor's would end up with them contracting rabies or anthrax.

The intermediary coughed loudly to signify the start of the meeting.

'Thank you all for coming. The 1990 annual general meeting of The Council is now in session.'

The Council, as it was known, was an alliance between four criminal organisations all operating in the revenge business. It existed for two reasons. The first was to maximise the revenue of each organisation through collaborative working and economies of scale. The second reason was to keep them all out of prison. The intermediary was most interested in the second reason, whereas he knew the others were only interested in the first.

He'd had the idea many years ago. How would it look if one day someone had a fatal accident and whilst the police were investigating the incident the victim's brother, son, daughter or father was beaten within an inch of their lives? The police may not always be the brightest sparks but they would be sure to take a much closer look at the first incident than they would have done otherwise.

As well as arranging the finer details and administrative aspects of The Boss Killers' contracts with clients, the intermediary also oversaw all the jobs carried out by the other three groups. This way he could ensure that if jobs had to be carried out on people in the same family, business, street, village or football team they were not done within a few days of each other. In short, through careful planning, he made their crimes appear more random than they actually were.

'Middleman, your report please.'

'A solid year for The Pugilists, intermediary. Revenues up fifteen per cent, net profits up twenty per cent. Fourteen arrests in total and two convictions but you already know the details of those cases.'

Indeed I do, thought the intermediary. One of The Pugilists, after beating a drug dealer almost to death, proceeded to smoke half the guy's stash of skunk whilst still at the crime scene, collapsing into an unconscious stupor minutes before the place was raided by the drugs squad. They were astonished to find their intended arrestee lying in a pool of his own blood and teeth next to an incoherent gibbering imbecile with blood all over his knuckles and a knife on his lap. The second Pugilist, who somehow failed to escape conviction, had decided it would be a good idea to stop and take a piss right in front of a CCTV camera after kicking seven shades out of an alleged snitch in an underpass. After several minutes of elaborate hand and finger gestures towards the camera, the Pugilist suddenly realised he was in fact no longer wearing his balaclava and was arrested the next day at his home address. Not the sharpest tools in the box, The Pugilists.

'As for the coming year, we propose a modest increase in our provisional count,' the middleman continued, sliding a sealed envelope across the table to the intermediary.

The count was the total number of contracts each group was permitted to take for the year. It was the most crucial element in the purpose of The Council as far as the intermediary was concerned. A cap on their activities had to be set to ensure it could all be managed. If there was no limit it was just a matter of time before standards slipped and they started employing complete muppets to do the extra work. In the case of The Pugilists, that would mean employing even bigger muppets than they already were.

'Thank you, middleman,' the intermediary replied. 'I will of course respond to you privately about the count once the final figures for everyone are settled.' The middleman, like the go-between and the secretary, suspected the intermediary of holding them back when it came to the count. 'Now, go-between, your report please.'

'Of course, intermediary. A reasonable, if unspectacular year for The Gang. Revenues up twenty per cent and profits also up twenty per cent. I have to say, as I did at this time last year intermediary, that once again we have failed to reach our count for the year and The Gang have asked me to express their disappointment and frustration at the lack of sales leads being passed onto me by other members of The Council.'

Here we go again, he's banging on about us not offering their services as a bonus product to our clients. How the hell do you cross-sell gang rape, for Christ's sake?

'As for next year, we are satisfied with the count providing we can get greater co-operation from The Council in meeting our targets for the year.'

'Thank you go-between, your comments have been noted. I remind all members of The Council that collaborative working and sub-contracting of other Council members' services is to be encouraged whenever it is possible to do so.'

Relieved to have got that one out of the way, the intermediary moved on.

'Secretary; your report please,' he snarled.

'Oh, is it my turn already?' She opened her notepad and read from it as if reading out a list of groceries on a shopping list. 'Count completed. Revenues up thirty per cent, profits up forty per cent thanks to a run of orders for canc...'

'We don't need the details thank you, secretary,' the intermediary interrupted.

'Very well,' she snapped. 'The Medics have instructed me to request a substantial increase in our count for the coming year.'

She slid an envelope towards the middleman and indicated with a smile that she would like him to pass it to the intermediary.

'I'm not touching that,' the middleman stated, whilst attempting to push his chair through the wall to increase his distance from the offending item.

'Yes, thank you secretary, I will consider your request and get back to you privately as usual.'

Almost over, the intermediary thought to himself. As the founding member of The Council, The Boss Killers were in the privileged position of not having to reveal their increases in revenues or profits. It was a key rule of The Council, along with the rule that nobody revealed their annual counts to each other, for it would only lead to bitter envy and speed up the onset of war.

'There was just one more thing,' said the secretary.

The intermediary raised his eyebrows; he knew he wasn't going to like this.

'Er yes?'

'As you know, my associates The Medics are qualified medical professionals at the top of their field. For a very reasonable rate we are prepared to offer the members of The Council access to a discounted private medical insurance scheme that would cover you for such eventualities as ...'

'This Council,' interrupted the intermediary with barely concealed rage, 'is not the time or place for the hawking of goods or services that are nothing to do with our core business. This is not a marketplace, secretary and I'd appreciate it if you didn't treat it like one.'

The secretary turned crimson and frantically scribbled into her petite leather-bound notepad.

'Right, well thank you all for coming and here's to another successful year of business and freedom. Unless there is any pressing business, that concludes the annual general meeting of The Council. I wish you all a safe journey.'

This was the cue for the others to leave. An angry secretary snatched her handbag and stormed out of the room and up the stairs. The go-between watched the monitor and waited until the car outside disappeared with the secretary inside, before he too wasted no time in making a hasty exit.

The middleman met the gaze of the intermediary and nodded.

'Got your hands full with those two, intermediary. Until next time,' and he too left the room, leaving the intermediary to contemplate his thoughts.

He knew the middleman was right and he also understood the sentiment behind his remark. If it came to war, The Pugilists would side with The Boss Killers. Better the devil you know.

The nerve of that woman, he thought. *As if any of us would receive medical treatment from people who dish out terminal diseases in exchange for cash.*

He looked at the two envelopes and opened them, making sure he used his gloves for The Medics' envelope. The Pugilists demand could be taken care of with ease; they could have asked for more and he would have agreed. Then he read the note from The Medics and frowned. Two years at the absolute most, possibly one. That's how long he had before The Medics would break up The Council and start a war. He would have to bring forward his exit strategy.

Chapter 9
Many Happy Returns

Stuart had promised Ross a birthday to remember. He hadn't specified why this would be the case but had stressed that under no circumstances should he murder Belvedere in the meantime.

This left Ross in a state of excitement at the prospect of some development on the Belvedere front but also frustrated at this restriction to his activities. He trusted Stuart though, so he returned the intermediary's business card to Adam for safekeeping.

Ross kept himself busy during the two-month wait for his birthday. He converted one of his spare rooms into a soundproof and lightproof mock-dungeon and populated it with an array of modern and medieval torture devices. If for some reason Stuart's plan, whatever it was, didn't work and if for some reason Belvedere happened to trespass into his flat then Ross felt sure that legally he would be on solid ground to claim self-defence by torturing him to death over a lengthy period of time with an assortment of elaborate punishment devices that just happened to be lying around in a room that just happened to resemble a specially constructed dungeon. He wasn't a hundred percent on the legalities though; he'd check it with Adam first.

Stuart was busy doing whatever it was he was doing with Rum and Black so Ross spent most of his time with Adam and Alice. They would drink in The Badger's Eyebrows, go bowling and visit the cinema to watch action movies. At first he didn't think anything of it but soon Ross began to suspect something fishy was going on with Adam. He kept on arriving late and leaving early. Sometimes he didn't turn up at all. Also, Adam seemed to be experiencing some kind of recurring muscle injury problem. He would cry out in pain and then soon afterwards make his excuses and leave. Ross had urged Adam to get himself checked out at the doctor's but he refused and said it would sort itself out. At least it would if Alice would stop wearing her steel toe-capped boots and sitting within kicking distance of him.

All this meant that Ross was spending rather more time alone with Alice than he was altogether comfortable with. Nothing had ever been said and they had never even kissed but Ross couldn't get away from the feeling that they were in a relationship, and he wasn't ready for that. It did at least have the effect of giving him something else to think about besides Belvedere. He wished his birthday would hurry up and arrive so he could see Stuart again.

Stuart had been busy. Project Belvedere, as it had been named, was coming along nicely. Rum and Black were proving excellent choices. So happy were they to be out of the broom cupboard and have something they could get their teeth into (hairy teeth in Black's case) that they were working around the clock. The project was complex though. They were entering uncharted territory and encountering more than a few snags. They were also all living in Stuart's flat. It was clear that Rum and Black's time in the broom cupboard had left them both with a not insignificant case of agoraphobia. Their financial situation was also much worse than they had let on. The university had terminated their contracts months earlier and they'd been squatting in the broom cupboard whilst trying to prove their worth and earn a new contract. By comparison, Stuart's spare bedroom was like a football stadium and they seemed more than happy to use it as both their home and place of work. Stuart was impressed with their intellect. He was less impressed with their basic standards of cleanliness and hygiene. His furniture was covered in hair; Black appeared to be moulting.

Stuart's original impression of Black had changed since they'd been working together. At first he'd thought Black was just the voice as well as the intellectual passenger of the partnership. This was wide of the mark. Black was the creative brains behind the project and his particular area of expertise was crucial. He specialised in creative thinking and the neurology involved in certain aspects of human-computer interaction. The time Stuart had spent working with Black had given him a whole new perspective on computing. He was learning so much.

Whilst Black was an accomplished computer programmer, Rum was the real genius in this area. His non-existent social skills were the result of his brain thinking largely in computer code, as opposed to actual human language.

The project team were confident of being ready for completion by their deadline, although they couldn't guarantee it would work and there was a high degree of risk. What they needed was an extensive period of testing and some independent volunteers. What they had was a miniscule amount of time for testing and because of the sensitive nature of the project, no volunteers. They would have to do the testing themselves.

****

DI Christmas was busy arranging the vast quantity of case files in his office into ordered piles. To the layman, it would appear that his office resembled a printer's warehouse with a slight Himalayan quality to it, but to Christmas everything was where it needed to be. Each pile had significance. It would be a cold day in hell before he let anyone touch his piles.

The latest pile he was working on was of particular interest. It contained dozens of fatal accidents that had in some way or other involved the medical profession. Maybe it was all just coincidence but some of these accidents looked a bit dodgy to Christmas. How could they be though, with so many official certificates from senior medical consultants? Christmas' head was telling him one thing but his nose another. His mouth, however, was telling him something very different. His coffee tasted of broccoli.

****

The fifth of March arrived, to the great relief of Ross. His resistance to Alice's charms was running thinner than a Hollywood actress on a fad diet. His birthday had fallen on a Friday and he arranged to meet a few friends for a jolly good evening of drinking at The Badger's and then it would be back to Stuart's for his surprise present.

Ross took the day off work and treated himself to a relaxation day at a spa, much to Alice's displeasure. The people administering the massage had better be male. If what he hoped was going to happen was true, it was a nice way to spend what could be his last day of freedom. Ross felt very relaxed after his day of pampering at the spa. He enjoyed the steam room and sauna very much. He hadn't been convinced by the healing qualities of the smelly mud bath though and he refused outright to undergo the colonic irrigation treatment.

****

When his spa day came to an end Ross met Adam, Alice and some friends from Browns at The Badger's Eyebrows to undo all the hard work of the spa staff. Some of the people from Browns were not regular drinking partners of Ross and were a wee bit wary of The Badger's unique ambience, somewhere between Victorian workhouse drinking pit, wild west whorehouse and gangsters' market.

Stuart knew where Ross was but was busy putting the final touches to Project Belvedere. He hadn't specifically mentioned to Ross about not getting shit-faced so Ross took this as a green light to do so. He challenged Adam to a drinking contest and thrashed him. Alice was on top form, drinking like a fish and abusing any students present.

'Oy egghead, get back to your lab, you work-shy dosser,' was just one of the many encouraging suggestions she offered tomorrow's leaders.

As his birthday present, Igneous offered to head-butt any person present for Ross' entertainment. For once it was a shame Belvedere wasn't present, he thought.

****

Stuart had asked Ross to arrive by 10pm. Having crammed a whole evening's drinking into a few hours, Ross thanked his party for their company and left for Stuart's. Alice insisted on accompanying him and Ross dragged Adam along to perform gooseberry duties.

A somewhat worse for wear Ross and an extremely worse for wear Adam arrived at Stuart's just after ten. Alice had been drinking all evening and was no worse for wear than when she started. Some people just have that ability.

Ross could hardly contain his excitement as they entered the flat. Stuart emerged from the office come bedroom come research lab, and closed the door behind him. Ross staggered around the flat, opening cupboards and doors.

'Where is he?' He spotted Stuart trying to conceal the entrance to his bedroom. 'He's in there, isn't he?' Ross said, beaming a wide grin and rubbing his hands together.

'Not as such,' said Stuart.

'What? Never mind your games, Stu; you've been teasing me for months. Is he in there or isn't he?'

'No. And yes.'

'You're not making any sense.'

Ross' brain was having enough difficulty functioning as a result of his earlier alcohol consumption without Stuart making him feel like he'd walked into an episode of The Prisoner.

There were three taps from the other side of the door behind Stuart. He replied by knocking on the door twice followed by a pause and then four further knocks. The door opened. Stuart stepped aside and beckoned Ross to enter.

'Happy birthday,' he said.

Ross edged past him suspiciously and scanned the room for any sign of Belvedere. He looked again. He still wasn't there. When he looked the third time he saw what was actually in the room: a lot of strange computer equipment, a small Asian man with missing teeth and fingers and what looked like a werewolf. A nervous Rum and

Black were sitting either side of an empty leather chair with a table in front of them. They moved another chair to the other side of the table, smiled at Ross and beckoned him to sit down.

'What's all this, Stu?'

'You want to kill Belvedere? Well I think I've found a way that doesn't involve you going to prison.'

'OK I'll play along,' Ross said, sitting down on the chair, 'but afterwards I want to know where you're hiding Belvedere.'

Stuart nodded. He prayed this would work. His calculations hadn't factored in the possibility of the subject being legless.

'What's he doing with those wires?' asked Ross, as Black approached him armed with a handful of electrodes.

'It will all become clear in a minute. Please, just trust me.'

Stuart was the only person alive who Ross trusted enough for those words to mean anything so, despite his trepidation, he complied. As he watched Black attach electrodes to his head, Ross was too busy wondering if either of Black's parents were human to notice Rum jab him with a syringe and inject the contents into his arm.

'Hey, what's he...' he started but didn't finish as he slipped out of consciousness. For a moment or two there was nothing and then he regained his senses. He opened his eyes.

'There you are, you bastard,' Ross shouted.

Belvedere looked up from his paperwork and smirked. At least, Ross thought it was him. It looked like him, but at the same time not like him.

'Mind your language, Ackerman or I'll have you suspended,' Belvedere sneered.

Something was a bit wrong with his voice. It sounded like Belvedere but it also sounded a bit like Stuart.

'What the hell are you doing in Stuart's bedroom?' bellowed Ross.

'This is my office, Ackerman and if you don't mind we were in the middle of your appraisal.'

Ross looked around the room. He was right. They were no longer in Stuart's flat but in Belvedere's office. His office seemed different somehow; it had something of a bedroom quality to it. *It must be the drink,* thought Ross. *I thought I was in The Badger's Eyebrows and then at Stuart's, but now I'm back in work. I must have blacked out.*

'Your performance has dipped noticeably in this quarter, Ackerman and I'm going to put you on an official warning to buck your ideas up.'

Belvedere was sounding more and more like Stuart.

I've had enough of this, thought Ross. He looked around the room and saw a large marble ornament; he'd never noticed it being there before. *That'll do.* He picked up the ornament and lifted it above his head ready to strike.

'What the hell do you think you're doing?'

'I'm going to bash your brains in, you piece of garbage. You're a self-important knob-head and I'm sending you to hell for what you did.'

Ross paused. It was time for the truth.

'Before I end you, tell me what she said.'

Belvedere looked at him blankly.

'What did she say, you fucking worm?'

Belvedere didn't move or say anything; he just sat there. A fury erupted in Ross that he made no attempt to contain.

'Tell me what she said,' he screamed.

The walls in the room moved and the lights flashed on and off. Belvedere disappeared, then reappeared for a moment and was then gone again. Ross looked around the room for him. He wasn't there. What was going on? He put his head in his hands and rubbed his eyes. When he took his hands away, he was back in Stuart's flat. He was the only one in the room. Then Belvedere appeared in front of him. Ross raised his hand above his head to bash him with the ornament but it was no longer in his hand. Belvedere disappeared once more. Ross was breathing heavily; he couldn't understand what was happening. The room was spinning, or the room was still and his head was spinning. He couldn't breathe. From nowhere Stuart, Rum and Black appeared beside him. He was sitting in the chair but he hadn't moved from where he'd been standing to get into it. They were all holding him down.

'Get away from me,' shouted Ross, fighting them off with all his strength. He swatted Rum away with one hand, round-housed Black with the other, jumped out of the chair and ran towards the doorway. He flung the door open and was immediately rugby-tackled by Adam. Stuart and Alice piled on top of him.

'No, no, he's here, I saw him. He *knows*.'

While Ross struggled for freedom Black appeared and administered another injection into Ross' backside. The sedative took effect and the flailing arms and legs lost their tension.

****

When he awoke the next morning Ross was back in his own bed. His head was pounding. *What a night. I've had it with drink once and for all*, he thought. The nightmare had seemed so real. Stuart and Alice sat beside the bed. He was glad to see them but wondered what the hell they were doing in his flat. He clutched his head in pain.

'You wouldn't believe the dreams I had last night. Did I pass out?'

'Yes,' said Alice. 'We brought you home.' Ross was relieved she used the word 'we'.

'So what happened?' he asked. Stuart and Alice looked at each other, wondering whether it would be best just to lie.

'You wouldn't believe me if I told you,' said Stuart. It was a red rag to a bull.

'Try me,' Ross sneered. He knew when Stuart was holding something back.

Stuart stood up and left the room. Alice gave Ross a look of love. He blushed, embarrassed at his present state. Stuart returned with Rum and Black. As soon as Ross saw them the flashbacks from the previous night began. He started hyperventilating. Alice held him while he struggled for breath.

'These men are at the forefront of virtual reality technology,' said Stuart. 'For the past two months we've been devising a computer programme so you could kill Belvedere in virtual reality.'

The rational part of Ross' brain consumed this information and took back control of his body. His breathing returned to normal.

'That was the present I promised you,' continued Stuart. 'How to kill Belvedere without having to kill him.'

Ross took all this in with great relief. It was a huge leap for his brain to accept but was preferable to the alternative: that he'd simply gone mad. He beckoned Stuart towards the bed and hugged him.

'Thanks for going to so much effort, mate. I appreciate it.'

'I'm just sorry it didn't work.'

'What went wrong?'

'Lots of things. The drugs didn't work the way they should have, the programme wasn't robust enough and in basic terms your brain rejected the reality it was presented with. We just didn't have enough time to get it perfect.'

'How much time would you need?'

'Plenty. There's no way I'd put you through that again unless it was tried and tested. The development work would need at least another couple of months to iron out the bugs. Then we'd need two or three months testing and another month to make the final adjustments. At least six months, I'd say.'

'Shit,' said Ross. He couldn't wait six months, not when he'd been so close to what felt like the real thing.

'I know, you can't wait that long. I'm sorry there's no other way,' said Stuart.

'Not unless you can get Mr X to help us,' laughed Black.

'Who's Mr X?' asked Ross.

'Oh ignore him, he's pulling your leg,' said Stuart. 'There's no such person. He's a myth. A legendary computing genius who can make the impossible possible. He's supposed to have an IQ of over 300. Getting his help would be great. If he existed, of course,' Stuart said, glaring at Black.

'But he does exist,' said Black. 'Rum's met him.'

Chapter 10
The House of Lard

Stuart shuddered, the memory of the ordeal Ross had just endured still fresh in his mind.

They were sitting at a dining table in The House of Lard, the UK's premiere restaurant dedicated to the obese diner. It had been Stuart's idea. The main lead they had for locating the elusive Mr X was that he was a salad dodger, so they had come to the mecca for salad dodgers. Stuart had booked in advance.

The House of Lard was a members' only establishment and Stuart just about fulfilled their strict criteria. He wasn't super-sized but he was fat, the minimum requirement for membership. Size was not judged on pounds or kilos at The House of Lard. Their bible was the Body Mass Index, or BMI, chart. If you wanted to eat there and your BMI wasn't in the red zone you didn't get in. The only reason Ross had got through the front door was because members were allowed to invite up to two 'unacceptable' guests. The criterion for unacceptability was somewhat subjective. Anyone possessing visible ribs had no chance of obtaining entry.

Everything about The House of Lard was anti-thin, or at least anti anyone whose clothes size didn't start with half a dozen X's. They were still a business though and recognised that lots of their paying customers needed the help of people who managed to get by on sensible diets. Many members were social outcasts who only ventured outside their house with the love and support of a friend or family member, usually their mum. Mums were treated like royalty at The House of Lard. If it wasn't for mums stuffing them full of chips and chocolate when they were kids, most of the restaurant's members would still be able to see their own feet.

The incident Ross and Stuart were still trying to recover from had occurred soon after they arrived for their eight o'clock reservation.

After some initial angry glares from the bouncers on the door, they were permitted entry following a lengthy scrutiny of Stuart's membership card. Ross' first impression of the place was favourable. The staff were immaculately attired in smart dinner jackets or stylish gowns and appeared courteous, despite being rushed off their feet. Even though they had a reservation, Ross and Stuart still had to wait in an enormous queue of diners waiting for their table. The queue had relatively few people in it, but was still massive.

As each group was escorted to their table, they were welcomed into the heart of the restaurant with a deafening chorus of cheers and applause, accompanied by some music of their choice. When Ross and Stuart approached the front of the queue there was a noticeable delay with the group in front of them being shown to their table. All of a sudden the lights went out. When they came back on a red carpet had been laid out the full length of the corridor. Along each side of the carpet waiters lined up to form a 'lard of honour'. The sound of clanging echoed from the kitchen as various cooking apparatus was discarded and the chefs scrambled out to join the end of the line of waiters. A moment later one of the doormen stepped forward and put his well-pumped arms to good use by smashing a mallet against a huge mock-antique bronze gong. The doorman then stood aside and announced at the top of his voice: 'All hail Roger Walters. Weight – fifty-six stone and three ounces, BMI 116. A superman among men. Let us all hail his greatness and the example he sets. We all aspire to be like Roger.'

The waiters, chefs and diners then joined in three choruses of 'All hail Roger'. As the brightness of the hallway lights increased further, it illuminated the waiters and chefs bowing their heads in respect. A few excited diners went a step further by prostrating themselves face down on the floor in submission. The opening bars of We are the Champions bellowed out of the restaurant's sound system and the largest human being Ross had ever seen was pushed onto the red carpet by three burly doormen who were using all their strength and only just succeeding in not going backwards.

Roger Walters was strapped into the largest custom-made wheelchair in the world. Like most of the diners' seats and tables at The House of Lard, the wheelchair was made from the strongest reinforced steel known to man. The specialist expertise required to build such a structure was beyond any traditional wheelchair manufacturer and had therefore been carried out by naval shipbuilders in Portsmouth.

As he inched down the red carpet to the sound of Freddie Mercury, Roger Walters, wearing an industrial-sized crown on his head, waved regally at his subjects. Anyone taking a closer look at his highness King Roger the First might have detected a slight sneer and general look of smugness and superiority. This wasn't immediately obvious though as the enormous amount of skin covering his face made all his facial expressions look more or less the same.

When he reached the end of the red carpet he was greeted by a huge round of applause from the diners. This came as a great relief to the doormen, who took the opportunity to catch their breath while Roger Walters basked in the adoration of his fans. A moment later he was wheeled around a corner towards an enormous private booth and the restaurant returned to normality.

Ross and Stuart stepped forward to the front of the queue of hungry diners. Stuart presented his dog-eared membership card and was again made to wait while it was given a thorough inspection. The waiter took his card and showed it to a more senior waiter. There followed a brief discussion between the waiters before they both made their way to a computerised booking system. The senior waiter pushed some buttons, looked at the data on the screen, rubbed his forehead in concentration, stared at Stuart as if this would provide the answer and then went in search of a yet more senior waiter.

Stuart was grinning inanely in an attempt to look jolly and affable but was only succeeding in looking nervous and shifty. A third waiter approached Stuart and Ross, his two junior sidekicks trailing behind.

Ross wondered if anyone was currently being served any food.

'My apologies for the delay, Mr Davies. It has been some time since we last had the pleasure of your company.'

'Er yes, it has been a while,' began Stuart, knowing they would make him beg for having the nerve not to dine there at least three times a week.

'It has been five years, Mr Davies,' replied third waiter, without a hint of sarcasm. First waiter was taking notes, in awe of third waiter's sheer presence.

'Gosh, has it been that long?' said Stuart, with unconvincing surprise.

'I've been working away a lot on business you see, overseeing our Malaysian operation you know. Ow.'

Ross accidentally on purpose trod on Stuart's foot. He knew that when it came to lying Stuart was the best in the world, provided that the world consisted of Stuart and no other human being, animal or plant life.

'Erm yes, well now that I'm back in town, so to speak, I'll be wanting to visit much more often,' he stumbled.

'So glad to hear it, Mr Davies. I will need to provide you with a new membership card and brochure. Much has changed since your last visit. In the meantime may I be the first to welcome you back to The House of Lard. I hope you have a pleasant evening and leave much heavier than when you entered.'

This was the traditional House of Lard greeting.

'My colleague will show you to the scales.'

Shit, thought Stuart. He'd forgotten about the scales. Every diner entering The House of Lard had to be weighed on the restaurant's custom-made scales. Custom-made by NASA's research and development department. Only the mums and carers of the larger members were excused this indignity.

The House of Lard was no mere restaurant. It was a safe haven for the huge and overweight. In this sanctuary its members could not just escape the ridicule of the outside world; they could be positively revered for their size. Here there was no name calling, no staring, and no prejudice of any kind against people of above average size. Anyone found guilty of this behaviour was barred for life. Here, there was something lacking in the lives of the average obese man, woman and child. Here there was respect. There was celebration of largeness. Pictures of famous over-sized celebrities adorned the walls – actors, politicians and former sportsmen and women who had let themselves go after retirement. A whole floor was dedicated to pictures of darts players past and present. Many were lifetime members. Trade unions stood up for the little man. The House of Lard stood up for the corpulent man.

Stuart stepped onto the scales, nervous about the reading but glad he was wearing his boots and heavy-duty denim trousers.

The House of Lard recorded the weight of every new member when they joined and required them to be weighed on each occasion they dined. This was to ensure they were still eligible for membership by way of adhering to the restaurant's strict BMI policy. It was also a way to keep tabs on its members. Detailed charts were produced showing their 'progress' towards ever-greater obesity. There were all manner of incentives for becoming fatter. Free meals and money off vouchers for the restaurant's partner stores, Lard-Mart, Lardland theme park, Lard 'U' Like and Fly Lard. You could even win a year's supply of lard and free subscription to Lard TV, including its pay-per-view adult channels catering for the niche porn markets of chubby chasers, morb-porn (featuring morbidly obese porn stars) and Claustro-porn (featuring shut-ins).

Rewards were not so generous for those members who were careless enough to not put on any weight or, heaven forbid, to lose weight. Punishments for these crimes included temporary termination of membership until the member could prove they had gained sufficient weight, right through to lifetime bans. That would not be the end of the matter though. For many of its members the prime social interaction they enjoyed with friends of equal and greater size was through the many clubs and societies owned and run by The House of Lard. Termination of membership, however temporary, removed the social outcasts from their only proper support network. They could no longer attend the clubs and other members were left in no uncertainty about what would happen to their membership if they were found to be associating with their former friends.

'You are nineteen stone and thirteen pounds, Mr Davies and your BMI is forty,' said third waiter. There was an audible background murmuring of acceptance.

'You have gained four pounds since your last visit.' Stuart breathed a sigh of relief as he stepped off the scales. 'I have to give you a first warning though, Mr Davies, as it's only a small weight gain and it has been over a very long time. You are allowed three consecutive warnings before I am required to place your membership on the temporary exclusion list.'

Third waiter smiled at Stuart and beckoned him into the restaurant. Ross stepped forward, unsure if he was allowed to follow Stuart or not. Third waiter motioned him forward.

'Ah, Mr Davies' guest, so nice to see a new face.' Ross had to admit it; third waiter was smoother than a Marvin Gaye album. 'Please, let me take your jacket sir.'

As he moved his hands over Ross' shoulders third waiter leaned next to his ear and whispered: 'If you've got any sense you'll get the hell out of here right now. Leave while you've got the chance.'

Ross was startled. Waiters weren't supposed to whisper warnings in your ear while taking your coat. He stood there in the hall, unable to decide on a course of action. Third waiter looked at Ross and darted his eyes in the direction of the exit.

'Can we hurry this up, I'm starving,' shouted a voice from behind Ross. It belonged to a diner further back in the queue who was absolutely, positively, definitely not by any stretch of the imagination in any danger of starving.

Third waiter couldn't understand why Ross was still standing there like a rabbit in the headlights. He resorted to plan B.

'Are you accompanying Mr Davies for any medical reason at all?' he enquired, nodding his head as he asked to indicate that Ross should answer in the affirmative. Ross looked blankly at third waiter.

There was a pause and then he replied: 'I'm his driver.' This came as a surprise to Ross as he was sure he hadn't made a sound. When he was not providing a world class standard of waiter service, third waiter was an enthusiastic amateur ventriloquist. He was getting quite good.

'Ah, you are his driver. Well no doubt Mr Davies requires driving for some irreproachable medical reason,' nodded third waiter, indicating that Ross should explain what that reason was.

Ross glared at the headlights of the oncoming juggernaut, completely mute. Stuart had by this time cottoned onto what third waiter was trying to do.

'Yes, I've got chronic wobbly leg syndrome,' he blurted out, immediately wishing he'd spent longer than a nanosecond engaging his brain to come up with a more impressive ailment.

'Er yes, wobbly leg syndrome, a most unfortunate condition and one which no doubt prevents you from driving, Mr Davies,' replied third waiter. He was being fed scraps by these two idiots but was determined to get Ross past the scales and out of harm's way.

'Oh yes, very serious,' continued Stuart, warming to the theme. 'Why, if it wasn't for Ross here I wouldn't get anywhere because of these accursed wobbly legs.'

Feeling some further justification was required, Stuart began shaking his legs and cursing them, like some demented extra from an early outtake of Monty Pythons Ministry of Silly Walks sketch. Third waiter had seen enough. He ushered Ross into the main restaurant and was a couple of steps past the scales when he was halted in his tracks by the stern figure of authority that was the restaurant manager, Mr Faulkes. *Merde*, third waiter thought to himself. *Well at least I tried.*

'I'm afraid I can't allow you in, sir,' said Faulkes to Ross.

'Is there a problem?' asked Stuart.

'Well, yes there is, sir. The fact is that wobbly leg syndrome is a fictitious medical condition that you've just invented.'

'I meant to say Restless Leg Syndrome,' said Stuart.

'That at least does exist, sir,' said Faulkes, patronisingly. 'However, we do have to consider that Restless Leg Syndrome is not a condition that would require a driver to accompany you on a short journey to a restaurant. Then there is also the fact that you didn't drive here anyway, sirs. You arrived by taxi, as evidenced by our excellent CCTV and the fact that all the door staff saw you getting out of a taxi. So in summary, we will be requiring your guest to be weighed, Mr Davies.'

Stuart grimaced; he'd hoped there would be some exemption to the rules for members' guests. Ross stepped onto the scales, unaware of what all the fuss was about. First waiter asked him to stand up straight while he made a note of the recorded height for Ross. He passed the note to third waiter. He'd been working at The House of Lard long enough not to need to go through this official procedure; he could tell a person's BMI just by looking at them. The scales showed the digital reading of Ross' weight and third waiter checked the large BMI chart on the wall behind the scales to confirm what he already knew.

'You are eleven stone and ten pounds and your BMI is 23,' third waiter whispered.

It was loud enough for Faulkes to hear. He turned to Ross.

'You are far too skinny to be granted entry as an unacceptable guest and I hereby ban you from ever frequenting this establishment again.' Faulkes handed Ross some official-looking paperwork and turned his attention to Stuart. 'Mr Davies, I am giving you a second warning for inviting such a guest to dine with you at the great House of Lard. You must have known he would never be admitted unless on medical grounds.'

Stuart looked close to tears. He hated confrontation and here he was being humiliated by an authority figure just for taking his best friend out to dinner.

First waiter led Stuart to his table while third waiter ushered Ross towards the exit. Ross felt a mixture of humiliation and fury at his treatment. Third waiter made sure he was out of earshot before he spoke.

'Why do you want to eat here, eh? This place, it – it isn't for normal people like you.'

'I just *need* to eat here,' Ross said, not wanting to divulge why.

Third waiter looked at Ross and saw the desperation in his eyes. He was from the old school of waiter service, the one where the customers' needs are of the highest priority, no matter how inconvenient that may be.

'Is it very important to you, sir?' third waiter asked, praying the answer would be no.

Ross thought of Belvedere and what he wanted to do to him right now. His plan had to work. He needed Mr X.

'It's life and death.'

Third waiter sighed. He leaned forward, put Ross' coat around his shoulders and whispered in his ear.

Ross stopped. He withdrew his hand from the exit door, did a sharp about-turn and marched back into the restaurant. Faulkes spotted him and gestured towards security. Before they could reach him, Ross bellowed at the top of his voice: 'Run the gauntlet'! I want to run the gauntlet.'

All noise in the restaurant stopped. Hundreds of pairs of eyes and ears turned towards Ross.

'You want to run the gauntlet?' Faulkes asked in disbelief. He wished it was his deputy's shift tonight; there would be all manner of forms to fill in. It had been four years since somebody had last asked to run the gauntlet and six years since anyone had gone through with it.

'If I run the gauntlet, you have to let me in,' said Ross, a steely determination in his eyes.

'Well, yes, but are you sure? You do know what this entails?'

Faulkes knew what was coming but he was pretty sure Ross didn't. Nobody in their right mind would volunteer to run the gauntlet. The last man to attempt it had been a hardcore masochist with a fetish for humiliation. He lasted about ten seconds. Third waiter had not had the chance to brief Ross on what 'running the gauntlet' entailed.

'Yes, I'm sure,' snarled Ross.

'Very well,' said Faulkes, fumbling through a staff training manual. He found the sheet he was looking for at the back of the manual under the heading Extreme Caution. He took it out, read the instructions and handed them to Ross to read. After reading them thoroughly Ross read them again. The next thing he did was to read them a third time and he followed this up by reading them a fourth time. He cursed the words for not changing no matter how many times he read them.

Faulkes pressed a small hidden panel on the wall. It rotated to reveal a red button under a shatterproof plastic cover. He took out a key and placed it into a lock next to the plastic. He then turned the key. The cover flipped up and he hesitated before pressing the red button.

There was a loud metallic noise that sounded like the moving parts of a machine clicking into place after a long period of inactivity. A thin sliver of darkness appeared along the centre of the giant wooden hallway of the restaurant. The assembled diners, waiters and doormen scrambled toward the walls of the hallway to get away from what was now a large chasm in the centre of the floor. The two halves of the hallway floor separated and continued their journey toward the walls.

'Stay behind the red lines,' bellowed Faulkes at the panicking crowd.

The long hallway had a thick red line at each of its sides, leaving a gap of about eight feet between the line and the wall. The advancing floor stopped when it reached the red lines. A gigantic rectangular hole was now in the middle of the hallway floor, revealing a long black abyss of nothingness. Then the noise started. It sounded like the world's largest disability lift raising itself out of the blackness.

When the noise stopped, Ross looked puzzled at what appeared to be an exact replica of the floor that had just divided to make way for this floor. At the far end of the new floor stood a small round table with a white packet upon it. Ross couldn't see from his vantage point what the packet was but he had a pretty good idea.

He looked at Faulkes questioningly and shrugged his shoulders. Faulkes looked bewildered. He looked around for someone to provide an answer. Nobody did. He looked behind him and then did a full 360 degree turn. This offered no further clues.

'One moment please,' Faulkes said to Ross. He picked up his walky-talky and pressed a button. 'Get me him,' he snapped. 'Yes, it's an emergency.'

There followed an awkward conversation between Faulkes and the owner of The House of Lard. Ross listened in.

'Yes, he wants to run the gauntlet.' Pause. 'Well I followed the procedure, I pressed the secret button.' Pause. 'Well see for yourself.' Pause. 'What do you mean, new procedure?' Pause. 'Where's the iron maiden, the lake of boiling lard? Where's the giant slingshot? And where's the goddamn polar bear?' Pause. 'Health and safety? What do you mean, health and safety?' screamed Faulkes. The next pause was longer. 'Yes, sir, I'm sorry sir, I meant no offence. Of course I approve and it's very wise of you sir, if you don't mind me saying so. I will attend to it straight away sir.'

Faulkes was sweating. He turned to Ross.

'You lucky sod. Your challenge is less hazardous but don't think for a second it's going to be easy.'

Ross smiled. Compared to the contents of the manual he'd just read whatever he now faced would be a doddle. Faulkes addressed the confused and somewhat disappointed gathering.

'This man,' he shouted, pointing at Ross, 'would like to enter the great House of Lard despite being thinner than a supermodel's fingernail. Should we let him?'

'No,' roared the restaurant diners and staff as one.

'Then make sure you don't make it easy for him,' yelled Faulkes to a raucous reply of cheers.

The crowd was warming up. Ross noticed many were being passed enormous plates of food and packets of lard by the staff. Faulkes waited another moment until he was satisfied that his army of big-boned soldiers were sufficiently well-armed. He spoke to Ross.

'When I blow my whistle you have six minutes to retrieve the treasure, return it here to me and utter the magic words.'

Ross nodded in acknowledgment. 'So all I have to do is walk over to the table, pick up that packet of lard and walk back?'

'Yes,' replied Faulkes, 'if you can manage it.'

'Piece of cake,' said Ross.

Faulkes blew the whistle. Before he could do anything Ross was stunned by a flying missile to the face. It was a piece of cake. Food of all varieties and courses rained down on him as he advanced towards the table. The noise was deafening as the diners, waiters and chefs screamed obscenities at Ross whilst hurling all manner of culinary grenades. He was hit by some sausages and a lamb shank to the torso, his face was stung by an obese child armed with a pea shooter, and whilst fending off a large quantity of raw semi-butchered offal with his arms he walked straight into the path of a well-aimed whole murder by chocolate gateaux right in his face. This turned out to be a blessing in disguise. As Ross kneeled down to wipe the thick chocolate out of his eyes, the air occupied by his head a second ago was surprised to find a whole pig's head sail through it. The chef who threw the pig's head stamped on the floor in anger, cursed his bad luck and set off back to the kitchen in search of a cow's head.

In spite of all this, Ross was almost at the table. Another few seconds of fighting his way through the wall of food and he would have it. He reached the table and stretched his hand out towards the lard. He was just about to grab it when he was knocked off his feet by a powerful force. Ross fought for breath but couldn't resist the pressure pushing him back. He wiped thick meat-smelling fluid out of his eyes and heard someone bellowing with laughter in his ear. He turned his head to witness Faulkes guffawing and pointing at him. He was back where he started.

Ross looked back at the table and saw first waiter standing behind it with second waiter right behind him holding his waist. They were both supporting an industrial-sized fire hose which was shooting out warm lard at high pressure in Ross' direction. He tried to get back up and slipped, falling heavily on his back. The floor was covered in wet dripping. How was he going to do this?

Faulkes grinned at Ross and gloated. 'You didn't think it was going to be that easy, did you, my dear boy?'

'I'll get it.'

'Huh! We'll see about that.'

With that, Faulkes held out a small remote control device and pressed a button. Despite the feverish cheers, laughter and verbal abuse, Ross recognised the unmistakable sound of hydraulics he'd heard earlier. A small section of the floor began rising, forming a giant slide with an increasing gradient. The table was now atop an elevated plateau at the end of the hallway. He would now have to traverse a lard-covered wooden floor and climb a flat lard-covered slope whilst being bombarded by leftover food and having warm lard fired out of a hose at him. Four and a half minutes had passed. Ross didn't like this; Faulkes wasn't playing fair. He needed help.

Seeing the table rise into the air was the last straw for Stuart. Nobody could succeed in running the gauntlet. He wished he could help his friend. He felt a presence behind him and heard the soft whisper of third waiter in his ear. Stuart pushed past the throng and ran towards the dining area, returning with several large glass tankards and an enormous plate.

'Catch this!' he yelled, throwing the gargantuan plate like a Frisbee towards Ross, who dived to catch it. Holding the plate in front of him like a shield, he advanced quicker towards the sloping floor as the jet from the hose sprayed off the plate, splashing the angry diners.

'Use the glass,' yelled Stuart as he hurled the heavy tankards a few feet in front of Ross. The tankards smashed into pieces on impact. Holding the plate in front of him, Ross stood onto the glass, the broken shards from the tankards wedging themselves into the tread of his boots, and for the first time he had a grip on the greasy floor. Hope renewed, he ran towards the start of the incline in the wooden floor and had enough momentum to keep running up the slope. First and second waiter were caught out by this move and couldn't react in time.

Ross' momentum carried him just far enough to stretch out his hand at the top of the slope and grab the packet of lard before he came tumbling all the way back down and skidded along the floor. Covered from head to toe in warm lard, he came to rest in a crumpled heap at the feet of an astonished Faulkes. Five minutes and fifty seconds had passed. Ross held out the lard to Faulkes. He didn't move a muscle.

'Magic words!' screamed Stuart.

Ross looked at Faulkes and grinned. 'Please sir,' he said, 'I'd like some lard.'

Five minutes and fifty-eight seconds had passed. Faulkes looked at his stopwatch, sighed, shook his head in disbelief and took the packet of lard from Ross' outstretched hand. He took a knife, cut off a piece the size of a fist and shoved it into Ross' open mouth. It took a few attempts and a huge amount of willpower to resist the natural gag reflex but, eyes streaming from the effort, Ross somehow managed to swallow the lard. He stood up victorious, his arms outstretched. Stuart punched the air with joy and then ducked for cover to avoid a flying cow's head.

Faulkes stared with malevolence at his adversary. Then, as if nothing had happened, he broke into a beaming smile and shook Ross by the hand.

'Welcome to The House of Lard, sir. I trust you will enjoy your dining experience with us this evening. Your waiter will show you to your table and respond to any specific requests you may have. Please take note of our specials menu as you make your way to the table. I recommend the goat surprise.'

Ross and Stuart were led away to a table by third waiter, after a brief stop at the bar for Ross to wash away the taste of lard by downing a pint of water.

The House of Lard operated a reverse hierarchy system for seating diners. Those members whose BMI was the highest and needed help to move about were housed on the ground floor. The second floor was reserved for the morbidly obese and those knocking on the door of morbidity with increasing volume. The third floor was for the mere obese, those with the lowest BMI readings. Here the fat cats were located at the bottom instead of the top.

The restaurant put a clever spin on this, stating in the member information that it didn't want its super-humans on the ground floor to be offended by the sight of the weak abominations on the upper floors, and that ground floor membership came with special privileges such as your own team of waiters to hand-feed you and tell you how great you were. All this was designed to brush under the carpet the real reason. No matter how hard they tried they just couldn't source a set of lifts that could withstand the punishment dished out by the restaurant's larger members. The structural engineer for the building had refused to sign off the safety report if the third floor was going to support such massive weights. It took a bribe the size of which a Tory politician would be proud of to get him to sign off the ground floor.

On the way to his table on the third floor, Ross was amazed by the staggering size of the restaurant. Each floor must have been the size of three or four football pitches. He remembered Faulkes' last words and decided to take advantage of his offer for any personal request to be dealt with. Whilst Stuart perused the menu Ross was given access to the private staff quarters where he showered and changed into the only spare set of clothes that was anywhere near his size. He returned to the table refreshed and resplendent-looking in his waiter's dinner jacket.

While he was in the staff quarters, Ross gambled on the generosity of third waiter and asked him if he knew of any member who might be known as Mr X. Although they were out of earshot, it was clear that third waiter was uncomfortable with this request. Ross hoped he hadn't pushed the man's helpfulness too far. He explained that the reason he ran the gauntlet was to try and find Mr X, who he had good reason to believe was a member. Anonymity of members' identities was sacrosanct at The House of Lard. Despite this, third waiter, seeing the pleading in Ross' eyes, agreed to see what he could do.

Ross went ahead and ordered the goat surprise while Stuart opted for a meat feast. All meals on the menu came in three sizes: small, medium and large. Diners were only permitted to order the size of meal consistent with the floor they were seated at, so as third floor diners Ross and Stuart were restricted to ordering small meals. As they waited for their order, they were now able to see the funny side of the earlier shenanigans.

'Honestly,' said Stuart, 'my heart stopped when I saw that pig's head flying through the air. It missed you by inches.'

'Let's just hope it's all worth it. I'm sure the goat surprise will be an experience of a lifetime but if we don't find Mr X then it's been a wasted effort and Belvedere's got a date with a load of power tools and a bath full of sulphuric acid.'

Stuart frowned. He didn't like this kind of talk. His friend was not rational when it came to Belvedere. All their hopes were pinned on finding Mr X. Could they trust Rum though, a man who refused to communicate with anyone without the assistance of an interpreter who looked like Bungle from Rainbow?

The meals arrived, wheeled in by two waiters on what resembled a surgical trolley used for transporting people to and from theatre.

'Excuse me, there seems to be some mistake. We ordered the small meals,' Ross pointed out.

The waiters looked at each other, grinned and raised their eyebrows in unison.

'These are the small sizes,' the waiter replied in as sarcastic a tone as he could muster, which was very sarcastic indeed.

The waiters departed, leaving Ross sitting there open-mouthed.

'How the bloody hell am I supposed to eat all this?' he barked at Stuart. The plates were at least three feet in diameter. Ross' plate contained a whole roasted adult goat, complete with head and limbs. He looked to Stuart for some sort of direction on how he should attempt to eat the beast.

'It's stuffed,' said Stuart. 'Here, let me.'

He took a sharp carving knife from the trolley and slit the goat's belly. A colossal quantity of meat and vegetables in a delightful-smelling sauce oozed out of the animal's stomach.

'Wow,' said Ross, impressed. It was enough to feed at least eight people. 'God, that's good,' he said, devouring the goat. 'No wonder this place is packed out. 'What's in the jug, gravy?'

'Lard. All dishes come with a side order of lard,' replied Stuart, in between mouthfuls of sausage.

'People pour lard over their meals?'

'They do here.'

****

Leaning back in his seat Ross let out a long satisfied sigh of contentment. He was full but his dish looked untouched. It was at this point third waiter returned. Ross could tell straight away it wasn't good news.

'I'm sorry, sir. I've searched our members' database and there is nobody with a first name or surname beginning with the letter X. I know most of the members as well as anyone here and I'm afraid it's not a name I've ever heard.'

'Well that's it then,' said Stuart, relieved at the prospect of departing.

Ross sulked. There had to be something else he could do. He looked at his reflection in the glass frame of a picture on the wall. A House of Lard waiter looked back at him.

'Don't bet on it,' said Ross.

He stood up and set off into the restaurant. Whilst Stuart spent the next hour apologising for his friend who had developed severe diarrhoea, and no it wasn't anything to do with the food thank you very much, Ross darted in and out of booths on all three floors. He waited tables, took orders, collected tips and assisted other waiters with some of the more enormous portions of food. He listened to every conversation of the diners and the waiters. He heard many interesting pieces of information but nothing to help him in his quest. A few waiters and diners studied him with curiosity, unable to recall where they recognised him from. Eventually Ross called it a day before he was unmasked, and returned to his booth.

'Let's go,' he said to Stuart, and the two friends headed towards the restaurant exit, both glad to be leaving The House of Lard.

Ross was impressed with how the huge hall had been returned to its former pristine condition in such a short space of time. Somewhere on the premises there must be a team of exhausted cleaners covered in lard.

The restaurant's cloakroom was located on the right of the hallway before the exit. Its desk sported bowls of sweets, chocolates, mints and other tempting freebies to send the well-upholstered diners on their way with a smile on their face. Ross was about to walk straight past but was hit by a strong feeling of fate at work. The cloakroom was being manned by third waiter. No other staff were in the immediate vicinity. He stepped forward. One of the bowls contained free pens and a variety of different sized House of Lard branded post-it notes. He took a pen and wrote something on one of the larger post-its. He shook third waiter by the hand, leaned forward and whispered in his ear. Third waiter nodded and took the note from him. Ross then thanked him again and departed The House of Lard with Stuart.

As they left the restaurant the doormen were considerably more polite than they had been on the way in and Ross received several slaps on the back and calls of 'well done' for his earlier efforts. They walked around the corner into the gigantic House of Lard car park and sat on a wall.

'So what do we do now then?' asked Stuart.

'You can go home if you want but I'm staying here for a while.'

'What for?'

'A phone call.'

In the restaurant, a large man made his way to collect his coat after enjoying a very hearty feed. He handed in his ticket to third waiter and was helping himself to some sweets and mints when something caught his eye. On the inside wall of the cloakroom hatch was a piece of paper stuck to the wall. In large letters, clear enough for all to see, were written the words:

Are you computer genius Mr X.? I need your help. Call me.

Ross had left the number of the new brick-sized mobile phone he'd bought a few days ago on the note. The man had a quick scout around to check nobody was looking and, when he was sure he wasn't being watched, he reached over, took the note down and put it in his pocket. He then collected his coat from the returning third waiter and made for the exit. Third waiter took the piece of paper from his pocket and dialled the number.

Outside Stuart continued to press Ross on the folly of his plan.

'Just because you bunged some waiter £50, it doesn't mean you're not going to be sitting here all night freezing your nuts off in the car park. It's over, Ross, face it.'

'You're right – so go home. You don't have to stay.'

Stuart knew Ross was calling his bluff; he had no intention of spending his evening sitting in a cold car park waiting for a fictitious person to make an appearance. He made his way towards the queue of portly taxis and stopped when he heard a noise. Ross' mobile phone was ringing. He answered it and had a brief but illuminating conversation with third waiter. The next man exiting the restaurant would be Mr X.

Chapter 11
Lo & Behold

The man descended the steps of The House of Lard. His bearing was one of contentment. Once again The House of Lard had excelled itself. The roasted sparrows were exquisite and the Wildebeest a l'Orange was to die for. At least it had been for the wildebeest.

He was still just about able to breathe, having resisted the temptation of the lard crumble. It may not look like it, but for a man who was barred from several all-you-can-eat restaurants, he was capable of extraordinary discipline. He was also a man used to having his wits about him. One day they would catch up with him, but they would need to get up earlier than an insomniac milkman to do so.

As he strolled towards the line of oversized taxis something made him stop on a sixpence. Figuratively speaking of course; in reality the number of sixpences required for him to stop on would be a number starting with one but ending with many zeros. His ears had heard it but his brain didn't believe it. It just wasn't possible. He carried on walking. Again he stopped. This time there was no mistake. Somebody was calling his name. So, it would be today. Mr X glanced around to look for the milk float. He prayed it would be the police; better them than the others. He scanned the horizon for the group of sharp suits he was expecting to see. There was no sign of them. He looked again. Still nothing. All that was there were a couple of scruffy-looking civilians. One of them stepped forward with his hand outstretched.

'Good evening Mr X, my name is Ross Ackerman and this is my friend Stuart Davies. I apologise for the intrusion into your leisure time but you are a very difficult man to track down.'

Mr X appraised the two, his mind racing through the possibilities. *Couldn't be Mafia, too well spoken for any of the London gangs, must be Old Bill but which one?* He could try bluffing, but if they knew who else did? He had to find out.

'Who are you – MI5, MI6, FBI?'

'Oh no, it's nothing like that, I assure you we are not from any law enforcement agency.'

Could be the Russians. Wouldn't put it past those shifty sods to come up with something like this.

Just to be sure Mr X called Ross and Stuart sons of backstreet Cossack whores in Russian and awaited the response. Stuart looked at Ross, who saw his blank stare and raised him a look of dumbfounded incomprehension. Stuart folded.

Definitely not Russian.

'What do you want?' The words were spat at Ross and Stuart.

Mr X was agitated. He was in an easily accessible public place with a couple of people who knew who he was. It wouldn't be long before some other people turned up and they would be armed with more than the good-natured bumbling act of this pair.

'We would like to speak to you about a business proposition,' Ross began. 'You see, we need a man of your unparalleled expertise for a project we are working on.'

So, it's gang related after all. Better play along. They may look like clowns but if they're smart enough to find me then they're not to be underestimated.

'OK gents, I'll hear you out but I do so under duress,' said Mr X. 'I don't appreciate being accosted in public car parks. First things first though, I need to know which gang you represent and who your top man is. There's a correct procedure for procuring my services and you'll be putting some dangerous noses out of joint by not following it.'

Ross and Stuart had a quick whispered conversation that was accompanied by confused facial expressions.

'Er, I think we're getting off on the wrong foot here,' said Ross, desperate to win Mr X over. 'I apologise for any confusion. I work for Browns of London, in the Fraud Detection department, and my friend Stuart here is Head of IT for Webley Snell Insurance brokers. With the help of a few colleagues we are developing a quite revolutionary software programme and we need the help of the world's greatest computer genius, which …'

Mr X started laughing with relief. He now knew he wasn't about to be killed.

'Bravo gents, I admire your audacity and ingenuity in finding me. So you want me to help you develop some software? Thanks but no thanks. I don't work for corporates. Believe me, you couldn't afford my services. There is, however, the small matter of how you found me though. Who told you?'

'That's private,' said Ross, trying to figure out how to turn this around. They needed Mr X.

'Very well.' Mr X took a mobile phone out of his coat pocket and began dialling some numbers. 'There are two numbers left to dial. If I dial them some people you really don't want to meet will be here in a few minutes' time. What they'll do is bundle you into a van, take you somewhere nice and quiet and 'persuade' you to tell them the name of whoever told you about me. It's up to you chaps but I'm trying to make it easier for you here.'

Ross' mind was frantic. What should he do? While he tried to decide, something unexpected occurred. In the blink of an eye Stuart stepped forward, retrieved a House of Lard fork from his pocket and thrust it against Mr X's neck.

'Press one more button and I'll rip your fucking throat out.'

Silence followed. It was accompanied by a complete lack of noise. During this time Mr X carefully handed the phone to Stuart. Ross' contribution to this scene was to remain rooted to the spot with his mouth agape. He'd known Stuart his whole life. As far as he was aware, this was the first time he'd threatened anybody and the first time Ross had ever heard him swear. Stuart's face had done a quick dash past red, stopped for a second at burgundy and was now a nice shade of puce. Mr X was breathing hard, beads of sweat rolling down his face.

Taking extreme care, Ross took Stuart's hand and eased it away from the jugular of Mr X. With a comforting arm around his shoulder, Ross gently moved Stuart away from arm's length of Mr X. Stuart shook with rage. Mr X shook with fear. Ross stood between them like the referee in the deciding bout of the inaugural Mr Witch Doctor UK championships. Leaving Stuart to calm down, Ross apologised to Mr X for his behaviour.

'I'm so sorry. He's my best friend, I've known him my whole life and I've never seen him like this before.'

'Look, I'll hear you out for your software project,' Mr X said, trying to regain his composure, 'but not here and not now. I'm not making any promises either.'

Ross thanked him and they agreed to meet the next day at his flat. Mr X looked at Stuart, still lost in his own world of uncontrollable wrath.

'I know professional killers who would have been too scared to do what he just did because of what would happen to them. He didn't think twice.'

'You threatened me. There's not much can raise him to anger but he's very loyal to me.'

'Then you're extremely fortunate. I hope you appreciate that.'

'Oh I do.'

****

In the enormous executive suite on the fourth floor, a safe distance from the scenes of debauched gluttony below, sat the proprietor of The House of Lard. His name was Dr Cornelius Corpulence. His title was not the product of years of agonising over a thesis on a preposterously obscure area of academic research but rather the result of some mutual back scratching between Corpulence and a friendly university vice-chancellor who saw fit to bestow upon him an honorary doctorate in return for a lifetime of free dinners at The

House of Lard. Both Dr Corpulence and the vice-chancellor had big bones and a serious gland problem.

From his lofty vantage point on the fourth floor, Dr Corpulence performed the twin tasks of running a global obesity empire and spying on his staff and diners via a state-of-the-art CCTV system. Assisted by his downtrodden assistant Jennifer, his sole purpose in life was to maximise the revenue and expand the size and influence of Lard Corp, the parent company whose tentacles penetrated every possible aspect of the obese human being's life.

From womb to tomb was the motto and marketing strategy of Lard Corp, a piece of information known only to a handful of trusted staff. Recruit them young, make them obese, keep them obese their whole lives until they die and sell them goods and services tailored to their needs every day of their lives between those two points.

The process started at birth with a range of affordable baby formula and weaning foods whose calorific content was way beyond acceptable levels. Extensive research had been conducted which exonerated the baby food products against any claims of producing obese babies. The research was funded by a subsidiary of Lard Corp. Then there was baby, toddler and children's clothing, all catering for the larger than average sizes of infant. Further into the lifespan came insurance companies specialising in cover for obese drivers, travellers and home owners, fast food diners and takeaways, extra large adult clothing, the manufacture of every food and drink product known to man, vitamin supplements and numerous companies delivering disability and mobility products and services for the obese human being. The vast web of businesses trapping its clients into an obese lifestyle also included theme parks, TV and radio stations, solicitors, medical clinics, rail and coach companies, car manufacturers, airlines and of course funeral directors. From womb to tomb.

In the middle of its megalomaniacal drive for world domination sat the cornerstone of the business, the jewel in the crown of Lard Corp: The House of Lard. The restaurant had a tendency to polarise opinions as to its merits. The *Full Plate Great Food Guide*, a publication produced by the Lard Corp-funded Fat Alliance pressure group to extol the virtues of various dining establishments catering for the obese diner, awarded The House of Lard its maximum score of five spit-roasted pigs out of five. By contrast, the *Avoid like the plague unless you want cardiac failure guide to eating out in London,* a government-funded healthy eating publication with an entirely different agenda, had awarded The House of Lard its maximum score of five clogged arteries out of five. Numerous attempts had been made to close the restaurant down on health grounds. In explaining the failure of these attempts, some critics pointed to the coincidental lifetime honorary House of Lard memberships of the local MP, leader of the local council and the Minister and Shadow Minister for Health.

On this fine evening it was not business occupying the thoughts of Dr Corpulence. He was taking a great deal of interest in the restaurant's video footage from earlier in the evening. The spectacle of an unacceptable guest running the gauntlet was not an everyday occurrence. It was imperative there would be no repeat episode. At the time he'd had a feeling that something wasn't quite right but now he'd watched the film over again he was convinced. Someone had been helping the challenger in their efforts. Someone who was blissfully unaware of the sudden change in their life expectancy.

****

Ross and Stuart were nervous as they waited for their meeting with Mr X. Ross thought the chances of him showing up after Stuart's performance were at best non-existent. Just in case though he gave the flat a damn good clean and made sure his most expensive gadgets and eminent literary works were on display. He didn't want Mr X thinking he couldn't afford his services, even though he couldn't, or that he was incapable of sophisticated intellectual conversation with a man rumoured to have an IQ of over three hundred, even though he wasn't.

Mr X arrived on time and was greeted by Ross. He was in the door a matter of seconds before he was set on by Stuart, though this was a very different Stuart from the day before. Rage had been replaced with remorse and it was a full five minutes before Ross and Mr X were able to persuade him that he really had apologised a sufficient number of times. To Stuart's surprise, Mr X presented him with a gift-wrapped set of prestige House of Lard cutlery.

'So you don't have to steal any more forks. If you attack me with them again though, I'll arrange to have you killed,' he said, smiling.

Ross and Stuart laughed at what they hoped was a joke. Pleasantries aside,

Ross made them all some tea while Stuart arranged a medium-sized picnic on the coffee table. At least it was medium-sized by the standards of Stuart and Mr X. It was enough to feed Ross for a fortnight. This gesture went down very well with Mr X who, by his rapid consumption of the enticing smorgasbord, appeared to have skipped breakfast. He hadn't.

With gluttony commencing at a nice rate Ross began to explain the background of the project they needed help with. Partway through his spiel he sensed that their cause would be better served if he allowed Stuart to take the lead. Near decapitation had produced a respect for Stuart in Mr X that Ross knew didn't apply to himself.

Stuart outlined how long Ross had wanted to kill Belvedere and their various unsuccessful attempts to eliminate his desire to do so. He didn't explain why Ross wanted him dead, just that he had a very good reason. He then explained what they had done to develop a virtual reality software programme. At this point the conversation turned technical as the two men discussed programming languages, mathematical algorithms, computer hardware and the minutiae of various pieces of code. Ross' understanding of their conversation could be approximated to that of his ability to speak fluent Mongolian and his contribution was downgraded to chief tea boy.

At no point did Mr X let on what he was thinking. He was

impressed though, particularly with Stuart. The initiative required to get the project up and running and managed to near success in an area of computing in which he knew little, to an unrealistic deadline and at great personal financial expense to himself, was a considerable achievement. Stuart's only reward was to save his friend from a lengthy prison sentence. Money didn't come into it. Altruism was a notion Mr X was aware of but had always been happy to leave to others. Now he was considering doing a job, an exceptionally challenging job even for him, without the prime motive to be remunerated by a figure so large it wouldn't fit onto the display of an average-sized calculator. Then Stuart let slip something that sealed the deal for Mr X. He was quizzing him on the application of complex algorithms in the code when Stuart absent-mindedly replied that he didn't know the answer and would have to check with Lo.

'Aha, at last. So the plot thickens, Watson,' said Mr X.

'What? Oh bugger.'

Ross returned with yet more tea and biscuits to an embarrassed-looking Stuart.

'What's happened?' he asked.

'I'm sorry, it just slipped out,' Stuart said, frowning.

'What did?'

'The identity of your mystery source, that's what,' said Mr X. 'So you managed to track down my old friend Lo, did you?'

'That's not how we found out about you,' Ross lied.

'Oh don't worry, I won't harm him. Me and Lo go way back. I thought he went back to Korea though. Where did you find him?'

Stuart explained about the Institute, the broom cupboard and his strange partnership with Black.

'That's an absolute outrage. Look, just so you can both relax, I'll definitely be taking on your job if you're working with Lo. I owe him one – well, two if the currency is fingers. I'm the reason he lost them.'

Ross and Stuart listened as Mr X explained his history with Rum. Many years ago when they were both ambitious programmers they were enticed into the shady world of contract hacking. They formed a partnership and soon established themselves, gaining work through word-of-mouth referrals. At the time computer hacking was in its infancy and they faced stiff competition from a growing number of hacking teams with the same idea. So they followed the work, wherever and whoever it led to. Which was how they found themselves in Beijing.

'We were recruited by a group of Chinese entrepreneurs to do some hacking,' Mr X explained.

'Black said they were Triads,' said Ross.

'They may well have been, I couldn't comment. I will say this though. They carried an awful lot of cleavers and hatchets about their person and to my knowledge none of them were employed in the butchery or slaughtering industries. At least, not the livestock or poultry slaughtering industries. Anyway, it seemed a straightforward hacking job; they needed some confidential data held on a company computer system. Then when it came down to negotiating they started playing us off against some local hackers and before you know it I've gone and agreed to a much tighter deadline than we normally worked to. It was stupid of me but I was ambitious and I didn't want anyone else to get the work.'

'So what happened?' asked Stuart.

'What happened is those bloody Triads failed to mention who owned the business we were hacking into. Only Li Noh, head of China's leading computer software development business at the time. The security system they were using was the most sophisticated I'd ever seen. Half an hour to deadline and we still couldn't crack it.'

'So they chopped off his fingers because you couldn't hack into the system?' Ross ventured.

'I hacked into it alright, had to invent a whole new language in half an hour to do it as well. They upped the stakes, didn't they? Tied Lo to a chair and said he'd lose a finger for every ten minutes I went over. I was twenty-five minutes over the time and they took two of his fingers. I had to listen to the screams. Focuses the mind that, I can tell you. They didn't pay up either. Lo was dumped at what was laughingly called a hospital and I was taken to the airport, given a one-way ticket back to Blighty and the old two-fingered salute. Taught me a lot, that did. Always worked alone since then, and the fees and deadlines I work to are always set by the same person. Me.'

Ross was surprised by his candour. Poor Lo, thought Stuart.

'So I'll take your job, but I have certain conditions and they're non-negotiable.'

'Name them,' said Ross. He was ready to agree to anything as long as it didn't involve a colossal sum of money he didn't have.

'I'll provide the expertise and equipment that you don't already have. I'll bring all the tools you need but it's up to you to do the programming. Lo's more than capable of that and Stuart's your man for heading up the whole thing. Lo's a brilliant programmer but he's no leader. You are,' Mr X said, pointing at Stuart. 'I'll be dealing exclusively with you and when required with the other two. Lo will prefer it that way.'

'Done,' said Ross.

'Next, no outsiders are to be brought in. It's just us and the programmers. Any testing will have to be done by you.'

Stuart frowned at this, remembering the failed attempt on Ross' birthday.

'Don't worry. The way we'll be doing this won't involve any drugs. It's much safer.'

'OK,' said Ross, delighted that so far no mention had been made of lots of cash or any of his vital organs being required by Mr X as payment for his services.

'Once the simulation is developed successfully for Ross, which it will be, the programme will be adapted for multiple additional scenarios. After the initial work is done this can be achieved quite quickly,' said Mr X.

'Er, how and why?' asked Stuart, not following where this was going.

'How, I'll come onto in a minute. Why is the correct question. Do you think Ross here is the only person who wants to kill his boss? Of course not. The potential for this is enormous. We are going into business, gentlemen, offering stress management services to the masses at a modest fee. Much cheaper than hiring actual contract killers, trust me on that one. How you run your business is up to you with two exceptions. I'll be most disappointed if you choose not to maintain Mr Lo Rum as your Head of Programming and Software Development and I'll be equally saddened if you choose not to pay five percent of your monthly net profits to Independent Technology Ltd as a retainer for their range of excellent computing consultancy services.'

'Er, who are they then?' asked Ross.

'They are me,' said Mr X. 'It's one of my companies. Officially I don't exist but a growing number of people who bear an uncanny resemblance to me have controlling interests in a portfolio of medium-sized profitable limited businesses.'

'Ah, I see,' said Ross, cottoning on, 'and do any of these businesses by any chance provide quality "laundry" services?'

'You know, I believe one or two may do.'

'Anything else?' Ross asked, praying there wasn't.

'Yes. The business we shall establish is to always remain limited. Bearing in mind the nature of the services we shall be providing, you don't want undue publicity. I can recommend some reputable accountants who are known for their discretion.'

'There wouldn't be the remotest chance they are owned by a person or persons who bear a striking resemblance to you, would there?' Ross asked with suspicion.

'That's uncanny. Have you ever considered a career in mind reading?' Mr X asked, without an iota of sincerity. 'Once everything is up and running I'll only get involved if absolutely necessary and it goes without saying that any mention of my existence will bring a swift end to our relationship.'

'All agreed,' confirmed Ross.

'Excellent. And now I suggest we celebrate by indulging ourselves in these fine chocolates.'

Mr X opened the box and competed with Stuart to not offer first choice of chocolate to each other.

'Excellent caramel fondant,' Mr X purred.

'Bet it's not as good as the walnut whip,' Stuart drooled.

Amid sexual-sounding groans of delight emanating from the two men, Ross attempted to gain their attention. Polite coughing wasn't working so he just came out with it.

'So when do you think it might be ready for me to try?'

Mr X didn't look up or appear to give the matter a second's thought. 'Oh, about a month,' he said, sniffing a triple chocolate brownie and savouring the aroma.

'What?' shrieked Stuart, his attention plucked from the chocolaty nirvana it had been inhabiting. 'That's never going to be enough time, is it?'

'Are you doubting me, Stuart?'

'Well no, but…'

'You're doubting me, aren't you?' Mr X was enjoying teasing Stuart.

'OK, if I'm being honest, yes. I don't think it can be done in that time.'

'He's absolutely right. What was I thinking? A month indeed. What kind of fool am I?'

Stuart sighed in relief.

'It will be ready in three weeks.'

'What?'

'Do you want to go for two weeks?' Mr X asked, daring Stuart to reply. 'Remember you're doing all the programming.'

A flustered Stuart flicked through an index of retorts and settled on silence. Ross was delighted. After what seemed like an interminable amount of time but was in fact just thirty seconds, Stuart couldn't hold his tongue any longer.

'OK, I'm not doubting your genius or anything but just how the hell are we going to do it in three weeks?'

'By using METATRON.'

'What the hell's that when it's at home?' Stuart barked in exasperation.

'The most advanced, most powerful, most flexible and intelligent computer programming language ever invented. It can do anything.'

'Erm, yeah that sounds great but how am I supposed to use a programming language that nobody apart from you has ever heard of?'

'Glad you asked. Classes start tomorrow at eight a.m. Bring the others and meet me here.' Mr X handed Stuart a business card. It had no name, just the address of some anonymous trading unit on an industrial estate. 'And now chaps, if you'll excuse me, I have much work to do. See you at eight, Stuart. Don't forget to bring the others. Best not tell Lo it's me or he might not come. Tatty bye.'

Mr X scooped up the remaining chocolates and disappeared.

'All in all I think that went rather well,' said Ross, rubbing his hands together in glee.

****

Training in METATRON didn't get off to the most auspicious of starts. When they arrived at the business unit Stuart had to screen off part of the large room to prevent anxiety attacks from the two reclusive programmers. He made a mental note to get them both to a shrink about their agoraphobia as a matter of urgency.

The appearance of Mr X didn't help matters. Lo's normal Zen-like state was replaced with a human impression of an active volcano. As the other men restrained him, Lo rained a torrent of Korean profanities on his former partner. He soon ran out of puff when his severely under-utilised vocal chords gave up the ghost. With Black interpreting, Stuart managed to persuade Rum to stay on board by outlining the long-term employment prospects and earnings potential for him. A fancy job title sealed the deal, with the proviso that he didn't have to speak to Mr X at any point. Given that Rum's normal propensity for discourse with anyone other than Black was rarer than a cannibal's steak, nobody thought this would be an issue.

METATRON training involved a three-day intensive crash course in the most complex computer code known to man. For a man who worked alone, Mr X was an excellent teacher. He walked them through the code, taking them from straightforward basic functions to the more advanced capabilities. He presented examples of the code's use and showed them how functions that would normally take weeks to programme could be achieved in just a few hours. Once they understood its basic capability, he took them onto its use for virtual reality. The technical capability of the hardware they were using, particularly in terms of its speed and memory capacity, was beyond anything any of them had seen before. Stuart wondered how Mr X had acquired it. His day job was to buy IT equipment and he knew for a fact none of this stuff was available on the commercial market.

Whilst the others got to grips with METATRON, Ross was busy with his own assignment. Now that the surprise element of the project was no longer required, he'd been instructed to bring back visual and audio recordings of Belvedere, as well as detailed depictions of the scenic backgrounds he wanted recreating. His task was made much easier by the state-of-the-art surveillance equipment supplied to him by Mr X, along with a dummies guide to installing bugging devices.

Under normal circumstances, finding a time when Belvedere was absent from his office would be a quest comparable to discovering the lost city of Atlantis. Fortune was on his side though, as it was time for Ross' monthly meeting with the Serious Fraud Office. He faked an important deadline and delegated the meeting to his boss, much to Belvedere's delight. Ross normally handled these meetings, at the request of the SFO. Not even professional organisations with legitimate reasons for seeing Belvedere wanted to do so. With

Belvedere absent Ross bugged his phone and placed several discreet microscopic cameras about his office, supplying live video feeds back to the headquarters of Project Belvedere.

Ross' second assignment was to attend a private health clinic for an MRI scan. After the debacle of the first attempt on his birthday, they weren't taking any chances this time. Comprehensive readings and reports of Ross' neurological activity would be acquired. As this had been arranged by Mr X, Ross shouldn't have been – but still was – surprised that the clinic was like none he had ever seen before. Another anonymous warehouse unit in another barren industrial estate. No indication existed that expensive medical procedures were taking place inside. The 'entrepreneurial' nature of the clientele made extreme discretion, bordering on invisibility, a key requirement for the clinic.

With the knowledge gained from their METATRON boot camp still fresh, and with everything they needed on Belvedere and Ross' brain, Stuart, Rum and Black set to work. They were amazed at how fast the programming was completed. Mr X made their work even easier by providing specialist software he'd devised for using METATRON in virtual reality applications. This included METATRON Clone for recreating convincing human characteristics such as appearance, mannerisms and speech, and METATRON Landscape for creating lifelike scenery and locations. The software, when programmed, could re-create virtual versions of real life places and people, using uploaded video, audio and still images.

The most complex and time-consuming aspect of the programming was getting the virtual world they'd created to interact and respond to the unknown spontaneous stimuli it would receive from the brain of a third party. Despite all this Mr X was as good as his word and Project Belvedere was ready for a full trial one day early. As punishment for being proved wrong, Stuart had to force himself to take Mr X out to dinner at The House of Lard. Sperm Whale Surprise was on special offer.

Ross waited outside Belvedere's office. Once again he was kept waiting by a fictitious conversation Belvedere was conducting, this time with a senior representative of the Bank of England. He took the opportunity to rearrange the superfluous leather chairs into a disordered arrangement. A petty act, but one he knew would drive Belvedere mad. Before long he was called in and took his seat, making sure he moved it just enough to be off-centre from the desk, requiring Belvedere to move his chair in order to face him.

There had been no explanation for the meeting. Ross knew it wasn't an appraisal but that was all he knew. Belvedere came straight out with it.

'I've called this meeting because certain allegations have been made against you and to make you aware that a disciplinary committee will be convened to hear the charges against you.'

'And what charges would these be, Charles?'

'I can't divulge them at this stage.'

'I see. And how then, if I may be so bold as to ask, will I be able to defend myself against charges without knowing what they actually are?'

Belvedere scowled. Ross always had a smart answer for everything. Well, he wasn't getting out of this one.

'You will be informed in writing of the charges and will be permitted to present your case against them to the committee.'

Ross formed a mental picture of the committee bouncing up and down, retrieving charge sheets from their pouches and saying 'g'day mate' while knocking back a cold tinny.

'And just for my own interest, who has made these as yet unspecified allegations against me?'

'That information is classified.'

Ross had a pretty good idea who it was. He glanced along

Belvedere's huge bookcase, filled with works that, at the most generous, could be described as colossally boring. He picked up the volume entitled Offshore Tax Havens: A Concise Guide. Ross had read this Inland Revenue publication before. It wasn't concise. As an insomnia cure, it rivalled the truly uninteresting A History of Librarians Volume 1, Complete and Unabridged.

'May I borrow this?' he asked. 'I think it would prove useful in a case I'm dealing with.'

Belvedere eyed him with suspicion. Flattery of his prized collection of reports was definitely a new ploy and he was unsure how to respond. *Ross doesn't do flattery,* thought Belvedere; *he openly hates me and uses every opportunity to undermine my authority.* He concluded that Ross must genuinely want the report. Perhaps this could be the start of a new, more cordial relationship between the two of them.

'By all means, if you can put it to some good use,' Belvedere said, finishing with a smile. This was an unfamiliar sensation for his cheek muscles and they recoiled in pain.

'Oh I think I can, Charles; yes I'm sure I can.'

Ross lifted the heavy report high in the air and brought it crashing down at speed on Belvedere's head. A stunned Belvedere stumbled to his feet and fell over. Deciding he needed more weight, Ross grabbed Money Laundering, All You Need to Know from the bookcase, added it to the tax havens report and once again set to work on Belvedere. Again and again he pounded at his skull with the weighty literature.

After several blows, Belvedere stopped moving. Still Ross attacked him. Now coming apart at the spines, the reports fell to the floor from his bloody hands when he concluded the motionless Belvedere must be dead. Ross was out of breath, sweat pouring down his face. Beating a man to death with his own fraud reports was more tiring than he'd anticipated. He stood over the late Charles Belvedere and took a moment to catch his breath. Then he beamed a magnificent smile. He'd done it. At last he'd done it. He savoured the moment.

'Again,' he shouted. 'Go again.'

Ross waited outside Belvedere's office. Once again he was kept waiting by a fictitious conversation Belvedere was conducting …

Chapter 12
Misdirection

In the six months since he first read Brown Free, Charles Belvedere had been busy. He had hobbies to cultivate. He chose beekeeping to start with, as it came first alphabetically ahead of fly fishing and magic. His efforts in his new endeavours were not quite the roaring success he'd hoped for.

He borrowed every book and video he could get his hands on from the library, took out a lifetime membership of Beesy Does It, the monthly apicultural bible, and joined a local beekeepers society. The society's tried and trusted initiation classes for beginners were too slow for Belvedere; he wanted to be an expert bee handler immediately. While the society was having a break in their class, Belvedere decided to advance his studies forthwith. He donned an idle beekeepers outfit lying on the floor and headed towards the hives. When the group returned from their break, they found Belvedere pelting down the hill being chased by a swarm of angry bees. Two days later, he received a letter from the society terminating his membership. They also asked if he could, at a convenient time, return the children's beekeeper outfit he'd stolen.

Undeterred by his initial failure to master beekeeping, or by the twenty stings he'd received, Belvedere was nothing if not determined. He purchased a beekeeper's outfit of the correct size and all the equipment he would need to manage his own hives. He then assembled a flat pack hive in his spare room and proceeded to stage two of his plan, the ordering of forty thousand bees. Belvedere didn't want to mess about; he wanted to make sure he had enough bees. He bought the bees through an obscure South American bee wholesaler advertising in Beesy Does It. He didn't bother to check the species of bee he ordered was the correct one.

One Saturday morning, his delivery of bees arrived and Belvedere couldn't contain his excitement. If all went well he would be swapping beekeeping anecdotes with the Chairman in a matter of weeks. About five hours later he was being treated in the Dermatology Unit at Westpoint General Hospital for 136 stings to his body, administered by a swarm of rare Peruvian Green Swamp Bees. Environmental health officers were keen to speak to him about where on earth he got the bees, as they were on a list of endangered species. They would have to wait their turn behind a queue of Belvedere's angry neighbours, several of whom were also rushed to hospital.

With a heavy heart and a sore body, Belvedere reached the conclusion that beekeeping wasn't for him.

****

After about eight weeks of recovering from the pain of his ordeal with the bees, Belvedere threw himself into the world of fly fishing. Again he acquired all the necessary books, instructional videos and equipment that a fly fishing novice would need. Once he familiarised himself with the basics, Belvedere perused *Trout and About* magazine for a list of fly fishing locations near to London. Satisfied with the selection of recommended chalk streams and stillwaters in Hampshire, Berkshire and Surrey, he chose an appropriate beginners rod, a selection of flies, and headed off to catch some fish.

For the next three months he caught a dawn train every Saturday and spent the weekend fishing. The long days of solitude, the fresh air and the sound and smell of nature did him the world of good. After a few weeks he even felt healthier. His lungs communicated with his brain that they would appreciate it very much if they could have a lot more of this and a lot less London smog, thank you very much. It was all good. There was just one problem. He was a spectacular failure in the art of catching fish.

He tried everything. He fished in rivers recommended for fly fishing. He studied his books and videos and replicated the instructions. He watched fellow fly fishers and copied their casting technique to perfection. He wore different clothes for fear of a particular pair of socks or trousers being unlucky. He changed his rod several times. He used flies with bizarre names like the Purple Head Woolly Bugger Fly and the Light Brown Booby Nymph Fly. It made not a jot of difference. He was the worst fly fisher in the whole history of bad fly fishers.

Putting his non-existent social skills to good use, he tried making friends with fellow fly fishers whom he'd just seen catching trout and pike, but no sooner had he joined them than they would be unable to catch a single sprat. People he was fishing with would make their excuses and leave, only for Belvedere to see them 100 yards further down the bank catching fish for fun.

Within a few months, word had circulated around the fly fishing community. Leaflets showing Belvedere's face with the words 'Avoid this man, he is cursed' were spread among the fishermen. Possessing a layer of skin so thick a rhinoceros would be jealous, Belvedere refused to give up without a fight. He sported a range of increasingly implausible disguises to continue his idiotic scheme, convinced that each time his luck would change. It didn't. Soon he was refused entry to the rivers and when he did manage to sneak in, he was detected and forcibly removed. Once again Belvedere had to admit defeat. The Chairman must indeed be a great man if he could master this infuriating pastime.

****

Browns of London was an old-fashioned institution. It prided itself on its traditional values. The average Browns client wasn't short of a bob or million. A typical customer voted Conservative, had attended public school and could lay claim to owning half of Staffordshire. Browns' clients did not expect their bank to be leading the way in ethical banking or employee profit-sharing schemes. This was just as well as Browns was not so much at the back of the queue for such corporate social responsibility concepts, they didn't even know there was a queue or where said queue might be located.

Browns' success was based on the strictest hierarchy. There were rules. Some were written, some unwritten. One of the unwritten rules regarded the use of lifts for its staff. Brown House consisted of five floors. It contained a lift at either end of each floor. It hadn't taken long after Brown House opened for one of the company's fundamental unwritten rules to be implemented. The lift on the left-hand side of the building was to be used by senior managers and members of the board. All other staff were required to use the lift on the right-hand side of the building. As a consequence, the right-hand lift was very busy and required regular servicing. To avoid any discrimination cases or tribunals being brought against it, when the right-hand lift was out of order, any disabled or pregnant members of staff would be invited to use the left-hand lift.

Charles Belvedere was a senior manager and had, as one of his perks, left-hand lift privileges. He used the right-hand lift though. Most people thought the reason he did this was to ingratiate himself with the workers and this only served to decrease his popularity amongst staff in the Fraud Detection department, an achievement given his popularity already suffered from terminal subsidence. This was not, however, the genuine reason for Belvedere's forgoing of his hard-earned lift privileges. Not long after being promoted to Head of Fraud Detection and receiving his left-hand lift rights, Belvedere conducted a time and motion study of his normal working day. Thanks to Ross, his office was at the extreme right of the third floor, the opposite end of the building from the rest of the Fraud Detection team. Belvedere's analysis concluded that over the course of a year he would spend over eight hours walking from his office to the left-hand lift and back.

This presented him with a dilemma. Belvedere was all for managers receiving special privileges and the left-hand lift was his ticket to a better class of person. He was desperate to use the left-hand lift and for two weeks he did. At the end of the two weeks he gave up and started using the right-hand lift. He was having panic attacks. He just couldn't live with the guilt of short-changing the company of two minutes of work every day.

The Chairman approved of the unwritten lift usage rule. Not surprising seeing as he created it. He glanced at his Rolex as he entered Brown House and walked towards the left-hand lift. It was five past seven and the building was empty, save for a few cleaning and security staff. He pressed the button next to the lift and it opened. Just before the lift door shut a figure darted inside. The Chairman didn't recognise him. The man started to speak but the Chairman wasn't listening. All he could think was *How dare this person use my lift. Don't they know who I am?* It then occurred to the Chairman that the stranger might want to attack him or hold him hostage; he was after all the most senior ranking person in the company. The man waved his arms extravagantly at the Chairman – who noticed he was dressed in strange attire – whilst pointing some sort of stick at him in a threatening manner. The Chairman retreated to the corner of the lift, holding his hands out in front of his face.

'Please,' he begged, 'spare me. I have a family. I have children. I don't have any money on me,' he lied, knowing full well he had over £800 in his wallet, 'but I can get you some from the bank. How much would you like?'

'No, no you don't understand,' the strange man said. 'Look.' The man edged closer to the Chairman and his arm moved through the air in the general direction of the Chairman's head. It struck him on the temple. At this point the stranger became even more animated, shouting incomprehensibly. When he reached his hand deep into his jacket, the Chairman, convinced he was about to be shot, lunged towards the controls and pressed the emergency red button. The lift plunged downwards at speed, jerked to a sudden halt and the doors flung open. The Chairman was relieved to see Stephen Cleary and his security team, armed and in position.

'Arrest this man, Stephen. He attacked me. Be careful though – I think he's armed.'

The security guards had already dived on top of the stranger before the Chairman had uttered a word. He was handcuffed and hauled away to the security office.

'Good work men, well done. I'll see you all get a bonus for this,' the Chairman lied.

'Thank you, sir. Are you alright? Would you like me to take you to hospital? You might have shock,' replied Cleary, a picture of calm despite the seriousness of the incident.

'No, I'll be fine Stephen. I'm just going up to the office. Pop up later, will you?'

When the Chairman reached his office on the fifth floor Deborah was already waiting with a large brandy at the ready. The Chairman drained the brandy in one gulp. His nerves were shot to pieces. Being attacked was scary. He would have to employ personal bodyguards. Female bodyguards of course, mainly in their twenties.

About 20 minutes later the Chairman's phone rang and Deborah answered. It was Stephen Cleary. She put him on speakerphone.

'What's the latest, Stephen, has he been banged up yet? Was he trying to rob the bank?' the Chairman asked.

Cleary sounded sheepish. 'Well, not yet sir. He's still here. We think he wasn't trying to rob the bank. He says there has been a big misunderstanding.'

'A misunderstanding? The man attacked me,' the Chairman bellowed. He was no longer in shock.

'Ah yes, well it seems that too may have been a misunderstanding, sir.'

'Stephen, I'm going to lose my patience in a minute. I've been attacked and you're saying there has been a misunderstanding. Is that it?'

'Yes, sir, that's it.'

'The man was armed, Stephen. You have confiscated his weapons, haven't you?'

'I'm afraid not, sir.'

'Why not? Explain yourself now – and it had better be good.' The Chairman was ready and waiting to shout 'You're fired!' at the first sign of an unacceptable answer.

'OK sir, this is somewhat awkward, I'm afraid,' Cleary began. 'I haven't confiscated any weapons because there are no weapons to confiscate. Not unless you count a pair of white doves, a string of handkerchiefs and a magic wand as dangerous weapons.'

'I, er ... what? I don't follow.'

'It seems that the person in the lift was trying to perform an impromptu magic show for you and it er ... well, it went a bit wrong.'

'Magic show?'

'Yes, sir, a magic show. He was trying to impress you. You know, with you being in the Magic Circle.'

'Er.' The Chairman's brain was racing. 'Oh yes.' Deborah frowned at him and waggled her finger.

'Sir, I don't want to overstep the mark here but with your permission I think it might be best all round if we hush this whole thing up. It could be very embarrassing for the company, what with who the man actually is.'

'Who is it, Stephen?' asked the Chairman, staring into space in stunned disbelief.

'It's Charles Belvedere, Head of the Fraud Detection department,' Cleary confirmed awkwardly. 'He's ever so sorry. Perhaps you could talk to him, sir. He's already offered his resignation.'

'Erm, can I put you on hold for a second, Stephen?' the Chairman asked, wishing the world would swallow him up immediately.

****

Belvedere sat in the security office sipping a cup of hot cocoa and being consoled by Cleary. He was so depressed he would welcome death in any form right now. He wondered if the guards would shoot to kill if he attacked one of them.

Instead of the triumph he had so anticipated, his big moment was an unmitigated disaster. The Chairman hadn't even recognised him! Belvedere blamed himself for this. What had started as a simple magic routine had, he decided, lacked the showmanship he was looking for. To address this he had visited a fancy dress store the previous day and purchased a theatrical magician's outfit, circa late nineteenth century, complete with flowing black velvet cloak, enormous hat and oversized wand. Having tried the outfit on he still felt something was missing. He therefore frequented a nearby joke shop and procured a black wig and novelty moustache to complete the man-of-mystery look he was trying to convey. By the time he finished applying the theatrical make-up, even he didn't recognise himself.

The second thing that had gone awry was that Belvedere had found himself so overawed in the presence of the Chairman he became an incoherent babbling fool. When attempting to perform a card trick he stuttered and mumbled like a first year student giving a presentation and his hands shook so much he dropped the cards. When his first trick failed he tried to get back on track by performing some sleight of hand. The Chairman just looked perplexed at the sight of a strange-looking man waving his arms about. Belvedere was dying on his feet in front of his hero. Desperate to rescue his act, he decided to remove a silver penny from behind his ear but when he tried to perform this trick, the frightened Chairman retreated and Belvedere slipped and stumbled forward. His momentum carried his already moving arm crashing into the Chairman's face.

Now experiencing a blind panic, Belvedere went for the coup de grâce and reached into his magic coat to remove one of the two white doves he'd stuffed into it earlier. Before he had a chance to dazzle the Chairman with his dove trick, he was being pinned to the ground by four security staff armed with guns.

Back in the security office, the incarcerated doves had escaped Belvedere's coat and were flying about the office, defecating on the CCTV monitors.

'I'm sorry about this, Charles but if the doves don't fly out of the window soon I'm going to have to shoot them. They're a security risk,' said Cleary, with as much sympathy as he could muster.

Belvedere shrugged. He didn't care about anything anymore. He was sure he would be sacked. All his dreams were shattered. Whether a dove shit on his head was the least of his concerns.

It had all started so well. Unlike the beekeeping and fly fishing, he was a dab hand at magic. He joined a nearby magic society, the Wizards of Westminster, and attended their meetings. The regular members of the Wizards were delighted with his progress and he received considerable praise and encouragement. His sleight of hand and misdirection were getting to a decent standard for a beginner; he'd mastered several basic card tricks and was starting to gain confidence in using magical props. His mentor in the Wizards told him that if he carried on showing this level of dedication and practice, he might one day be able to perform his own magic shows, maybe even go professional. This was all music to Belvedere's ears but as far as he was concerned, magic was just a means to an end.

Displaying an impressive inability to learn from previous catastrophic mistakes, he once again decided it was time to run before he could walk. He set a date to deliver his private performance for the Chairman and frantically worked on his act. When it seemed he would not be ready on time with just a few days to go, it didn't occur to Belvedere to change the date to give himself more time. Procrastination was for losers.

'Perhaps you could talk to him, sir. He's already offered his resignation,' Belvedere heard Cleary say into the phone.

He briefly emerged from wallowing in a fog of depression to eavesdrop on the phone conversation between Cleary and the Chairman, desperate for the tiniest microscopic crumb of hope. He wished Cleary hadn't mentioned about his offer to resign. If they sacked him he could always contest it, or at least try for a generous redundancy and a good reference, or any redundancy and a good reference. He was prepared to settle for no redundancy and a bad reference.

'What's he saying, Stephen. Have I got to clear my desk?' Belvedere asked, his voice a pathetic shadow of his normal pathetic self.

'He's put me on hold, Charles. Hasn't decided anything yet, I don't think,' Cleary replied.

****

'I told you that newsletter would blow up in your face, didn't I? But would you listen? Oh no, you always know best, don't you? Magic Circle indeed,' snapped Deborah.

'OK. You were right, OK. Now tell me how to sort this mess out,' the Chairman pleaded, showing Deborah his best innocent schoolboy look and charmer's smile. Like she had so many times before, she fell for it.

'First things first - you can't reprimand him. This has to be swept under the carpet unless you want the whole company to know you lied in the staff newsletter and you can't recognise your own senior managers.'

The Chairman sulked; he couldn't believe he was going to let off the hook a man who had just thumped him.

'Very well,' he said. 'What else?'

'Well...' began Deborah.

****

'More gateaux, Charles?' the Chairman asked.

'Oh no thank you sir, I couldn't eat another thing,' Belvedere replied.

'Please Charles, less of the sir. Call me Teddy.'

'Yes, sir, I will, sir,' Belvedere bumbled, his anxiety levels at an all-time high.

A relaxing evening of fine food and polite conversation with the

Chairman and his wife at their luxurious country estate. It should have been an ecstatic occasion for Belvedere, the fulfilment of his lifelong dreams. Instead, he'd spent the entire evening stressed out of his gourd as he attempted, and failed, to master the subtleties of dinner party etiquette. It had started when he arrived. The sinking feeling he experienced as he realised he was the only one wearing a dinner jacket was soon followed by the horror of seeing all the Chairman's butlers and house staff. He could feel them all looking at him, the stench of failure and inadequacy oozing out of his every pore. His paranoia reading was off the chart. He wasn't imagining it either; he really did see the Head Butler smirk as he handed him a bottle of supermarket champagne.

'Er thank you, sir. I will add it to our collection in the cellar.'

Of course he's got his own wine cellar Charles, you ignoramus. It's probably stuffed with priceless vintage champagne – but oh no, he's bound to want to crack open this rubbish you just bought from Tesco.

The internal argument Belvedere was having with himself reached fever pitch as he was led into the dining hall and faced with two challenges that would test the ability of his heart not to explode to its very limit. First, he was introduced to the Chairman's wife. Conversing with the opposite sex wasn't Belvedere's strong point. It also didn't make the list of the top million things he was useless at; he would need some actual experience of how bad he was at it to make that particular list. Then there was the cutlery. Knife, fork and spoon. He knew where he was with knife, fork and spoon. Instead he was faced with what looked like half the world's collection of antique silver in various shapes and sizes, a few of which vaguely resembled knives, forks and spoons.

With the help of frequent trips to the lavatory for pep talks and the shameless copying of everything the Chairman, his wife and the butlers did, Belvedere somehow made it through the meal. His attempts at conversation met with mixed failure. The minutiae of Fraud Detection, complaints about the location of his office and requests for longer working hours were not appropriate topics of conversation for the dinner table, he discovered.

'Would you care to join me for a brandy in the billiard room, Charles?' the Chairman asked, as the staff cleared away the remnants of the meal. Belvedere was so happy at the request he wanted to cry. So he did.

'You don't mind, do you, Mrs Chairman?' the Chairman asked his wife.

'You boys go and play. Thank you for a lovely evening, Mr Belvedere,' the Chairman's wife replied, giving him a peck on the cheek before she left the room. It was Belvedere's first ever kiss. Moments later both men heard the roar of rubber on gravel as what sounded like a high-powered sports car was driven away at speed by an irate wife keen to rescue what was left of the evening.

'Your shot, Charles,' the Chairman said to Belvedere in the billiard room.

Belvedere went to get out of his chair but he couldn't. A strong feeling of dizziness flooded through his brain as his muscles became so relaxed he was unable to move them. He tried to communicate this to the Chairman but he no longer possessed the power of speech.

'You don't look so good, Charles. I think I should call you a doctor,' the Chairman said with concern as he left the room in search of help.

As if by magic, a doctor appeared outside the billiard room. At least he called himself a doctor; in reality he possessed no formal medical qualifications at all.

'You're sure this will work?' the Chairman asked.

'How much did you spike his drink with?' the man asked.

'The full amount of course, just like you said.'

'Then he'll be putty in my hands. It's a very effective drug, makes people highly suggestible. In a few hours his whole memory of the last week will be whatever I tell him; this evening, the incident at the bank the other day, none of it will ever have happened.'

'Thank God for that,' said the Chairman, lighting an enormous Cuban cigar in celebration. 'Because if I have to spend one more second in the company of that odious excuse for a human being then I will not be held accountable for my actions.'

Chapter 13
Lift Off

Ross tapped his fingers on the desk and hummed to himself to calm his nerves. He looked at his watch. Almost time. He wished he could fast forward an hour so he could be sitting in a pub trying to break his record for most pints drunk in an hour.

There was a knock on the door. Ross took a deep breath and tried to compose himself.

'Come in.'

The door opened and Alice entered.

'Hi Alice. Please take a seat.'

'Miss Houghton,' Alice said, correcting him.

'What?'

'It's Miss Houghton, Ross. Not Alice. We've been through this before. This is a formal interview for the post of Sales Director and I want to be treated the same as all the other qualified applicants for the post.'

'Er, yes of course. Please take a seat, Miss Houghton,' Ross said, his stress levels increasing by the second.

Alice sat down as Ross pretended to scrutinise her CV. None of this had been his idea. He'd already offered Alice the job of Sales Director for the newly formed Executive Stress Relief Ltd on several occasions. Alice had insisted that she would only take the position if she earned it on merit after a thorough and formal recruitment process. She was now regretting it. What if one of the other applicants was better than her? This fear had been at the forefront of her mind when it came to choosing her interview attire. She had to make an impression. She plumped for shock and awe tactics.

Ross peeked at Alice from behind her CV. She was dressed like she was about to step onto a porn movie set. Her hair was tied back and she was wearing a pair of secretarial glasses. *Alice has perfect 20/20 vision. What's she doing wearing glasses?* thought Ross. Her nympho secretary look was completed by a white blouse several sizes too small for her, cut lower than a mole's basement and revealing a substantial amount of cleavage, none of which was supported by a sturdy bra. Then there was her skirt. It was black and complemented her blouse and high-heeled shoes. The only trouble was it was shorter than a Glaswegian's temper. Ross was also pretty sure that stockings and suspenders weren't appropriate attire for Sales Directors. There was more flesh on display than in an Amsterdam doorway.

Ross was making a pig's ear of the interview.

'Erm, so Miss Houghton. Erm.'

'So I expect you've read my CV,' Alice said, helping him out.

'Er yes, I erm, that is to say, um…'

'And you want to know how my experience qualifies me for the job?' Alice asked herself on Ross' behalf, pouting at the end of her question.

'Er yes.'

Oh my lord, she's wearing scarlet lipstick. She's pouting. Did she just wink at me?

'Well, I've been working in sales for a number of years now. I regularly exceed my targets. My figures are very impressive. Would you like to see them?' Alice asked, letting her hair down and slowly twirling a strand around her finger.

'Umm. Yes. Impressive figures. Hmm. Umm. Er, hmm.'

Alice was being very patient. This was some sort of psychometric test Ross was setting her. She was impressed with how seriously he was taking the situation. Unbeknown to her, Ross was having a full-blown inner argument with his brain.

'Just work, will you? Give me some proper words, dammit. I sound like a Neanderthal.'

'Don't blame me. I'm trying my best but the rest of the body's not listening to me anymore. The groin's in charge now, mate; you need to stop thinking about her, that's what you need to do.'

'I'm not thinking about her.'

'Oh yeah? Look at her. Go on, just look at her.'

Ross couldn't look anymore. He had to get out. Despite wearing underpants and trousers two sizes too big for him he still couldn't stand up. There was nothing for it. He looked out of the window at some non-existent emergency taking place outside, a shocked expression on his face. As soon as Alice followed his gaze he took the opportunity to dart out of the room and escape the claustrophobic atmosphere of sex. Another minute and he would have jumped on her.

He found what he was looking for in an as-yet unopened box of books in the storeroom. He opened the book and read. It took several minutes for the antidote to work but eventually Ross felt the pressure ease in his trousers and his brain return to something approaching normality.

'Thank you, Charles Belvedere,' he said, as he closed the massive volume that was *Insurance Fraud: A historical critique of detection methods, by Charles Belvedere.* No brain could withstand the banality of one of Belvedere's reports.

Armed with his kryptonite, Ross returned to the office and completed the interview. As long as he referred back to it every few seconds the somnifacient effects of Belvedere's report managed to neutralise the strong sense of sexual bewitchment coming from the other side of the desk.

Alice got the job but Ross thought it prudent to wait an appropriate period of time before he gave her the good news, just to give her the chance to change into something resembling clothes.

****

Recruitment for Executive Stress Relief Ltd was now complete. Stuart was IT Director, Lo Rum was Head of Programming and Software Development, Matthew Black was Creative Director, Adam was Director of Legal Affairs and a man named Alan West had accepted the post of Operations Director. His appointment had proved to be a spectacular success. In his first few days he secured an enormous business premises at a scarcely believable low rate of rent. The building had lots of offices which were perfect for converting into virtual reality techno pods for the discerning businessman wishing to murder his superiors after a long day of pointless meetings. The property also had ample room for expansion. It was an absolute steal. Alan West had brokered the deal with Ted Armour, an old contact of his in the commercial property market. Both men bore more than a passing resemblance to Mr X.

Initiating the recruitment drive hadn't been all plain sailing though. After the success of the trial simulation carried out by Ross, keeping his bargain of going into business with Mr X had been the last thing on his mind. The first thing on his mind was killing Belvedere. Stuart, Mr X, Rum, Black, Alice and Adam had all been unprepared for the effect on Ross that murdering Belvedere would have. They expected him to experience a feeling of closure now he'd achieved what he had yearned for, for so long. Not a bit of it. For three weeks Ross lived in the virtual world created by METATRON. Again and again he killed Belvedere, pausing only to eat, sleep, use the toilet and occasionally bathe.

While they waited for Ross to return to the real world, Rum, Black and Stuart set to work. They created a series of standard situations with numerous alternative scenarios that could be chosen to suit the requirements of the client. Black worked on the creative details of each simulation, Rum did all the programming, while Stuart dealt with any technical issues as well as helping the other two. His Korean was really coming along.

In time, Ross grew bored with the repetitiveness of his interactive snuff movie. His desire to kill Belvedere in new and exciting ways forced him back into the world of human beings. If he was to continue murdering Belvedere in ever more elaborate scenarios, he would need his team of programmers to build them for him and they couldn't live on fresh air. They needed paying. The idea of making a successful business out of violent fantasies began to take hold.

****

It was the greatest day in Charles Belvedere's life. Ross asked to meet him in private and just came straight out with it. Belvedere didn't waste time trying to persuade him to stay. He rushed to his computer to type up an official letter for both of them to sign and make it official. Before he could finish typing the first sentence, Ross produced a letter he'd already typed, approving a year's career break for him, and they both signed it. And that was that.

He'd considered just resigning but was persuaded by Stuart to hedge his bets just in case things didn't work out with ESR. This didn't bother Belvedere in the slightest. He had a full year of scheming ahead of him. By the time Ross returned the door would not so much be still open as replaced with one made of reinforced steel four feet thick, complete with alarms, barbed wire, more locks than the Manchester ship canal and guarded by a pack of hungry wolves. Ross had no intention of returning; he had Belvederes to kill.

****

Jennifer Ellis sat at the desk in her office on The House of Lard's executive floor and tried to concentrate on the tables of sales and expenditure figures for the various divisions and subsidiary companies that comprised Lard Corp. It wasn't easy with the noise coming from the adjacent office.

She didn't require absolute silence to carry out her work and meet the demanding deadlines of Dr Corpulence, but her brain struggled to concentrate when subjected to screams of agonising pain from somebody being tortured just a few feet away on the other side of the office partition. She shouldn't have to put up with this. She was an accountant with an MBA and yet here she was working for a respected businessman and popular public figure who just happened to be a ruthless sadist who didn't think twice about torturing and murdering his own staff. The screams grew louder.

Listening to the howls of pain was even more difficult than normal for Jennifer, as she knew it was third waiter being subjected to the abuse. She had certain feelings for third waiter. She often watched him on the security film, graceful as a ballerina as he glided across the dining room, his immaculate dress and effortless charm enough to make her turn the electric fan on in winter.

It was no coincidence that Dr Corpulence's hired goons had chosen the office next to Jennifer's to carry out the act. It was a gentle reminder from the good doctor about the kind of punishment awaiting those who dared to cross him. Jennifer had more reason than most to fear Dr Corpulence. As his number two in all matters of business, his official accountant and private secretary, she was privy to all his dirty little secrets; the infinite range of fraud, theft, money laundering and other crimes too numerous to mention that Lard Corp engaged in on an industrial scale. The fate that awaited her should she ever inform the authorities would be so much worse than merely being tortured for helping a customer gain entry to the restaurant; the crime third waiter was accused of.

She'd seen the video footage herself and concluded there was no evidence at all of his involvement. The partition thudded and bent backwards from the force of third waiter being thrown against the other side of it. Jennifer couldn't take any more. As she approached the office to protest, the door opened. His face bloodied and beaten to a pulp, third waiter was dragged out of the room by two enormous men with stern facial expressions, followed by an even more enormous man who was grinning from ear to ear. It was Dr Corpulence.

'Sorry my dear, did we disturb you?' he asked, with all the sincerity of a timeshare salesman.

Jennifer tried to reply but couldn't. Fear had gripped her. Hearing a man being tortured was one thing. Seeing the physical evidence close-up was another matter. She was petrified.

'Oh, do you have to?'

'Kill him? I'm afraid so, Jen. Got to keep the rule of law, haven't we? Can't let our discipline slip otherwise where would we be, eh?'

She tried to fight back the tears. She wanted to scream at him to stop, but she knew that would just make things worse for them both.

'Oh, I see. You've got a soft spot for our waiter friend here, haven't you?'

Corpulence furrowed his brow in thought, as if seeking the answer to some phenomenally complicated riddle. 'I tell you what. I'll make you a deal. I won't kill him on one condition.'

Jennifer's eyes lit up in hope. Perhaps there was still a chance his life would be spared.

'You have to push him down the stairs. If he survives the fall I'll pay his medical bills. Now you can't say fairer than that, can you?'

Third waiter was dragged by his hair to the precipice of the metal stairwell only accessible to staff. With tears in her eyes, Jennifer looked to the heavens for guidance. If she didn't push him Corpulence would have him killed, and if she did push him he might die anyway and she'd be guilty of murder. Corpulence had her over a barrel.

'It's OK, Jennifer,' third waiter spluttered, blood trickling down his chin as he spoke, 'you can do it.'

Jennifer closed her eyes and said a short prayer for the life of third waiter. Then she pushed him down the stairs.

****

Executive Stress Relief Ltd opened for business with an initial portfolio of ten simulations available for purchase. The building work was complete and they were now the proud owners of a dozen state-of-the-art simulation pods. George Arthurs, Managing Director of the builders, was another rotund associate of Alan West.

Although he was in charge, Ross left all the day-to-day details to his Director of Operations. He suspected that the meetings between Alan West, Ted Armour and George Arthurs would be extremely amicable and concluded in record speed. It was now over to his Sales Director to bring in the business. This was the part of the venture they all knew would be tricky.

Ross had spent a great deal of time discussing marketing strategies with his Sales Director, much to her delight. Their situation was precarious. They needed quick sales but because of what they were offering, placing an advert in the local rag along the lines of *'Want to bump off your boss? Then call Executive Stress Relief Incorporated'* would have the Old Bill round quicker than the opening of a new doughnut shop.

Their strategy would have to be one of building up a discreet following through word of mouth recommendations. A host of possible methods to achieve this were discussed and all but two were dismissed. The first tactic would be to offer free trials to a hand-picked group of friends and former work colleagues. These were people they trusted not to call the police, but at the same time they were the type of people who liked to talk about the latest thing they had just tried; *'You mean you haven't done it yet? Oh you must, it's amazing. I can't think what I ever did without it.'*

The second method Ross was less comfortable with, but was certain would be a success. They would pimp Alice out. Initial efforts at pimping Alice failed. Ross blamed himself. He took the phrase too literally, insisting she wore her interview outfit. The aim was to get Alice noticed among wealthy ambitious businessmen. She got noticed, of that there was no doubt. However, once she started handing out business cards at functions and networking events for an organisation called Executive Stress Relief Ltd whilst dressed like a strippergram, the organisers of said events had no option but to ask her to leave – after taking a handful of business cards and promising to visit her very soon, of course.

It was time for plan B. An adjustment to the wardrobe and the business cards was matched by a more reluctant, passive approach to networking. She would let them come to her. It worked. Alice's new persona of elegant, demure businesswoman about town proved very popular with men of all descriptions. She was chatted up and invited to dinners, functions and business clubs. She joined numerous exclusive tennis and golf clubs and was pursued by an army of male admirers. Her head wasn't turned by any of this attention; she still only had eyes for Ross.

Alice had a plan. She knew who she was looking for. There were two primary targets. The first was the loud, cocksure executive on his way to the top and without a care who he had to step on to get there. He was all ambition and couldn't wait for those above him to retire. He was the easiest to spot for Alice. She called him Dom. The second target was the man who went to work every day, did his job and never complained. He was reliable, trustworthy and hard-working. He was also always overlooked for promotion in favour of some aggressive, back-stabbing, greasy-pole climbing Dom who took the credit for work he hadn't done and passed off everyone else's ideas as his own. Alice called this second target Kevin. She knew there were a lot more Kevins out there than Doms but while Kevin had a pathological yearning to kill Dom, his natural shyness meant he couldn't bring himself to approach Alice.

The net yield from all this activity was of such a magnitude as to be singularly unimpressive to the small business adviser assigned to Ross by his bank to look after the account of Executive Stress Relief Incorporated. For once he bore no resemblance at all to Mr X. His name was Nigel and after his initial excitement at the prospect of ongoing cash flow difficulties and payments in kind to curry his favour in order to extend a line of business credit for what he assumed to be an upmarket massage parlour, his interest waned when he learned it was something to do with computers and speculative neurological experiments with no immediate likelihood of prodigious profits.

Nevertheless, there were bookings. Ross' friend Paul from Browns' Fraud Detection team had taken up their introductory free trial offer and enjoyed slaying Belvedere so much that he put in a recurring monthly booking. They had their first paying customer. The rest of the Fraud Detection team soon followed. It didn't take long for word to spread beyond the Fraud Detection team and soon more staff from Browns were queuing up to put Belvedere out of his misery. Senior managers were putting it down as miscellaneous expenses against their training budget. No flood yet – but the tap was starting to drip.

Alice's efforts had even drawn a few Doms to the headquarters of ESR Ltd. Even though their personal preferences inclined towards the excessively violent, they never booked again. Dom was much more interested in the real thing. Good news for the intermediary.

The lack of Kevins taking bookings led to a change of strategy for Alice. They were too reserved to go straight for full murder. She needed a nice juicy carrot to dangle in front of them. And so was born a new product range.

Humiliate™ was a suite of simulations aimed at the population of Kevins who wanted to dip their toe into the warm and pleasant water of virtual boss comeuppance. Set at a very affordable entry-level price, clients could enjoy the experience of turning the tables on their boss in simulations ranging from *Deep Embarrassment™* through to *Moderate Ridicule™* and finally *Degradation™*. Alice's instinct was spot on. Kevins descended on ESR. They brought with them an army of Sarahs; their oppressed office sisters and revolutionary soulmates. Sarah was no stranger to being treated like dirt, or to having the desire to execute her line manager.

The standard *Humiliate™* products were popular but were soon overtaken by the very specific requests of ESR's newest customers. They knew what they wanted. Black was impressed with the creative mind of the average Kevin. So much so that he hired his favourite Kevin, who just happened to be called Kevin, to work full-time on product development for the *Humiliate™* range. Ideas flowed.

Conference™ saw Dom heckled during his big career-defining conference speech. As usual, he didn't know what he was talking about and Kevin saw to it that all the prominent industry figures witnessed the spectacle of Dom comprehensively failing to recall facts and figures that a schoolboy would know, as well as failing to answer even the most basic questions about the industry. By the time Kevin had finished with Dom his career was over – humiliated and shown to be the unintelligent, opportunistic, bullshitting egomaniac that he was.

Directors' Report™ was another off the production line. Dom was presenting a key business development report to the Board of Directors. Naturally, he hadn't written one word of the report himself; that task had been delegated to Kevin. Due to an unavoidable technical glitch on his computer, he'd been unable to finish the report until the early hours of the morning and the first Dom got to see of it was five minutes before the meeting when Kevin, who by sheer coincidence was also taking the minutes, presented it to him along with hard copies for each of the directors. When the moment arrived, Dom stood up to address the board, making great play of the extensive research and many painstaking hours he'd put into the report. Without any assistance, of course. The first couple of pages were written to a high standard as Kevin knew that was all Dom would read beforehand. By page three, however, Dom was already looking like a complete knob. By page six he was sweating like a pig. He didn't get to reach page ten before he was escorted off the premises – instant dismissal for gross misconduct.

Dom had been played like a grand piano. He'd read several pages of the report before he cottoned on that it was not just littered with spelling mistakes but was about a completely different industry to the one in which his company competed. When the report switched to the language of Urdu, and then Klingon, Dom realised he'd been stitched up. The list of financial irregularities and extramarital affairs by each of the board members on page nine ensured Dom didn't get a chance to attack Kevin.

Word spread amongst the quiet network of Kevins and Sarahs. *Conference*™ and *Directors' Report*™ became ESR's best-selling products along with other Kevin creations such as *Tribunal*™ and *Office Party*™.

It wasn't long before Alice's sales strategy reaped its rewards. Once the Kevins got to sip the frothy golden nectar from the cup of boss degradation, they soon wanted to take a long, deep glug of moral poison from the tantalising luxurious decanter in the expensive drinks cabinet. There followed a high conversion percentage of Kevins and Sarahs from *Humiliate*™ products to those simulations categorised in the *Terminal*™ range. The Kevins proved very loyal. They soon became hooked on murder.

Business was booming. Ross was delighted. Alice was still out there making contacts and networking with growing confidence and increasing arrow-like radar for the frustrated hordes of downtrodden office workers. Black and Kevin were enjoying themselves so much with each new creation that Ross had a job getting them to leave at the end of each day. In the end he gave up and handed them both a set of keys. Stuart and Lo had been busy programming all the new simulations.

Despite the incredible artificial intelligence of METATRON, with its ability to learn from each new simulation and do most of the programming itself, Stuart and Lo were still stretched. Every new booking required some tinkering with the programme to personalise it to the client, plus Kevin and Black were coming up with new products all the time. There was also the occasional deviant request for Belvedere death scenarios from Ross. They needed more programmers. The nature of what they were doing and the stipulation from Mr X that he would only permit people he trusted to use METATRON, coupled with Ross' strong suspicion that Mr X might have them killed if they disobeyed, meant ESR Ltd couldn't exactly advertise for programmers in the local paper. A compromise solution was negotiated by Ross. They would recruit from the extended family of Mr Lo Rum.

While not much to look at, or indeed listen to, Lo Rum was

something of a legend in his family. The story of his missing fingers had achieved mythical status, and even though the current version of the story doing the rounds bore little resemblance to what had actually taken place, it nevertheless inspired the next generation of Rums. They were all budding computer programmers. When the call came from Lo that he needed trusted programmers for a lucrative, top-secret project, it took several days of intense negotiations, fighting and gambling before the family agreed on the most suitable candidates.

Mr X made it clear to Lo that they were his responsibility. Lo spelt things out even clearer to his family. If any of them got the idea of using METATRON for their own ends or selling it to the highest bidder they would be hunted down like dogs by the rest of the remaining army of psychotic, hatchet-wielding Rums.

Mr X hadn't been seen since the first days of ESR, preferring to play a back seat role in the organisation. A massive back seat. His associates, however, had been busy. Between them Alan West, Ted Armour and George Arthurs had all been involved in expanding the floor space of ESR Ltd to increase capacity. Two more floors were in the process of being added with planning permission for a further four already approved. Soon they would have over 80 techno pods available.

Things were going so much better than Ross had expected. By the end of month four they were making a tidy profit. It was enough to pay a generous salary to everyone. Ross would never again have to go back to Browns and work for Belvedere. Life was good. Nothing could go wrong now.

Chapter 14
The Big Fish

The start of a new year was the busy season for the intermediary. The Christmas break gave people time to reflect on their lives and make resolutions for the year ahead. I must lose weight. I must spend more time with my family. I must have my boss murdered by strangers. Over half of his organisation's bookings for the year were normally taken in the first few months. Things had been slow so far this year but he was sure they would pick up soon.

He was driving to his next appointment and was a bit concerned by the address. The services of the people he worked for did not come cheap. They specialised in the affluent, corporate end of the market. This was where the people who could afford their services were located. Where they were not located was in dingy, high-rise council flats in the sky. The intermediary parked his car and made his way to the block of dingy, high-rise council flats. He took the lift to the fifteenth floor and found the flat he was looking for. He was a few minutes early so he waited.

He'd just come from a successful meeting that had led to a booking. He'd have to be careful who he used for this job as the heat would be all over them. The Chairman of Browns was a big player in the corporate world. The intermediary's professional pride was pleased they were catching the big fish. At least high profile clients were not something he was going to be concerned with in the meeting he was about to have.

The lady he'd just met was certainly bitter. *Hell hath no fury like a woman scorned,* thought the intermediary. It seemed crazy to him that, with all the subordinates beneath him plotting to take his place, the Chairman would go and dig his own grave by having an affair with his own PA, stringing her along and then getting caught having a threesome with a pair of dolly birds at the Christmas party. *Still, you live by the sword; you die by the sword,* he thought – pork sword in the Chairman's case. If he had a pound for every booking made by disgruntled mistresses...

He checked his watch. It was time. He stepped forward to ring the bell but the door swung open before he got the chance. *Now that's punctual,* the intermediary thought, impressed. Jennifer Ellis ushered the intermediary into the flat and offered him a cup of tea.

'I'm sure you're surprised by my request to meet here,' she began, 'but you see, he has my flat watched, and I think he's bugged my phone. This is my sister's place. If he knew I had a sister, she'd be in danger so we changed her name years ago and now we have to meet in secret.'

Jennifer made the teas and handed one to the intermediary, who thanked her.

'Is he the target?' asked the intermediary, taking a seat and sipping his tea.

'Yes,' said Jennifer.

'And who is he?'

'Dr Corpulence.'

The intermediary almost choked on his tea. 'Dr Corpulence of The House of Lard?' he asked, praying the answer would be no.

'The very same.'

The intermediary was lost for words. It didn't do for a man in his position to be lost for words; it didn't quite give the right impression of a man representing a human arsenal of professional life-enders. This was big. Much bigger than they'd done before. Dr Corpulence was always on TV. An impossible job. *Not impossible,* he thought, rubbing his chin, *but bloody difficult. At the very least tricky.* He settled on tricky. He could live with tricky.

'You certainly pick 'em, miss. It's going to be tricky; I'll not lie to you.' He looked around the flat, taking in its surroundings.'

'I don't mean to be rude, miss, but this will be our biggest job yet. Lots of risk involved, you see.'

'Yes, there will be.'

'Well then, you understand my caution. Not everyone could deal with a job this big. Some would say they could but take my word for it, they couldn't.'

'I have no doubt that's the case.'

'It's just that, well, not to put too fine a point on it…'

'Can I afford it?' asked Jennifer, finishing his sentence.

'Well, yes.'

She smiled at him. 'I'm the good doctor's personal assistant. I do a lot of his dirty work, and believe you me; his work is very dirty indeed. I'm one of just two people with full access to the private financial accounts of Business Conglomerate Holdings.'

The intermediary gave a blank expression and shrugged.

'Business Conglomerate Holdings owns, amongst its numerous other parent companies, Lard Corp. Lard Corp owns over 200 businesses worldwide. Over 98 per cent of the entire global obesity market for goods and services. Getting hold of the money won't be difficult. Staying alive for more than a few hours after he finds out I've taken it – and he will find out – that's the tricky part. But that's my problem.'

The intermediary found himself in an awkward situation. His client would be better off if he didn't take the job. It would be best for all concerned if he talked her out if it.

'Look miss, are you sure you want to do this? I mean, he always seems such a jolly chap when you see him on the telly.'

Jennifer told him about the incident with third waiter, how the doctors said he'd never walk again.

'You always get that with these top business people, miss. Ruthless bastards, I'm afraid. You can't deny he's providing valuable services to a lot of vulnerable people though. I saw him the other day opening another of those day centres for the massively fat, or whatever you call them. He can't be all that bad.'

Jennifer laughed out loud. *God, if the world only knew what he's really like. The man's pure evil.*

'My brother used to eat at The House of Lard,' said the intermediary. 'He loved it there. Treated him like royalty, they did.'

'Where is he now?'

'Six feet under, love. Passed away a few years ago, he did. Huge bunch of flowers from Dr Corpulence there was. He didn't have to do that, did he?'

Jennifer wanted to tell him but was scared to. Living in fear was a way of life for her. 'How discreet are you?'

'Wouldn't be very good at my job if I wasn't, would I?' said the intermediary, feeling on pretty safe ground here. He was old school. Never talk. Never, ever talk.

'If you tell anyone what I'm about to tell you I'll be dead the same day,' she said without any fear. She was simply stating a fact.

'Miss, I've been tortured by the Old Bill and the Mafia. I didn't tell 'em shit. How'd you think I lost this?' He showed her his left hand. It wouldn't have been much good if he needed to count to five.

'OK,' she said, 'but I warn you, you're not going to like it one bit.'

She sat down on the sofa and opened up a laptop computer on top of a coffee table. She entered a password.

'Every member of The House of Lard has a personal file. I have access to the restricted section of their files. Now what was your brother's name?'

He told her and she entered his details. Once she had his restricted file on screen, she turned the laptop around and pushed it to the other side of the coffee table where the intermediary was sitting in an armchair.

'Read,' she said, and she made her way to the kitchen to fetch a bottle of whisky. She poured him a large measure and placed it on the table, along with the rest of the bottle. Then she lit a cigarette, took a deep drag and prayed she'd done the right thing. They sat in silence. He drained his glass and poured another.

'Who's this?' he asked. She could hear the lump in his throat.

'That's Mr Michaels, one of the many social workers on his payroll.'

The intermediary shook his head in disbelief. Then he exploded. 'What the bloody hell's he doing with a copy of my brother's will? It's not even signed,' he bellowed.

'It's a forgery. Corpulence employs the best forgers in the land. Did your brother by any chance leave his entire estate to the nursing home he stayed at?'

'I wasn't invited to the reading so I never heard the will, but I heard that's what he did, yeah.'

The intermediary was finding it hard to get the words out. This was bringing back painful memories; feelings he'd buried deep inside. Jennifer sighed; she was going to have to fill in the blanks for him.

'Sometime before he died did you receive letters from your brother severing all ties?' she asked, knowing the answer.

'Yeah. I tried to see him but they wouldn't let me in. I wrote to him, called him, but he never responded. I carried on paying his nursing bills but it wasn't long after that he passed away. We never made our peace.'

Jennifer took a deep breath. 'The letters were faked, just like the will was faked, just like the social workers' referral to the nursing home was faked. Once your brother retired he no longer had an income and therefore wasn't much use to Corpulence. So just like he's done thousands of times before, he had him referred to a nursing home, had his will forged and all his assets went to the home. You have to understand, he's a dangerous and controlling sociopath. He owns the nursing home and dozens of others like it. He owns the solicitors who manage the fake wills. He owns the private company that provide the social workers who specialise in obesity cases. He owns the bank that held your brother's money and he owns the funeral directors who buried him. He even owns the florist who supplied the flowers for the funeral. Every penny your brother earned ended up in the pockets of Corpulence. From cradle to grave, that's his motto. You won't want to hear this but you need to hear it. For the last few months of your brother's life he was kept prisoner in a so-called nursing home. No visitors, no privileges. Meanwhile they starved him to death and stole all his money. It's all above board and I'm the only one who can prove any of this.'

Jennifer took the bottle of whisky from the intermediary and took a swig. Then she lit another cigarette. The intermediary was purple with rage. His knuckles were white as he gripped the sides of the armchair harder than any armchair had been gripped before. A supreme effort of will was taking place within him, to not bludgeon to death everyone within a ten-mile radius. He was also thinking very hard.

'So I'll imagine you'll want to take this case as a matter of urgency then,' she said, quite keen for the about-to-explode intermediary to leave as soon as possible. 'When do you need the money by?'

The intermediary took a deep breath and exhaled slowly. He knew from years of experience the importance of mastering his anger.

'That won't be necessary.'

'What?'

'My organisation is booked up, I'm afraid, so we won't be able to take this case. If anyone asks, you never met me. This conversation never took place. Thank you for the drink.'

The intermediary stood up and made his way to the door. Jennifer flung herself in front of it, blocking his path.

'Please, you've got to do it. I can't take it anymore. He's evil.'

She grabbed him and fell to her knees, pleading for help. He never spoke, instead flashing his eyes at her. She saw it and recoiled in fear – the cold, dark look of a killer. Jennifer had seen into his soul. She stepped aside, finally enlightened. He opened the door to leave.

'Wait,' she said. Jennifer dashed into the bedroom and returned with a small piece of paper that she handed to him. It was a photograph. 'He never goes anywhere without it. Bring it back to me safe and in one piece and nobody will ever know.'

The intermediary stared at the photo in utter incredulity. He shook his head as he marched out of the door. Jennifer poured another drink and allowed herself a relieved smile. The intermediary had refused to take out a contract on Dr Corpulence. This was to be a private job. No contracts, no money exchanging hands, no paperwork. Whatever he had in store for the doctor wasn't going to be pleasant.

Chapter 15
The Boss Killers

Deborah watched as the Chairman ogled the attractive young air hostess at the check-in desk. *Enjoy it while it lasts, you lying, cheating, lecherous old thief.*

'Let me help you with that bag,' the Chairman offered, stepping in so close to the air hostess as to afford a much better view of her cleavage. His good deed for the day done, he returned to exchanging pleasantries with Deborah.

'Should be a good flight,' he said, rubbing his hands together with excitement. 'I've ordered the Lobster Thermidor and several bottles of Bollinger to get the party started early. Had a word with the pilot and we've been promised absolute privacy,' he said, tapping the side of his nose and grinning lustily. *That's right, you lap it up you blackmailing, controlling, poisonous witch; I've got your number.*

Check-in complete, they retired to the executive lounge for complimentary drinks before boarding Browns' private plane. Its destination was a top global finance conference in the Maldives. Despite a passenger list of just two, the Chairman had still insisted on an air hostess to cater for their not very onerous in-flight needs, even specifying the vital statistics required of the successful applicant. As luck would have it, the agency that supplied Browns with airline personnel for their business trips had just taken on a young lady matching the Chairman's exact requirements.

One unsatisfying sexual encounter followed by an expensive seafood and champagne dinner later, Deborah and the Chairman slept like babies in the king-sized bed that, due to some administrative blunder, had been ordered by Browns to replace most of the passenger seating.

****

'So what comes next?'

Apprentice Number Eighty racked her brains. She'd only joined the organisation two weeks ago. In that time she'd been on a crash course in air hostessing, and was now shadowing Number Twelve on a live contract. The Boss Killers didn't mess about when it came to work experience.

'Let's see. We've taken care of the pilot with a lethal dose of cyanide in his dinner, and the targets are both sleeping off a general anaesthetic added to their champagne. Erm, do we just point the plane at the nearest mountain and jump out?'

'Haven't you forgotten something?'

Apprentice Number Eighty screwed up her face in concentration.

'Parachutes?' she ventured.

'Well done. Wouldn't want to jump out of a plane at twenty thousand feet without one, would we?'

Apprentice Number Eighty blushed. At this rate she would never graduate from apprentice to full Number Eighty status.

'Don't worry about it,' Number Twelve reassured her. 'You're learning the ropes and it's a tough school. Trust me, if we didn't think you could cut it you wouldn't be here. Look at the positives. You've done a great job of keeping the Chairman's attention diverted. He's been so busy staring at your tits he hasn't even noticed that a completely different co-pilot to the one he was chatting to earlier boarded the plane. Fortunately I'm an expert pilot of many years' standing and in time, if you work hard and keep your head down, that's the kind of specialist training you can look forward to.'

Apprentice Number Eighty breathed a sigh of relief. The occasional crumb of praise was essential for her peace of mind when surrounded by assassins all the time.

'Besides, fat old men are something of a speciality of ours, and with a pair of baps like those I guarantee you'll never be out of work.'

The intermediary had tried his best. He'd sent them on courses, given them *How to* booklets and they'd all taken part in role-play sessions. They were still a long way from adhering to discrimination in the workplace and equal opportunities employment legislation though. That they had female employees at all was a huge step compared to many of their competitors. The Pugilists and, for obvious reasons, The Gang were male-only domains.

Deborah awoke groggily from her drug-induced dreams. She tried to move but her legs refused to play ball. The force of the freezing wind was biting at her face. Confused, she managed to turn her head and realised she was still dreaming. The sight of the air hostess waving at her before jumping out of the plane confirmed this was the case. The blistering wind in her face was so realistic though. A horrible thought struck her. Reaching into the pocket of the unconscious Chairman, she located his wallet and found what she was looking for.

'Shit,' she said as she held the intermediary's business card in her hand, recognising it as the same as the one in her purse. 'What a pair of bloody fools we've been.'

In the few seconds of life remaining before the plane crashed into the mountain, she held the Chairman's hand tenderly, tears forming in the corners of her eyes.

****

Matthew Black was struggling to breathe. He placed his hands on his lap and knelt forward with his head bent over his knees. He was beyond nervous. His whole body was shaking with fear.

The source of his trepidation was sitting on his sofa sipping a glass of wine, unaware of the private battle taking place inside his bathroom between Black and his central nervous system. It was a woman. Black was no stranger to women of course, but this woman was different in one very important way from the women he usually interacted with. She had a pulse. Black's usual experiences of the opposite sex were through glossy gentlemen's magazines and occasional encounters with erotic dolls. All that had changed since he met Mr X. Nowadays he met women every day. Beautiful women, sexy women, all of whom wanted to please him. The trouble was they were all figments of his imagination, brought to life thanks to the genius of METATRON.

The woman sitting outside waiting for him to do who knows what was very real indeed. He couldn't understand why this was happening to him after all this time. Her name was Alison and, by most people's standards, she was an attractive woman. To Black she was a goddess. She was Bardot and Monroe all rolled into one. Black's standards were not the highest. He would have happily settled for so much less. Alison had both her arms and legs, and could see, hear and talk. All bonuses to Black. He would have dated a blind, deaf monoped with webbed fingers and a club foot. Alison had beautiful unspoilt, soft, silky skin and a perfect smile. He would have jumped at the chance to take out a third-degree burns victim with a cleft palate. Alison had a toned figure with exquisite round breasts and smooth waxed legs. Black would have settled for a bearded lady who was a ground floor member of The House of Lard. Alison was none of these things though; she was a total stunner.

Black just couldn't understand what was going on. This was their second date and already they were back at his flat. What was more, she had done all the running. She had turned up at ESR one day and shamelessly chatted him up. Other people had been present to witness it; she hadn't cared. Naïve he was, but Black was not stupid. This sort of thing had happened to him before, though always as a result of a wager with a third party. The usual conclusion to these situations was prolonged pointing and laughing at Black from the woman in question, followed by Black running away in humiliation. Alison hadn't laughed at him once.

Black looked at himself in the mirror. A hairy man looked back at him. *That's not right,* he thought. It was time for honesty about who he was and what he was. A very, very hairy man looked back at him. *Still not quite true.* Quite probably the hairiest man walking the face of the earth looked back at him. *Almost there.* He took a deep breath. Without doubt the hairiest, agoraphobic, scared virgin in the entire world looked back at him. *That's better.* Relieved that he was at least being honest with himself, Black puffed out his chest, combed his facial hair, and walked out of the door to face the fear and maybe, just maybe, get to lose his cherry.

Black was unaware that his first meeting with Alison had not been down to chance. Rum and Stuart had stumbled upon his private adult simulations and decided to help their friend. They were well aware of the size of the task they were taking on. Black was absolutely petrified of women and, perhaps more importantly, he looked like the offspring of a grizzly bear and a chinchilla. Registering him in the personal ads wasn't a viable option. Instead, they ventured deep into the world of very, very niche pornography to find what they were looking for.

The Bear Club was a small group of individuals who met once a month to indulge their fetish for hairy bodies. Stuart and Lo attended one such meeting on the premise of being fans of the more hirsute gentleman. It was there they met Alison. The men who were paraded and drooled over by the members of *The Bear Club* were bald compared to Black. Alison didn't need much persuading. She almost fainted when Rum showed her a picture of Black.

****

Black wasn't alone in enjoying an evening of romance. Adam too was on a hot date, although so far his evening wasn't going too well. He was sure this would all change, just as soon as his date actually turned up. There was bound to be some very reasonable explanation for her tardiness. She was after all just an hour and a half late. He'd had the waiter check several times that a serious road traffic incident hadn't occurred in the surrounding area within the last few hours. The waiter assured him this was not the case. Adam ordered another beer, his seventh so far. He was steaming drunk. Any minute now she would arrive.

They had met just a few nights ago at The Badger's Eyebrows. Adam had been trying to chat her up for some time with little success.

She seemed more interested in the criminals present. Her attitude changed when he dropped into the conversation that he was a Director of ESR. After that she was all over him like a rash.

Adam knew she was a gold digger. It was that word, 'Director'; roughly translated it meant 'filthy rich'. Adam didn't care if she thought he was a millionaire if it improved his chances of getting into her knickers. He would come clean about his not being Donald Trump, just as soon as he'd succeeded in banging her. Lots and lots of times. They went back to her place and did the deed that very night; he couldn't believe it. To keep the pretence up he even gave her a tour of ESR and wangled a last minute booking for her. They were supposed to meet up this evening at La Gondola, a fancy Italian restaurant in the West End, to be followed, Adam hoped, by a night of hot steamy sex. Instead, he was sitting alone and drinking himself into oblivion while the waiters glared at him and ostentatiously checked their watch every time they caught his eye. He would give her another half an hour, then stagger back to The Badger's in case she'd gone there by mistake.

Ordinarily, it being Saturday night, Adam would have arranged to see Ross at The Badger's but that never happened these days. He was always too busy with ESR business. Adam didn't click with that ESR crowd at all. Bunch of geeks and freaks as far as he could see. Ross was always having to cancel meeting Adam at The Badger's because of some urgent meeting he had with one of his new cronies. Adam didn't trust that Alan West at all; there was something about him that wasn't quite right. The same went for Ted Armour and George Arthurs. He wouldn't be at all surprised if those three were hatching a devious plan together to swindle Ross in some way but he couldn't quite figure out how. Maybe they were all related? And why were they all so *bloody massive*?

He'd put his brain right onto it and come up with the solution just as soon as he could see straight. His first priority, however, was to get up off the floor. What the hell was he doing lying face down on the floor?

****

The tradition of Sunday was something that Stuart Davies adhered to with religious zeal. Sunday lunch down the local, washed down with a pint or nine, and then back home for a date with his sofa, a box full of tuck, and afternoon repeats of Columbo.

The thing that Stuart liked most about Sunday was its historic status as a day of rest. It was there in black and white in the bible. Who was Stuart to argue with millennia of tradition? He demonstrated his wholehearted support for Sunday tradition by never, under any circumstances, getting out of bed before noon. Everyone who knew him was aware of this. So who the hell was calling him at eight in the morning on a Sunday?

He ignored the ringing but they just kept calling. He could of course just go and unplug the phone but that would involve actually getting out of bed. Unable to stand the irritating ringing any longer, or the loud banging on the wall from his irate neighbour, Stuart emerged from his warm nest intent on giving the culprit both barrels for depriving him of his usual twelve hours sleep on a Sunday.

He picked up the phone and was greeted by a screaming incoherent Korean on the other end of the line.

'Slow down Lo, I can't understand what you're saying. What's that? People, is that? Lots of people, you say? Hundreds of people?'

****

Ross grinned to himself, enjoying the moment. There was nothing like a nice relaxing day's fishing. Sea fishing, as it happened. Nice big boat, beautiful blue sky and a sea full of big sharks just waiting to be reeled in. He had just the bait to tempt them. He'd had a special bespoke rod made for the occasion.

It took all his strength; even a pint-sized weasel like Belvedere was heavy dangling on the end of a massive fishing rod. A satisfying splashing noise was made by the blood-soaked Belvedere as his body entered the water. His kicking feet would attract those hungry sharks any second and then it was dinner time. Ross waited with anticipation. He would have to wait a long time.

Belvedere was saved from his watery grave by the loud ringing of Ross' phone. He awoke from his slumber wondering who the hell was ringing him at this time on a Sunday morning. He answered the phone with some trepidation. Calls at this time of day were never good news.

'Hello?'

'Ross, it's X. Sorry to call so early but it's an emergency. Get yourself down to ESR straight away and call the others to get down there too.'

'What are you talking about? What's going on?'

'You'll see when you get there. On the way make sure you pick up a copy of today's Chronicle and turn to page 16. That will explain everything.'

'OK, but can you give me a clue? I need to know what I'm walking into here.'

'The cat's out of the bag. That's what's going on, Ross. Someone from inside ESR has been talking to the press.'

****

When the phone rang in Black's flat it didn't wake him up. He hadn't been asleep yet. It had been a long night, most of which had passed by in a haze of sex, sex and more sex. His groin was numb. Sometime in the middle of the night when his poor private parts could take no more punishment he'd injected himself in the knackers with an anaesthetic. He estimated he'd lost at least a stone in weight in a single evening.

Black had waited all his life for Alison to come along and he didn't want to mess things up by not giving her enough sex. It didn't occur to him that it would be perfectly reasonable to ask for a short rest. In a state of acute delirium and starvation, he answered the phone and said a short prayer of thanks when he heard of the emergency at ESR that required his immediate attendance.

'I'm sorry honey, there's an emergency at work. I've got to go.' He didn't know what else to say. Should he ask her to see herself out? What was the protocol here?

'Don't worry, you big sexy bear. Give me your key.'

Black obeyed.

'I'll do us a nice dinner for when you get back.'

'Er great,' said Black, confused. 'There isn't much food in though. A few Pot Noodles and some crisps, I think.'

'I'll go and do a shop. Leave it to me.'

Right, thought Black in disbelief. *In the space of a few days I've met a sex maniac with a thing about bears who now seems to be my girlfriend and is moving in with me. Wonder what today holds?*

He left for ESR with the plan of finding a 24-hour all-you-can-eat diner on the way.

****

When Ross arrived at ESR headquarters in the semi-abandoned industrial estate there were cars everywhere. Bikes too. It was Sunday morning – what were they doing here? He watched as groups of people gravitated toward ESR. Each of them was clutching a copy of the Chronicle.

Ross reached over to the passenger seat to retrieve the copy he'd bought a few minutes earlier. He turned to page 16 and read.

In Search of The Boss Killers, By Julie Levet

Where would we be without violence? Violence is big business, a massive global industry fuelling free market capitalism that keeps us all in the very nice standard of living we have grown accustomed to, thank you very much.

Just think about how much of our economy is dependent on violence and aggression. Defence equipment manufacturers, arms manufacturers and dealers, armed services personnel, policemen and women, security guards, bodyguards, lawyers, surgeons and other emergency medical staff, the computer gaming industry and a good deal of the entertainment industry. Our need for violence keeps these people in jobs.

The violence industry is as old as they come, definitely what you would call a mature sector. It's reached saturation point and there's no room for new players now. Too late, sorry - you should have got in on the ground floor. Don't you believe it.

On the outskirts of London there is a little known trading estate called Turbary Industrial Park. One of its newest residents is ESR Ltd and they are changing the face of this oldest of industries forever. Also known as 'The Boss Killers,' ESR Ltd provides a very modern and new slant on an age-old need, and this reporter is the first to get the inside track when I gained an exclusive interview with a company source.

'It's like this,' begins my source. 'Everyone hates somebody. Most people hate their boss. A lot of people would like to do something about it, you know. They'd like to do them in. They fantasise about it all the time. We just help their dreams come true. It's all legal, no laws are being broken and nobody gets hurt. In fact we're probably saving lives because if it wasn't for us some of these people could be acting on their urges.'

ESR Ltd is a high-tech provider of virtual reality simulations for the frustrated executive. Been passed over for promotion? Had someone claim credit for work you did and then fired you afterwards? At ESR you can fight back.

In the interests of proper investigative journalism I booked a session with them to see for myself what all the fuss is about. It was the most unbelievable experience of my life. I could choose from a tantalising smorgasbord of humiliation or murder scenarios, such as shooting, poisoning, drowning, stabbing or strangling to name just a few. They then take a motion capture scan of my body size and movements, a recording of my voice, and I either provide them with a home movie, photograph or recording of my intended victim, or I can choose from a database of countless options for facial appearance, voice, mannerisms and personality. I'm then taken to a small booth where a non-invasive chip is attached to the back of my neck and I'm instructed to close my eyes and count down from ten to zero.

When I opened my eyes the world changed. I was standing at the location I had selected and was in the presence of the person I had chosen to kill. For legal reasons I won't divulge who it was I murdered that day, or how I did it. What I will say is this: it was no simulation. It didn't look or feel like I had committed murder - I had committed murder. It was as real as anything I've ever done in my life. I was liberated and felt a rush of euphoria. I had killed and gotten away with it. Nobody was hurt. No laws were broken.

Violence is alive and well in the modern world and I for one am very glad of it. On behalf of the downtrodden workers everywhere I say long live The Boss Killers.

Bloody hell, thought Ross as he finished reading. All word of mouth, no publicity, that's what we agreed. It wasn't impossible that a journalist had stumbled across them but it did look very much like somebody had been talking.

Ross locked his car and walked towards the entrance of ESR. He didn't get very far. As he tried to step past a group of men who appeared to be standing at the side of the road chatting, a substantial hand blocked his path.

'I don't think so, pal. We were here first. You can join the end of the queue like everyone else.'

'Queue?'

The man stepped aside to reveal the longest queue Ross had ever seen. It led to the doors of ESR.

'Bloody hell.'

'You're not wrong there, mate. Reckon we'll be here for a while.'

Ross looked up and down the enormous queue until his eyes stopped at a particular individual about ten or fifteen people ahead of him in the queue. He was Stuart-shaped. Risking the wrath of the queue, Ross skipped ahead and pulled Stuart out. He made sure they were out of earshot before he told Stuart to follow him, as he had a key for the service gate at the back of the building. They had just rounded the corner and were out of sight of the horde when something odd happened. A man dressed all in black leather and wearing a helmet stepped in front of them and thrust a package into Ross' chest.

'Special delivery for Mr Ackerman. Courtesy of Mr Alan West.'

Ross looked at the man, then at the package and then back at the man.

'Sign here please,' the helmeted figure requested.

Ross signed and took the package. 'Wait a minute, courier.'

'Yes?'

'How did you know I was Mr Ackerman?'

'Mr West told me to look for two men, one a, ahem, well, a larger gentleman, sir. He said you'd be skulking around the back somewhere.'

Ross and Stuart entered the building through the rear entrance and headed for the main offices. When they got there they found the employees of ESR cowering in the dark, having closed all the blinds and switched the lights off to avoid detection from the massed ranks outside. There was Kevin, Lo, and all the other Rums. The only person not cowering was Alice. She didn't do cowering.

'What's this all about, Ross?' she asked.

'This,' replied Ross, showing them page 16 of the Chronicle. 'Kev, go and photocopy this a bunch of times so everyone can have a read please.'

Kevin returned moments later with numerous copies of the article and handed them round. Ross watched them all as they read the Chronicle. He was looking for any telltale signs of guilt. He didn't spot it in any of them. Who was missing? Mr X, Alan West, Adam and Black. He knew it wasn't Mr X and he felt pretty confident Alan West was also in the clear. Mr X was meticulous, obsessive in his preparations and, given his circumstances, the last thing he would ever do would be to draw attention to himself. So it was Adam or Black.

Before he could give the matter anymore thought his attention was diverted to a disturbance. Two disturbances, as it happened. Having finished reading the article Lo had stormed out of the room and returned with what could best be described as a bloody great big machete. As he watched Lo screaming in Korean at his siblings whilst pointing the machete at them and holding his incomplete fingers in the air, Ross found himself caught in the classic conundrum every man faces some day in his life: not wanting to be party to a man butchering several other men and women to death, whilst at the same time having no desire at all to step in front of a crazed machete-wielding Korean with a lazy eye and several fingers missing.

'What's he saying, Stu?'

'Something about his fingers. I think he might be threatening to chop off all their fingers if he finds out it was one of them who spoke to the press.'

After a few minutes of scuffling amongst the Rum family, the victorious Rum stepped forward, knelt down on the floor and laid his hands flat on one of the office desks. The others formed an orderly queue behind him to have their fingers chopped off.

'Well, I think we can safely say it wasn't any of the Rums. Stu, can you try and talk to him please and tell him we know it wasn't them.'

With the prospect of a mass be-fingering avoided, Ross turned his attention to the other disturbance outside. A figure was attempting to get to the front of the queue. Every time he tried to advance, a wall of bodies blocked his path but then scattered when the queue jumper got nearer to them. In one hand the figure was clutching a family-sized bag of hamburgers from a nearby drive-through Burger God®, and in the other hand he was clutching his groin. He was making slow progress. The combined physical efforts of ESR Ltd just about managed to secure safe entry for Black whilst keeping out the army of restless prospective murderers.

They retreated to the safety of the main office and Ross explained the current situation to Black. This took longer than it should have done, as Ross found the sight of a man – who looked like at least one of his parents did its business in the woods and was attempting to cram more than one hamburger into his mouth at a time whilst holding a large bag of ice against his privates – somewhat off-putting.

'Is that absolutely necessary?' asked Ross, pointing at the ice.

'I'm afraid it is,' replied Black.

Stuart and Rum exchanged knowing glances.

'So, it looks like this is down to either you or Adam. Met anyone new of late, have you?'

'Well yes, as it happens.'

'Somebody who approached you and became amorous very quickly by any chance?'

'Er yes.'

'Been talking to them about ESR, have you?'

'Yes,' Black replied, blushing and shaking his head as the penny dropped. He knew it was all too good to be true. Now all he had to show for his night of passion were a group of friends he'd betrayed, and an about-to-drop-off manhood. Ross shook his head in disappointment.

The earlier furore of Rum's outburst and Black's entrance had made Ross forget about the package from Alan West. He opened it and removed a photograph of a woman with a note attached to it. He read the note.

To help you uncover your rat, this is Julie Levet.

Ross studied the photo. He couldn't be too hard on Black. She was very attractive, and when you looked like he did ... well.

'Is this your new friend?' Ross asked Black, giving him the photo.

Anticipating the sight of a grown man (allegedly) having a breakdown, the others circled Black like vultures. His response made them all jump.

'No,' he screamed, dancing around the room waving the photo above his head. 'That's not Alison. She loves me, she really loves me!'

In a state of unbridled ecstasy, Black continued to do a solo conga around the room until the pain in his groin stopped him in his tracks. He limped to the nearest chair and shoved the bag of ice down the front of his trousers.

Ross was shocked. This was all his fault. Adam was his friend, nobody else's. He'd have to sort this mess out.

'I'm very sorry for accusing you. Please accept my apologies.'

Black held up a hand in acknowledgement; he had more pressing matters.

'Right everyone, I know who did this and I'm off to sort it out. Thank you all for your hard work and continued loyalty. There will be an extra bonus this month for everyone.'

'What about that lot outside?' asked Alice, pointing to the window.

'We are in business, ladies and gents. We open the doors and take their bookings of course.'

'But there's hundreds of them. How are we going to process that many new orders?' asked Stuart.

'If you've got any more computer programming relatives, Lo then there's a job waiting as soon as you can get them over here,' said Ross, addressing Rum.

'Yes, sir,' said Rum. He set about martialling his family and pointing at the phones in the office.

Ross slipped away in pursuit of Adam, leaving a confused Stuart wondering how come the last sentence from Ross had not required a translation into Korean.

Chapter 16
Moral Majority

Adam's name was mud. When Ross confronted him later that day about the Chronicle article, a hungover Adam refused to believe that he was responsible.

That all changed when he saw the photo. What was wrong with the women of the world? Here he was, an affluent, eligible and, if he did say so himself, handsome bachelor and the only action he could get was as the victim of a tabloid honey trap. As a result, he'd almost ruined his friendship with Ross and made himself look like a right knob in the process. He had a lot of making up to do.

Mr X had gone to ground. Media interest in ESR was mushrooming and he couldn't risk being anywhere near the heat. He was wanted in over 30 countries, and that was just the authorities. Of greater concern were the bounty hunters employed by the gangs on the receiving end of his past activities. While he was still under the protection of the other gangs he'd been working for at the time, he knew that their diligence in maintaining this protection after he'd completed his work for them was patchy at best.

He therefore delegated METATRON training duties to Lo for the squadron of Rums now arriving on each new incoming flight from Korea. Those relatives remaining in Korea were working full-time on tracing the Rum family tree to unearth more eligible recruits for Rum Enterprises Incorporated, which was now the fastest growing computer programming training organisation in Northeast Asia.

The surge in demand for ESR services as a result of the Chronicle article was giving Ross headaches. Managing the bottleneck of orders was just about in hand thanks to the new Rums and the recruitment of several new receptionists and admin staff who were trusted friends of Alice. Alan West had been working overtime on a more permanent solution to the problem.

Planning permission for further development of the current ESR site was at a standstill with the local council. Planning officers, who earlier had been more than happy to accept sizeable donations to the charity of their choice, had come over all moral when news of the Chronicle article broke. West was nothing if not persistent. With the help of Ted Armour, he'd succeeded in locating a new, much bigger site in a neighbouring borough with full planning permission, and was in the process of drawing up contracts with the builders. The size of the new site and the speed with which completion was required meant that West had to recruit a larger building firm to work alongside George Arthurs Builders Ltd. Ross met with Cedric O' Reilly, the owner of the new building contractors, to finalise the details. There was something about him. He looked awfully familiar.

Completion would be in two months' time and would extend capacity by an extra 400 techno suites. Ross hadn't done the maths yet but he felt sure that, if they weren't already, pretty soon they would all be multi-millionaires. In the meantime, he had to beef up security at ESR. Camera crews were arriving, keen to jump on the media bandwagon. Ross had just the man for the job.

****

'This is Chip Copperhead, reporting for CNN at the headquarters of ESR Limited in London, England, where we can exclusively reveal to viewers the story of a new phenomenon sweeping London. Boss killing. That's right folks, inside this building ordinary men and women are killing their bosses thanks to the computer geniuses behind ESR who have created a new video game so realistic that people are queuing up to commit murder.'

The camera panned to a long line of people outside the main entrance to ESR.

'Let's go and have a closer look to get the inside track. Hi there, buddy. How you doing? I'm Chip Copperhead from CNN. Can we maybe film inside the building and speak to one of your guys about the business?'

'Sorry sir, nobody comes in unless I get the all clear.'

'Hey yeah, that's great you know, security is real important but I'm from CNN,' said Chip, flashing his press badge 'and our viewers would really appreciate your co-operation.'

'You can't come in, sir.'

A throat-cut gesture from Copperhead indicated it was time to stop shooting at this point.

'Listen buddy, do you know who I am? Why don't you run along, get your boss and stop being a pain in the ass?'

The man guarding the door stepped forward and beamed a toothy smile – or rather, it would have been a toothy smile if he had any actual teeth.

'Jesus Christ, look at his teeth. Er, I can see you're busy right now so we're going to leave you alone but we'll be over here if you need us. Great job, by the way. Keep up the good work,' said Chip, retreating to a safe distance. 'Did you see that fucking guy's teeth? Mike, tell me that camera's not still running, you goddamn asshole ....'

'Well that was Chip Copperhead there reporting from London. We apologise if any viewers were offended by Chip's remarks. And now in domestic news, the President today issued a new warning about the state of the economy...'

****

'How do I look?' asked Adam.

'Yeah, great,' said Ross. 'Just remember what we discussed, will you? Keep to the script and, whatever you do, don't get verbal diarrhoea in front of all those cameras.'

'I've done this before, you know. I've been trained for occasions such as these. You worry too much. Right, let's do it. Wish me luck.'

'Good luck.'

You're damn right I'm worried. If it wasn't for you we wouldn't be in this mess in the first place. Oh God, what am I thinking letting him speak to the press?

Adam stepped past ESR's one-man security department and strolled towards the waiting media scrum. He was wearing his most expensive double-breasted pinstripe suit, red silk tie, shirt, cuff links and braces. He looked sharper than a sack full of ripe lemons.

'Ladies and gentlemen, thank you for your patience. I have a brief statement to read on behalf of ESR Ltd. Certain allegations have been made in the media about the business activities of ESR. First, I wish to make it clear that ESR is a legitimate, privately owned business, registered with Companies House. We are a responsible law-abiding business and we pay corporation tax, VAT and income tax. Furthermore, our clients' privacy is of the utmost importance to us and if any media organisation were to reveal the identities of our clients, then that could only be obtained through illegal methods and we will report that organisation to the authorities, as well as taking the strongest legal action possible against said organisation and the individuals responsible. We also wish to clarify that the name of our business is ESR Ltd. It is not called *The Boss Killers* and never has been called this by anyone representing ESR Ltd. We will take legal action against any organisation misrepresenting our registered business name by referring to ESR as *The Boss Killers*. We are an honest, law-abiding business providing a realistic, high-quality video game experience for video game enthusiasts. Thank you for your time and I will not be taking any further questions.'

Looking calmer than a Buddhist monk on beta blockers, Adam sauntered back towards the ESR building. Watching his performance on television was a relieved Ross. *That was smoother than an otter's wetsuit. We'll never hear the end of it though.*

****

That evening Ross and Stuart met Mr X at a desolate car park in the middle of nowhere on 'urgent business'. Neither of them knew what the nature of the urgent business they were meeting him about was.

What was even more galling for Ross was that not long before he was due to meet Mr X he had concluded a meeting with Alan West about the new building. He had to drive another twenty miles to meet with Mr X. Ross was finding the whole charade of Mr X's alter egos tiresome and vowed to broach the subject with him at the next available opportunity.

'If we don't act right now then ESR will be shut down and some of you may go to prison,' said Mr X, getting straight to the point as usual.

'How do you work that one out?' asked Ross. 'We're making money hand over fist and you heard Adam earlier – we're not breaking any laws.'

'That's irrelevant. We're making a lot of money doing something that the moral majority find repugnant. It's just a matter of time before the establishment comes after you. Fortunately you employ a quite brilliant consultant who anticipated all of this occurring long ago, and has devised a rather excellent plan to ensure we all continue to live in Fat City.'

Ross looked at Mr X. He suspected he was not only a permanent resident of Fat City, but had served several successful terms as mayor.

'Tell us this great plan then, genius.'

'Project Future.'

'Project Future?' asked Stuart.

'That's right.'

'What's that then?'

'There are three groups of people that are going to come after you. The media, politicians and the police. They represent the moral majority. Now that your existence is known, the media will soon turn on you. They will do this because murder makes a nice juicy news headline, even though we aren't committing murder, and juicy headlines sell papers and boost ratings. Also, you are successfully doing something that, while not illegal, is pretty questionable morally. Anybody who fails to live up to the morals of the Archbishop of

Canterbury is fair game for the media. Funny really when you consider the average hack has the personal moral compass of a mass murdering despot. Politicians will jump on the bandwagon of whatever's in the media to appear popular, and the police serve the state so they do what politicians tell them to. We have a short window to get a pre-emptive strike in.'

Stuart and Ross looked at each other in the hope that one of them had the faintest idea what he was talking about.

'Sorry, you've lost us. What is this pre-emptive strike and how do we do it?' asked Stuart.

'It's already done. We need to win over a select few individuals with influence. I've prepared some special simulations for a handful of VIP guests who will be arriving at ESR from tomorrow. All the details are in here, including the passwords for the programmes on the mainframe.' Mr X handed Stuart a folder.

Ross and Stuart were open-mouthed as they flicked through the folder.

'Bloody hell, isn't that...?'

'Yes it is.'

'And that's...'

'Yes.'

'Right. Er thanks, you know, for all your hard work and that.'

'You're welcome. Lay out the red carpet for this lot and try to be nice to them. They'll be arriving via the back entrance at the stated times. And make sure none of them see each other as one or two are in each other's simulations. Anyway, I'd better get going, a few more things to do.'

Ross wondered what those things might be, and the probability of them increasing the frequency of his visits to the toilet. He prayed he would never make Mr X's shitlist. The man scared him.

'One more thing. Keep a close eye on that lawyer of yours. He did OK today but he enjoys the cameras a bit too much for my liking.'

Ross nodded in agreement; he'd been thinking the same thing

himself.

'Oh, before you go. One question. Why Project Future?' asked Ross.

Mr X grinned. 'Because if it fails none of you will have one.'

****

Mr X was right. As usual. The next day the papers were full of quotes from MPs, local councillors and the police about the evidence of 'moral decline', when it's deemed acceptable for entrepreneurs to profit from encouraging normal people to commit murder. Questions would be asked in parliament during Home Secretary's questions on Friday, and senior police were quoted as saying they would be launching a preliminary investigation into the legality of ESR, and the possibility of bringing charges for incitement to commit murder. The press were camped outside the building.

Adam was rushed off his feet but had never been happier. He was in demand like never before. Honey traps were being set right left and centre. Adam ate the honey on offer, whilst being careful to avoid the trap. He was playing with fire.

****

The heavy press presence made the success of day one of Project Future all the more remarkable. Project Future was a five-day operation.

Days one and two targeted the media, days three and four national and local government and day five the police. Day one, Tuesday, dealt with the Sunday press and the investigative television programmes. Mr X had thought hard about the strategy. He understood that the Sundays set the agenda for the week's news in the daily nationals. They have a whole week of investigating a story. It was Tuesday, they would already have their teeth into ESR, but it was still early enough in the week to change that.

One by one they arrived in secret, exiting blacked out cars into a concealed temporary garage structure at the rear of ESR, which had been assembled by Ted Armour Builders Ltd.

Mr X's instructions had been planned down the minutest detail. Alice was given chaperone duties and was dressed to impress. She gave each guest a brief tour of ESR headquarters, ensuring there was enough time for the middle-aged hacks to be alone with her. It was important they were given ample opportunity to cop several eyefuls and make not very well concealed attempts to come on to her. Alice played her part to perfection. She was careful not to lead any of them on, and was courteous and flattered at the attention, whilst at the same time ensuring each of these episodes was in the correct location to be captured by the elaborate, discreet CCTV system recently installed by a company specialising in counter-espionage. Another personal contact of Alan West not known for ordering too many salads. Ross took on the same role as Alice for the female VIPs and male ones who preferred the company of attractive gentlemen.

Each VIP was required to sign a contract stating they would not reveal any details of the simulation they were about to experience. The contracts were not worth the paper they were written on but this was merely part of the 'wet behind the ears, naïve, law-abiding company' impression they wanted to portray to the media guests. Mr X knew full well none of them would honour the contract; they had deep pockets and could easily afford massive legal teams.

Before the simulations began, the coup de grace was applied. Ross entered one of the booths and acted out the first simulation ESR ever did, that of himself bludgeoning Belvedere to death in his office with his own fraud reports. Ross knew it so well he didn't need the simulation to be running for him to get into character. This was just as well, given that it wasn't running. Whilst this was taking place, the VIP was in the technical programming room, observing that there were no monitors or computers anywhere playing Ross' simulation. At this point Stuart would explain how the vast number of future simulations that were being worked on at any one time, along with all the simulations taking place in the techno booths, meant that no IT system in the world had the memory to store all this data, and therefore there was no room to save all the past simulations for more than a few hours. Each simulation would be saved to disc only and not the company hard drive, otherwise the entire system would crash. To evidence this, several computer screens displayed large numbers of files being erased after they'd been saved to disc. The disc was presented to the client at the end of their session as a memento of their visit to ESR.

At the end of Ross' non-existent simulation, a disc ejected from a machine and Stuart demonstrated the proof of what he had been saying by inserting the disc into a computer and playing the old simulation of Ross killing Belvedere. Each of the guests were amazed at the realism of what they saw and jumped at the chance to participate themselves. At the end of their session, they were given their disc and asked if they had any further questions. At this point, each of them was so keen to get back to their offices or studios and start work on the story, they couldn't leave quick enough. When they did get back, however, they soon found out they'd been done up like a kipper by one of the greatest criminal minds the world had ever seen.

There on their desk was a sizeable package waiting for them, courtesy of ESR. Inside was a copy of the CCTV film showing them drooling over and coming onto Alice. Also included was a letter. It stated that their session had indeed been recorded and that if any future negative stories about ESR were published or broadcast by their organisation, the film of their indiscretions would be sent to their wives and children. Copies of the simulation would be sent to their family, friends, work colleagues, employers and of course the person who was the victim of their virtual crime. In most cases this was either their editor, a more senior reporter or a rival journalist or broadcaster.

As the media are not known for taking this sort of treatment lying down, the letter continued that ESR was grateful for their time and by way of compensation, they were prepared to offer them full lifetime membership of ESR for free, subject to the continued support of their organisation. It concluded by suggesting they may find the contents of the envelope of interest for their upcoming editions or programmes. The envelope contained details of various embarrassing indiscretions of high-profile members of the government and shadow cabinet. These included concrete evidence of illegitimate children, extra-marital affairs, a penchant for young boys, and detailed breakdowns of several MPs' fraudulent financial affairs. When the exercise was repeated for the dailies on Wednesday that took care of the media.

Thursday and Friday saw the turn of the politicians. The local councillors were easy enough to win over, thanks to substantial donations to the charities of their choice combined with copies of confidential paperwork for various lucrative land deals awarded to companies who just happened to employ the services of the very same councillors on long-term retainer consultancy contracts. The MPs were a different kettle of fish. You didn't rise to a senior position in national politics without being monumentally paranoid and having already fumigated your closet of all potential skeletons. None of them tried it on with Alice or Ross and only about half of them opted to take part in the simulations. This meant two things. First, the offer of free lifetime membership was neither here nor there, and second, the material with which they were about to be blackmailed had better be phenomenally good. It was.

****

The Home Secretary, Sir Anthony Reaves, was speechless at the sight of the photo that fell out of the envelope inside his package. It was a nice one of him snorting cocaine out of a prostitute's bum crack. Not the sort of image that the man responsible for the war on drugs would want to be made public. The leader of the opposition was left equally mortified by the historical photos of his overseas private meeting in which he was accepting packages from Baku Otam, the ousted African despot wanted for international war crimes. Somehow he just couldn't see how he was going to explain this one to his friends in Amnesty International.

By the time it was the turn of the police, their interest in ESR had slipped off the radar, thanks to the sudden explosion of sensational exposés and the Home Secretary's resolute insistence at the dispatch box that ESR had no case to answer. Just to be on the safe side though, those senior officers who did keep their appointments were rewarded with a treasure trove of evidence against the suspected perpetrators of several fatal police shootings.

In the space of a week, ESR was given a clean bill of health, with the media consensus being that they were a normal, albeit eccentric, computing company and that there really was no story here. The only member of ESR unhappy about this sudden lack of interest from the media was Adam. His celebrity was fading. In a desperate attempt to cling onto his media profile, Adam printed thousands of business cards and was handing them out like confetti. They listed the contact details for ESR with his name and position as spokesman for 'The Boss Killers'. When he discovered what Adam was up to, Ross was unamused and terminated his contract.

****

The middleman poured himself a generous measure of single malt and rolled it around the glass a few times before putting it out of its misery. He grinned as he held one of Adam's business cards in one hand and a telephone in the other. Yet again he was trying to ring one of the approved 'safe' numbers for the intermediary. There was no answer.

For two weeks now he'd been trying to contact him. The Council was furious about all the news coverage of The Boss Killers. They knew it was just a matter of time before some clever hack or The Old Bill stumbled across the real Boss Killers and then they would all be in the firing line. The middleman had persuaded the others to let him track down the intermediary and sort this business out. If he didn't succeed soon he would have to prepare his troops for war.

****

The intermediary took a deep swig of his cocktail and laid back down on his front. His drink was called 'brain fog', an appropriate name given that he hadn't been sober since he boarded the plane to Goa two weeks ago. The meeting with Jennifer had knocked him for six. He'd had to get away from it all.

He groaned in relaxation as the skilled hands of the masseuse danced over his ageing body. Knots were unravelled and tension released. If the masseuse didn't move her hands from his inner thigh soon there would be a new build up of tension in close proximity. He tried to remember how long he'd been here but to no avail. Everything had gone fuzzy. Every time he closed his eyes his starving brother's face looked back at him, pleading in his eyes. It was no good; no matter how hard he tried, he couldn't escape those eyes. He was going to have to go back and face the music.

****

The middleman had had enough. He couldn't stall The Council any longer. From inside his jacket pocket he retrieved his most valuable of assets. It was small, black and contained the names and numbers of all The Pugilists. He picked up the phone and started dialling.

Chapter 17
Welcome Home

As the plane touched down on the runway at Gatwick Airport, the intermediary took the opportunity to enjoy the last few moments of his holiday by sinking a quadruple whisky. That would keep the DTs at bay for at least a few more hours. He hadn't been sober at any point since he left England three weeks ago. He took his hand luggage and exited the plane. The cargo of bleary-eyed passengers walked in unison along the gangway and into the main terminal. It was a close fought contest but the winner of the completely inappropriate attire competition was a senior gentleman who'd opted for a safari hat, flamboyant Hawaiian shirt, shorts revealing far too much upper leg flesh for a man his age, and a pair of flip flops that were only being held together by dirt. It was the intermediary.

After negotiating several miles of endless airport corridors he arrived at the baggage reclaim area and for once was not kept waiting until the last suitcase. He passed through the 'nothing to declare' gate, even though he had over fifty grand of cash in his luggage, and was carrying two carrier bags of hand luggage that made frequent clinking noises. Before he made for the exit, a short detour to the airport safety deposit boxes was required. Here he deposited most of the cash and collected several personal items, including one of his many books of names and numbers. How the police would like to get their hands on his little black books. He also retrieved his mobile phone, a modern necessity for a man in his position. With trepidation he switched the phone on. There were seventy-six missed calls and forty-two messages. Not good.

The intermediary had been a naughty boy before he departed. The condition by which his holiday had been approved by his employers was that he took his mobile phone with him, and got on the first plane back to Blighty if there was an emergency. He'd agreed to this but had negotiated that all day-to-day matters could be handled by his assistants, and that he was only to be contacted if it was a matter of life and death. His life and death, to be precise. He then absent-mindedly left his mobile phone in the safety deposit box and buggered off to Goa for three weeks. He knew The Boss Killers would not be pleased.

His plan was to go home, straighten himself out, and begin what would be a long day's work – but he couldn't do anything until he'd had a hot shower and drunk a catering-size jar of coffee granules. He looked like a beach bum's granddad. He smelt like a beach bum's great, great, great, great granddad.

As he exited the airport, a group of tall, heavyset men appeared on either side of him. An identical group of equally tall, heavyset men appeared in front and behind him. With the intermediary the jam in a tall, heavyset men doughnut, they all walked towards the open door of a waiting parked Mercedes with blacked out windows. The vehicle was black and the men were all wearing matching black suits, shoes, ties and sunglasses. The intermediary wondered who had placed a bulk purchase with the mail order goon squad company. Whoever it was, they really liked the colour black. He didn't make a fuss as he entered the rear of the car. He knew if it was serious he would be dead already. His most pressing priority was to uncover just who it was he was dealing with here. The vehicle interior offered precious few clues. He was seated alone, separated from the driver by blacked-out interior glass. On closer inspection, the intermediary noticed it was bulletproof glass.

That's quality workmanship. Too many tin-pot organisations wouldn't have thought of that, but it's those little details that make all the difference.

In front of him was a small glove compartment, which he opened. 'Bollocks,' he said, as he took out a balaclava.

****

The Mercedes pulled into an exclusive private road and stopped outside a lavish four-storey private residence. The intermediary stumbled out of the car and staggered drunkenly up the immaculate stone staircase, holding onto the wall for balance. Outside the maple front door he checked his reflection in the gleaming paintwork, to confirm that he was indeed wearing his balaclava. The words Maple Arch Private Clinic were inscribed on a small gold plaque next to the door.

So I'm entering The Medics' dominion.

The front door opened at his push and he entered a grand hallway, complete with matching patterned burgundy carpet and flock wallpaper. Orchids and lilies lined the length of the hallway, at the centre of which was the most extravagant indoor fountain the intermediary had ever seen. At the end of the hall, sitting inside a small alcove comprised of luxurious marble for no other reason than because they could afford it, was the receptionist.

'Second floor, first on the right,' she said, without looking up.

The intermediary was impressed. At an establishment that clearly only catered for multi-millionaires, a man stinking of booze and body odour, wearing a hideous party shirt, flip flops and a balaclava didn't even merit a derogatory look of disdain. That's an altogether better class of underling, he thought.

He took the lift to the second floor and entered the meeting room. Whatever his preconceptions had been, he was not expecting this. The room was enormous. In its centre was a giant antique boardroom table that could seat at least 50 people. At the far end of the table the secretary and the go-between were sitting next to each other. Four times his arm's length was sitting next to the secretary as far as the go-between was concerned. In front of the intermediary was the middleman, an empty chair next to him. The battle lines had been drawn.

'Good morning, intermediary. So nice of you to join us. Please do help yourself to some refreshments,' said the secretary, gesturing to the corner of the room behind the middleman.

The intermediary rubbed his already sore eyes to check he wasn't hallucinating. It was just that he thought he'd seen an expansive buffet area offering full English and continental breakfast, a salad bar, egg station and china bowls of seasonal fruits and berries, all served by a smiling man wearing a spotless white chef's apron and hat. On the second look it was all still there, except this time there was also a chocolate fountain and a small Chinese noodle bar.

'So how have you been, intermediary – and more to the point, where have you been?' the secretary began, in between mouthfuls of ham and onion omelette.

'As your hired goons just picked me up from the airport, I shushspect you already know the answer to that question, secretary.'

He was both annoyed and impressed that they knew he was returning from holiday, given he'd been using a false name and passport he hadn't divulged to anyone, and had not made a single soul aware of his destination.

'As you can no doubt guesh, I have been on holiday. This was approved by the Bosh Killersh. Ash the next meeting of The Counshil was not due for another two monthsh I shaw no reashon to bother you with the detailsh. All ongoing operational mattersh were handed to my able ashishtant who I trust sherved you well in my abshensh.'

The secretary and the go-between exchanged confused glances. Holding his hand in front of his nose and breathing shallowly, the middleman attempted to shuffle his chair ever so slightly away from the intermediary. He was alone in his own council.

'Are you pissed?' the secretary asked.

'A little bit, yesh. Sho whatsh the emergenshy that you have to hire a goon shqad to bring me here from the airport?'

'Bookings are down, intermediary.'

'Thatsh it, is it? Bookings are down?'

'You don't consider that to be an important matter?'

'Yesh, yesh of course. What's the damage then?'

'Eighty per cent drop on last year for The Medics,' replied the secretary.

A shocked intermediary was mid-gasp when the go-between interrupted him.

'Ninety-five per cent.'

All eyes turned to the middleman, who muttered 'Ninety per cent,' whilst ensuring his hand maintained a protective force field for his nose.

'I take it we can all assume your organisation has been affected as well, intermediary?'

He knew it had; there had been just a handful of bookings all year so far. The economy had taken a turn for the worse, but in the intermediary's experience this was no bad thing in their line of work. He nodded his reply to the secretary's question. As he did, he began to feel peculiar. His brain went into slow motion, as if he was caught somewhere between consciousness and sleep. All his muscles experienced sharp stabbing pains, whilst his body instantaneously underwent a massive rise in temperature. His hands trembling, he jumped out of his seat, ripped his shirt off, and launched himself towards the small restaurant in the corner of the room. He grabbed the first of several large jugs of iced water and, discarding his balaclava, proceeded to drain the contents of the two-litre jug in one go. He poured another jug, including the ice, over his head.

'You! Full English and three quadruple espressos. Now,' he barked at the frightened chef.

Sobriety was approaching and the intermediary was determined to speed up its arrival. He could handle drunkenness and he could handle sobriety, but that bit in between was evil and nasty and needed to be stopped in its tracks immediately. Death by food poisoning was preferable to his approaching hangover.

'So what is it? What's going on then?' asked the intermediary, returning to his seat as if nothing had happened.

'Perhaps it has something to do with this,' replied the secretary.

She threw a folder across the table towards the intermediary. He opened it and saw a stack of newspaper clippings from recent weeks, all about the ESR story. The intermediary read, pausing only to shovel in mouthfuls of cooked breakfast that he washed down with espresso. There it was in black in white, and in some cases colour: *The Boss Killers*. This was serious. It was at this point the middleman interrupted.

'Council needs to be aware that this matter is in hand. The Pugilists are, as I speak, in the process of dealing with these so-called Boss Killers. I can assure you we shall not be troubled by them again.'

A door opened at the far end of the room and a man stepped in. He approached the secretary from behind, whispered something in her ear and then disappeared. He had at all times kept a very close eye on the go-between.

'There is a call for you, middleman. If you exit the door behind you a colleague will show you to the phone.'

The middleman and the intermediary exchanged worried glances. Mobile phones were banned from Council meetings as an unwelcome distraction, besides which, the intermediary, secretary and the middleman had no desire to ever have to listen to any conversation the go-between had with members of The Gang. Instead, an emergency number was always made available for the duration of the meeting. The middleman left the room to take the call, knowing, like the others did, that whatever it was would not be good news. In his absence, an uncomfortable silence fell over the meeting. The intermediary did his best to punctuate this with loud guzzling noises as he polished off the rest of his breakfast and espresso. His body was grateful for the sustenance and instructed his brain that what it would like right now was a nice long sleep. Something in the region of two or three days' worth would do the trick. The secretary did a fake cough and looked at the intermediary, gesturing towards her own face as she did so.

'I'm well aware I'm no longer wearing a balaclava, thank you very much, secretary. Am I setting your heart alight with my rugged good looks?'

She sneered at the intermediary with attempted superiority. Meanwhile the door opened and the middleman returned. He was ashen-faced.

'Bad news, middleman?' enquired the secretary, with as much genuine concern as she could muster, which was numerically identical to the number zero.

The Council was no place for bullshitting so he told it to them straight. 'The Pugilists have failed in our mission to bring a swift conclusion to the activities of ESR. Heavy losses have been incurred.'

The room fell silent. This was a not inconsiderable piece of information to digest. The middleman had admitted, in so many words, that The Pugilists had just suffered an arse-kicking, and if ESR were capable of doing that to the biggest bunch of bloodthirsty psychopathic badasses in the land, then they were a much bigger problem than any of them could have imagined. The intermediary gave his colleagues a few seconds to volunteer their services before he took control of matters.

'The Boss Killers – that is to say, the organisation I represent – are most grateful to The Pugilists for their endeavours. We will now take care of this business as a matter of urgency.'

The secretary and the go-between had a brief and impolite concealed conference whispered behind their hands. Yet another Council rule broken.

'We would like this matter resolved by Monday,' stated the secretary.

'Monday it is,' replied the intermediary, with indifference, in part due to his lack of knowledge of what day it was.

With that, the meeting was brought to a swift conclusion and the semi-naked intermediary helped the shocked middleman to his feet. Outside, the intermediary got into a cab the receptionist had ordered for him, and gave the driver an address, after having first instructed him that all of his family would be killed if anyone were to ever learn of the destination he'd just been given.

As the cab exited the private road, the intermediary had a lot to think about. He had until Monday to resolve this ESR business or war would be declared. There was a lot to do in a short space of time. A less experienced intermediary would plough straight on but he knew better. Precision planning of such important matters as these required a clear head. Before he could hope to attain such clarity there was something else apart from food, caffeine and sleep that he needed. Peace of mind. He had a scratch that needed itching.

****

The Pugilists didn't do subtle. Their complete lack of subtlety was one of the things they were best known for. That, and keeping the wheelchair manufacturing industry in business by providing it with a steady supply of new customers.

When a gang of balaclava-clad Pugilists approached the offices of ESR you didn't need Nostradamus around to predict there was going to be trouble. Those waiting their turn in the ever-present queue to place their order decided that this might be a good moment to go and wash their car, weed the garden, or attend to other vital matters that couldn't wait another moment. As they approached the building entrance, the chief Pugilist spelled it out even more clearly to the few brave opportunistic stragglers who hoped to take advantage of the situation by jumping the queue.

'Anyone who doesn't want to spend the rest of their life in a wheelchair had better piss off.'

The stragglers dispersed at speed, apart from one man in a wheelchair who hadn't felt particularly threatened by the last statement. A lone security guard stood his ground as the mass of Pugilists advanced towards the entrance.

'We admire your bravery, son. We all do, don't we, lads?' His colleagues murmured their agreement. 'We've got many mates in the security trade. Lot of us first started there ourselves. I'm telling you this because I want you to know we respect you, and your profession, and we appreciate your dilemma. You're paid to protect your employers. But this is one of those times when you need to use your loaf. Look at the numbers, son. What chance do you stand? You're brave, we can see that, and we pay good money for brave fellas like yourself who can handle themselves. Step aside and you'll be making a wise career choice. Stay where you are and I need to tell you we'll hurt you so bad your own family won't recognise you. What's it to be, big man?'

The security guard stood his ground.

'You've got balls fella, I'll give you that. Do you know who we are?'

The guard shook his head.

'We're The Pugilists, son. Heard of us, have you?'

The guard nodded.

'Looks like we're going to have to beat some sense into this one. Come on lads, let's get started.'

The chief Pugilist stepped forward and threw a punch, with an arm so massive it looked deformed, squarely onto the jaw of the guard. He instantly recoiled, screaming in pain. Every one of the bones in his fingers and hand was broken. The guard grabbed the screaming Pugilist by the lapels and head-butted him so hard his skull ruptured, blood spurting out of a gaping chasm in his head as he hit the ground like a lead weight. His whole body convulsed for a few seconds and then he was dead.

The remaining Pugilists looked at each other in shocked disbelief, wondering what to do next. This had never happened before. The security guard smiled at them, light gleaming off the pieces of broken bottles that passed for his teeth.

****

Ross was busy sorting through his ever-growing mountain of paperwork when an assortment of flustered Rums burst into his office in something of a panic. Several attempts by them to communicate something that seemed of an urgent nature were unsuccessful as Ross failed to decipher their pidgin English. He really did need to learn Korean. Where words had failed the universal language of pointing triumphed as Ross was brought up to speed with developments outside the building. He witnessed the stand-off between The Pugilists and Igneous, and reached the rapid conclusion that diplomacy would be a wasted effort in this situation. They needed help and they needed it fast.

He knew the proper response was to call the police. He also knew that they were operating on the right side of the law by a margin so fine as to be invisible to all but those whose ancestors had mated with hawks. He had also just overseen the entrapment and blackmail of several senior members of parliament and the police force, and his Head of Security not only had a criminal record as long as a Frenchwoman's armpit hair, but was also known to have an involuntary cranial reflex to the presence of police that involved 'head-butt first, ask questions later'.

Ross picked up the phone and called his fixer of last resort.

****

Not more than two hours after Ross made his phone call, life returned to normal at ESR. It was as if the earlier confrontation between Igneous and The Pugilists had never taken place.

The dead bodies had been removed to a location Ross had no desire to be informed of. The critically wounded, who had been unable to accompany the seriously wounded in The Pugilists' retreat, had been dispatched to various hospitals for emergency treatment. The pavement that formed the approach to ESR had undergone a transformation that would make every local council's Head of Finance seethe with envy at its speedy conclusion. Paving slabs splattered with blood just a few hours earlier had been replaced with brand spanking new ones. The enormous temporary marquee that been erected to screen off all this activity from the general public whilst it was taking place had now been disassembled.

Trucks belonging to Cedric O' Reilly building contractors departed from the scene, taking with them the final evidence of what had taken place here. Once again, Ross was in awe of Mr X. The man was very good indeed.

****

Belvedere completed a memo congratulating the Chairman on yet another excellent decision. It was the fourteenth he'd sent in the last week. After the world learned of the tragic death of the Chairman, Belvedere had dutifully adhered to an appropriate period of mourning. It was, by sheer coincidence, the exact same amount of time it had taken Browns to appoint a new Chairman. That greasy pole wasn't going to climb itself.

****

Raymond Van Hagen sat alone at the bar in the Coach and Horses, sipping his pint with the quiet contentment of a man who appreciated the simple things in life. Today was his day for pure indulgence. Already he'd been for a swim and enjoyed a nice lunch in a delightful noodle bar. Before frequenting the Coach and Horses, he'd taken in a Bruce Lee double bill at the flicks and now he was enjoying an evening nightcap.

It was something of a ritual for Raymond. Once a week, every week, he would take a day out of his hectic life to lap milk from the saucer of self-indulgence. It was never the same day. Neither did he frequent any of the same establishments or locations. He never dressed the same or used the same cab firm or driver, and his accent, general facial appearance and name would change each week. This week he was Rotterdam's Raymond Van Hagen. Last week he was Eric Birtles from Blackpool and next week he would be Giuseppe Minestrone from Naples. It was out of necessity, rather than schizophrenia, that he took such measures. Raymond Van Hagen was taking a holiday from himself. He had created a monster, and now the only way he could escape was to lose himself in a day of anonymous simplicity once every seven days.

Pint drained, he soaked in the atmosphere of ordinariness for a moment longer before exiting the pub. The full moon illuminated the night sky, making the already calm evening close to perfect as Raymond strolled along the road. He stopped at a hot dog stall at the side of the road, unable to resist the enticing aroma of fried onions.

'Large hot dog, please. Plenty of onions and mustard.'

'Yes, sir, coming right up,' replied the vendor.

Raymond gazed up at the sky, so still, so peaceful. 'Feels a bit muggy tonight. Wouldn't be surprised if a storm's on the way.'

'You're not wrong there, mate.'

Raymond heard the change in tone of the hot dog vendor's voice, and the simultaneous screech of tyres, but it was no good; he was too slow to react. A moment later it was all over and the car sped off with Raymond bundled into the boot and the intermediary sitting in the back seat, still wearing the vendor's apron as he chomped on Raymond's hot dog.

****

The last thing Raymond saw outside the Coach and Horses, before his head was covered with a sack, was the gruff weatherworn face of the intermediary, with its several centuries of life etched into its grizzled features. As Raymond was awoken by searing pain in his temple and ribs, he was greeted by that very same face. He tried to escape but gave up when he realised he'd been tied and handcuffed to a metal pole that joined the floor to the ceiling. The person responsible for restraining him was presumably blacklisted from attending every theatre in the world playing host to escapology acts.

The intermediary grinned at him with the comfortable air of a man who doesn't care if he lives or dies. In the absence of any feasible escape plan, or anything else to look at, Raymond returned his gaze. He knew he was in as much trouble as it was possible to be in. A quick glance around the room told him he was in some sort of large, empty industrial building or factory. He had three options as he saw it. Beg, bribe and threaten.

Something about this place gave him the eerie feeling that he wouldn't be the first living being to be killed there. The smell was rancid. The lighting was poor but Raymond thought he could make out some old dark patches on the walls and floor that looked like blood. That it hadn't been concealed was very worrying indeed.

'I think there's been a big mistake. I don't know who you are or what you want but whatever it is I'm not the person you're looking for.'

'Is that so?'

'Yes, I believe it is, so if you could just, you know, let me go then I'll be on my way and won't say another word about the whole affair.'

The intermediary didn't reply. He just stared at Raymond for what seemed like an age. Then he began to undress. Watching a stocky, balding pensioner removing his shirt and trousers to reveal his muscular, tattooed body was a sight more disturbing to Raymond than what he'd already been fearing might happen next.

'Now listen, there's no need for this,' he gibbered, his mouth trembling. 'Whatever you're planning – and I've got a pretty good idea now – please don't. I beg you.'

His begging was genuine now. If the choice was between begging and being raped by an old man then Raymond was happy to wear out the knees in his trousers in penance. Having stripped down to his briefs, the intermediary picked up his clothes and left the room. When he returned Raymond was relieved to see he was at least clothed again. The relief was momentary and soon turned to terror when his brain received the input of the new attire and processed it into the potential ramifications for his wellbeing. Looking like a cartoon caricature of a deep sea fisherman, the intermediary was wearing a thick bright yellow waterproof Mackintosh, matching yellow waterproof hat and trousers and a pair of black Wellington boots.

'Just so you understand, I'm not about to go fishing or attend a nautical-themed fancy dress party. I was pressed for time and this was the best I could do. Don't want to get blood all over my clothes, you see.'

Raymond gulped. His brain went in overdrive as he tried to devise a remotely feasible escape plan. The intermediary helped raise Raymond's heart rate to unsustainable levels by removing a tarpaulin from a bundle on the floor to reveal its contents. It was further bad news for Raymond. The intermediary ran his fingers over the array of metallic devices, unable to decide which one to choose first. He ignored the surgical and dental equipment and the various hammers, chisels and electrical gardening tools. Instead, he picked up a plain black box. It had a lead emerging from the back of its base. At the end of the lead was a plug. The front of the box was of greater interest to Raymond. Protruding from holes at each side of the front of the box were two long electric wires. Crocodile clips were attached to the ends of the wires.

'You might recognise this,' said the intermediary. 'It's not a million miles away from your average car battery charger, except it's been modified to beef it up a bit. You see, when you're in my game, you come into contact with some right clever sods. Real geniuses, they are. So when I say "Any chance you can knock me up some clever gadget to electrify the shit out of some bastards that need taking down a peg or two, but make sure it's not enough to kill them," then they say "Sure, no problem".'

Raymond's face was soaked with a mixture of sweat and tears. He was terrified.

'Please, I beg you, don't do this. I'm not who you're looking for.'

'I think you are.'

'I swear I'm not. I ... I'm someone else.'

'That's the most truthful thing you've said so far, but you're going to have to do better than that,' said the intermediary, slipping on a pair of thick rubber gloves.

'I'll tell you anything. Please. What do you want from me?'

'Who are you?'

A simple question, yet one that Raymond dare not answer. If he said nothing, it was clear he would be tortured. If he lied, he would almost certainly be tortured. Telling the truth looked like his best option for sustained living. Telling the truth would provide a whole new set of problems though. If this man was actually looking for him – and there were many who were – then he faced certain death if he told the truth. If, however, this man wasn't looking for him and had made a mistake then he might just be able to buy his way out of his predicament. He'd already ruled out threatening; this wasn't the sort of man you could threaten.

'Who do you think I am?' ventured Raymond, testing the water.

'Haven't got time for these games. You've got three seconds to come clean,' the intermediary said, as he pulled a pair of industrial safety goggles over his head and plugged the box into the extension, which was already plugged into the wall.

Fearing the pain he was about to be subjected to, Raymond opted for the truth.

'OK, OK, you win. I'm Dr Corpulence.'

The intermediary put the electric wires down and stood with his hands on his hips, a confused look on his face.

'You don't look like Dr Corpulence. He's a great big fat man.'

'I am Dr Corpulence and I can prove it. I've got money. If you let me go I'll pay you whatever you want. Name your price and it's yours.'

'You're lying.'

The intermediary advanced towards Raymond, holding the electric clamps in his hands. He stopped a few feet away. Raymond could feel his hair standing on end from the electricity.

'I'm Dr Corpulence. I'm Dr Corpulence!' he screamed in desperation, his one hope resting on the intermediary believing this fact.

The box was switched off and placed on the floor. Raymond panted with fear and relief.

'I believe you. I always say honesty is the best policy, especially for someone in your position. There's just one small problem though.'

'What?'

The intermediary removed his gloves, inserted his fingers into his mouth and wolf-whistled. Chubby legs supporting his enormous obese body, Dr Corpulence waddled into the room and stood beside the intermediary.

'Oh fuck,' Raymond blurted out. The game was up.

'Dr Corpulence, meet Dr Corpulence.' The intermediary gestured towards Raymond. 'That's taken the wind out of your sails, hasn't it?' he gloated. 'Just so you know, it wasn't easy getting you two into the same room. Seventeen people we had to torture to get to you. As you've probably already guessed, your personal make-up artist now has a new employer.'

Resigned to his fate, Raymond was surprised to find his overwhelming emotion was that of relief. He'd been trapped inside an obese prosthetic body for longer than he could remember, a prisoner to his own lustful pursuit of more and more money and power.

'Now my dear, Dr Corpulence and I have some unfinished business. It's time for you to be on your way.'

'I'd like to stay please,' replied Jennifer.

'I'm afraid I must insist you leave. Trust me, this will give you nightmares.'

A disappointed Jennifer Ellis left the room wearing the prosthetic body suit of Dr Corpulence, a bright new future ahead of her. There would be some changes to The House of Lard, that was for sure. Firing Faulkes was first on the list.

'Now then. Even though you're a lowlife, lying, manipulative, murdering, thieving bastard, I'm feeling generous so you can choose,' said the intermediary, pointing at the various torture implements before him. 'You've got ten seconds otherwise I choose.'

No longer caring, Raymond nodded his head towards a heavy lump hammer.

'I can see your reasoning there. Big tool. Should get the job done nice and quick. Good choice.'

His back turned to Raymond, the intermediary bent down to pick up the hammer but moved past it to another object.

'Fooled you,' he laughed, as he turned back to Raymond with the chainsaw roaring in anger. 'Now let's see what you look like without any arms.'

Chapter 18
Ambition

Sergeant John Major sat at his desk and sipped his coffee. It tasted of figs. He was not happy. The whole point of being in the police force was to arrest people. His preference was to kick someone's door down at six in the morning, trash their house and shove a gun in their face. Instead, he was sitting at his desk making boring phone calls.

Christmas had given him a long list of people to call. Mechanics who serviced cars just before they'd been driven off a cliff, plumbers who serviced gas boilers just before all the building occupants died of carbon monoxide poisoning and manufacturers of various mechanical devices that had inexplicably malfunctioned or exploded, killing their owners in the process. It was tedious stuff for Major. He wasn't a 'back office' copper. He much preferred the traditional 'pounding the street, busting heads' approach to policing. What made things worse was that all the calls he was making checked out. He wasn't getting anywhere nearer to the satisfying sound of metal crunching on skin that came from slapping a cold pair of handcuffs onto a suspect.

Christmas was keeping something from him, he was sure of it. Major had always been loyal to Christmas through thick and thin. Lately things had been thinner than a bulimic catwalk model during Paris fashion week. He felt mutinous. Christmas was out following up a lead. That was another thing. Christmas had been hoarding all the best leads and leaving him with the boring office tasks. Major had had enough. It was time to act.

As DI Christmas' sidekick, nobody paid any attention to Major entering his superior's office and rifling through his files. He wasn't sure what he was looking for but felt confident he'd know it when he saw it. Christmas was meticulous and careful when it came to his files so Major was relying on some luck. An exhaustive search of the case files didn't reveal anything; Christmas was too clever for that. Major was about to leave when his copper's nose spotted something that shouldn't have been there. His computer was still on. *That's just careless,* thought Major. *There's the piece of luck right there.*

He switched the monitor on and saw that the screen was locked. He would need the password. What would Christmas use as his password? Major racked his brain for several minutes trying to come up with the answer; he knew he would only have three attempts to get it right. The answer presented itself to his grateful brain. Of course, what else would it be?

He typed the word 'summertime' and was granted access to the personal files of DI Harry Christmas. He didn't need to search any further; the file was already open. It listed all the cases they were investigating in chronological order, with notes of clues and leads next to each case. Some of the leads Major hadn't seen before. He scrolled to the bottom of the document and read:

```
Conclusion

Statistical analysis, along with considerable anomalies,
rules out likelihood of the majority of these cases being
genuine accidents. Considerable but as yet circumstantial
evidence that these cases are linked. Most likely
scenario is that these deaths (at least 150 identified so
far, many more suspected) were perpetrated by highly
sophisticated underground hit squad adept at arranging
murders to look like accidents. More hard evidence
required to form a credible case. Proceed with extreme
caution.
```

Major's eyes lit up. The words 'underground hit squad' and 'at least 150 cases' raced through his brain. He began to salivate. This is the big one, John. This is going to be the biggest arrest in the last hundred years. And you're the one who's going to make it.

****

Major twitched as he waited for his contact to arrive. *He's late. He's never late.* The individual in question was Ronnie Winters, a minor criminal who dabbled in this and that, but had his fingers in enough pies to be of interest to the police. That he was still free to engage in these illegal activities was entirely down to the protection provided to him by Major.

Winters was Major's snitch. He was a very useful snitch as well. His information almost always checked out. The reason for this wasn't because he had the ear of all the gang bosses; it was because he had the ear of the street. Winters was a criminal, everyone knew it. He'd been around so long that even though he was small potatoes, he had the respect of the underground.

Major had been looking after Winters for years now. He'd always been a perfect handler, keeping Winters out of prison and keeping an eye on his old mum, who still lived in Killman Street, one of the roughest parts of London. Winters was approaching retirement and all contributions to his retirement fund, such as those made by Major in return for information, were most welcome. He needed Major. He was too old to do any more time; he wouldn't make it through another long stretch. Now Major was going to do something he swore to Winters he would never do. He was going to lean on him.

Winters part strolled, part limped through the park, choosing a random bench to sit at to watch the afternoon sun and listen to the birds. By sheer coincidence, it was the exact same bench Major was already sitting on.

'What's the emergency?' asked Winters. He was nervous. This wasn't the usual arrangement.

'You were supposed to be here half an hour ago,' growled Major.

No niceties, no 'How've you been keeping, Ronnie?' You're going to lean on me, aren't you – like you always said you wouldn't. You coppers are all the same.

'Been in hospital, haven't I? Another check-up on my prostate. It's not looking too good as it happens, nice of you to ask.'

Major looked at him. He didn't look well; definitely lost some weight. *Can't be helped, John. You've kept him safe all these years. Now it's payback time.*

'What do you know about an underground hit squad that specialises in accidents, hundreds of them?'

Shit, this is bigger than the usual stuff he wants. I know plenty but I'm not telling you, sunshine.

'Can't help, I'm afraid. Sorry. That's a bit out of my league, that one. I wouldn't know where to start.'

That was just a bit too quick for it to be believable. He knows something. Even if he doesn't he knows someone who does.

'That's very disappointing,' replied Major. 'A man of your knowledge, I would have thought you might know something at least, even if it wasn't very much. It's a big case, this one. Massive. Taking all my time, it is. Lot of pressure from the top, you see. I'll do my best but I can't guarantee I'll be able to pop round to Killman Street while all this is going on.'

Winters remained silent.

'Also, thought I should warn you, your name cropped up a few times in connection with some stolen video players. If I could just make a breakthrough in this case it would really free up my time to get rid of any evidence they might have on you.'

Still no word came from Winters.

I don't have time for this, thought Major. *Christmas could be out there right now finding the clue he needs to crack the case.*

'I'm sorry it's come to this, Ronnie but if you don't come up with something for me on this hit squad pronto then I'll plant some drugs on you and get you sent down for five years.'

Winters glared at Major. *He's done it, the bastard's leaned on me. He said he wouldn't. I'm not going inside again, never. At my age, with my prostate and the arthritis, I'll be coming out in a wooden box. You'll pay for this. I'll make sure of that.*

'You sure you want to be doing this, Sergeant? These people are hardcore. They'll kill us both.'

'I'm dead sure. Don't worry about your safety. I'll put you in witness protection. They'll never find you.'

These kids... Must think I was born yesterday. You're the one who'll be needing protection, sunshine – not me. I'll be long gone.

'It doesn't look like you give me much choice. Give me a few minutes. I'll need to make a few calls, see what I can find out.'

'Good man.'

What an idiot. As if anyone would find out underground secrets by ringing someone up and asking them. You never ask for information. You make sure you're in the right place at the right time and you hear things. That's how it's done.

Winters walked away from the bench and out of earshot of Major to make his confidential calls from a nearby phone box. He rang five numbers.

The first was Heathrow Airport, to book a one-way ticket on the next available flight to Thailand. He then called his brother Pete to tell him the good news – that he was on his way to live with him at his beach house on Koh Samui. The third call was to his bank to transfer all his money and savings to his brother's account. He then called the most important number. It was one he'd never called before, and prayed he'd never have to. It was the underworld's equivalent of 999, and financed by the gangs. If something big was going down you called a special number to warn them. The people at the other end of the line would then make sure everyone who needed to know was told immediately. Of course there were consequences to calling this line. It always meant that someone somewhere had been talking to the police and the people they had been talking about would be somewhat eager to invite them in for a polite conversation, followed by a free amputation service. The deed was done. Winters made a fifth call to a taxi firm and offered them quadruple fare to be at the park gates in three minutes' time. He then returned to Major.

'You're in luck. I've got something for you. The man you want is meeting someone in a pub on Hurst Street at two o'clock today. I'm not sure which one. That's the best I can do. He'll be getting off the tube at Watkin Station about quarter to, ten to two and walking from there. Make sure you're there to follow him.'

Winters began to depart. *That taxi had better be there.*

Major chased after him. 'Wait. How will I know which one he is? What does he look like?'

'Late fifties but would pass for ninety. Bit chubby round the waist. Crew cut hair. Looks and sounds like he's smoked five trillion ciggies. Face like a welder's bench.'

Winters continued walking at pace and didn't turn back. He could see the taxi now. He hoped his brother could hook him up with a decent prostate doctor over there. Preferably one whose fingers didn't have the same circumference as an overweight toddler's forearm. A young Thai girl wouldn't go amiss either, as long as she didn't turn out to be a ladyboy.

Major was excited. He was going to beat Christmas to the kill. This would be a day all officers would remember for years to come: the day Sergeant John Major blew the underworld wide open. He looked at his watch. It was quarter past one. There wasn't much time. He rushed back to his car and drove off at high speed, his brain greedily anticipating the arrest. What it should have been doing was processing the clues Winters had given him, turning the car around and driving in the opposite direction. Hurst Street. Watkin Station. There was only one pub he could be going to.

****

Major perused the journalistic offerings and confectionery products available at the news stand outside Watkin Station, taking his time with the difficult decision of his imaginary purchase. It was forty-four minutes past one; he hoped he wasn't too late. He still had the tricky job of identifying his target. Fortunately for Major, the intermediary wouldn't be hard to pick out. Very few people departed at Watkin Station. The traffic tended to be one-way, that way being any direction leaving the area.

The intermediary emerged from the station. He glanced around to see he wasn't being followed and stomped off down the road. Major followed him at a distance, pleased that his advanced training in surveillance and undercover techniques had once again ensured he had the drop on the criminal. *When will they learn? We have the best police training in the world. Of course they're not going to see us.*

Major's heart was racing; this was what it was all about. No more desks or phone calls, he was on the street, in hot pursuit of a criminal. If only more of his life could be this exciting.

The intermediary stopped and entered a large derelict building. On approaching the building Major could hear much noise coming from inside. Could this be a giant squat or perhaps a crack den? Closer inspection of the building's exterior confirmed that it was in fact a public house, in a dilapidated state of repair. A rusty metal signpost was missing the sign bearing the name of the pub.

Major thought of his options. He *should* call for back-up, he knew that, but if he did someone higher up the food chain would waltz in and make the arrest. This was his collar; he wasn't stepping aside for anyone. He should at least have a look inside, see how the land lay. If things looked a bit dicey he could always leave and call for back-up. He placed his hand on the door and hesitated for a moment. Something in his brain was screaming at him to turn back. It was something to do with the name of the pub. It was on the tip of his tongue.

There were a number of theories about the origin of the name The Badger's Eyebrows. Students who drank there insisted it was named after a Monty Python sketch that had been cut from the show before it was aired. Other theories suggested it was a Chinese culinary delicacy, a rare crop of skunk cannabis, an unsuccessful nineteenth-century racehorse and another way of stating that something was very good, as an alternative to saying 'the dogs bollocks'.

One of the more surreal explanations was that it received its name from the landlord of The Dolphin, the former name of The Badger's, after a late night drugs bust. The rumour went that the landlord, Joey Clay, had branched out into a bit of small time dealing and when his pub was raided by the drugs squad late one night, in a state of panic he swallowed the last of his stash: 46 LSD pills. Unable to find any evidence the police left him alone. When Joey's wife returned from visiting relatives three days later she was confronted with the pitiful sight of a petrified Joey hiding in the closet. He was shaking and pointing at a demonic pair of giant badger's eyebrows that only he could see.

Major stepped inside. For a few moments he forgot about the intermediary as his senses attempted to take in, and mentally catalogue, the hundreds of separate instances of crime taking place. There was no doubt about it, he would have to call for back-up. A quick scan of the pub's interior confirmed one important fact. There was no sign of the intermediary. Major had lost his target. In a panicked state, he rushed to the one place he had yet to check. Major entered the gents and walked past the vacant urinals to the shabby cubicles at the end. He pushed the doors of the two cubicles open. Empty. He stared perplexed at the empty cubicles. Where was he? A loud slamming noise preceded the appearance of the intermediary, who stepped forward from his hiding place behind the entrance door to the gents' and stepped in front of the door, blocking Major's exit.

'Looking for me are you, pig?'

Major spun around, startled. He'd been rumbled.

'What, er, no I'm looking for a friend, erm Joey, supposed to meet him here.'

'In the toilets? You an uphill gardener are you, son?'

'Er, no of course not, I'm erm...'

Major was flustered; he was going to pieces.

'You coppers are all the same. Couldn't catch a cold.'

'I'm no cop, you bastard. I told you, I'm looking for my mate.'

'Yeah, yeah. Joey, you said. You know there was a guy called Joey who used to live here a long time ago. Joey Clay, his name was. He drew this.'

The intermediary stepped aside and pointed at the back of the gents' door. There was a series of scratch marks in the paintwork which together looked a bit like a badger. It had massive eyebrows.

Major looked at the door and began to shake. 'Oh fuck,' he shouted.

'You're right there, sunshine.'

Major darted for the exit. He was no match for the intermediary, who absorbed the impact and, with lightning speed, turned him around and threw him back onto the hard floor. While Major regrouped for another attempt, the intermediary took in a deep breath. Before Major hit him a second time the residents of The Badger's Eyebrows all heard the scream. It stopped them in their tracks and sent a shiver down their spines. The landlord reacted first, sprinting to the pub's entrance and bolting the doors shut. The regulars, as one, moved at pace towards the gents' toilets, checking their assorted tools and weaponry as they did.

It wasn't the volume of the scream that had prompted such a response. There were always screams in The Badger's Eyebrows. It was the word that had been used. The word that was prohibited on pain of death. The intermediary had chosen it with care. He could have screamed 'Help'', 'Fire!', 'Rape!', 'Thief!' or 'Murder!' and nobody would have come to his aid. Screaming 'Police!', however, was an entirely different matter.

Chapter 19
Saturday Night

Number One checked his watch again. It was the fourth time in the last minute he'd done so. Killing was as natural and easy to him as breathing. It had been a long time since he'd had to consciously think about what he was doing. Until now.

He knew he should just get on with it. It was easier said than done though, even for one of the world's greatest assassins. This was no ordinary job. As the number one operative in The Boss Killers, it was customary for him to be given the toughest assignments. It was all in a day's work for Number One. Except this time.

He'd agreed to the job and, as usual, had signed the contract to say he'd do it. In a break with standard protocol, he'd even been given the full background as to why the target had to be taken out, something that went against their standard procedures. The intermediary had insisted. He wanted Number One to know what was at stake. Number One understood the reasons. He agreed they had to do it, and he knew he was the best man for the job. His heart was pounding though. His hands trembled. He lit a cigarette, took a long, slow drag and breathed the welcome smoke into his lungs. This was a momentous moment in his life and in the life of the organisation he loved so much and had given his life to. If he made a mistake, they were all well and truly in the brown stuff.

He finished his cigarette and began his walk towards death or immortality. After about ten minutes he arrived at his destination, and strolled into the entrance of New Scotland Yard. He flashed his ID at security and received a nod of approval. First hurdle negotiated. The intermediary had excelled himself by supplying a phoney police ID that would pass the highest scrutiny at such short notice. He took the lift and exited on the third floor. It was half past eight in the evening and already dark outside. He'd been assured the main shift would have left and there should only be one or two bodies left. His target would be working late. He always worked late.

****

The DCI sat at Christmas' desk, his face showing the concentration of a man attempting to complete the Times cryptic crossword. His head rested in his hands. What the hell was Christmas up to? It was most important he found this out so he could take the credit for it. A few more high profile cases solved and he would be knocking on the door of making Chief Superintendent. He'd been meaning to have a good snoop around Christmas' office for a while now but the opportunity never presented itself. The man simply never went home. In the end, the DCI took matters into his own hands by ordering Christmas and the rest of the team onto a top secret emergency counter-terrorism exercise. They'd be away for the rest of the evening. All except Major of course, who'd done a disappearing act. He was looking forward to disciplining that earnest little shit.

The DCI thumbed through the mountain of files that masqueraded as Christmas' desk. What was he doing spending so much time on these dead-end cases? Christmas had been quiet of late. This pleased the DCI, as he despised the man, but his silence was ringing alarm bells. He would be most displeased if Christmas succeeded in taking credit for his own hard-earned achievements. He tried to read the notes in the margins of the case files.

How can anyone read that tiny scribble?

Years of detective work told him that perhaps that was the point; Christmas didn't want anyone reading his notes. The DCI searched through Christmas' desk and found what he was looking for in a drawer. He put the reading glasses on, again placed his head in his hands, and strained his eyes in an attempt to decipher the version of hieroglyphics Christmas had used for his notes.

****

Everything was going like a dream. Number One had reached the floor and found the target without anyone giving him even a sideways glance. Luck was on his side. Not a soul was about. Glancing around one more time to ensure he was alone, Number One removed his gun from his jacket and attached the silencer. With years of training, the quality of which the police could only dream of, Number One used all his stealth skills to approach Christmas' office undetected. He removed the picture of Christmas from his inside pocket for a quick last glance. It wasn't a great picture but it was the best the intermediary could manage at such short notice.

Number One knew that pictures were never a perfect likeness. He approached the office signposted for Detective Inspector Christmas and saw a man sitting at the desk, reading. His view through the half-closed shutters wasn't great, but was good enough to make a firm identification. The man was wearing the same glasses as the man in the picture and was sitting at his desk. Who else was it going to be? Number One opened the door and fired twice. It was done. Now came the difficult bit. How the hell was he going to get all these files out without raising suspicion?

****

Adam arrived at The Badger's Eyebrows well ahead of the agreed time of nine o'clock. He was supposed to be meeting Ross and the others from ESR for an official corporate social celebration, or as Adam preferred to call it, a gigantic lash-up. He'd been surprised and delighted to get an invite and hoped it might be a chance to worm his way back into Ross' good books.

The plan was to start with a few in The Badger's and then go clubbing, preferably somewhere where the ladies were loose and the quality of the disco lighting appalling. Adam wanted to get a few drinks in early to loosen up a little. All those ESR nerds with their weird techno talk and half English, half Korean language made him nervous. He needed a few cheeky shorts before he could face them.

He was also hoping to tout for a bit of business before the others arrived.

Wilson, Wilson, Wilson, Wilson and Wilson had been unimpressed by Adam's appearances on television, radio and in various newspapers as the apparent spokesperson and legal representative of an organisation known as The Boss Killers. Adam was not contracted by Wilson, Wilson, Wilson, Wilson and Wilson to represent such an organisation, and indeed the firm deemed it most inappropriate that they should be associated with the controversial, and quite possibly illegal, activities of said organisation. Mr Wilson in particular was said to be spitting feathers about the whole episode.

As a result, Adam's contract of employment with Wilson, Wilson, Wilson, Wilson and Wilson had undergone some significant changes. Before it had contained lots of terms and conditions – unsurprising for an employment contract with a firm of lawyers specialising in employment contracts. Now there were no terms. No conditions either. This was mainly due to there being no contract. No contract meant no salary. Adam was unemployed and broke. He still had all his business cards though, the ones he had printed by the truckload when he was in demand by the media. In between his medicinal drinks, he proceeded to hand them out to anyone who didn't move quick enough, together with a quick spiel about how he was the famous lawyer for The Boss Killers and was now available at very reasonable rates.

The intermediary sat in a secluded corner of The Badger's Eyebrows, aiming daggers at his glass of concentrated orange juice. What he wouldn't give right now for a bottle of single malt and a funnel. He'd been back in the country less than 48 hours and already he'd put in a shambolic appearance in front of The Council, spent a whole evening torturing a man to death and then, just when he'd been looking forward to getting down to some normal business, he found he'd been followed by the rozzers. This was a serious problem.

Under normal circumstances, the intermediary liked to keep a nice healthy distance between himself and his employers. He only spoke to them directly or met with them if it couldn't be avoided. This was one of those times. If Major was on to him then he was on to them and they had to be told straight away. He put the call in to his contact at The Boss Killers within a few minutes of confronting Major in The Badger's toilets. To his great fortune, the first people the intermediary was joined by after shouting 'Police!' were a couple of off-duty Pugilists he knew from way back. They were able to hold off the baying mob for just long enough for The Boss Killers to arrive and whisk them away. What followed made the intermediary realise that, when it came to torture, he was a mere amateur compared to the ruthless professionalism that Major was subjected to. That he had managed to withstand the pain for even a matter of minutes before he gave up the name of Christmas was an effort worthy of respect. The intermediary had spent the rest of the afternoon trying to put the pieces of a plan together for the most dangerous and risky job they'd ever attempted. He'd done his best. It was out of his hands now.

The afternoon's excitement had meant he was now way behind on his promise to deal with ESR. He'd called in all the remaining favours he was owed and had come up with nothing. It was actually quite strange, as if someone with considerable influence had got to his contacts first. The one contact who might have something was late for their appointment. A rare occurrence indeed. Something was amiss. This ESR business was critical to all their futures and so far he had sod all to go on.

Fate, it seemed, was not without a terrific sense of humour. That, or something very similar to that, was the gist of the intermediary's thinking as Adam presented himself and handed the intermediary a business card.

'You know, you might be just the person I'm looking for. You see, I do need a lawyer and you must be good because I saw you on the telly the other week. Can I buy you a drink?'

Adam beamed with pride. The fish was on the hook. It was time to reel him in.

****

Ross, Alice and Stuart didn't stay long at The Badger's Eyebrows, but it was long enough to detect the atmosphere. It was downright ugly. A quick drink, for traditions' sake, and they would be off.

They were meeting the others at Big Hair, the planet-sized club up west dedicated to the sounds and fashions of the seventies. Even on a good day The Badger's was no place for a sizeable group of naïve Koreans to be hanging out. A quick trip to the gents' and one of the black market corner traders would have sold the lot of them to the nearest gangmaster. Black would be traded on the illegal endangered species market.

Ross finished his drink and told the others it was time to leave. His sixth sense told him that if they didn't have Igneous with them they'd be in serious danger. One man in particular was eyeballing him. He looked like a retired bare knuckle boxer. Stuart and Alice drained their drinks and followed Ross out of The Badger's Eyebrows, all three of them wondering where the hell Adam was.

The intermediary was fuming. He had until Monday to fix the mess he was in and here he was letting his target walk out of the door. After the incident with The Pugilists he wasn't taking any chances where Igneous was concerned. His brain felt like it was about to explode. Major, Christmas, Dr Corpulence, The Council and now Adam and ESR. He was spinning too many plates. As all their faces whirled around his brain, a few got jumbled up.

'Of course.'

The intermediary skulked off to the bathroom, took out his enormous mobile phone and dialled a number.

'Keep him alive and no more damage. There's a change of plan. I'll tell you when I get there.'

****

The first annual ESR works night out was in full swing and going well. It was a year to the day since Ross had piloted the simulation created by METATRON.

ESR was now such a massive entity and demand so relentless that to take a single night off – and Ross was under no illusions that this would be accompanied by the following morning for most of them – took a lot of planning. The previous day's incident with The Pugilists had nearly made him cancel proceedings. Mr X had been concerned about an evening of unbridled debauchery so soon after a gang of criminals had tried to kill them all, but had permitted the evening to proceed on the proviso that Igneous attended. Exchanging pleasantries with work colleagues in a social context was not Igneous' scene but he agreed to tag along and keep an eye on them, provided he could spend some of the evening helping the bouncers on the door. The Rums had come dressed like the cast from a seventies blaxploitation movie. The male Rums were all sporting oversized afro wigs, flowery shirts with massive collars, flared trousers that were at least ninety per cent flare, and platforms that made them all a foot taller. A few sported brown kipper ties. The female Rums wore dresses that included every primary and secondary colour known to man, arranged in no particular order.

While Ross chatted to Stuart and Kevin, he watched the Rums attack the dance floor. It was an impressive sight. The more reserved of the Rums remained seated near the bar, chatting to Alice and her friends. Ross sipped at his drink. It was still early in the evening and whatever happened, he felt an obligation to be there at the end. The way the Rums were going it looked like someone needed to be sober later on. Stuart wasn't drinking at all. It would be an early night with a clear head for Stuart. He had a big day tomorrow. Kevin was drinking like a man who has just been told by a doctor that if he doesn't drink as much alcohol as possible in the next half an hour his genitals will fall off. There were lots of ladies present and he needed some Dutch courage just to be in the same postcode as them. The way he was going his courage would pretty soon have acquired not just Dutch citizenship but also that of Germany, Belgium, France, Italy and Poland. It was advancing on Russia in a pincer movement.

As he watched the carnage unfold, Ross thought about Adam. He was coming to the conclusion that their friendship was at the end of the road. He hadn't wanted to sack him but what choice did he have? He'd pretty much begged Adam to come tonight because he wanted him there as a friend, and even then he hadn't turned up. Ross was woken from his thoughts by a disturbance in the club. The throng of inebriated clubbers parted as one and reformed again. Ross thought he heard screams. He stood on his chair to get a better look.

Alison didn't want them to be in any doubt whatsoever. Black belonged to her. Not just her boyfriend; she *owned* him. Yes, there were pretty girls here, but they had better realise that if they so much as looked at him she would rip out their eyeballs. She was pleased she was doing such a good job of scaring the hell out of them with her vicious stare and snarling teeth. Why else would they be screaming and running away? The end of the throng parted and Alison and Black appeared, a gap surrounding them noticeably larger than that around anyone else on the premises. They took a seat next to Stuart and Ross.

'Women!' shouted Kevin, jumping out of his seat and staggering towards the dance floor. Alison was disturbed that neither Ross, Stuart nor Black even acknowledged his actions.

'Thanks for coming, guys. You both look great.'

Alison beamed with pride and gripped Black's arms even tighter.

'Can I get you both a drink?'

Before they could answer, Sandra, one of the ESR admin team and friend of Alice, rushed over to their table.

'Ross, you'd better come quick and sort this out.'

'What's up?'

'It's the Rums. They've challenged Alice to a drinking contest.'

'Ah.'

Something wasn't right. Something was very wrong. The place was crawling with police. This was not an unusual occurrence for a building that was the headquarters of the capital's police force. When Christmas approached the building though, it was after midnight. It was also by now a Sunday. A skeleton staff should be all that was on duty at this time. The others would be out and about getting stuck into some serious criminal activity. Some of them would even arrest a few criminals. Those that were not on duty, not upholding or breaking the law, and not at home in bed, went by the name of Detective Inspector Harry Christmas.

'Identification please, sir.'

Christmas showed the man his badge. He didn't recognise him. Security was tight and he wasn't even in the building yet. He was ushered inside and onto another security checkpoint. This one was manned by a man whose jaw enjoyed easy listening, trainspotting and making model aeroplanes out of matchsticks. It really was that square. He took Christmas' badge and inspected it for a lengthy time, all the while staring daggers at him.

'He's clean. Send him up right away. They're waiting for him.'

Another man with a ninety-degree-angled jaw grabbed Christmas by the arm and accompanied him to the lift. *This must all still be part of the counter-terrorism training*, thought Christmas. Credit where credit was due; the DCI had gone to town with the authenticity of the thing.

When he arrived on the third floor and approached his office the penny dropped. This was no exercise. The whole floor was teaming with forensics. Everywhere he looked men and women dressed from head to toe in white outfits were busy dusting for fingerprints, taking pictures and bagging anything that didn't move into evidence bags.

What the hell is going on?

A tall figure pointed a finger in his direction and beckoned him forward.

'Christmas?'

'Yes?'

'I'm Commissioner Grange.' The man held out a hand to shake. A petrified Christmas took it. 'We need to talk.' Grange ushered Christmas into an empty office further down the hall. 'Where were you between eight and ten this evening?'

'Operation Fulcrum.'

'Operation Fulcrum?'

'Yes, sir.'

'Remind me again of the details.'

Christmas couldn't believe it. Here he was talking to the Commissioner. He'd only ever seen him on television before.

'It's the counter-terrorism training exercise. I've been taking part in the operation all evening, sir. Since about four o' clock, sir.'

'Fulcrum, Fulcrum ... Oh yes, of course. Fulcrum. That's Inspector Roberts' unit, isn't it?'

'Smith, sir.'

'Yes of course, Inspector Smith. Over Wealdstone way, isn't it?'

'Clapham, sir.'

'Yes, I know it. We'll have to check all this of course.' Grange stood up and yelled. Several officers ran to his call. 'Call Inspector Smith, Operation Fulcrum over at Wealdstone...'

'Clapham, sir.'

'Yes, over at Clapham. Check his alibi. Quick, Sergeant.'

'Yes, sir,' replied the Inspector.

Grange sat back down and smiled at Christmas, who had adopted a policy of not speaking unless instructed to do so. Several minutes passed in tense silence. There was a knock at the door and the Inspector returned.

'He's clear, sir. Inspector Smith confirms he's been with them the whole evening.'

'Thank you, Sergeant.' The Inspector retreated, hoping he hadn't been demoted. 'I expect you want to know what's going on.'

'Yes, sir.' Christmas replied.

'Sometime between eight and ten this evening DCI Richards was murdered.' Christmas turned pale.

'Shot twice in the head.'

The blood drained from Christmas' face.

'In your office.'

The room began to move ever so slightly. Christmas felt an urge to lie down and slow his breathing while listening to the sound of whales communicating with each other.

'Your file says you're a bloody good detective. A knack for solving unsolvable crimes. It also says you're a social misfit and a physical coward. You hate confrontation and faint at the sight of blood.' Christmas sighed. He wished he could protest at his unfair treatment. Alas, he knew it to be true. 'Afraid you're going to have to conquer that fear tonight. There's a crime scene that needs your eye for detail and we can't wait any longer.'

Grange led the way and Christmas followed, stopping in his tracks when he saw the horror show that used to be his office. The door was open. Light flashed as the crime scene photographer snapped every millimetre of the room.

'Tell me what you see, Inspector,' Grange said.

His features switching between grey, crimson and damson, Christmas attempted to master his desire to vomit and scanned the office.

'What's there that shouldn't be, Inspector?'

'Well, without wishing to state the obvious, sir, the DCI.'

'Correct. And what does that tell us?'

Christmas knew the answer but it didn't make any sense.

'That I may have been the target, sir?'

'Wonderful work, Christmas. You'll make DCI yet. He's sitting at your desk, in your office, wearing your reading glasses, and was presumably reading your case files. We can reasonably assume therefore that it was you who was supposed to be sitting there, can't we?'

'Yes, sir,' replied Christmas, despair in his eyes.

'Who would want you dead, Inspector?'

Christmas shrugged.

'Look again please. The clues are there, are they not?'

Christmas concentrated and again looked around the office. It wasn't easy for him. He had to somehow ignore the corpse sitting in his chair with half its head missing. There. He saw it; or rather, he didn't see it.

'I take it from that look in your eyes that you've found it?'

'Yes, sir.'

'Well, Christmas?'

'The files on the desk, sir. The pile should be much higher. More than half the files have been removed.'

'Excellent. So I think we can safely say that you were the target. We can also conclude that the perpetrators of this crime are somehow related to the cases you were investigating. A shame you don't have one of those photographic memories so we could know which of the files were taken.'

'No need, sir. I have copies of every file, sir, so I can work on them at home.'

'Ah, you're that DI Christmas.'

'Sir?'

'Never mind, Inspector. Now listen carefully, man. Something this big can't be kept quiet for long. In a few hours I'll be speaking to the press. I'll tell them about the brave detective cut down in the line of duty. Best not to mention that a criminal wandered into New Scotland Yard, murdered one of our top men and waltzed off with armfuls of evidence. I will have to give them a name though. Your name, Harry.' Harry. It had been over ten years since anyone in the force had called him Harry. 'We want whoever did this to think they succeeded. Understood?' Christmas nodded. 'Meanwhile, Inspector, I'm going to give you every available man to pursue your investigations. You're onto something, and it's big. I'll be sending over at least fifty bodies in your direction in the morning, Christmas. I want you to find the people who did this.'

'Yes, sir,' said Christmas, unable to contain his pride. At long last he was being recognised by the top brass.

'Well? Was there something else, man? Spit it out.'

'It's just that ... well, this might be a coincidence, sir, but my colleague Sergeant Major, who was working these cases with me ... he was supposed to be on the training today but he never turned up.'

'Hmm. Forgetful fellow, is he?'

'No, sir.'

'Sickly chap?'

'Not in seven years, sir.'

'He hasn't had a day off sick in seven years?'

'No, sir. Sergeant Major takes his responsibilities as a police officer very seriously. His arrest record is second to none.'

'Ah, that Sergeant Major.'

****

Ross read his speech again. It was a good speech. In it, he thanked everyone for all their hard work over the last year and told them how he was lucky to have such a dedicated and talented team. He felt a lump in his throat reading it. What he didn't feel was nervous. There was no prospect at all of him having to deliver the speech. At least not this evening.

The workers he was so proud of were making something of an exhibition of themselves. Ross frowned as he watched several security staff dragging away a demonic-looking Alison. After she'd attacked yet another innocent woman for having the nerve to smile in the same proximity as Black, the bouncers gave in and decided they would have to go, even if they were with Igneous. His head bowed, an embarrassed Black trudged after his psychotic girlfriend in the general direction of the exit, and then onto the nearest constabulary. Black would end his relationship with Alison if he wasn't so petrified of what she might do to him for even entertaining such thoughts.

Elsewhere, Igneous was giving Kevin a master class in how to chat up women. There was a surprising amount of fresh air head-butting for such a conversation. Ross foresaw several possible outcomes for Kevin from following the wise teachings of Igneous. He hoped not to be around to have to witness any of them.

The Rums were out of control. All of them were now on the dance floor, leading a mass of bodies in frenetic dance routines that they were making up as they went along. The DJ had long since given up trying to dissuade the mad clan of Koreans by slowing the pace down, and had instead opted to play a relentless assault of high-energy house music in the hope of inducing cardiac failure. The dance floor had turned into a ferocious, sweaty no-man's land, suitable only for the most fearless of disco warriors. Several incidents of bulbous hair-related injuries had been reported. What the situation required was the steady, authoritarian hand of Mr Lo Rum to bring his house to order. This was not possible, however, due to Lo accompanying Hi Rum and Long Rum in an ambulance, tearing along at high speed in the direction of the nearest hospital to have their stomachs pumped. Alice sat down next to Ross, a mischievous, alcoholic grin on her face.

'Did you have to?'

'Have to what, dear?'

Inhibitions had gone out of the window, down the drainpipe, along the alleyway and hopped onto the number nine bus.

'Put two of my programmers in hospital. It'll be days before they're back on their feet – that's providing there's no lasting liver damage.'

'All that's damaged is their pride, lover. They knew the risks. Nothing wrong with a bit of healthy competition among work colleagues.'

Ross raised his eyebrows. 'Really?'

'Oh get over yourself, you pompous prick. At least they had some pride to lose. Big work night out and you're still sipping shandies. You used to be hardcore but now you're a boring bastard. Boring old fart looking down your nose at everyone having fun.'

Ross looked around for moral support. The spaces next to him were vacant. Stuart had gone home early to prepare for his big day and Adam hadn't turned up in the first place. Everyone else was having fun. A brief moment's thought clarified matters in his mind.

'Right, you foul-mouthed, hollow-legged bint. Line them up.'

****

'You're not going to believe this but I've got good news for you.'

Tears streaming down his bruised face, a desperate Adam looked up into the eyes of the intermediary. It hadn't taken them long to break him. Some of The Boss Killers thought it might be a new record. All of 24 seconds before he was screaming like a baby and offering to do whatever they wanted.

'You can go home now.' Adam didn't understand. 'On two conditions, of course. Break either of them and you'll be straight back here, except next time we won't be so nice. These boys,' the intermediary said, pointing at Adam's torturers 'are good, don't get me wrong, but if you break the terms of your release then I'll get some real pros to work you over.'

Adam shuddered. His soul didn't come at a high price. The intermediary bought it with his last sentence.

'First, it goes without saying that this never happened. You never seen any of us and if anyone asks where you got the bruises you tell them your friends at ESR gave them to you.' Adam nodded his agreement. He hoped the second condition would be as easy. 'Second, you call the police from your home tomorrow morning. Make sure it's early. You ring them and you read this word for word.'

The intermediary handed Adam a piece of paper.

'Take your time when you read it to them. Need to make sure you take at least five minutes to read that script – and don't change it either.'

The intermediary handed Adam a stopwatch.

'Just so you can check you're being slow enough with your call. Feel free to cough a lot, sneeze, big pauses between sentences, that sort of thing.'

The script didn't make for pleasant reading. Adam liked it a whole lot more than he liked being killed though.

'I'll do it,' he whispered.

'I know you will. Just in case you get any ideas, you should know your phone's tapped, so if you try and tell anyone we'll know. You'll be watched as well, so don't try and make a run for it.'

The intermediary gestured towards the door. Scared out of his wits, Adam tiptoed past the intermediary and the other Boss Killers and made a run for it.

'You sure you can trust him?' asked Number 26.

'That one would sell his own granny to save his skin. Seen more backbone on a jellyfish.'

****

The lock moved. Ross tried again. It moved again. How could a door lock move?

'I can see ya, ya bastard. Stop moving now.'

He lined the key up one more time and thrust his hand forward. It moved again. Ross had forgotten about his magic door. For some reason he always remembered about it when he was pissed. Coincidentally, that was also the only time his door lock ever moved. Sometimes another three or four locks appeared at the same time. They would take turns to bamboozle him with their trickery.

'Give it here,' said Alice.

After three attempts, during the first two of which the lock moved again, she slotted the key into the lock and the pair of them collapsed into the hallway of Ross' flat. Alice tried to stand up. It proved more difficult than should ever be the case. The hallway was alive. It was moving from side to side, shaking her from one wall to the next and back again. Ross crawled on his hands and knees along the hallway.

He'd forgotten how to walk. He needed the toilet. Straining every sinew, he crawled into his living room and just made it in time to reach his emergency Saturday night bucket. A warm sensation spread down his legs. He hadn't made it in time after all. Alice collapsed next to Ross on the floor. She was too inebriated to notice the pool of urine surrounding him. Within a minute the two of them were unconscious.

Number 16 waited a few minutes until the heavy breathing turned into snores. He then slipped from behind the door in Ross' bedroom and into the hallway. He caught a glimpse of the comatose bodies and smiled.

'You two are in for a surprise in the morning.'

He left as quietly as he arrived, his work for the evening complete.

Chapter 20
Sunday Morning

Ross had the strangest dreams. Really vivid. He dreamt he was cuddling a semi-naked Alice on his living room floor. It made a nice change from torturing Belvedere. He felt terrible. Several attempts to get back to sleep and wake up feeling peachy failed. He opened his eyes. He was cuddling a semi-naked Alice on his living room floor. Ross knew what was going on; this was one of those recurring dreams. A bit more sleep and everything would be back to normal. Ross closed his eyes and managed to drop back off for a few minutes. When he woke up things became much clearer. He was cuddling a semi-naked Alice on his living room floor. It would appear this was actually happening.

What had happened last night? He remembered drinking shots with Alice in Big Hair, and there was something about a dentist's chair. After that it was just a blur. Had they done it? He couldn't remember.

Alice was still out for the count. Ross risked a quick inspection of his genitals. It didn't clarify things one way or the other. Boy, did he feel rough. He needed sugar. Salt was also required, as was fluid of some description. He tried to think. Whatever had happened there was nothing he could do about it now. What he could do was make sure Alice didn't wake up on his living room floor to the sight of Ross looking and feeling like faeces. If they had become intimate last night he should at least try and make her feel special in the morning. The very least he could do was a top class fry-up. That would sort them both out.

Gently, he picked Alice up, carried her into the bedroom and placed her carefully in his bed. A quick audit of his kitchen revealed none of the ingredients required for breakfast. He'd been living off takeaways for weeks now. It was six in the morning and it was a

Sunday. His shopping options were limited. It would have to be Khan's. He changed his booze- and urine-stained clothes and set off in search of pork, eggs, bread, milk, tea, mushrooms, beans and several litres of lemonade.

Khan's was a bit of a walk so Ross set off at a brisk pace. This soon turned into a moderate-paced trot followed by a slow crawl a teenager being asked to do chores would have been proud of. What was he going to say to Alice when he got back? He hoped something appropriate would spring to mind. At the end of his road he turned left, crossed over Everest Drive, and turned right onto the High Street. In the distance he could see the welcoming lights of Khan's. A few cars drove along the road. The pavement was absent of pedestrians. As he approached Khan's the silence was broken by a loud ringing noise coming from a public phone box. Ross wondered who on earth would be ringing a public phone box on a deserted street on a Sunday morning. He walked past the phone box, stopped, turned around, stepped into the phone box and picked up the receiver.

'Hello X.'

'Stay there and I'll come and get you. I'm in a black Sierra. If anyone else approaches you, run away as fast as you can.'

The phone went dead. Why did all his conversations with Mr X end up like this? Thirty seconds later a black Ford Sierra tore around the corner and screeched to a halt.

'No time to discuss. Get in the back and hide under the blanket.'

'Is hello or good morning too much to ask?'

****

Alice was also having strange dreams. The Koreans she was engaged in a drinking contest with collapsed one after another onto the floor and had to be put into the recovery position until the paramedics arrived. Then she was attempting to rouse Ross from his coma for some adult fun. For some reason the next part of her dream involved lots of shouting and doors being kicked in.

When Alice woke from her dream it was to the unwelcome sight of a gang of armed police officers standing over her pointing guns in her face. She took a moment to gather her thoughts.

'Get the fuck out of here, you gun-loving fascist bastards!' she screamed.

The police maintained their position.

'And stop staring at my tits, you bunch of homos. Bet it's the first tits any of you lot have seen since your mum's when you were babies. Speaking of babies, I've seen more meat on a premature newborn baby's little finger than any of your cocks. Bet you can't get it up. Even if you did, no one would notice unless they had a microscope. Take your hands off me, you perv! Bet that made you come.'

Between them, the officers managed to restrain Alice and escort her out of the flat, into the police car and back to the station for questioning. The abuse continued the entire journey.

****

It had been a long night for Black. He'd had to escort Alison to the station and wait there while she was interviewed and released with a caution. The club hadn't pressed charges; they were just glad to be rid of her. All the fighting and arguing in the club had worked Alison into something of a frenzy. She'd been so pumped up she forgot she'd moved in with Black and had ordered the taxi back to her own flat.

When she eventually got to sleep Black was relieved to find her freezer stocked with an extra large bag of frozen peas, which he wasted no time in putting to good use. He was still sitting there, popping painkillers and nursing his groin with frozen vegetables when the doorbell rang. Black answered the door and had an envelope thrust into his hand by an anonymous leather-clad courier. He opened it up and read.

```
The police have raided your flat. Everyone from ESR under
suspicion of murder. Nowhere safe. Don't call anyone. All
phones are bugged. They don't know you're here. Stay here
until further notice and keep a low profile. Good luck. X
```

Black sat back down and replaced the ice on his groin. Unable to leave the flat until further notice. *She'll be awake soon.* He shuddered with fear.

****

'Morning Christmas, how's the investigation going? Good I hope?'

'Excellent, sir,' lied Christmas.

His bloodshot eyes and bin full of empty cartons, drained of fluid that had allegedly been coffee, gave away how much sleep he'd had. He took another sip from his latest cup. It tasted of pilchards. The previous cup tasted of egg.

'Well, let's have the details then,' ordered the Commissioner.

'We received an anonymous call this morning from a man claiming to know who was responsible for the murder of DI Christmas.'

'And?'

'And we managed to trace the call, sir. He was on just long enough. Brought him in a few hours ago. He's from that computer company ESR, the one that was in the news the other week.'

'Never heard of them,' the Commissioner lied. The memory of the contents of his briefcase from ESR made him shudder.

'Well, according to the informant, ESR is just the public front for a gang of assassins. He's given us names and addresses of the main suspects. The team have raided their properties this morning.'

'Have they now?'

This was turning into a nightmare for the Commissioner. ESR could ruin him at the drop of a hat if they wanted to. A DCI had been murdered though. If it came to it, he would fall on his sword.

'And what have these raids yielded, Inspector?'

That wasn't a question Christmas wanted to answer.

'Well sir, we have two arrests so far.'

'The arrests. They are the prime suspects, I take it? The residents of the properties?'

Christmas winced. 'Not as such, sir. The main suspects weren't present.'

'What? Well who have we got then?'

'Alice Houghton – we believe she's the partner of Ross Ackerman, the Head of ESR. We think she might be something to do with the sales side of the operation.'

'Think, eh. Time is of the essence, man. We need answers. Who knows where this Ackerman is by now? Is she being interrogated?'

'Oh yes, sir. She's not being terribly co-operative though.'

'Well lean on her, man. Never mind good cop, bad cop. I want bad cop, bad cop. Scare the hell out of her. She'll crack, they all do. Just got to push the right buttons, that's all.'

'Yes, sir.'

Christmas thought of the progress of their interviews with Alice so far. He dreaded the thought of having to play the tapes in court.

'Tell you what, why don't I have a try?'

'Sir?'

'I'll lead the interview, Inspector; show you how it's done eh.'

'Er the thing is, sir, I think ...'

'Are you the Commissioner now?'

'No, sir.'

'Right, then leave the thinking to me. I'll be back in a jiffy.'

****

The Commissioner strolled nonchalantly into the interview room, sat on the table and looked down at Alice. He'd show them how it was done; the old school way, none of this pussyfooting about rubbish.

'Right Houghton, tell me where Ackerman is right now or you're going to the big house for perverting the course of justice. Pretty girl like you,' the Commissioner said, pausing the tape recorder as he ran his fingers through Alice's hair, 'they'll pass you around like candy. I'll tell them you're a snitch. By the time you get out you'll have had sex with more women than George Best.'

It had been a good performance; he was proud of it. Alice leaned towards the Commissioner and sniffed at the air.

'I can smell come. Did you just jizz in your pants when you were making that little speech? Probably the nearest you've ever been to a woman without having to hand over a massive wad of cash.'

'Listen to me!' the Commissioner bellowed. 'If you don't start talking you're going down.'

'You'd know all about going down, wouldn't you, plod? Bet you went to public school. Have to fag for the older boys, did you? You loved it; your mouth was never your own. The only one who's going on trial here is you, for shagging that herd of goats down the farm when your wife refused to drink two bottles of gin and stick a peg on her nose so you could get your end away.'

The Commissioner took a moment to gather his thoughts in the face of the tsunami of abuse. He lit a cigarette, inhaled the smoke and considered his interview technique. Arrogant bad cop had died on his arse; it was the turn of concerned, caring good cop. He leaned in towards Alice and quietened his voice.

'Listen Alice, we know you're not responsible for any of this and I want to let you go, really I do. But Ross is in big trouble. He's in danger and we need to get to him right away so we can protect him. You understand that, don't you?' Alice shrugged, her face still beautiful despite the best efforts of last night's smeared make-up. 'Just tell us where he is and you can go free right now.'

Alice placed her head in her hands and thought hard about the proposition put to her. A difficult decision reached, she took a deep breath and looked up into the eyes of the Commissioner.

'OK, if he's in trouble I'll tell you where he is, but first there's something I need to know.'

'Yes, of course, anything,' replied the Commissioner, greedily anticipating the juicy nugget that was about to crack the case wide open.

Christmas shook his head on the other side of the two-way mirror. He knew what was coming. Sixteen officers referred for counselling.

All of them had interviewed Alice.

'Did it hurt?' she whispered.

'Sorry, I didn't quite catch that. Did you ask "Did it hurt?"?'

'Yes.'

'Did what hurt?'

'When you had the sex change operation? Did you go the whole hog and have the lot chopped off or is there still a little bit down there? Did you do it because you fantasise about cocks but you don't have the balls to be gay or is it because your knob is so small you thought you might as well be a woman because at least if you were a lezza you might have a chance of seeing some minge?'

'Where the hell is Ackerman?' the Commissioner screamed, smashing his fists against the table, his face a deep shade of beetroot.

Alice grinned. 'He's round at your house banging your wife, or at least he will be when the queue of off-duty bin men and down-and-outs who haven't had a bath for months have finished with her. Don't worry, he's taken a plank with him to strap to his back so he doesn't fall in when he's on the job.'

Veins bulging in his neck and blood pressure off the scale, the Commissioner stood up and turned to leave.

'Had enough have you, plod? I can go all day if you like. The circus called. They asked when you're going back to join the freak show cos their ticket sales are down. The clinic called; the lab results couldn't detect any sign of a penis so could you go back cos they've got a bigger microscope to have another look. Your wife called, she said "Woof, woof, woof woof woof".'

'Interview suspended until further notice. Commissioner Grange has left the room.'

The Commissioner slammed the door of the interview room in retreat and stormed off back towards the incident room where Christmas was waiting. Neither man acknowledged what had just occurred.

'What about the other one then? What information has he given up?'

Christmas fixed his grin. 'Not a lot, sir. He doesn't speak a word of English. We have an interpreter in with him but so far he hasn't responded to any known languages. He just sits there smiling. I don't think we're going to get much out of him to be honest.'

'I see. Is there the faintest possibility you might have some good news for me, Inspector?'

'Yes, sir. So far we've recovered a gun from Ackerman's flat. Ballistics are testing it now, against the bullets recovered from the DCI.'

'A gun? Good, good. Anything else?'

'Well yes. We've retrieved large amounts of evidence, sir.'

'Evidence? What sort of evidence?'

'It looks like it relates to some murders. Dates, names, locations, methods used, that sort of thing. Some trophies from the crimes as well.'

'Really?' replied the Commissioner. This was unexpected. 'How many murders are we talking about here, Inspector?'

'It's hard to say, sir; we're still sifting through the evidence. If I had to guess though, I'd say about 80 so far.'

'Eighty! Wow. Think I'd better have a sip of that coffee.'

'Er, I wouldn't if I were you, sir.'

****

Christmas watched from behind the two-way mirror as Adam sang like a canary.

'There's something you're not telling us, isn't there?' said good cop.

'I wouldn't waste your time with this one. He's all talk but he doesn't know a damn thing,' said bad cop.

'Look, I've told you everything. You'll find everything you need if you just raid Ross and Stuart's flats.'

Adam was flustered. He thought he would have been released by now.

'We did that already – except they weren't there, were they? All we got was some crazed bitch with Tourette's syndrome and an Asian mute with some missing fingers and a lazy eye. Neither of them has told us a goddamn thing.'

'What? They should have been there. They were supposed to be there.'

'So where are they then?'

'Stuart will know where Ross is. They must be together somewhere. Did you get the others? The Korean guy you're holding is called Lo Rum. All his relatives work for ESR. They're all computer programmers. Most of them live at the ESR building. You have raided that, haven't you?'

Christmas ran out of the observation room and ordered the raid on ESR. Why hadn't he done that already? Sleep deprivation was impairing his judgement. Something wasn't right with this whole business. He wondered if Adam was a crank. He was falling over himself to give them information. Preliminary checks on the suspects revealed nothing that would suggest any of them were criminal masterminds. What did he mean they were supposed to be there? He needed more caffeine.

A junior officer accosted him in the hallway and handed him a couple of notes. They'd found a clue in the flat of Davies that might shed light on his whereabouts. The second note confirmed the gun that killed the DCI was a match to the one found in Ross' flat. Christmas marched into the nearest office and picked up the phone.

'Get me the Commissioner.'

****

'Where are we going?' Ross asked.

'Out of London. I can't tell you where, but it's safe to say a long way from here.'

'Nobody likes a nice drive more than me but can we do this another time? I had quite an important night last night and I need to get back now, thanks.'

Mr X frowned. Ross wasn't firing on all cylinders. Half a cylinder would be an improvement.

'You don't seem to be quite grasping the seriousness of the situation here. You are wanted on suspicion of murdering a DCI. Every policeman in London is looking for you.'

'Looking for me? Why?'

'Not just you. All of ESR. Someone has set you up. The police have raided your flat, Stuart's flat, and they've probably raided ESR too.'

Ross yawned. His body was crying out for salted meat and sugary fluid. 'This is super interesting and that but can you just drop me back now? I need to see Alice. Got to talk to her about last night.'

Mr X sighed. It was like trying to have a conversation with a toddler. Everything had to be repeated and nothing was taken in until you pressed the right button.

'Alice is under arrest, Ross. The police have her. You might never see her again.'

Slowly the words entered Ross' ears and rolled around his head a few times until his brain seized them and converted them into thoughts. Through a desert of dehydration, the penny rolled on and on until it found the slot. Then it dropped.

'We've got to save her. I need her. I mean, I need to talk to her.'

'I'll save her, I promise. There's nothing we can do for them now though. We can't just storm the police station.'

'Why not? I'll do it. Let's go.'

'Admirable courage, but foolhardy. We can't very well help them if we get arrested, can we? First thing we need to do is reach safety. After that we regroup and then we play the game my way.'

'They've got Stuart as well?'

Earlier conversations were now being granted access to Ross' brain.

'Yes. I already told you they raided his flat the same time they did yours.'

'But Stuart wouldn't have been there. It's his big day today.'

Ross almost came through the back of Mr X's seat as the car screeched to a halt.

'What are you talking about? That's next week,' snapped Mr X.

'No, it's today. They had to bring it forward a week. The stupid venue double booked them with a Jehovah's Witness convention so they had to change the date.'

With acute urgency, Mr X pressed a few buttons on his radio and listened.

'All in position now, sir. We've got the place surrounded. Nobody can get out.'

'Good,' said another voice. 'Now remember this is an undercover operation so I want you all to keep a low profile and blend in. There are over one thousand civilians inside but our job is to bring Stuart Davies out safe and in one piece. Nice and professional, boys. Let's go.'

Mr X switched the radio off, put the car into gear and drove off. The two exchanged no words. It had only been there for the briefest of seconds but Ross had seen it. The rage in his eyes.

****

'You can go in now,' said the officer posted outside the interview room. 'Might want your notebook though. Talk the head off you, this one will.'

The solicitor ignored the sarcastic tone in the man's voice and entered the room. He took his seat and explained to his client the predicament he faced. He also explained how several of his relatives had also been arrested, and the rest were about to be raided. Lo remained silent. A quiet noise floated through the room and settled in the brain of the solicitor. The noise formed words. It sounded like 'They will fight to the death,' spoken in perfect English. It was unclear where the noise had come from other than it had not been from Lo's mouth. He was known not to speak any English.

'You should know,' said the solicitor, 'that I'm not a duty solicitor. I've been appointed by a mutual acquaintance. He sends his regards and has asked me to pass on a message to you.'

Lo raised his eyebrows.

'Whatever it takes I promise to get you off. I never give up on a friend.' Lo was impressed. The man spoke Korean very well indeed. 'A token of my employer's sincerity.'

The solicitor reached into his briefcase, retrieved a jar and handed it to his client. Lo Rum held the jar in his hands, moisture collecting in his eyes. It had been many years since he had last seen them. They were withered, decayed and had seen better days but there was no mistaking them. They were definitely his fingers.

'Tell them to stop the raid,' he said.

****

Constable Smith of the riot police was getting tetchy. He hated delays. All ready to go he was, adrenalin pumping through his veins. There were heads that needed busting and he was just the man for the job. Why hadn't the order been given? Inside the building an angry horde of Koreans hung out of the windows, waving machetes and screaming impressive war cries. They looked up for a fight. The riot police had had a few false alarms of late but this had the makings of a really good dust-up.

The squad car pulled up outside the ESR building. Christmas exited the car and opened the back door for Lo to step out. Christmas took a seat on the bonnet of the car and folded his arms. He watched as Rum walked alone to the entrance of the building. A barricade of tables and chairs inside the doorway was moved aside and Lo was dragged in by many arms. Minutes passed in silence. Then the door opened and out came Lo, followed by a long line of well-behaved, unarmed Koreans. Smith was fuming. Not a single voice of dissent was raised as they obediently filed into the waiting police vans.

'Search the rest of the building,' ordered Christmas.

Smith and his colleagues didn't need a second invitation. They returned moments later carrying a comatose Kevin and a man who appeared to be attempting suicide by laughing himself to death. It was Igneous. In The Security Guard's Definitive Guide To Protecting Your Employer's Life And Property, the chapter on The Most Appropriate Preparation Methods For Police Raids did not include the following advice: *consume an industrial quantity of magic mushrooms*. For some reason Igneous had assumed it had.

Alice's friends went less quietly. The Rums waiting in the vans could hear their screams. Some of their words were unfamiliar to the Rums. They weren't included in the syllabus for GCSE English.

****

For as long as Stuart could remember he'd had a dream. He wanted to embrace and share his passion with like-minded individuals from all over the world in an extravaganza of love and devotion. He'd been planning it for years. The meteoric rise of ESR meant he now had the funds to make his dream a reality.

One More Thing was the realisation of that dream. Everything had been going swimmingly until, out of the blue, the conference centre called and told him they'd double-booked him with a Jehovah's Witness convention and could he please take the previous weekend instead. He'd been rushing round like a blue-arsed fly all week.

'Good morning, gentleman. Welcome to One More Thing. Here is your programme for the day. It contains all the different sessions and a map of the venue. Love the outfit by the way; it looks like you slept in that raincoat.'

DI Christmas smiled at the compliment. It was his personal raincoat.

'Now, I need to draw your attention to some special highlights of the day,' continued the enthusiastic steward. 'The competitions for Best One More Thing Impression, Most Dishevelled Raincoat and Most Confused Facial Expression Whilst Questioning a Suspect will be happening right throughout the day but the results won't be announced until the grand awards ceremony at four. That's when there will also be a live lookalike contest and the much anticipated fans' favourite episode. I almost forgot, please help yourself to these; we've been given special dispensation to smoke them indoors. There are plenty of ashtrays dotted around but feel free to use your coat pockets or your own hair.'

The steward handed Christmas and his fellow undercover police officers each a handful of enormous Cuban cigars and a lighter. At great expense Stuart had negotiated a relaxation of the building's no smoking regulations. All of the building's fitted smoke alarms had been dismantled. Stuart had signed all manner of legal disclaimers drawn up by the conference centre's lawyers. As luck would have it, the Chief Fire Officer for the building had won an all-expenses paid fortnight's holiday for four to the Bahamas. He didn't even realise he'd entered a competition for one.

The detectives branched out into the main exhibition area and tried to look inconspicuous. DI Christmas had never seen anything like it. Every person he saw was dressed like Columbo and doing a Columbo impression. There were tall Columbos, short Columbos, black Columbos, Chinese Columbos and female Columbos. The air was thick with cigar smoke.

It wasn't going to be easy for the detectives to find their target. Everyone looked like Columbo. Christmas needed a plan. Scanning the horizon, he drummed his fingers on top of his head and concentrated. When he emerged from his thoughts he noticed a small group of Columbos had formed in front of him and were watching his every move. They erupted in spontaneous applause.

'That was amazing.'

'He's a dead cert to win the competition.'

'It's like Peter Falk was in the room with us.'

'Let me shake you by the hand. Best Columbo impression I've ever seen,' said a Mexican Columbo, grabbing Christmas' hand and almost

253

removing his arm from its socket with the vigour of his handshake.

A sheepish Christmas put his finger to the side of his forehead then pointed in the direction of the assembled Columbos in acknowledgement. Applause erupted again.

It took some time for them to locate Stuart. Navigating around the conference centre was a dangerous exercise. Delegates were constantly bumping into each other and falling over as a result of their impromptu displays of absent-mindedness. Christmas also kept losing his undercover team. The trouble was they looked like Columbo and so did everyone else so distinguishing his detectives from all the other people wasn't easy because they all looked like Columbo. The situation resolved itself and they tracked Stuart down to the judging panel of the One More Thing competition.

****

'Well that's me about done, I think. Yep, so sorry to have bothered you again, sir. You have yourself a good night. Wait a minute, where is my head at? There was just one more thing, sir, if you could spare a moment.'

'Thank you, contestant number 37. Judges?'

'Very good voice. I liked your accent and I very much enjoyed the "Where is my head at?" ad lib. Good work and well done to you.'

'A commendable effort,' added the second judge, 'but I think your notebook work could do with a bit more practice. You found it too quickly for my liking.'

'And our head judge?'

'I agree that your accent is very good and I liked your script, but your coat isn't dishevelled enough and you need to do more work on your bumbling. It was all a little bit too polished for me,' Stuart finished. He was having the time of his life.

Christmas had seen enough. He attempted to approach Stuart unobtrusively. 'Excuse me, sir,' he whispered in Stuart's ear, 'could I have a word with you in private? It's a bit erm ... well, delicate.' He flashed his badge at Stuart.

'Oh now this is very good,' Stuart boomed. 'A trademark unexpected entrance, an almost apologetic opening approach. Your accent is rubbish but everything else is top draw. Excellent use of props with the police badge and your coat is an absolute disgrace. First-rate bumbling. You're a real contender for first prize.'

Christmas wanted to leave now. Being continually praised for a Columbo impression that he wasn't doing was making him paranoid. He gestured to the others for assistance. It was all very confusing. Columbos appeared at the side of Columbo to arrest Columbo while a crowd of Columbos looked on. As Stuart was marched out of the room he continued to praise the police for their original and realistic routine. Not until he was being booked in at the station and thrown into a cell did the thought occur to him that something might not be quite right.

****

Christmas was on his way back from arresting Stuart when he got the message. He proceeded to the canal, where he was met by the Commissioner.

'Let's hope this is a false alarm,' said the Commissioner.

A more thorough search of Ross' flat had recovered a watch matching a description of the one Major was known to possess, and a map indicating a canal that was of some interest to Ross. The police had put two and two together. It was their job to do that sort of thing. Divers had been dispatched to the scene.

A diver emerged from the murky waters, gesticulating towards an area of interest.

'They've found something.'

Please, not Major. Anyone but Major, thought Christmas.

It took several divers to lift the discovery to the water's surface and then onto the bank. It was a large bundle wrapped in a black tarpaulin. Christmas and the Commissioner watched as the forensics team moved in. Taking care to preserve the evidence, they untied the cover and unwrapped the package.

For a few moments nobody said anything. It took many seconds for their brains to comprehend what their eyes were telling them was there. Then the reactions came. Some stayed rooted to the spot, unable to move. Others turned away. Christmas vomited. He wasn't the only one. The air turned blue with profanities. There were threats of violent acts of revenge. Nobody was reprimanded. There was no manual, no standard operating procedure for a situation like this. The Commissioner was in shock. Christmas put his arm around him. It was a tender act of kindness from a man possessing no social skills. The Commissioner let Christmas help him back to the squad car.

'I can tie things up here, sir,' Christmas said, patting him on the shoulder.

The Commissioner stared ahead blankly in silence, his face ashen as the car drove him away.

Years of training took hold, giving Christmas the strength to carry on. *They need you. He needs you.* There were procedures to follow. Things that needed to be done if it went to court. He took a deep breath and took charge. Christmas took great care in examining the body. He retrieved a wallet from the trouser pocket. It was Major's.

'Goodbye old friend,' he said, placing his hand on the shoulder of the body. He tried not to look at the trotters that been surgically attached to the ends of Major's arms and legs to replace his severed hands and feet. The face of the pig's head stitched onto Major's neck stared back at Christmas. It was smiling.

Chapter 21
Amy Jones

Amy Jones was born on the first of May 1960. She grew up as the only child in a wealthy middle class family, her father a doctor, her mother an osteopath. The young Amy was doted on by her parents. Exotic holidays abroad, weekends at the seaside, trips to the zoo and all the time she was never once left to be cared for by anyone other than her mother and father. As is often the case with children who get so much of their parents' time, Amy was spoilt, and it wasn't long before she discovered she could wrap her parents around her little finger.

Amy was a bright girl. She attended St Mary's Academy for Young Ladies, a private Catholic school for girls, where she soon established herself as the leading student in her year, finishing top of her class in every subject apart from physical education, which she had no real interest in. After a quiet start, Amy became popular among the other girls after her natural stubbornness revealed itself in the form of a strong rebellious streak against the many strict rules in force at St Mary's. Her disputes with the school authorities led to numerous detentions, lines and other punishments.

Her parents were unimpressed. Particularly when they were called in to hear how Amy had been the ringleader of a Year 8 strike. The whole year had refused to learn anything until their demands were met. These included an immediate revoking of the ban on confectionery products and make-up, an improvement in conditions for Alan, the school cat, and more liberal use of 'Hail Marys' and 'Our Fathers' for minor rules infringements. Amy was suspended for a week.

When she was 14 years old Amy's charmed life took a darker turn. She contracted glandular fever and was ill for four months. It was a most difficult time for Amy's parents. They nursed her through the whole ordeal. The emotional strain of having to watch their beloved child so weak and fragile broke their hearts. Amy didn't leave her bedroom for two months. Slowly, she regained enough strength to sit up, and eat and drink unaided. In time, she grew stronger as her body fought the virus, and her parents thanked God that the life they had created, and had been forced to watch slipping away from them, was now returning to their little girl.

Amy prayed that she could once again have the health she now knew she had so taken for granted. Her dreams were filled with the mundane, boring, everyday chores that she would now give anything to have the strength to carry out if her body would just let her. Health is wasted on the healthy, she discovered at a young age. Towards the end of the fourth month of the illness Amy began to feel a little better. Then one day she went to bed and slept for 36 hours. When she woke up she felt something that had been missing for so long she had forgotten what it felt like. Energy. Wonderful, wonderful energy. She jumped out of bed, screamed in delight, ran down the stairs and flew into her parents' arms. She had some making up to do.

Amy returned to school and attacked her studies with a determination and vigour her teachers had never seen before. They thought she'd been trying before but now they could see she'd just been coasting. Four months of missed studies were caught up in two weeks. She wasn't hanging about. Amy also tried out for, and made it onto, every sports team the school had. She'd never seen the point in sports before. Now she knew, and could feel it in her soul, in a way none of the other girls ever could. Sport was a celebration, a thanks to God for the beautiful gift of health and energy. Amy was an automatic choice for captain on every team. Her energy levels, aggression and sheer competitive spirit made her team mates scared to fail. Opponents were swept aside, beaten before they began.

As she entered her final year of school Amy was elected, unopposed, as Head Girl. She ran a tight ship. Anyone who wasn't giving their all was reported to the Head, and that was just the teachers. They got off lightly compared to the students. She worked hard, she played hard and she dragged the school with her, whether they liked it or not. St Mary's Year 11 won the local, regional and national finals for netball, hockey, lacrosse, tennis and athletics. The school recorded its highest ever grade average at O level, finishing in the top five for the whole of the UK. By this time the headmistress had been relegated to mere figurehead status. Amy was running the show. When she requested an end of year disco for the school, complete with a DJ and invitations sent to all the boys in Year 11 at the nearby comprehensive, the school board and the PTA considered the request and duly obliged. Amy wasn't interested in boys, but most of the other girls were and they deserved a reward for all their hard work. She would go along and have a laugh and a dance with her friends but she wasn't going to bat her eyelids and go all gooey over some boy.

The night of the disco arrived and the girls of St Mary's were buzzing with excitement. Some had already arranged dates with the invited boys. Others arrived in a big gang, their final time together before they would go their separate ways. Amy hadn't gone to the effort that some of the girls had but she still had standards; she was Head Girl after all.

The DJ did his best but, as with all teenage parties, he was fighting a losing battle to start with. Boys lined one side of the dance floor, girls the other. The girls were waiting for the boys to come over and ask them to dance. The boys were all looking at each other and wondering who was going to be the brave one to cross no man's land and risk looking a fool in front of everyone. Amy wasn't interested in any of that; she was happy chatting to her friends and trying to cajole a few of them into dancing. She wasn't having the influence over them she usually did; there were boys present. *They'll soon get bored looking at these boys*, she thought to herself, *and then we can all have a nice dance.*

In the absence of much else to do whilst she waited for her friends to stop looking at the boys, Amy allowed herself a quick look at the boys. She felt sorry for the girls who would end up with some of these rogues, particularly that one ... look at his nose. Two-thirds of the way along the line something odd happened to her neck. It had stopped moving to the left. She tried moving it to the right. It wouldn't budge. She was staring at a boy.

Amy Jones, stop staring at that boy this instant. Her head wasn't listening. It was too busy staring at the boy. She felt very hot all of a sudden; her heart was beating like crazy. What was wrong with her? The boy was staring back. They were both staring at each other. *Oh my God, he's coming over here. Say no if he asks you to dance. Just say no.*

'Excuse me, would you care to dance?' the boy asked.

'I'd love to,' replied Amy.

What the hell was that? Stop dancing with this boy this instant and stop giggling like a soppy schoolgirl!

The other boys and girls breathed a sigh of relief and it wasn't long before the dance floor was full of couples. The rest of the evening was a blur to Amy. The boy spoke to her, she spoke back. Their eyes never left each other. For some strange reason, after what felt like a few minutes, the evening was over. The boy asked her for a kiss and, despite feeling certain she had said no, she flung her arms around his neck and kissed him. When it came time to leave something unthinkable became apparent to her. Amy was in love. She couldn't bear to be without him for a single second and would rather die than not see him again. They agreed to see each other the next day and Amy returned home in the car with her father, in floods of tears. She didn't sleep a wink. She met the boy the next day and they spent the whole wonderful day together. They soon became inseparable.

It wasn't long before Amy's parents demanded to meet this amazing boy their daughter never stopped talking about. Her father knew this day would come but he thought he had a few years left yet before she would be bringing boys home. As they sat, making small talk over dinner, Amy's father saw how the boy was looking at her, saw his eyes and what was in them. It wasn't lust, which was what he was expecting to see. It was love. It was caring. He also saw a protective ferocity in the young man's eyes that made him both relieved and profoundly jealous. This young man would kill anyone who tried to hurt her with his bare hands. He knew he'd lost her to this boy.

****

Five years later Amy stood at the front of the church and declared her love for the young man to the world. As the vicar pronounced them husband and wife, Amy's parents cried with joy and pride. Her father hugged her tight for the final time before they signed the wedding certificate.

'Congratulations, Mrs Ackerman. I hope you'll be very happy together.'

Chapter 22
Wanted

It was mid-afternoon when the black Ford Sierra came to a stop in a lay-by at the side of a wide, deserted road. There was no sign of life. No cars, no signposts, no buildings, no people.

'We're here,' said Mr X, squeezing his massive frame out of the car. He stretched his arms and legs and took in a deep lungful of air.

It had been a long drive. The previous evening's prodigious alcohol consumption and small amount of sleep had caught up with Ross and he had soon fallen into a deep slumber. He emerged in a sleepy daze from the car and performed a series of exaggerated stretches. Something was bothering him but his waking senses had yet to specify the source of the problem.

Mr X collected some things from the boot of the car and moved towards Ross, a pair of dark blue workman's overalls clutched in his large outstretched hand. Mr X had already changed into another, much larger, pair of overalls. Ross took the overalls and looked blankly at him. His senses were screaming.

'What's with the overalls?' he asked.

'We walk from here. It's just around the corner but we have to put these on first.'

Ross looked at the overalls and turned them over. The words Creekmoor Sewage Plant were printed in large white letters on the back of the overalls. Upon reading these words a large drawbridge was lowered in Ross' brain and a massive steel portcullis raised. The sensory neurons responsible for smell flew across the drawbridge at light speed screaming *What's wrong with you? Couldn't you hear us? We've been banging on that door for ages! It's hell out there.* A small war subsequently broke out between the neurons and Ross' central nervous system. As the neurons advanced on his brain, Ross was unable to control the feeling of nausea that accompanied the return of his nasal function at a heightened level. He doubled up and was sick on the grass verge. Mr X rushed to his aid. He gave Ross a towel and smeared some pungent-smelling cream under his nostrils.

'I'm sorry, I should have given that to you straight away. I thought you must have had a cold or something because you didn't seem to notice the smell.'

Ross straightened himself and wiped his mouth with the towel. His mouth and stomach felt like they'd just been forced to eat a doner kebab whilst sober. He felt rougher than Godzilla's ballbag.

'Please tell me what's going on,' pleaded Ross.

'I'll tell you everything, but first you have to put these on,' said Mr X, picking the overalls off the floor and handing them to Ross.

Reluctantly, Ross put the overalls on.

'You'll feel better when we get inside. You can't smell it then. And try not to breathe too much either. It makes your mouth taste of shit.'

Ross wasn't sure how he was supposed to breathe less than the required amount but he tried his best to follow the advice. Mr X strolled down the road, beckoning Ross to follow. When Ross caught him up, he began to explain.

'The reason we are here, in this godforsaken crap hole in the middle of nowhere,' he began, 'is for a meeting.'

'A meeting with who?' asked Ross, confused.

'A meeting with some acquaintances who might be able to help people like us.'

'People like us?'

'People like us, Ross. People who need to get the hell out of the UK fast and can't just pop down the road to the nearest travel agents. No, what we need, my friend, is professional assistance from what you might call a non-traditional source.'

Ross listened intently, understanding everything except the words. He was getting a nasty sensation in his stomach, and it wasn't just the taste of faeces.

'You're going to have to help me with this one, X. Why are we at a sewage plant?'

Ross thought it a reasonable question to ask. He had a strong suspicion he wasn't going to like the answer.

'The people who own this sewage plant provide a range of hard-to-access services for desperate criminals such as ourselves.'

'Why would they do that?'

'It could be because they're good Samaritans who want to help out their fellow man in their hour of need – or it could be because they're a bunch of crooks who run a lucrative people smuggling business, amongst many other illegal activities, fronted by a sewage and water treatment plant.'

'Do you mean this isn't a real sewage plant?' Ross asked, with ever-decreasing comprehension of what was going on.

'Wipe that cream away from under your nose, take some nice deep breaths and then tell me you're not convinced there are industrial quantities of untreated excrement very near to where you're standing. It's real alright. Around that corner is the Creekmoor sewage plant. Ranked fifth out of ten in the UK sewage plant league tables. It's run with just enough efficiency to avoid being investigated by Ofwat for poor standards, and just enough negligence to avoid inspections by Ofwat for best practice. The owners don't want any unnecessary attention, you see.'

'Who are the owners?'

Mr X frowned and tried to change the subject. 'Bet you got a shock when you breathed that air in, eh.'

Ross wasn't falling for it. 'Who are the owners?' he repeated.

Mr X sighed. 'The Mafia.'

Ross stopped, frozen to the spot. For a few seconds his bowels forgot how to work and he came very close to doing something he hadn't done since he was a toddler.

'The Mafia? The goddamn Mafia? You're supposed to be helping me escape, not getting me killed. Are you serious? You're taking me to see the Italian Mafia?'

'Not the Italian Mafia, Ross, no. I'm not that crazy. They're one of the lesser Mafias. Real specialists though. Great at smuggling. Got it down to a fine art, they have.'

'Italian American Mafia?'

'No.'

'Columbian Mafia?'

'Nope.'

'Then who?'

Mr X paused. 'Belgian Mafia.'

Ross entered the words Belgian Mafia into the box in his brain and hit the search button. It returned zero results.

'Belgian Mafia? Are you winding me up?' He rubbed his face with his hands, trying to comprehend this new information.

A solitary song thrush swooped down from the sky, landed on the Ford Sierra and prepared to break the eerie silence with exquisite birdsong. It cleared its throat, took a deep breath and promptly keeled over and died of asphyxiation.

'I'm sorry, but I'm struggling to take this in,' Ross continued. 'Are you telling me that the Belgian Mafia run their operations from an efficiently run sewage plant in ... in wherever the hell we are?'

'Not to be underestimated, your Belgian Mafia. So you've never heard of them. What does that tell you, eh?'

'That they're a poor man's Cosa Nostra?'

'Poor man's? You're joking. These boys are expensive. I could get the Italians for half the price but where would that get us, eh? Probably both drowned in pasta sauce for humming the Godfather theme, that's where. The reason you've never heard of our soon-to-be best friends, Ross, is because they never get bloody caught, that's why. *You* may not have heard of them but in the underworld these guys are legends. There's nothing they can't smuggle. And when you're wanted for multiple murders you need specialist smugglers to get you the hell away and keep you hidden. That's why we're here. Why do you think Belgian chocolate's so expensive? Ninety per cent of it passes through these guys' hands. They're coining it in.'

Mr X stopped walking. He looked to his left. There was a narrow gap between the lines of dense mature trees at the side of the road. Ross followed his gaze and understood that this was to be their destination. He squinted at the gap in the trees and could just make out a huge metal gate at the end of a well-concealed path. He thought of all the welcoming scenes he would like to feast his eyes on at this moment. None of them included a crappy path squeezed between some trees next to a sewage plant in the middle of nowhere. He took a deep breath and stepped onto the path. Mr X put his arm across Ross' chest and stepped in front of him.

'Not so fast. It's best if I take it from here. Follow my lead and don't say a word unless they ask you a question. The Belgians are not like the Italians; they only use violence as a last resort. Don't be under any illusions though; these boys can be a right bunch of nasty bastards when they want to be. Keep your mouth shut, let me do all the talking and for God's sake don't make any jokes about chocolate, waffles or the European Union. With a bit of luck, in a few hours time we'll both be on our way to freedom. If things don't go so well though, we'll both be dead in about ten minutes.'

Ross shuddered. It was too late to turn back now. In his head he started to say the Lord's Prayer as he walked after Mr X towards the gap in the trees.

'Before we go in, there's just one thing I want to know. If this might be my last few minutes of life, I wouldn't mind knowing the real name of the person that's about to get me killed.'

'You want to know my name?'

'Yes.'

'It could get you killed.'

'I'll take that chance.'

'Very well. It's ...'

Chapter 23
War

Ross hated boats. If it was up to him he'd build gigantic bridges to link up all the continents. His current residence was aboard a cargo ship containing luxury chocolate products. The ship, the chocolate, and the company that made it were all owned by the Belgian Mafia, as were the customs officers at the port where they would soon be docking.

Ross looked through the contents of his bag to take his mind off the unpleasant gurgling sensations in his stomach. The bag contained everything he needed for his new life, until such a time as he could return to his old one. The photographs on the passport and driving licence of Jean-Marc Chivre bore an uncanny resemblance to Ross. The bag also contained a new birth certificate, employment history with references, a full set of Belgian academic qualifications, as well as a complete family tree. He was married to Justine and owned a small working farm that they ran with Jean-Marc's uncle, a large-framed gentleman whose appearance was strikingly similar to Mr X.

Ross fantasised about dry land and eating nothing more exciting than bread. He never wanted to drink alcohol again. His poor stomach had taken an almighty hiding since yesterday. It wasn't helped by the overpowering smell of hot waffles emanating from somewhere on the boat. The Belgian who kept popping his head in stunk of B.O. He pointed it out to Mr X but he said he couldn't smell anything. Mr X didn't smell too clever either for that matter; maybe that was why he didn't notice. The room they were in smelled funny as well. It had an ensuite bathroom. Ross had showered four times already because of the terrible stench coming off him but the bathroom was making him feel sick because of its putrid smell. The shampoo, the soap, the water and the towels all had a nasty, pungent aroma. Everything stunk. What the hell was going on? Inside his body

Ross' olfactory neurons advanced on his central nervous system. Neither side was backing down.

****

The intermediary watched the black Mercedes pull into level seven of the multi-storey car park and stop in the designated space. A minute passed before it flashed its lights three times. Another minute passed. The intermediary flashed his torch seven times. Thirty seconds passed. The car flashed its lights nine times. The elaborate sequence complete, the intermediary wandered over to the car and took his place in the passenger seat. He showed a piece of paper containing a six digit code to Number Three before handing him a briefcase. He then ate the paper containing the combination to the case.

'Everything you need is in there. All the names, addresses, numbers and photos of The Medics and The Gang. I've included The Pugilists as well for good measure. We don't want to target them but you need to know who they are so we don't take out our own partners. Keep me up to speed with your progress. I'll be contactable around the clock from now on using one of the safe numbers. If you need me to do anything just say the word.'

He wasn't enjoying this encounter. The Boss Killers were ready for murder at a moment's notice at the best of times. During wartime you could end up getting killed just by being in the same county as them. He was relieved it was coming to this. The other gangs were no match for The Boss Killers when it came to war. There was no way they had the intelligence on The Boss Killers that he had on them.

'Thanks. We should be fine though. The boys have been waiting a while to get stuck into that lot.'

The intermediary nodded. This would be a good time to leave.

'Could have done with this a week ago though,' Number Three said, tapping the case.

'Come again?'

'After our meeting I'm due to meet The Boss Killers to hand out the jobs and give a bit of a rousing speech to send them on their way in high spirits.' Number Three paused, turned towards the intermediary and looked him right in the eye. 'So far six have called in sick. From hospital. Five more have gone AWOL. Not the best of starts, is it? Healthy lads don't normally get struck down by meningitis and rabies, do they?'

The intermediary swallowed hard. The war had begun.

****

Stuart was in a desperate state. He hadn't slept a wink. His eyes were red and puffy from crying and bloodshot from lack of sleep. Stuart wouldn't ever categorise himself as brave. He had too many phobias. Pretty high up his personal fear list was being stuck in a prison cell for a crime he hadn't committed. Just above that was being stuck in a prison cell for a crime he hadn't committed, with the largest, angriest-looking tattooed man he'd ever seen. He tried not to think what the man might be in for. He was pretty confident it wasn't false accounting. The man stepped down from his top bunk and began to dress. Stuart cowered in his bed; he'd yet to remove his clothes from the previous evening. A loud bell rang out. A few seconds later, there was the sound of a key in the lock and the door opened.

'Come on, you horrible lot. Shower time. Don't keep me waiting.'

Shower time. Those two words had just been elevated to Stuart's number one all-time fear. He followed the man-mountain out of the cell, down the corridor and into another corridor. He tried not to look around. He could feel the eyes of the other prisoners on him. He risked a glance. Some stared. Others smiled, and not in a welcoming sense, Stuart thought. A few blew kisses and made indecent hand gestures towards him. His heart raced. His hands shook. There was just no way he was ever going to make it in prison.

They arrived at the shower block. Suggesting he didn't fancy a shower probably wasn't going to cut any ice. Ten prisoners, including Stuart, were escorted into the shower block by two prison officers.

Stuart's pulse raced as he watched the other prisoners strip. There was no escape. He was just going to have to grin and bear it. He took his clothes off and walked towards the furthest shower. If he had to do it, this would go down as the fastest shower in history. In seconds it started. Whispers. Sniggers. He heard the words 'fat' and 'arse' several times. A muscular man walked towards him. The man was smiling. It wasn't the only indication he was happy. He stood before Stuart, stretched his arm out in front of Stuart's face and opened his clenched hand.

'Oops. I seem to have dropped my soap. Could you be a pal and get it for me?'

Stuart was so gripped by fear he couldn't move. What happened next was both fast and confusing. The would-be rapist felt a sudden, urgent need to test the strength of the wall by hurling his entire body at it. He was encouraged to do so by an enormous hairy fist. It belonged to Stuart's cellmate and new best friend. A second later the showering continued in total silence. Neither the prison guards nor the other prisoners appeared to have witnessed the incident. Stuart was invisible. He dried himself, dressed and returned to his cell.

Shortly afterwards he was ordered to take breakfast. After breakfast, he returned to his cell. Nobody had looked at him once. Later that morning his cell was unlocked.

'Follow me,' ordered his giant cellmate.

Stuart wasn't about to argue. A few minutes later, they arrived at a cell in an isolated part of the prison. They entered the cell and were greeted by an elderly gentleman.

'My name is Hill, Don Hill. Most people call me gov or sir,' said the old man. His face was covered in scars. 'I run this prison. The governor thinks he does but he's in a minority of one.'

Stuart stood to attention and tried to look respectful.

'I don't normally see new faces but you're a special case. You should know that you are now under my protection.'

Stuart was confused. His new policy of displaying zero facial expressions was in danger of being broken. He'd already struggled to hide his amazement at the size and luxury of Hill's cell. It was marginally smaller than Stuart's flat.

'That means no one in here can touch you. Willie here will see to that,' Hill said, gesturing towards Stuart's new best friend. Stuart didn't have him down as a Willie. 'I can't move you to a bigger cell just yet but if you need anything at all you've only to ask. This isn't for the good of my health, mind; I haven't gone soft if that's what you're thinking. You've got wealthy friends on the outside, Stuart. We're being paid top whack to look after you.'

Confusion remained in Stuart's brain for a few more seconds before it was elbowed aside by realisation. He had a strong feeling that his mystery benefactor was known to the world by a single consonant near the end of the alphabet.

****

Alice was having her own introduction to prison life. Unlike Stuart, she hadn't spent her first night crying. Other people might do tears, but not Alice. The police transporting her to the prison, the prison staff and the governor had all encountered at first hand her colourful use of the English language and seemingly infinite catalogue of profanities. Alice was allocated a single cell.

The combination of her stunning good looks and relentless aggression towards the prison authorities made her an instant hit with the other inmates. When they discovered she was charged with murdering a policeman, removing his head, feet and hands and replacing them with those of a pig, her status could not have been any higher. Alice was wary of the other women though. She knew what went on in prisons. It would be a cold day in hell before she became anyone's bitch. Her paranoia about this eventuality occurring led to the unfortunate incident on her first full day that cemented her soon-to-be legendary status.

Alice had watched too many prison movies. She'd convinced

herself that something was required of her to prove herself to the other prisoners and gain their acceptance. At lunchtime she picked a fight with the biggest, butchest-looking woman she could find, and clobbered her senseless. While the prison officers attempted to prize her off the unfortunate victim, Alice shared with everyone present, at record volume, her strong views on prison romances.

'Any lezza tries to touch me up I'll rip out your womb and shove it up your arse.'

It earned her a few days in solitary confinement, loss of privileges and the collective fear and awe of the entire prison. How was she to know the woman she'd just destroyed was her own private bodyguard?

****

The governor of Belmarsh prison read the incident report. The damage to the wing was considerable. He'd have to find the money from somewhere to pay for it. So much for the new table tennis table.

'What are their demands?' he asked the senior officer.

'They say they want the immediate release of their leader from solitary, reinstatement of privileges and return of his private possessions.'

'Is that it?'

'Yes, sir.'

'They've caused a full-scale riot just because of that?'

'It seems so, sir.'

'Who is the man concerned?'

The officer read from his duty list. 'A Mr Lo Rum.'

The governor shook his head. He'd had nothing but trouble from the Koreans since they were assigned to him three days ago. He'd apply to have them transferred but they'd already been through three prisons before he drew the short straw.

'What possessions are we talking about?'

'Well, erm, it seems that Mr Rum had somehow brought in, ahem, his severed fingers, sir.'

'Good God.' The governor paused. 'Give them what they want,' he said, after considering the matter for a grand total of seven seconds. 'Straight away. But tell the snitches they asked for the world and we knocked them down.'

Anything for an easy life.

****

The Commissioner had recovered from his shock at witnessing the abomination that was Major's body. Everyone from ESR who'd been arrested was charged and imprisoned. Even though they had hard evidence against just a few of them, the pressure had come down from the top. His assumption that they would all talk to save their necks wasn't working. The only thing they were giving the police was silence. All apart from Adam. The less they talked the more he talked. His ramblings were becoming less and less coherent. Somebody knew something.

The Commissioner was under tremendous pressure. The lure of the pound was too great for some and the true nature of what happened to Major had been leaked to the press. They were having a field day. The Commissioner responded by declaring war on the gangs. Every suspected gang member and criminal was hauled in. Official rules on acceptable interview techniques went out the window. As did regulations on casual beatings, stop and search, arrest warrants and raids on properties. It was war. The gangs had gone too far this time and the Commissioner intended to show them just who the biggest and baddest gang out there really was.

****

It wasn't a good time to be in a gang. The pressure coming down on them from the law was too much for some. Gang members with old scores to settle took advantage of the situation. Snitching was at an all-time high. Survival was the name of the game now. By the time the war was over there wouldn't be many left standing. Those gangs that weren't busy being beaten by the police or snitching on each other were lining up behind the members of The Council.

As a collective, The Council was a powerful organisation. It had considerable resources, expertise and experience. When they had finished tearing each other apart there would just be one gang left standing. Being a friend to the victor would bring a great many advantages to the gangs that backed the winning horse. New alliances could be forged. Small gangs could increase their power and influence overnight. If nothing else, the introduction of other gangs to the mix would ensure the destruction of The Council and the removal of some dangerous competitors. It was time to pick a side.

****

The secretary sipped her chamomile tea and took a bite out of a rather splendid Danish pastry. She was feeling pretty pleased with herself. The weeks spent planning had paid off. A blow had been struck at the heart of The Boss Killers. The Pugilists who hadn't already been decimated by Igneous were now being arrested at will by the police.

The great advantage of The Medics over the other gangs was that they were above suspicion. A few more days of strategic strikes and The Boss Killers and The Pugilists would be finished. After that, she'd shop The Gang to the police. She now had the resources to win the war. Gangs were lining up to offer their support. When it was over, she'd offer a few tasty crumbs to a select few to keep them sweet. The terms of a new alliance had already been drafted. They didn't offer prospective partners of The Medics much of a deal. The secretary didn't care. They could take it or leave it. She had bigger fish to fry. The States. That's where the big bucks were. An untapped market. After that, the world. Governments would beg for their services. All this awaited as soon as The Boss Killers had been dispatched.

The second wave of attacks was planned and ready to go. Her extensive research indicated there were 27 members of The Boss

Killers. Fewer than she'd thought. Eleven were now dead or incapacitated, and by the end of today that number would be at least 20. She was just waiting for an appointment to confirm the details. They were late.

****

The UK's Chief Medical Officer to the World Health Organisation (WHO) read the report again. It beggared belief. The Secretary of State for Defence was on his way over with his top adviser on chemical weaponry. In 48 hours, the infectious disease centre had reported incidents of rabies, meningitis and anthrax, all within a small geographical area. The initial lab tests gave a strong indication they were genetically manufactured. Somebody was deliberately infecting people with contagious fatal diseases. There was something strange about the victims as well. They were all suspected criminals. The Home Office had been notified. The Defence Secretary was going straight on from this meeting to an audience with the Prime Minister. The national alert for terrorist activity had been raised from moderate to high.

****

The hunt for Ross continued. He'd been elevated into the list of top ten most wanted British criminals. DI Christmas was heading the search for him, whilst also managing the case against those already arrested and charged. He was also doing something he knew would get right up the nose of the Commissioner. He was trying to solve the crime.

It didn't add up. None of those arrested had a criminal record, apart from the skinhead known as Igneous of course. His involvement with ESR was only recent though. There was no doubting he was capable of murder but the thing with Major and the pig was beyond the capabilities of a mindless thug like Igneous. The rest of ESR were spotless.

There were other concerns too. None of the known criminals they'd been leaning on for information had ever heard of anyone from ESR. It wasn't a code of silence thing either; they genuinely had no idea who they were. Then there was the question of motive. Christmas knew his case files inside out. Nobody from ESR appeared in any of them. They weren't under suspicion for any of the apparent accidents he was investigating. There simply wasn't a motive. The computer business was making a fortune. He'd met their business bank manager and the Fraud Squad had been through their accounts with a fine toothcomb. Apart from some large payments to a consultant they'd so far been unable to locate, it was all above board and very profitable. Evidence related to a number of suspicious deaths had been collected in the apartments of both Ross and Stuart. It dated back several years. At that point, both men were in full-time employment. Christmas had interviewed former work colleagues for both of them. Glowing references all the way. No evidence had been found of unusual financial transactions involving their accounts during the time before they formed ESR.

The only evidence they had on Ross and Stuart was what they found in their flats. That could always have been planted. He had dozens of witness statements that Ross and the others were out partying the night before. Other than that, it was just Adam's word to go on. That was starting to look about as solid as a cheap, flat-pack wardrobe. Christmas had come to the conclusion that it just wasn't possible for their prime suspects to have had anything to do with the crimes. He needed to go back to square one. His case files. Where had Major gone the day he disappeared?

****

The emergency meeting of the government's special crisis cabinet was in session. The Commissioner had been invited, as had the Chief Medical Officer to the WHO. By now they were all aware of what had happened to Major.

The Chief Medical Officer gave an update on the containment strategies in place to manage the sudden outbreaks of fatal contagious diseases. A further development had occurred since the Prime Minister's most recent update. There had been a reported incidence of the Black Death, the first for three centuries. Someone in The Medics had messed up.

The Commissioner was up next. He reported that during a two-hour period yesterday twenty-six senior members of NHS and private clinic staff had been murdered. Within the same two-hour period a further twenty-eight medical staff had suffered an apparent series of bizarre accidents and were now in a critical condition. It was also his displeasure to inform them that reported incidents of gang-rape had increased by 900 per cent in the last week. Some of the suspected perpetrators of these abhorrent crimes had themselves been murdered. He assured the Prime Minister he was doing everything within his power to restore law and order and bring those responsible to justice.

The Home Secretary followed. He reported that a recent riot by a group of Korean prisoners was unrelated to these other incidents.

****

DI Christmas had the breakthrough he was looking for. It wasn't good news. The Commissioner had been called to an urgent meeting with the Prime Minister, and there was no way on earth Christmas was going to proceed with his desired course of action without his approval.

The gangs were at war with each other. Survival was the name of the game. In return for an immediate flight out of the UK to an undisclosed location, and a guaranteed legitimate job for life with a decent income, an informant in fear for his life had given him what he was after. Major's last known whereabouts. Hurst Street. Not a good place for a police officer to be. Particularly one heading in the direction of The Badger's Eyebrows, which Christmas now knew Major was. Orders for a raid on The Badger's would have to come right from the top. The thought of it made him shudder.

He took a medicinal bottle of whisky from his desk drawer and poured a generous measure into his coffee to calm his nerves. Even with the added whisky, his coffee still tasted of cabbage.

****

Igneous woke up with a thumping headache. It was a unique experience for him. He was in a police cell. Thinking wasn't something Igneous had to do a lot of. It tended to get in the way of head-butting. He racked his brain to try and remember what had happened. A series of flashbacks shed a small amount of light on the situation. He was drinking with Kevin. There was some acid involved. Then magic mushrooms. Then some skunk. After that, he couldn't remember a thing. Wait. There was something about a fight with some coppers.

After three days in a drug-induced coma, Igneous hadn't been in the best of moods when he woke up. He put three officers in hospital before they subdued him with a potentially lethal dose of horse tranquilizer. That was two days ago. Now he was awake again. It wouldn't be long before someone would be along to check on him, and no doubt administer a further dose of drugs. He had to leave. Going out in a massive tear-up with a load of rozzas was definitely the way to go as far as Igneous was concerned, but not here. If he was going to make a last stand it would need to be somewhere where the odds were stacked more in his favour. Somewhere a man could kill another man with his bare head and the regulars would carry on drinking.

Igneous stood up. Like a builder checking for load-bearing walls, he tapped his head against each of the walls in his cell.

'That's the one.'

Head down, he stood with his back against the opposite wall and charged.

****

The Commissioner returned from his meeting with the Prime Minister somewhat chastened. He'd been told in no uncertain terms that they expected all this business with the gangs to be brought to a swift conclusion.

He'd only just made it through the door of his office before he was confronted by Christmas with the news. It was right up there in the top two things he didn't want to hear, just behind 'Say hello to my little friend'. Raiding The Badger's Eyebrows was like pressing the detonator on a bomb – from inside a factory that manufactures bombs. He closed his eyes and hoped it would all go away. The porcine features of Major's corpse glared back at him. He didn't join the police to let anyone get away with that. A few deep breaths and generous measures of whisky later, he approved the raid.

Christmas was given strict instructions by the Commissioner to take no chances with the raid. He made it clear that, when he next met the Home Secretary to provide an update on progress, if he wasn't threatened with disciplinary action for gross heavy-handedness he would be very disappointed. Christmas took him at his word. One hundred and fifty officers were dispatched to the raid. They were joined by a further one hundred specialist riot police. Fifty of the Met's finest armed officers were thrown in for good measure. Hurst Street was cordoned off at both ends to prevent reinforcements joining the enemy cause and to stop any would-be escapees. The army of law enforcement descended on The Badger's Eyebrows.

From the Commissioner first approving the raid, to them arriving en masse to the location, the whole operation had taken just under two hours. The effect of their speed and efficiency was precisely zero – to the power of zero. When they arrived on the scene The Badger's Eyebrows was ready and waiting. Windows and doors were boarded up. Several layers of heavy-duty, industrial metal fencing had been erected around the building, stretching back 50 feet from the pub walls. The place was fortified better than a presidential palace in the middle of a civil war. In between two of the rows of fencing a family of rare breed pigs trotted along, searching for swill. The symbolism wasn't lost on the officers.

The Commissioner studied the fortifications and pondered what his first move should be. *If only he'd read his copy of The Art of War by Sun Tsu, instead of just displaying it on his bookshelf to make everyone think he was a strategic genius.*

****

Jean-Marc Chivre was enjoying the quiet pace of rural life. His farm had a large stock of cattle, pigs and sheep and over 30 acres of seasonal crops. As head of the farm, he should have been rushed off his feet tending to animals and cultivating the land. An ever-increasing number of farm hands and extended family took care of this for him. So far he'd learnt how to milk a cow and been promised a sheep-shearing lesson. There wasn't much else for him to do.

Jean-Marc's uncle Albert was much busier. When he wasn't on the phone making overseas calls, in fluent English, he was greeting a steady stream of agricultural suppliers arriving at the farm. They drove agricultural vehicles and wore wellies, checked shirts and woolly jumpers that had seen better days. Some of them carried hoes. Somehow though, no matter what they did or how they dressed, there was always something of the gangster about them. It had been a stressful time for Albert Chivre. Hundreds of phone calls had been made. With the help of the Belgians he'd spent a fortune on bribing the police and dozens of criminal informants. It wasn't money well spent. All he'd got from the police was the latest on their investigations into the deaths of Major and the DCI. This amounted to squat. The police knew no more about who'd framed Ross and Stuart than he did.

The underworld was at war with each other. Getting quality information out of it was proving difficult. His usual sources were too busy dying, being arrested, or contracting fatal diseases to help him. Opportunism was rife. In such circumstances, taking a large sum of cash to give duff information to a desperate overseas organisation was not the taboo it would usually be. Guaranteeing the safety of Stuart and Alice had been his solitary successful act to date. He received regular reports back from the prisons. By all accounts, Alice was now running the women's prison and the Rums were being given a wide berth by anyone who wasn't Korean and didn't possess the surname Rum.

Another supplier arrived with news. Albert considered the financial rewards of moving into the Belgian agricultural vehicle supply market. Compared to his earlier distress on the ship, Jean-Marc was now at relative peace with the world. Since arriving on Belgian soil, hostilities between his olfactory receptor neurons and his central nervous system had been suspended and a peaceful compromise had been reached. The net result was that the neurons had agreed to stop taking the piss and return to Jean-Marc a sense of smell typical of that of a human being, instead of one belonging to a drug-detecting bloodhound.

From the safe distance of his cosy haystack, he watched Albert in conversation with yet another supplier. Jean-Marc had acquired a nice straw hat and was busy flicking a piece of hay around his mouth. All he needed was a pair of denim dungarees and a banjo to complete the look. He sat up and looked closer. Albert was animated. The news was either very good or very bad. Albert punched the air and roared in triumph. It was good news. Jean-Marc jumped off his haystack and ran towards him.

****

Inside The Badger's Eyebrows the troops prepared themselves for battle. All morning there'd been a conveyor belt of arrivals. People. Arms. Food and drink. Industrial fencing. Personal body armour. The place was packed to the rafters with the dregs of society. The drugs of society were prevalent too. The police were on their way. The landlord took the opportunity to make a brief speech.

'Now ladies and gentlemen, as you know I run a legitimate business here and don't condone illegal activities of any kind.' A Mexican snigger wave circled around the bar. 'It's a tiring job, as I'm sure you can imagine. I'm going to go upstairs now for a little sleep. On the off chance that anything illegal might occur while I'm sleeping, I naturally won't have been here to witness it. You should know I'm a very heavy sleeper. Sometimes I don't wake up for whole weeks.'

Speech over, the landlord finished attaching his bullet-proof vest and securing his army helmet and climbed the wooden hill with his favourite teddy, which was metallic and gun-shaped. It wasn't that he was a coward, far from it. If he wanted to have the remotest chance of keeping his licence he could have no part in what was about to happen. His regulars would always need somewhere to drink, and for that they needed a landlord who wouldn't bar them just because they were a load of criminals committing crimes on his premises.

****

The Commissioner didn't like the look of the heavy barricades surrounding The Badger's Eyebrows. Someone had tipped them off about the raid. He did what all good senior managers do at times of critical decision-making. He delegated the task to a subordinate who was paid much less than he was. Christmas was the lucky recipient of the personal development opportunity.

Christmas' qualifications and experience for meriting the responsibility of leading a major police operation such as this were exclusively limited to 20 years of sitting behind a desk looking at paperwork. He tried to remember his basic police training for riot and hostage situations. A mediator. There should be a mediator somewhere to make contact with the hostile party. Christmas sent for a mediator. As it turned out the mediator was already at the scene, hiding in one of the riot police vans and hoping that nobody would remember that a mediator was required. The mediator liaised with Christmas and was handed a megaphone. One always appears in these situations. He took a deep breath.

'This is the police. We have a warrant to search the premises. Can we speak to the landlord of The Badger's Eyebrows?'

A short, silent pause followed.

'He's asleep,' a voice shouted from inside the building.

The mediator looked at Christmas and shrugged. None of his training scenarios had included that response.

'Can you wake him up?'

Another silent pause.

'No, now piss off,' the voice shouted back.

The mediator turned red with embarrassment. Everyone was looking at him.

'Now look here, we are the police. We have your building surrounded and we are armed. If you all come out now with your hands above your heads, nobody will be hurt.'

The mediator felt proud of his brief monologue. *Show them we mean business, that's the ticket.* The silence that followed was electric.

'You're armed?' the voice questioned, a hint of concern detectable in its tone.

'Yes,' replied the mediator.

A loud cracking noise broke the silence, followed by a heavy thud. The thud was the sound of the mediator's body hitting the floor. The crack had been the sound of the gun firing the bullet that passed through his brain.

'So are we,' shouted the voice.

A chorus of cheers and profanities erupted from inside The Badger's Eyebrows. Christmas ordered his forces to advance.

****

The intermediary looked at his watch. Quarter past eight in the evening. What the hell time did this guy finish work? His plan to frame Ross and ESR to get the police off his tail and avoid a war had failed. The war had started anyway. The only difference he'd made was that, instead of one very clever inspector and his sidekick taking an interest in a great many suspicious accidents, now the whole Metropolitan Police Force were interested in a great many suspicious accidents and were busy arresting anyone and everyone with the slightest links to crime. Criminals weren't stupid. Sooner or later they would identify the source of all the heat that was being brought down on them.

He needed the investigation into Major's and the DCI's death to end yesterday. He needed Ross Ackerman. If his sources were to be believed, it wasn't good news on tracking him down. The word was he was under the protection of the Belgians. If that was true they'd never find him. His contingency plan had been to draw Ross out by threatening to harm those he was closest to. Again he'd been beaten to it. His prison sources had confirmed Stuart and Alice were untouchable. Somebody somewhere was thwarting all his plans. He wasn't quite at plan Z yet but was approaching the letters of the alphabet highly sought after by professional Scrabble players.

If love wouldn't bring Ackerman out of hiding, maybe hate could. The intermediary watched as Belvedere descended the stone steps of Browns and headed for the bus stop. Keeping a tight hold of the gun inside his jacket pocket, he followed at a distance.

****

Christmas sank into the chair in his new office. He was exhausted. The Commissioner had been clear in his instructions for the raid on The Badger's Eyebrows: make it quick. Two days later the siege was still raging with no immediate sign of either side gaining the upper hand. The lack of progress had led to the Commissioner replacing him as operational head of the raid. He'd been taken off the case. At least now he could concentrate on solving the crime. Well, he would if he could keep his eyes open. He guzzled more coffee. It tasted of trifle. Perhaps things might seem clearer if he had a quick power nap at his desk.

There was a knock at the door. A figure dressed from head to toe in black leather, and wearing a black crash helmet, thrust a package into his hand and disappeared. Christmas was too tired to be confused and he didn't quite have the energy to be perplexed either. He opened the package and removed two sheets of paper. `You're barking up the wrong tree with ESR. All your questions will be answered if you arrest this man.`

Christmas looked at the photo of the intermediary. He didn't recognise him. An address and map were also included. This was it. He could feel it. Sleep could wait. With what little authority he had left, he rustled up a few officers and set off in hot pursuit.

Chapter 24
Belvedere's Folly

The day of Belvedere's heinous crime was a Tuesday, the day of the weekly Fraud Detection team meeting. It began well for Ross. He made love to Amy in their king-sized bed in the early hours of the morning. They were trying for a baby. Amy had drawn up a strict schedule of lovemaking in order to maximise their chances. Ross wasn't complaining about all the extra sex. His groin might have something to say if it knew what the schedule had in store for Thursday though.

They made love again in the morning before Ross showered, changed and left for work. If he was late Belvedere would report him to the HR department, as he had done on other occasions. Anyone would think Belvedere was Ross' boss the way he carried on. The rush to leave in time meant Ross forgot to tell Amy he loved her. He would make it up to her later that evening.

By contrast, Belvedere spent the morning reading one of his many management self-help books whilst constructing numerous plots to overthrow Ross as Head of the Fraud Detection team. It was 1986 and Belvedere was all in favour of personal advancement at the expense of others, providing the personal advancement was being experienced by him.

It was two years since Ross had been appointed Head of the Fraud Detection team ahead of Belvedere. He was still fuming about the decision. How could they choose Ross over him? He was the senior man. It was his turn. His right. Instead, they gave it to this young, inexperienced novice, fresh out of university. So he got a first at a red brick university. So he sailed through all the aptitude and team building tests Browns threw at him at their management recruitment day. So he was popular amongst the other staff and management at Browns. So he was good looking and married. Why should any of this matter? A great injustice had occurred. It was clear to Belvedere who was to blame.

The Fraud Detection team meeting was a get-together for the team to discuss progress on their workload, allocate new cases between team members and raise any issues, fraud related or otherwise, for Ross to feed back to the banks' senior management. There was work to discuss but Ross tried to keep it social, putting on a nice mid-morning spread of cakes and biscuits, which always went down well. Belvedere saw this meeting somewhat differently. It was his opportunity to ridicule Ross for everything he'd done and said in the previous week, always pointing out how a more experienced team leader would not have made such schoolboy errors.

The meeting was scheduled for an hour and, as Browns was committed to providing a permanent fraud reporting hotline during work hours, Ross always had a temp in to man the line for the duration of the meeting. This week, however, he'd decided that as punishment for his comments at the previous week's meeting, and also for his memo to the Chairman expressing his dissatisfaction at Ross' performance, Belvedere would cover the phones for the team meeting. The man was getting on his tits.

The meeting started at eleven. The members of the team decided to honour Belvedere's absence by not being in any hurry at all to get through the business of the meeting. Five minutes after the meeting began, an angry Charles Belvedere picked up a phone call on Ross' direct number that had been transferred to the emergency fraud reporting line while the meeting took place.

'This is an emergency call for Mr Ross Ackerman from Westpoint General Hospital. It's most urgent I speak to Mr Ackerman.'

The decisions we take in a split second can change the direction our lives take forever. Hatred and bitter envy racing through his veins, Belvedere made such a decision.

'This is Ross Ackerman speaking,' he said, hoping to learn of some embarrassing or disabling ailment Ross was suffering from that he could use to his advantage.

'Mr Ackerman, my name is Dr Stuart from the Accident and Emergency ward at Westpoint General. I'm afraid I must ask you to prepare yourself for some grave news.'

This sounded serious. What was left of Charles Belvedere's goodness had long since been overwhelmed by his depraved ambition and, instead of rushing to the meeting room to inform Ross, he continued with his folly.

'I'm ready.'

'Mr Ackerman, your wife has been involved in a very serious road traffic accident and is in critical condition. She has received serious head trauma, her spine is broken in several places and she is suffering heavy internal bleeding. I'm so sorry to tell you this over the phone but, even though we are doing everything we can for her, the internal bleeding means she is suffering from multiple internal organ failure.'

Belvedere was speechless.

The doctor sighed before adding, 'In all likelihood your wife has an hour at the most. I'm so sorry. She is still conscious and is asking for you. We have an emergency portable phone with her for occasions such as these. She may not have long left to be able to talk to you before she loses consciousness. After that I implore you to please get here as fast as you can to be with her at the end.'

'Er yes, of course.'

There was a pause and then the sound of medical staff shouting instructions to each other. The voice of Amy followed, breathless and groaning with pain.

'Ross, is that you?'

'It's me, my love,' replied Belvedere.

Deep, deep down inside him, well hidden from view, the last remnant of Charles Belvedere's decency died of shame.

'I'm so sorry, my darling,' panted Amy. 'I've got to leave you, my love. I'm broken.'

Her words were becoming slower and more slurred, her breathing heavier.

'I ... I love you, my husband. Forever.'

Her body losing its flimsy grip on life, Amy summoned all her strength to utter her final words.

'Tell me you love me one last time.'

'I love you,' replied Belvedere insincerely, looking round to make sure nobody could hear him.

'Be happy, my sweetheart,' Amy whispered, her voice trailing away until it was inaudible.

No further words came back from Amy as she slipped from consciousness for the final time.

'Please get here soon,' said the voice of a member of the medical team to Belvedere before the phone line went dead.

Now operating on a level devoid of any human compassion for his fellow man, Belvedere lusted greedily about the opportunity for personal advancement that a grieving Ross would present him with. To avoid having to answer any further calls from the hospital, Belvedere used the single telephone line reserved for emergency incoming fraud calls to make a series of inconsequential outgoing calls relating to various non-urgent matters. After almost an hour, he decided it was time to break the news to Ross. It was a world class performance by Belvedere. He burst into the meeting room and, with his best-feigned concern and sense of urgency, told Ross in front of the whole Fraud Detection team that he had to hurry to the hospital as his wife had been involved in a serious accident.

Westpoint was an eight-minute drive from Browns. Ross did it in three. Almost driving into the hospital reception area in his delirium, he jumped out of his car and sprinted in shouting Amy's name. He was rushed to the emergency theatre by a nurse. He burst into the theatre and saw Amy lying still on the operating table. He looked at the medical staff, desperate to understand why nobody was doing anything. They couldn't look him in the eye. Tears streaming down his face, a shocked Ross knelt beside the battered body of his wife.

The medical staff left the room. He held her hand against his cheek, then leaned over and gently kissed her brow. He was too late. She'd gone.

'I'm sorry, my darling. Please forgive me,' Ross begged, his eyes pleading with the vacant dead eyes of his beautiful wife.

Then the enormity of what was happening caught up with him. In a second he was hit with every emotion it was possible to experience. Loss, grief, shock, anger, love and guilt. Guilt. He should have been there at the end and he wasn't. As he started to hyperventilate, a doctor observing through the window recognised the signs and rushed into the theatre just in time to catch him.

****

Belvedere worked hard through the rest of the day, bringing an impressive number of case files to conclusion. Even by his own high standards it had been a productive day. HR had given the rest of the Fraud Detection team the option of leaving early and, being too upset at the news coming back from the hospital, they had all taken up the offer. Belvedere had shown his dependency and reliability in a crisis by holding the fort for them. He would soldier on as best he could through this distressing time.

In the afternoon Belvedere met with HR and volunteered to be the team's temporary Acting Head to take the pressure off Ross needing to return to work too soon. Assuming Ross would only be absent for a short period, they agreed.

****

Armed with a stack of pills to combat the shock, Ross left the hospital in a daze – but not before a brief and unpleasant encounter with Amy's parents. They would never forgive him for not telling them in time for them to say goodbye to their daughter. Over the coming weeks and months their relationship would suffer irreparable damage. The alcoholic world Ross was about to enter was not one in which responsibilities of any description would be tolerated. Amy's parents would have to handle all the funeral arrangements and Amy's affairs.

Sometime just before midnight on the day of his wife's death, an inebriated Ross collapsed through his front door. After a brief sleep he slumped against the hallway wall and, after numerous failed attempts, managed to unscrew the lid from one of the many bottles of whisky he had purchased earlier that day. Voluntarily, he staggered through the entrance gates to oblivion.

****

Charles Belvedere beamed with pride as he once again inspected his new business cards. He'd ordered them less than five minutes after he'd spoken to Amy and was impressed at how soon the printers had been able to supply them. Of course, he had offered them three times the usual rate for same day delivery. Acting Head. There it was in black in white.

Out of respect he didn't remotely feel for his grieving, soon-to-be former boss, he would leave it a week before removing the word Acting from his next order of business cards.

Chapter 25
Peace (and love)

Number Seven paid for his mug of tea and sat down at a booth in Dave's Café, an establishment known more for its criminal clientele than the quality of its catering. The booth that Number Seven had chosen to drink his tea in already had a diner sitting at the other side of the table. By sheer coincidence it was Number Nine. Neither acknowledged the other.

'What's the intermediary playing at?' Number Seven snarled. 'Why haven't we made a move on The Gang yet?'

'Keep your voice down,' whispered Number Nine. He scanned the café for prying ears. Apart from an old man with a walking stick and a hearing aid, it was empty.

'Don't worry about him; he's deaf as a post. Didn't even hear Dave calling his order just now,' said Number Seven. 'Just keep your cool and stay patient. Our friend knows what he's doing. There's been a new development. The word is The Medics are about to hit The Gang. It's a double-cross. Secretary doesn't trust them. Mark my words, in a few days they'll all be feeling a bit Tom and Dick.'

With that, Number Nine finished the last of his breakfast, stood up and left. Number Seven followed soon after.

The old man continued reading his newspaper, spilling beans down his shirt as he ate his breakfast. After several minutes, he leapt to his feet in a manner that belied his advanced years and darted out of the café. A hundred yards down the road he stopped running when he reached the phone box. A number was dialled and the phone placed back on the receiver after a single ring. The phone in the phone box rang seconds later. The old man picked it up.

'It's me. I need to speak to the go-between. Yes, it's urgent. I've got some important news.'

****

Willis felt peculiar. The doctor told him to take a little time and drink a cup of water before he drove home. It wasn't unknown for patients to have an allergic reaction to immunisations, he'd warned him. The war would be over soon. They were all planning their escapes to warmer climes until the heat died down.

Willis pulled over at the side of the road. His immune system was strong but, while he was waiting for it to overcome the injection it had just received, he would have a small sleep on the back seat. He was sweating heavily. His vision was blurred. His limbs felt like they belonged to someone else. Something was wrong. Nobody felt like this from a tetanus jab. What the hell had he been injected with? The inside of the car span round in his head as he fought to remain conscious.

This couldn't be happening. The secretary had promised immunity to all members of The Gang. He'd been double-crossed. The go-between would have to know. Willis strained every sinew in his body to haul himself upright. He reached the glove compartment and pulled out the huge mobile phone. Hands trembling, he called the one number pre-saved on the phone.

'Please come and get me,' he sobbed, sweat pouring down his face. 'The Medics have double-crossed us. I think I'm dying.'

The phone fell from his clammy hand and Willis collapsed back onto the seat. He slipped out of consciousness and died in his sleep a few minutes later.

****

'Next patient please,' said Number Nine.

He'd had a good day. First, he'd given an award-winning performance as a naïve gangster who couldn't possibly have suspected the old man reading his upside-down paper in the café was an impostor. He'd followed that up with a starring role as the caring doctor giving his patient their essential inoculations for overseas travel. It was good to know all those years in RADA hadn't been wasted. He still had it. His next patient entered.

'Good afternoon, Miss Small. How can I help?'

'It's my breasts, doctor. They're so massive they're causing me back pain. Can I have an operation to make them smaller?'

'Perhaps I'd better have a look,' said Number Nine. He could get used to this.

****

The intermediary returned to his safe haven with several bags of shopping. He'd decided to stock up and stay hidden until the war was over. It wouldn't be long now. The Medics had been decimated and, if everything went to plan, pretty soon The Gang would deliver the final blow.

He was proud of his work. Getting The Gang to turn against The Medics was particularly inspired, he thought. The black arts of misinformation and propaganda were often overlooked by inexperienced managers such as the secretary and the go-between. There was a reason he'd been intermediary for The Boss Killers for so long. He was good at it. He'd been through wars before. They hadn't.

Pleased with himself, he reached into his drinks cabinet and poured himself a large single malt. He felt safe here. Nobody knew the place existed except him. It wasn't listed in any phone book or located on any map and it didn't have its own postcode. There wasn't much natural light, but what did you expect living a hundred feet underground? It had taken him years to find the place. He'd been saving it until such a time when he needed to disappear. It would all be over soon. Then he really would disappear. Somewhere nobody would find him.

There was a noise. It was barely audible to the human ear but the intermediary heard it. He was the only one in the room and he knew he didn't make it.

'OK whoever you are, show yourself.'

He drained the whisky and prepared himself for the worst. *Please*

God, let it not be The Gang.

DI Christmas stepped into view. 'Detective Inspector Christmas,' he said.

The intermediary turned to face him and saw the badge.

'You're under arrest.'

'What for?'

Christmas stepped back a few paces, knelt down and touched a tile on the wall. It looked like all the others. There was a sound like steam escaping and the wall parted to reveal a secret room. Gagged, handcuffed and shackled to a chair, Belvedere was visible for all to see.

'That for starters,' said Christmas, pointing at Belvedere. 'There are these as well,' he continued, holding up several of the files stolen from his office the night the DCI was murdered. 'So that's kidnapping, false imprisonment and the murder of a senior police officer. Not looking too good, is it?'

The intermediary considered his options. He had two open to him. 'I take it you're not alone?' he ventured.

Several armed officers emerged from the secret room Belvedere was being held in. That ruled out option one. Preparation. It was what the intermediary's life had been all about. His time inside had taught him one invaluable lesson. Always be prepared and always have a plan.

'OK, you've got me. If that's all you want you can take me now.'

Christmas remained silent. Something good was about to be said.

'However, if you want to solve those,' the intermediary said, pointing at the files in Christmas' hand, 'and hundreds of other murders, rapes, beatings and a whole load of other crimes that will shock the world then I'll give you all the info you need.'

Christmas thought for a moment. This was the man he'd been looking for all this time.

'What do you want?'

'Immunity from prosecution. To go into witness protection somewhere safe. Preferably near wetlands with some nice hides so I can watch the birds. Sort that out for me and I'll help you put away half the criminals in London.'

'It's a deal,' said Christmas.

He didn't know how, but he'd do whatever it took to clear it with the Commissioner.

****

'This is your final warning. Vacate the building. Walk out slowly with your hands above your heads.'

The raucous laughter from the inhabitants of The Badger's Eyebrows was not the desired response, but was somewhat expected. The siege of the pub had proceeded with the least amount of success it was possible to achieve for a period of seven days now. Reinforcements had been brought in on both sides. It was stalemate. Every time the police advanced, they were repelled by a well-motivated and armed band of rebel warriors with no moral qualms about killing police officers. The whole sordid episode was a deep embarrassment to the Commissioner. Enough was enough; it was time to bring matters to a swift conclusion.

'This is your absolute final warning,' the Commissioner shouted into the megaphone.

'You and whose army, pig? We've heard it all before,' came the response.

The Commissioner stepped back several metres and made a slow, deliberate gesture with his arms. About a minute passed before they all felt the earthquake. It was a small tremor but the force increased with each passing second. Inside The Badger's, glasses fell off tables and smashed as the building shook. Just as the force of the quake reached a crescendo, it suddenly stopped. The Commissioner returned to his post and raised the megaphone to his lips.

'The British army,' came his delayed answer. 'You have ten minutes to vacate the building.'

Inside The Badger's Eyebrows, the mood had changed from exuberance to dejection. They had no fear of the police and were prepared to die fighting them. A squadron of state-of-the-art Challenger tanks was another matter. They weren't going to wait around to be bulldozed to death or blown to small bits. It had been a good fight, they could be proud of their efforts, but it was now time to call it a day. Hugs and handshakes were exchanged all round and some forward-thinking dashes to the lavatories were made to conceal precious valuables that were small enough to be hidden in the one place the authorities preferred not to look. Then, after a quick prayer of thanks from the singing vicar, they all filed towards the exit and into the smug clutches of the enemy. All except one.

Igneous refused to leave. One man against the might of the Royal Armoured Corps was not much of a chance but it was one he was prepared to take. That it was a solitary deluded rebel remaining mattered not a jot to the Commissioner. The tanks were ordered into The Badger's.

What should have happened was that Igneous should have been killed within a matter of seconds after the first tank clattered through the front wall of the pub. When the smoke cleared from the mountain of rubble, the Commissioner and the rest of the assembled Met officers stood agape as they witnessed the uncommon sight of a bald man head-butting holes in the tank's impenetrable armour. The landlord of The Badger's Eyebrows had a bird's eye view of the cranial carnage as his bed crashed through what used to be his bedroom floor. At least, he would have done if he hadn't been such a heavy sleeper.

****

The secretary paced around the room. She was nervous. A meeting with the go-between was the last thing she wanted but he'd been most insistent. Security had been beefed up just to be on the safe side. She'd offered to have him picked up but the go-between had requested his own transportation.

The black limo pulled into the private road and stopped outside the clinic. The go-between and his bodyguard exited the car. It was within the rules for him to be accompanied by one bodyguard when visiting the premises of another organisation during wartime. The go-between ascended the stone steps and pressed the buzzer to request entry. The door buzzed open.

'Now,' he shouted.

The doors of the limo burst open and members of The Gang swarmed into the clinic. The secretary watched with horror as they surged through the clinic, dispatching her security guards with ease. She locked the door to her office and called the police. Prison was much more desirable than whatever The Gang had in store for her.

By now the whole clinic was aware of the commotion and was busy defending themselves. The intruders met with stiffer resistance as they ascended the stairs in search of the secretary. The Gang took cover as a volley of medical missiles rained down on them. Syringes full of nasties, stethoscopes, saline drips and aluminium bed pans were all hurled in their direction. A few Medics had armed themselves with tranquilizer guns. Not having received any formal artillery training, the projectiles mostly missed their intended targets, but a few were successful in taking out The Gang. Just five Gang members remained when they reached the top of the stairs. Once they were there, the Medics' resistance was quashed with ruthless professionalism. The Gang substituted their usual method of punishment with beatings. They were saving their energy for the secretary. Crouching and quivering behind her desk, she prayed for a miracle as they pounded on the door of her office. It gave way.

'No point hiding, secretary. We know you're there,' the go-between said, as he and the other four Gang members entered the room.

The secretary stood up to face them, giving her best impression of defiance under the circumstances. It was a pitiful attempt.

'What do you want?' she stammered.

'I think you know what we want,' the go-between replied, grinning.

'Please, I beg you, don't do this. We are winning the war.'

The go-between wasn't listening. 'Now I don't want you to get the wrong impression about what we do, secretary. People watch TV and they think, "Oh, that's not so bad." I guarantee this will be bad.'

The rest of The Gang smiled demonically.

'Don't you worry though,' the go-between continued. 'My boys have had years of training. We can keep going for hours, sometimes days.'

The secretary slumped to her knees, clasped her hands together and began to pray. She'd done terrible things in her life, unforgivable things. At that moment she prayed with more passion and desperation than any other human alive. The Gang advanced.

'Armed police. Put your hands in the air – now.'

The Gang turned around and saw the unwelcome sight of a dozen armed police officers pointing large guns at them. They put their hands in the air. Very rarely is it a difficult decision to submit to an order when the alternative is to have your head blown off. The secretary's prayers had been answered. Her ordeal was over.

DCI Christmas walked into the room and arrested The Gang. A hysterical secretary flew into his arms. Never had she been so grateful to anyone in her whole life. Christmas showed his compassionate side by arresting her. Everyone else in the building that was still alive was arrested; they were all guilty of something.

Several days passed before the secretary recovered even the slightest bit of poise after the shocking events of The Gang's ambush. When the hysteria and adrenaline subsided, her body crashed and she had to be taken to hospital for treatment. By that time she'd already told Christmas everything she knew.

In the days following the arrest of the intermediary and the secretary, the UK's prisons bulged under the weight of new convicts. The Boss Killers were arrested. The Gang, The Medics and The Pugilists were all arrested. Many others who were caught in the crossfire or joined with one of the feuding Council members in the hope of rich pickings were also arrested. The war was over.

****

It was a beautiful sunny day. Ross and Mr X watched as the small charter plane touched down on the runway of the private airfield. The plane came to a stop and a set of mobile stairs was wheeled onto the runway and aligned next to the plane. The door opened and out stepped Detective Inspector Harry Christmas. Ross and Mr X greeted him.

'Mr Ackerman, I presume,' Christmas said to Ross. He was in high spirits. 'I congratulate you on your successful escape and hiding from the authorities and I apologise that you were forced to take such action. No doubt you will be relieved to know that all the charges against you and your friends have been dropped and we now have those responsible for the terrible crimes you were accused of in custody. I would be most delighted if you would care to accompany me back to London.'

Ross looked at Mr X. Mr X looked at Christmas. From a distance, the Belgians also looked at Christmas, through the sights of their rifles aimed at his head and heart. Ross and Mr X were still under their protection. Christmas just looked chipper.

'I do beg your pardon,' he began, reaching into his jacket pocket.

'Slowly. Do it very, very slowly,' Mr X barked.

'Er yes, of course.'

In super slow motion, and with exaggerated hand movement, Christmas retrieved the envelope from his pocket and handed it to Ross, who gave it straight to Mr X. He examined the envelope.

'It's got the official seal. Looks genuine.' He opened the envelope and read the letter. 'It's legit. All charges dropped and a full pardon. Signed by the Commissioner of the Met himself. Congratulations. You're a free man.'

Ross breathed a huge sigh of relief. Freedom was underrated. Behind his back Mr X made the merest of hand movements. The Belgians relaxed their trigger fingers, had a smoke and partook of some luxury dark chocolates.

'Yes,' said Christmas, 'we got an anonymous tip-off giving us the identity and exact location of the man responsible for setting you up. He goes by the name of the intermediary. That ring any bells by any chance?'

Mr X performed a world class impersonation of a man without a clue.

'I'd like to shake the hand of the person who sent us that information,' said Christmas, looking Mr X in the eye. 'Very interesting chap, this intermediary. Fingers in lots of pies, as you might expect. Had an interesting theory about who might have shopped him. He thinks it's a computer genius called Mr X.'

Ross swallowed hard and attempted to look vacant.

'We don't believe him, of course,' continued Christmas. 'Everyone knows Mr X is just a myth,' he said, looking at Mr X and smiling.

'What about the others?' asked Ross, keen to change the conversation.

'The Koreans have all been released. The prison governor was glad to be rid of them by all accounts. Your friend Kevin is still recovering in hospital from a suspected drug overdose and your secretarial staff have all been released without charge.'

'Was Alice with them?' Ross asked.

'I'm afraid she's still incarcerated.'

'What? Why?'

'She has refused to leave prison until she has concrete proof that you are alive and well. We have reassured her that this is the case but she won't leave until she sees you.'

Ross smiled. She always was a stubborn mare.

'And Stuart?'

Christmas turned to face the plane, waved and then beckoned with his hands. 'Why don't you ask him yourself?' he said, grinning.

Somewhat bedraggled, and looking a good deal thinner than the last time they'd both seen him, Stuart descended the staircase and walked straight into a bear hug from Ross, followed by a hearty handshake. Uncomfortable with human emotion, Christmas removed himself to a safe distance until the scene was over.

'How you doin', mate? I'm sorry you had to go through this. It's all my fault. I promise to make it up to you – anything you want.'

'It's good to see you,' said a smiling Stuart. 'First repayment is you're taking me to the nearest all-you-can-eat dining establishment and we're not leaving until I've scoffed so much I need an oxygen mask to breathe. Prison diet sucks.'

'You got it. Think you owe this man a big thank you first though.'

Ross stepped aside. Stuart and Mr X stood facing each other in silence for several seconds. Then they embraced. Ross smiled. He knew Stuart would have been eaten alive inside without protection. Mr X had more than earned Stuart's gratitude. The embrace continued. *He certainly has got a lot to be grateful for,* thought Ross. At least a minute had passed and the embrace continued. Both men had tears streaming down their faces. Ross watched, confused by the scene. He could feel a knocking sensation in his brain. A thought was trying to escape. The thought had always been there but for some reason it had been locked away in a part of his subconscious that refused entry to visitors. The knocking continued. The embrace continued. After years of incarceration, the thought's time had arrived. His brain gave way and released the thought.

'Ahhh. So that's it.'

A puzzle thirty years in the making was solved. Hundreds of flashbacks of past incidents poured into Ross' conscious mind. In this moment they finally made sense. The embrace ended. Stuart wiped the tears and snot from his face with his jumper.

'Is this going to change anything?' he asked, a worried tone in his voice.

'Course not,' Ross laughed. 'How dense am I?' he asked. 'How long have I known you? All this time staring me in the face. I'm sorry, Stu.'

'I thought you must have figured it out after all these years of no girlfriends.'

'Sorry, mate. I'm pretty thick, aren't I? I thought you were just ...

well, shy around women.'

'Nobody's that shy, Ross.'

'I know. I'm going to be apologising about this for the rest of my life, aren't I?' Stuart nodded.

'Hang on. What about that time you shagged big Sally from HR at the Christmas bash?'

Stuart shuddered at the thought. 'I told you then and I'm telling you now, she gave me a drink and the next thing I remember is waking up in a broom cupboard with her on top of me. That doesn't count.'

Ross turned to Mr X and recognised the look he was giving Stuart. It was one of love.

'You know, I did sometimes wonder why an international criminal genius would decide to help us.'

Mr X grinned. 'If it wasn't for him I would have had you all killed.'

'I see. Well I'm glad you didn't. I take it we won't be seeing you for a while?'

'I'll be keeping a low profile, wait until the heat dies down, you know.'

'Yeah, sure. I am – that is, we all are very grateful for everything you've done for us.'

'No sweat. It wasn't entirely without its perks. Made quite a lot of money, didn't we?'

'Yeah, we did.'

There was an awkward silence. Ross got the distinct impression he was being a gooseberry.

'Er right, I'll leave you two to it.'

He started to walk away when he suddenly remembered something.

'Erm, I don't suppose you could do me a small favour? Pretty please.'

Mr X shook his head. 'I think you're all out of favours, don't you?'

Stuart frowned at him and raised his eyebrows.

'Oh go on then. What is it?'

****

It was late in the evening by the time Belvedere returned home from work. He'd tried to stay later but security had turfed him out of the building around nine. Human Resources were doing their best to use his kidnapping as an excuse to keep him away from Browns. He'd agreed to see a counsellor, provided the appointments were in his office and he could continue to work whilst answering questions.

As he did every night, Belvedere retrieved an unhealthy ready meal from his freezer and placed it in the microwave. Time spent cooking was time he could be spending working. He opened his briefcase and took out the latest copy of Fraud Rigid, the leading journal for the fraud detection industry. It had just hit the desks that day but it was essential that he read the entire issue from cover to cover so he could memorise key passages of text and pass them off as his own thoughts in the coming days.

The microwave pinged and Belvedere retrieved his dinner. As he did so, he felt the strangest sensation. A sudden sharp, stabbing pain occurred in his right buttock. His muscles relaxed and he felt a strong desire to lie down on his bed. Once again Mr X had delivered the goods. It had taken just seconds from the syringe entering Belvedere's body for the drug to take effect. Ross entered Belvedere's bedroom and saw him lying down on his bed, helpless from the effects of the drugs. He gave serious consideration to slipping his hands around the man's throat and squeezing hard. He thought back to their one and only physical encounter years earlier.

Less than a month after the death of Amy, Ross returned to work on light duties. It was too soon. Cheated out of the opportunity to go to work on the driver responsible for Amy's death when, unable to live with the guilt of his actions, the man took his own life, Ross instead turned his violent attentions to Belvedere. The sight of him swanning around the office like he owned the place, wearing a broad smile at all times, was too much for Ross to cope with. When Belvedere reprimanded him for returning a minute late from his lunch break, Ross, who hadn't been sober since the last time he'd been in work, snapped and launched a full-frontal assault on the new Acting Head of Fraud Detection. Belvedere escaped with a black eye, broken nose, fractured skull, two broken ribs and severe abdominal bruising. He was back in work the next morning at eight o' clock.

The tribunal that followed had something of the Australian marsupial about it. It failed to reach a unanimous verdict on what had happened due to inconclusive evidence. All the staff present at the time – and there were many – had been otherwise engaged on vital work duties and either failed to witness any attack or swore blind that Belvedere attacked himself. A compromise solution was reached, mainly to stop Belvedere reporting the incident to the police. He was made permanent Head of the Fraud Detection team. Ross was given three months' gardening leave and sent to an anger management counsellor.

Mr X had explained that once the drug was administered the victim would remain conscious but be in a state of such deep relaxation that they would be unable to move. The part of their brain used to lie would be deactivated during this time. *Now for some answers.*

'Hello, Charles.'

'Is that you, Ross? I feel most peculiar. Just having a lie down for a bit if you don't mind.'

'Not at all, not at all,' Ross said. 'There's something I've been meaning to ask you for a while now. On the day my wife died did you pretend to be me when the hospital called the office?'

'Yes I did. I thought they might tell me something I could use against you. I wanted your job, Ross, and I didn't care what I had to do to get it. Is it hot in here?'

With difficulty, Ross controlled his urge to bash Belvedere's brains in. 'I see. How long did you wait until you told me about the accident?'

'It was about an hour, I think.'

Ross bent over, put his head between his knees and slowed his breathing. There was still more to discover. He needed to calm down.

'Did you speak to Amy?'

'Yes.'

He knew it. He'd always known it. *It would be so easy now to just slip my hands around his throat and strangle the bastard.*

'What did she say, Charles?'

Belvedere didn't answer straight away. He closed his eyes in concentration.

'Ross, is that you?' he whispered in Amy's voice.

'It's me, my love,' he replied in his own voice.

'I'm so sorry, my darling. I've got to leave you. I'm broken.' Amy's voice was becoming weaker. 'I ... I love you, my husband. Forever. Tell me you love me one last time.'

'I love you,' said Belvedere.

'Be happy, my sweetheart.'

The voice faded into silence. Belvedere had tears in his eyes. The venomous anger disappeared from Ross. The years of punishing himself for not being there. The guilt and the pain. Trying to guess what her final words might have been. Turning the pain into rage against Belvedere. Finally he knew the truth. He collapsed to his knees and wept. After about half an hour of bawling his eyes out he stopped. He was exhausted. The deed was done though. He'd got what he came for. He looked at Belvedere and for the first time in a long time, the desire to murder him was absent.

'Why did you do it, Charles?'

'Because I was jealous of you, Ross. You had the job I wanted. You were younger than me, better looking, intelligent. Everyone liked you and you had a beautiful wife. What did I have?'

Ross looked at the pathetic excuse for a man before him and for the first time felt pity for him. He was just about to leave when a thought popped into his head. This was too good an opportunity to miss.

'Tell me, Charles, what qualifications did you have when you applied for the job at Browns?'

****

When Belvedere woke up he had the mother of all headaches. He took two Paracetamol and returned to bed. Noticing that it was already light, he risked a glance at his alarm clock. It was half past nine. It took his brain a few seconds to interpret this information. Half past nine and light equals morning. A sensation he had never before experienced in his adult life was upon him. Charles Belvedere was late for work.

He showered, dressed and commuted to Browns at record speed. It was still after ten thirty by the time he got there. If he proceeded straight to his office and shut the door it was just possible he might have enough time to arrange a fictitious early morning meeting before anyone noticed. Like an experienced drunk, he tiptoed along the corridor to his office, mindful to avoid all known squeaky floorboards and creaking doors. He needn't have bothered. He arrived at his office to the sight of four burly security guards packing up all his belongings into several enormous storage containers.

'Here, what do you think you're doing? Those are my things. Unpack them at once,' bellowed Belvedere. 'Don't you know who I am?' he sneered haughtily.

'Charles Belvedere?' enquired one of the men.

'Yes,' he replied in surprise.

The man handed him an envelope. He got as far as opening it and reading the first line – Dear Charles, Your employment with Browns has been terminated with immediate effect – before two of the guards grabbed an arm each and escorted him off the premises.

He sat on the pavement, scratching his head in confusion. Late once in fifteen years and they'd sacked him. It didn't make any sense.

He took the letter out and read it. There it was in black and white: he was fired. Hoping some further explanation might be forthcoming, he turned the letter over. It turned out there was. On the back of his dismissal letter was a photocopy of a typed note. It had been typed by Ross Ackerman. The note had then been placed in the pigeonhole of every member of staff at Browns. Belvedere read the note.

```
Charles Belvedere is a Fraud

To the good staff at Browns of London. Charles Belvedere,
Head of the Fraud Detection department at Browns, is
himself a fraud. He has no formal qualifications of any
description. No fraud detection qualifications, no
degree, no HND, no A Levels, no O Levels and no CSEs.

This makes him the least qualified member of staff
employed by Browns, including the cleaners. He has failed
every examination he has ever sat. He did not attend
Oxford University or Eton as he has boasted on numerous
occasions. Neither is he a member of the aristocracy and
distantly related to Her Majesty the Queen, as he has
often claimed. His real lineage is much less prestigious.
His mother was a waitress in a greasy spoon café and his
father a bus driver.

On the day of the death of Amy Ackerman, wife of former
Fraud Detection Head Ross Ackerman, Belvedere took the
call from the hospital and waited a full hour before
passing on the message to Ross that his wife had at best
an hour to live. He also pretended to be Ross Ackerman to
hospital staff and to Amy as she said her last words in
agonising pain.

Belvedere's real name is ...
```

****

'Bum-Face. Barry Bum-Face.'

The queue of men in the job centre burst into laughter at the announcement of the name and looked around for the identity of the unfortunate Mr Bum-Face. One man wasn't laughing.

'Barry Bum-Face. Step forward please, we haven't got all day.'

Cringing with shame, the man who had hitherto presented himself to the world as Charles Belvedere approached the desk for his unemployment benefit application interview. There were times – many, many times – when he had wondered just what the hell Grandma Bum and Granddad Face had been thinking when they decided to lumber their future generations with such a ridiculous surname. Even the clerk was sniggering; he'd heard some corkers in his time but this took the biscuit.

The man formerly known as Charles Belvedere was broken. Fifteen years of service and he'd been tossed aside like an old newspaper. No leaving party, no words of praise from the new Chairman, no clock. There would also be no reference and no severance pay.

A select few at Browns had known of Belvedere's deceit for years but had agreed to conceal it on account of him never taking his entitlement to annual leave, always working at least double his contractual hours, and never asking for a pay rise. When the rest of the company discovered that the Head of the Fraud Detection team was himself a fraud, it was a step too far for Browns. Within days the outside world would know. Action had to be taken. A career in fraud detection was no longer an employment avenue open to Barry Bum-Face, at Browns or anywhere else. They tended to object to that sort of thing.

'So what skills do you have?' the clerk at the desk asked Bum-Face.

He thought hard. Fraud and anything to do with banking was right out. What else was he good at?

'I can do magic,' he offered.

'That's good,' replied the clerk. 'I'll put you down for children's entertainer vacancies. We get a few jobs in now and then for the family holiday parks.'

Bum-Face groaned. He hated kids.

****

It was a beautiful morning. Ross placed a broadsheet newspaper on the damp grass and knelt down on it. From his rucksack he retrieved an assortment of gardening tools. With the help of a pair of shears, a trowel, a dustpan and brush and a bottle of fluid whose purpose was to exterminate unwanted garden nasties, he spent over an hour tending to the area and making it presentable. What was it with the weed killing industry? Why was the manufacture and supply of products that might actually kill weeds so seemingly beyond them?

His work complete, he packed away the horticultural paraphernalia and inspected his handiwork. It was good. Better than adequate, but not brilliant. Some colourful perennials were required: daffodils and tulips, perhaps some foxgloves.

'I'm sorry it's been so long,' he said to no one in particular. 'I've been a fool. Made a complete pig's ear of everything, haven't I? Friends have gone to prison for me and I went and almost got myself killed. And all for what? So consumed with my own selfish rage I didn't stop and think of the consequences. I've been lost for so long I didn't know where to start looking for a way out.'

Ross looked into the bright blue sky and breathed it in. He'd been taking nature for granted. Looking at it now, in its breathtaking majesty, he felt at peace with the world for the first time in a long time.

'I'm putting that all behind me now. I've decided not to kill Belvedere. I haven't let him off the hook for good but I'm not going to waste any more time hating him and blaming him for the past. What's done is done. It's time to move on.'

He knelt down and placed the dozen red roses at the foot of the headstone.

'I loved you more than any man ever loved a woman.' Tears rolled down his cheeks. 'One day we'll be together again, my love. Save a nice cloud for us, won't you.'

Ross kissed his hand and placed the kiss onto the face of Amy in the framed photograph that lay against her grave. Wiping the tears from his face with a handkerchief, he braced himself and took the first step into the next chapter of his life. It was time to be happy.

****

Ross leaned against the side of his car, arms folded, sun shining on his face. He glanced at his watch. They were late. All good things and all that. He could wait a bit longer.

The quiet was punctuated by a loud clanging noise followed by the sound of very large, very old cogs springing into action. The giant iron doors parted, revealing inmate number 9764538. When the doors were extended, inmate number 9764538 remained motionless, military-style canvas bag slung over her shoulder. With head bowed, a clenched fist was thrust into the air in protest. A tribal roar of approval erupted some way in the distance behind inmate number 9764538.

Moments later inmate number 9764538 stepped across the prison's threshold and into freedom, where she was instantly replaced by Alice. Ross embraced her. It was still the embrace of friends. Conversation could wait. Ross had assumed that the first priority would be to get Alice the hell away from prison in the minimum amount of time possible.

As they drove on, Alice regaled Ross with tales from the inside. It was some story. The threats, the fights, the beatings – it had been a rough ride for the other inmates until they gave in and submitted to Alice's will. She'd been in effective control of the prison for weeks now. Even the governor had to request her approval on key decisions. Alice was just beginning another story when the car stopped and Ross got out.

'Won't be a minute.'

He disappeared into a building and left Alice in the car. She'd been doing a lot of thinking in prison. There tended to be a great deal of time for such activity. She'd come to the conclusion that she'd been too passive where Ross was concerned and vowed that once released she'd stop waiting for him to do the running. Ross returned from his sojourn and opened the car door for Alice.

'We've got a party lined up for you a bit later but there's something I could use your help with. It won't take long, I promise.'

Ross led a confused Alice into the building and straight towards the elevator. A quick glance around confirmed to her that this was a hotel of some description. The elevator reached the fourth floor and Ross led her along the corridor and stopped outside a door.

'What do you think?' he asked, after they entered the room.

It was a large suite with a separate lounge and balcony.

'Er yes, very nice,' Alice replied, unsure of what it was she was supposed to be commenting on.

'Come on, it's in here.' Ross led them into the bedroom and sat on the bed. 'It's a super king-size. I'm thinking of getting one. Big decision buying a new bed. Lots of important factors to consider: size, comfort and of course durability.'

He started gently bouncing up and down on the bed.

'I mean, they all look good, don't they, but just how much of a proper pounding can the springs take? That's the real question, isn't it?'

Ross looked into Alice's eyes. It was the kind of look that said in no uncertain terms that domestic purchases were the last thing on his mind. It was the look Alice had been dreaming of for years. If facial expressions alone could convey a sentence then the one Ross was wearing went something along the lines of *You've got ten seconds to get out of those clothes before I rip them off with my teeth.*

Alice blushed and momentarily lost her breath. Then she launched herself at him.

****

'Waiter.'

'Yes, sir, how may I help?'

'There is a fly in my soup.'

The waiter inspected the soup for the rogue insect. He didn't find it.

'Of course, sir. I will attend to the matter at once.'

The waiter removed the offending dish from the table and left the room. He returned seconds later with a fresh bowl of soup and placed it on the table. The diner considered the new dish before delivering his verdict.

'It needs work, waiter, a lot more work. Seven is the most I can award your performance and, as you know, the pass mark for this module is at the very least ten out of ten. Perfection, waiter. Perfection is what we teach here. It matters not how close you are to achieving it. If it's not perfect it just won't do.'

Third waiter was a hard task master. He was instructing the next generation of world class waiters. They couldn't expect an easy ride.

'Three main areas you need to address. First, your general demeanour. Your mouth is smiling but your eyes are not. I'm simply not getting the impression that being in my presence is the single most joyous event in your life so far. Second, you inspected the soup. This suggests you don't believe my assertion that it contains a fly. It is of no consequence what the complaint is, waiter. If I had stated that my soup contained a water buffalo I still expect you to instantly agree with me that my soup does indeed contain a water buffalo. Third, you returned the soup to my table a little too soon for my liking. The customer must believe that you are bringing them a new bowl of soup and not just leaving the dining room, counting to five in the kitchen and returning to them the same bowl of soup in which they spotted a fly.'

The student waiter was crestfallen. He bowed in gratitude to third waiter before trudging out of the dining room with his tail between his legs. Third waiter looked at his watch and inspected a laminated sheet of paper in the folder in front of him. It was the timetable of lessons for the lucky cohort of student waiters who had been accepted into his Waiter Finishing School. He had a couple of hours to kill while the students would be perfecting their cutlery laying, wine serving and customer toadying. He laid the table for two just in time for his guest to arrive.

Third waiter pulled the chair away from the table and waited for his guest to take her place. He then pushed the chair towards the table, poured tea for the two of them and invited his companion to select an accompaniment to the tea from the exquisite array of delicacies on the sweet trolley. His guest also happened to be the benefactor of his waiter school, as well as being his fiancée. Having completed his serving duties with the usual standards of absolute perfection, third waiter limped back to his chair. Several operations and extensive physiotherapy had enabled him to walk without the use of sticks.

Jennifer sipped her tea and gazed into the eyes of third waiter. Soon they would be married and, once she'd finished liquidising and disposing of Lard Corp's assets, they could buy a small tropical island somewhere and live happily ever after. Until then the suit remained under lock and key, only seeing the light of day when, for legal reasons, Dr Corpulence was required to make an appearance. She looked forward to the time, not long from now, when she could burn the suit and with it the memory of the tyrant who controlled her life through fear for so long.

****

Detective Chief Inspector Christmas eased into his brand new comfy leather chair and placed his hands behind his back and his feet on top of his new mahogany desk. It was enormous. As was the rest of his office.

He looked at the mountain of paperwork and pondered whose desk he would dump it on while they were busy elsewhere. The Commissioner had taken the bulk of the credit for the victory over the gangs. Christmas was more than happy with his promotion though. He celebrated by booking the whole of December off as holiday leave for the next twenty years. Life was good.

He took a deep mouthful of coffee. It tasted of coffee, with a slight tang of lard. His first act as DCI had been to fire the catering staff. He used their lack of culinary skills and inability to produce anything edible as justification for his actions. The new staff were much better. The menu was a little extravagant for his personal tastes but the food did at least taste like it was supposed to. The one slight drawback was a tendency for everything to have a slight lardy aftertaste. Christmas smiled contentedly and drank the rest of his coffee. Rome wasn't built in a day.

****

Despite overwhelming evidence of his guilt in cases of fractured skulls too numerous to mention, and millions of pounds worth of damage to property and military equipment, Igneous' convictions were overturned on appeal.

A powerful group representing influential scientific and industrial interests lobbied on his behalf. As per the conditions of his release, Igneous spent three days a week taking part in scientific experiments and research and development projects, usually involving his cranium testing the strength, density and durability of various experimental plastics and metal alloys. He featured in numerous metallurgical research papers published in prominent academic journals.

When he wasn't otherwise engaged in this important groundbreaking work, he spent his time head-butting houses to death.

****

The intermediary finished assembling the small observational camera in the correct position and sat down on the long grass to eat his sandwiches.

The witness protection scheme had arranged for him to disappear somewhere hard to find. He was an unpaid volunteer for a five-year research project studying breeding patterns of rare migratory birds in the remote islands off the north west coast of Scotland. It was not the glamorous reward that a supergrass supplying priceless information that had led to the conviction of the UK's most notorious and prolific assassins might expect.

The island was a bleak, desolate place, frequented only by the occasional group of hardy twitchers and several million birds. The police thought the location was a punishment for the intermediary for years of arranging murders, but he took a different view. He had found his very own slice of heaven.

****

Ross gave a deep sigh of relief. The vicar had just read the bit about speaking now or forever holding your peace. Nobody had spoken up. He hadn't been worried that there would be any objections before the service began but that was before he saw Alice walking down the aisle. Since that moment he'd been experiencing acute anxiety. Surely somebody would stop the ceremony to say something like, 'Hey, this isn't right. What's the most gorgeous woman on the planet doing marrying this oik?'

The rest of the service went off without a hitch. Ross managed to speak the line about knowing no lawful impediment why he couldn't be joined in matrimony without getting his tongue in a twist. When he married Amy he was so nervous he declared that he knew of no lawful peppermint why they should not be joined in matrimony. Another moment of concern was Stuart's decision to perform his latest Columbo bumbling routine when trying to locate the rings. An extensive search of all his pockets followed by an even more extensive search of the exact same pockets eventually unearthed them in the very first pocket he searched in the first place. Alice was amused. Ross wasn't.

Once the vows were complete, the vicar got as far as 'You may...' before Ross grabbed Alice for a lengthy sensual kiss. He'd done it; she was his. Alice hadn't stopped smiling since the time Ross proposed, a minute after they'd finished destroying the luxury hotel bed on the day of Alice's release from prison. A queue of hotel guests had complained about the noise and the falling masonry. Structural engineers had been required to check the hotel's foundations were still intact.

It had been a perfect day. Stuart looked resplendent in his top hat and tails and couldn't wait to tear into Ross with the best man's speech. Alice had been unable to choose between six of her friends so had picked all of them as bridesmaids. Igneous happily accepted security duties. A few opportunistic paparazzi had got more than they'd bargained for, opting to seek emergency dental surgery instead of taking any further photos. Kevin had managed to overcome his nerves and fulfil the basic requirements of an usher by pointing people to the left or right. The Rums had turned up in such numbers that they had to be distributed between both the bride's and groom's pews. The wedding guests in attendance who were not employed by ESR were surprised at just how many Korean relatives Ross and Alice both had. Sat amongst the Rums were Black and Alison. Black had agreed to take Alison back on the condition that she saw a sex therapist. Squeezed underneath the church pew just below where Black was seated was a coolbox containing several bags of frozen peas.

As the bride and groom took the applause of the assembled guests, a part of Ross felt a tinge of sadness at those absent for his big day. Adam was still imprisoned for perverting the course of justice. While Alice would happily arrange for him to be eaten alive by starving wolves, a part of Ross would still like to see his old friend one more time and try to make the peace. He was also disappointed Mr X hadn't made it to the wedding. Alan West had also declined the invitation, as had George Arthurs, Ted Armour and Cedric O'Reilly.

Among those who had accepted were several anonymous corporate and banking faces who were invited for the long-term goodwill and public relations of ESR. One of them sat on the back row trying to look inconspicuous. Eric Kevin Salisbury was finance director for ESR's firm of auditors. Ross caught his eye as he scanned the crowd of well-wishers, cameras flashing all the while. Even at a distance, he could see Eric was a large-framed gentleman. There was something about him. He looked awfully familiar.

Acknowledgements

Thanks go to my sister for inspiring me to write and to my wife for looking after the kids so I could write and taking care of me when I was seriously ill.

To those friends who have supported me over the years and listened when I needed an ear I give thanks. Thanks to Paul Luxton for reading the first draft of this story and not saying it was rubbish.

Huge thanks and love go to everyone at the Wednesday night Kinson writing group for your honest feedback, advice and ideas; especially Ian Burton, Emma Norry, Wendy O'Mahoney, Della Galton, David Wass, David Kendrick, James Coates, Jackie Winter, Barbara Featherstone, Nancy Henshaw, Charlotte Joyce and Kay Hopkins.

Thanks also to my editor Alison for helping me get over the line.

About the Author

Keith Gillison has red hair and isn't very tall. A graduate of Aston University and the Chartered Institute of Marketing, he spent seventeen years working in marketing, eleven of them for a large organisation. For legal reasons he can't talk about that. He once sold steel mortuary trays to funeral directors for a living. He's quite good at table tennis. His prized possession is a signed photograph of Peter Falk. He suffers from anxiety and was diagnosed with Chronic Fatigue Syndrome.

He likes to write stories; some funny, some dark. His stories have been published online and in print. He wrote this novel for his sister – who he loves very much and misses every day. His future plans are to write more stories and novels and, as a matter of urgency, attend a course entitled 'Author Biographies – what not to write'.

This is his first novel. He thinks novels should be entertaining, and he hopes you were entertained by reading this one.

Printed in Great Britain
by Amazon.co.uk, Ltd.,
Marston Gate.